THE
DREAM
SEEKERS

THE
DREAM
SEEKERS

A Novel

Grace Mark

WILLIAM MORROW AND COMPANY, INC.
NEW YORK

It is the policy of William Morrow and Company, Inc., and its imprints and affiliates, recognizing the importance of preserving what has been written, to print the books we publish on acid-free paper, and we exert our best efforts to that end.

Library of Congress Cataloging-in-Publication Data

Mark, Grace.
   The dream seekers / by Grace Mark.
     p. cm.
   ISBN 0-688-11223-4
   I. World's Columbian Exposition (1893 : Chicago, Ill.)—Fiction.
  I. Title.
   PS3563.A6625D7   1992
   813'.54—dc20   91-34417
                                                                   CIP

Printed in the United States of America

First Edition

1 2 3 4 5 6 7 8 9 10

BOOK DESIGN BY M. C. DE MAIO

To Norman, the love of my life;
Anne, my daughter and friend;
and my precious mother, Chloe

For being such an important part of my dream.

Acknowledgments

The author is grateful to the many historians and writers who have found "America's most American city" fascinating and written about it, most especially my husband, Norman Mark, whose book *Mayors, Madams, and Madmen* introduced me to the quixotic beauty of Chicago's reformers, as well as its more notorious reprobates. Herman Kogan's books were especially helpful, as were the studies of Clarence Darrow done by Arthur and Lila Weinberg and Kevin Tierney. I also wish to thank Rabbi Leonard Mishkin for sharing what life in Russia was like when he was a boy, and Spertus Museum of Chicago for the assistance of their excellent librarians. A special thank you to Jane Cushman, the agent who breathed life into the project, and to my editor, Lisa Drew, and Bob Shuman for their enthusiastic support at William Morrow.

THE
DREAM
SEEKERS

1

Chicago

May 1, 1893

PHYLLIS WOKE UP RELUCTANTLY. That damned baby in the flat upstairs was crying, and the sound made her head hurt. She straightened her legs on the lumpy bed and felt an ache shoot across her back. Silently she cursed her last customer from the night before. A brute, he was. A large ironworker who had used her so hard against the frame of a darkened doorway that she'd actually been afraid.

Without lifting her head, she looked over at her boyfriend. Tony was lying on top of the covers and, except for his boots, was completely dressed. She smiled at him lovingly. Even in his sleep, Tony Rinaldi looked every bit the high roller.

Tony had unbuttoned the high collar of his ruffled shirt so that his noisy breathing was impeded by nothing more than the rolls of fat that vibrated beneath his chin. His dark eyebrows were crimped together in an expression that made him look as if he were confidently placing a bet at one of his tables. She stroked his arm. Every once in a while he beat her up after he'd lost a large sum. But that was understandable, wasn't it? A man needed his outlets.

Phyllis scratched her arm where a corn husk had poked

11

through the mattress and irritated her. She pulled herself out of bed and glanced at herself in the mirror. Like Tony, she had slept in her clothes. Her dull brown hair was matted, and her face was puffy from the strain of too many tricks and too much cheap liquor.

"Ugly," she whispered at her reflection, suddenly saddened to see what was happening to her.

Phyllis untied the drawstring on her purse and rummaged around for her comb. The coins from last night's work jingled through her fingers. *Jeez, I must have done half the visiting males in the city last night,* she thought. *By the time the fair ends in six months, I'll be rich.*

She poured water from the white pitcher into the bowl and splashed it on her face. Then she wet her comb and tried to pull it through her hair. The water plastered it down, giving her the appearance of grooming. *That's as good as it's going to get,* she told herself.

Phyllis looked back at her boyfriend with an expression of loving indulgence. His jaw had come slack, and he was snoring openmouthed.

He ain't a bad guy, Phyllis thought, smiling fondly as she picked her dirty yellow coat off the floor. With this happy thought in mind, she walked down the hall, opened the outer door of his flat, and stepped into the alley. Time to get back to work.

It was chilly outside. Chilly and damp. Phyllis locked Tony's door, pulled her coat around her shoulders, and glanced at the sky. It looked like rain. What a rotten shame. Rain on a day like this, when more than a quarter of a million people had come to Chicago for the opening of the fair. Ah, well, there was always a silver lining. If they canceled the ceremonies, all those men would have nothing to do but gamble and buy sex. That meant more for Tony and more for her.

It occurred to Phyllis to wonder how much money she had made last night. Better to count it here where she was alone than out among the crowds. As Phyllis stood in the doorway, poking around in her purse, counting and trying to keep the amount straight, she did not notice that she was not alone.

Across the alley, lying where he had passed out behind a group of trash cans, another soul had awakened. He watched her with fascination through bloodshot eyes. She was such a prize standing there all alone. He barely dared breathe for fear of scaring her away. His head hurt with a throbbing that was maddening, but that wasn't what filled him with such an overwhelming rush of anger. The anger had been with him for a long, long time.

Quietly, almost silently, while he kept his eye on her through the slit of light between the trash cans, he drew his legs toward his body. Then he softly pushed himself onto his feet. Damn! His knee cracked so loudly he thought the sound would fill the alley.

No. She hadn't heard. She still stood there, fidgeting in her purse.

Good. It was always best to go after the prey when they were unaware. The surprise sometimes held them like invisible chains, making them unable to move. He stood, moving so slowly that she failed to notice him. Then he stepped out from behind the trash cans.

Phyllis finished counting her money and tightened the purse strings. *Eight dollars*, she thought. *There ought to be more than that. I'm sure I did more than sixteen last night. Dern! If that Tony stole some of my—*

Suddenly she felt a presence near her and looked up. Standing beside a group of trash cans, a tall, dirty man in strange clothes was staring at her intently.

A shock of fear pulsed through her body. She gasped, and instinctively her hand flew to her heart. Then she inhaled, trying to get over the jolt of the surprise. The most valuable thing she owned was that little purse, so she hid it behind her.

The man smiled to himself. This was going to be easy.

Slowly, fixing her eyes with his, he stepped into the alley. Phyllis stared back, afraid, not sure what was happening. As long as he stared into her eyes, she felt compelled to stare back. She didn't dare turn her back and run, for she thought it would encourage him to lunge for her. He stepped again. His movements were smooth and stealthy, a hunter moving in on his quarry.

Phyllis's heart raced crazily. She stepped backward, feeling for the door she had passed through. There it was. Thank God.

Now for the knob. Her hand found it, turned it, and she

shoved her body hard against the door. It didn't open! With a sinking realization, she remembered that she had locked it.

The man saw all this and understood. She was trapped. Still staring deeply into her eyes, he curled his lips back and bared his teeth. Phyllis shuddered. The expression on his face was remorseless, the way an animal might look before it killed.

She was so frightened now that her legs nearly buckled. She wanted to bang on the door and rouse Tony, but she didn't dare turn away. Still facing the man, she slapped her hand backward against the strong, locked panel. She could barely hear the sound for the pounding of her heart. Time seemed to be standing still and racing forward at the same time.

The man took another step forward. He knew that she would soon start to scream. He loved that sound, the sound of terror rushing through a woman's throat. But not now. Not here in an alley crowded in with tenements. Not where faces would appear at windows and see him and remember. He pulled a knife from a leather sheath at his waist.

Phyllis saw the gleam of the large blade and knew. Now frantic, she turned away from him and pounded on the door as hard as she could.

"Tony!" she screamed hoarsely. "Tony, for God sake, open the door. Tony! Hurry!"

In a flat across the alley a woman heard Phyllis's scream and turned over in bed. Christ, those two were always fighting. The gambler was always knocking his woman around and locking her out.

Phyllis realized that Tony would not wake up in time—not in time to save her from this red-eyed apparition and his knife. She pushed herself away from the door and tried to run. The man sprung forward powerfully and lunged for her. Phyllis dodged. He missed her shoulder but caught her yellow coat. Attached to him by the coat, Phyllis spun away crazily in a half circle, across the alley. When her coat slipped from his fingers, the release hurled her against the trash cans. As she hit them, they crashed loudly.

That goddamn noise, the man thought. His mind instinctively told him to trap her behind the shield of the trash cans.

Then time became very slow for Phyllis. She tried to push herself from the cans and force her trembling legs to carry her up the alley, but they moved so slowly it was like a dream. Slowly, slowly. And he was so fast.

In one motion he reached her. He grabbed her arm and turned her to face him. She looked in terror at the implacable hatred in his eyes. As the knife came down, she saw it gleam. She put her hand up to stop it and felt pain sear through her hand. Blood spurted. He grabbed her hand and pushed it away from him, slamming it, pinioning it against the wall.

Her heart fluttered with fear. The knife flashed again. The knife hurt so much when it tore through her abdomen, so much that it shocked her. Then, for one peaceful instant before she died, she felt nothing. Only wonder and astonishment. Her eyes opened in a questioning stare, searching him for the answer. Why? Why? Her eyes locked open, life floated from her, and her body jangled the cans as it toppled to the ground.

The man watched her face intently as she died. His knife was stuck in her, and as she fell, she drew him along with her. They were so close in this embrace that his hot breath covered her face. In the silent alley the trash cans clattered noisily once again.

He freed his knife from her and wiped it on her coat. Then he saw her purse and picked it up. From an apartment across the alley a voice yelled, "Jesus, can't ya keep it quiet? I'm tryin' to sleep!"

The man was startled. He hesitated for a moment before he stuffed her money into a pouch at his waist. Then he dropped the purse on her with a contemptuous gesture and hurried away.

Isabelle Woodruff sucked in her breath and arched her back. She was standing straight, bracing herself against the ornately carved walnut dresser in her elegant bedroom. The heavy blue velvet draperies were still closed against the dim morning light. An expensive gas chandelier glowed overhead.

"Don't worry about me, Helen," Isabelle said to her powerfully built chambermaid. "Just pull as hard as you can." Isabelle tightened the muscles of her lean stomach until they ached.

Helen made a disgusted look before she pushed the buttonhook through the hole at the back of Isabelle's waist. Lately she had taken to showing her disrespect for her mistress outwardly, though, of course, in subtle ways that were barely noticeable.

Helen's attitude didn't make Mrs. Woodruff angry; it just seemed to confuse her. The woman actually tried to carry on politely as if she hadn't noticed. As far as Helen was concerned, that just showed what a fool she was.

Helen slipped the end of the hook around a button at Isabelle Woodruff's waist. She yanked it abruptly to pull the button through the hole.

Sssssssss. Isabelle inhaled and clenched her teeth. "Oh, please," she said under her breath.

Helen pulled the hook and then—to vent a little of her hostility—jerked it again. It would have pleased her if the button had ripped off, but she contented herself with the little gasp of pain that escaped Mrs. Woodruff's slender throat. Helen was even a little disappointed to see that the button had slipped into place.

Isabelle turned to search Helen's eyes. She could sense the violence beneath her maid's demeanor, and it disturbed her.

"Sorry, ma'am," Helen said matter-of-factly to conceal her delight. "Now that one's in, the other's should be easier."

Isabelle turned and offered her back to Helen again. "I can't understand why this dress is so tight," she said to distract herself from her maid's odd behavior.

Isabelle had been carefully measured by Marshall Field's best seamstress before Mr. Field himself had ordered the marvelous dress from Paris. It had irritated Field that this young banker's wife hadn't purchased one of the ensembles he had in stock. But what was he to do? The woman had brought him a magazine with a drawing of the dress, and he always tried to give his customers satisfaction. "The customer is always right" was the guideline on which he ran his business, and it had made his store the biggest in Chicago.

Now with more buttons fastened, Isabelle was barely able to breathe. It occurred to her that she might faint before the day was over, but that was not a serious matter. Swooning and other signs of feminine weakness were still in fashion, although in the last few years, what with those Bloomer girls in their ridiculous flowing breeches, women's dresses had become much less full.

Isabelle remembered the dress she had worn at her wedding. There had been so many yards of embroidered white satin in the skirt that she had been forced to lean forward just to reach the extended hands of the wedding guests. That had been a little more than six years ago. In March 1887.

God, what a fool she'd been. Almost everything she'd hoped to find in marriage had failed to happen.

Isabelle had assumed that marrying one of Chicago's most established bankers would put her into a swirl of parties and friends. But it had not. She was lonelier now than she had ever been.

She tried to make friends, but her invitations were usually met with polite rejections. If they were accepted—if she was lucky enough to stage a little luncheon in her home—she was usually disappointed later by not being invited back in return.

Instead of rushing gaily from society luncheons to afternoon teas, Isabelle found herself in a large house with a staff of servants who paid little attention to her. She was alone even at night. For reasons she had never been able to understand, her husband had moved out of their bedroom when she became pregnant, and he had never returned.

Ah, well, she thought. She shook her head to rid herself of those troubling remembrances. This was going to be a good day. She wanted to look pretty, so she turned her mind to pleasant thoughts.

I have my little son, James, she told herself. James made up for a lot. And she did live in a splendid three-story mansion on fashionable Michigan Avenue—a showplace that as a schoolgirl she could only have dreamed of. Though she had few social companions, Isabelle was hoping that the fair would help change all that.

The fair. The 1893 Columbian Exposition. It marked the four hundredth anniversary of Christopher Columbus's discovery of America, and Isabelle felt excited just thinking about it. She had seen the outside of the fairgrounds—dozens of magnificent buildings that covered thousands of acres. Huge, beautiful structures covered in white stucco and masterfully embellished with gilt. And it was said that the inventions inside were truly amazing.

Social reformers called the fairgrounds the Gilded City and

criticized it because it was so at odds with the dreary brick buildings that made up Chicago itself. But as far as Isabelle was concerned, the fair represented the future. In less than a decade the world would be entering a new century. If the inventions were any indication of the changes the new century would bring, the modern age would be dazzling.

Today the fair was opening with a full program of pageantry and speeches. The most important, powerful people in the world had come to Chicago just to be there. Even the direct descendants of Christopher Columbus, the Duke and Duchess of Veragua, had come all the way from Spain for the ceremonies. They had arrived only yesterday in one of George Pullman's luxurious sleeping cars.

That was why wearing the exquisite green silk Charmeuse dress that Helen was buttoning was so important to her. Today, during the opening ceremonies, she would be sitting on the speakers' platform with prominent people: the Marshall Fields, the Potter Palmers, the Cyrus McCormicks, Governor John Peter Altgeld, Clarence Darrow, even President Grover Cleveland himself. This was her chance to show those women, those arrogant society matrons who always looked down on her, that she was a woman worthy of their attention.

Isabelle felt so nervous that her palms were moist. "Are we almost finished, Helen?"

"We," Helen said curtly as she gave the dress one more yank, "we are doing the best we can."

There was such disdain in Helen's voice that Isabelle looked away. What had she done to make Helen dislike her so? Helen's contempt was all very restrained—nothing Isabelle could put her finger on—but it was there. Isabelle just didn't understand it.

When she had first married Phillip, Helen had been warm, had even made her feel a little less lonely. But now her attitude was so hostile it made Isabelle uncomfortable. Isabelle wanted to dismiss her, but once when she asked her husband to remove her from the staff, he had rebuked her stiffly.

"In our class," he had said, "we don't fire a servant—unless it's for a very *major* infraction."

Isabelle turned back toward the large ornate mirror, and Helen returned her attention to Isabelle's dress. As the maid pulled the last button into place, she glanced at the reflection of her mistress.

Helen hated to admit it, but Isabelle Woodruff was indeed attractive. She was young—certainly no more than twenty-seven or twenty-eight—and her hair seemed to float around her face like a gleaming cloud. It was such an unusual color that even here under the gaslight, it glowed a rich gold. But outside in the light, Helen knew it would take on the lively sheen of strawberry blond. Mrs. Woodruff was tall, too, at least five feet six inches, and her waistline was so slender that Helen could not understand how a woman could have had a child and still look like that.

Helen glanced at herself in the mirror and felt angry all over again. Her round body was covered with an apron, and even to her own eyes, she looked like a pillow tied with a rope. Beside Isabelle Woodruff's classical profile, Helen's pug nose looked comical, squatting as it did in the middle of her round, freckled face.

No wonder Phillip Woodruff had married this woman! She looked like quality. Deep down, Helen knew that Mr. Woodruff would never consider marrying someone from Helen's class—even if he weren't already tied to Isabelle. But it rankled her to think that the fancy Phillip Woodruff took his pleasure in *her* bed while this redheaded wife of his got the use of his money.

Sometimes Helen enjoyed imagining Isabelle's surprise if she were to catch her husband bouncing his skinny rump on top of her. Or even better, if his wife walked in while she was tying Phillip's ankles to the footboard of her bed. Then she'd see something! Helen had dreamed of arranging that scene many times. She hadn't, of course, because she knew that if she were caught, *she'd* be the one who paid the price—not the fancy mister. Not the fancy missus either.

Isabelle suddenly felt such a surge of animosity from her maid that she wanted to escape the room.

"I'm going downstairs to wait for Phillip," she said.

"As you wish, ma'am," Helen answered curtly.

"Please make sure my son is dressed and ready to leave when my husband returns," Isabelle said coldly, matching her maid's tone. "We want to be sure to get to the Lexington Hotel

to meet President Cleveland and the duke and duchess before
the parade begins."

Josef Chernik took his sister's hand in his and held it up to
make his point. "I promise," he said to his parents, using the
intertwined hands to demonstrate how careful he would be. "I
promise nothing will happen to Hannah."

His mother smiled in spite of herself. Even now, when she
wanted to impress her son with the seriousness of her concern,
the love Josef had for his younger sister brought joy to her face.
Even the little girls, Mashke and Frieda, grinned.

What a wonderful family God had blessed her with! They
had always stuck together, not only back in Russia, where life
was always dangerous, but also here in Chicago, where the
danger was different.

"All right" she said indulgently. "I trust you. But no silly
business."

This gentle admonition was not enough for Yankel. He
loved his son, Josef, of course. But *trust* him! A boy who even
as a child had to be dragged kicking and screaming to *cheder*. A
boy whose impetuousness had forced them to flee their home.
Trust him? Ridiculous.

"You hear your mother?" Yankel demanded. "No silly business. And no trouble! If you don't have enough money to get
in regular, you come back. No sneaking in. This family needs
no more problems with the police."

Josef closed his eyes in irritation. Wouldn't they ever let
him forget? Wouldn't they ever get over hiding from the police
in Russia? Here he was, a man of twenty-two already. He had
been slaving for five years to help the family survive, yet they
still treated him like a child. He was old enough to have his own
family—and would have—except that without his earnings, his
parents would be unable to feed his three sisters.

His father certainly had no head for business. He had been
raised only to read and study. That was how it was back in the
little *shtetl* where he grew up. In Svislovich a brilliant student
was respected, and his father had been so brilliant that Rachel's
family saw him as a good catch even though he had no way to
support her. For such a scholar everyone chipped in. Even the

poor relations gave whatever they could to help Rachel support her family.

But when the family had fled from Svislovich to Lithuania, the money and the assistance had stopped. In the large ghetto of Vilna Yankel and Rachel had barely eked out a living. Rachel sewed and Yankel tried setting up a store, but he had no luck with it. So Yankel, the scholar, had learned to make caps for his cousin Moishe.

Josef tried to overcome his irritation. "Father, I assure you. There will be no problems with the police."

"And you will not let your sister out of your sight?" his father insisted. "Remember, only last week a hoodlum tried to grab Chaim Salkind's daughter for God knows what bad purposes. If Chaim hadn't been nearby, the girl might be gone."

Josef nodded. He knew how serious this was. Here in the slums of Chicago's Nineteenth Ward, white slavers were a constant problem. Especially when a girl was as pretty as his sixteen-year-old sister, Hannah.

Yankel saw concern cloud the faces of Hannah and Josef and stopped his lecture. Was this a way to raise children, to teach them to live in fear? No. He had said enough. Josef, he knew, would give his life to protect Hannah.

"Then go," he said briskly. "Enjoy and learn. There will be many fine things to see, and it will be a good opportunity to understand more about America."

Once it was decided that Josef and Hannah would be allowed to go, the younger sisters clamored and whined until Yankel shouted them into silence. "You girls, be quiet! You are too young to go to such an event."

When Josef and Hannah were finally dismissed, they hurried to the worn gray landing outside the family's third-floor tenement and raced down the stairs as if they had escaped from a prison. Josef looked at Hannah and laughed. She was so thrilled her eyes were gleaming.

"Oh, Josef, I was so afraid they'd change their minds. I would have *died* if they hadn't let me go!"

Josef loved to see his sister so full of excitement. Of all the people in the world, he loved her most dearly. During those years of hiding in the ghetto in Vilna, Hannah was the only person he had been able to talk to. He had been constantly afraid that the police would come for him. When he stayed in hiding, he became bored and anxious. When he ventured out, he always felt a mild, underlying terror.

But whenever he thought he would go crazy from all the fear and dread, there was Hannah. Even as a child she could listen like an adult without getting upset the way his parents would. Somewhere, concealed behind her soft green eyes was something solid and imperturbable. Hannah was strong.

When the Chernik family arrived in Chicago, they had moved into a dismal area of tenements already crowded with Eastern Europeans. Josef had watched Hannah quietly accept the noise and the crowds. He had seen her adjust to the dark two-room apartment with no sign of disappointment. He had taken her to the neighborhood public school to learn English and watched her walk inside with no sign of fear. She had embraced every change so calmly that Josef knew she had an inner strength far more resilient than his.

Yet even today she was only sixteen. Her dark hair still curled around her exquisite face the way it had when she was a child, and through those remarkable flecked eyes she observed the world as intently as an infant. If the family had been able to afford clothes that set off Hannah's beauty, she would have drawn attention like a magnet. So it was just as well that she kept her dark hair hidden under the cheap cotton babushka. Attention in the overcrowded, corrupt Nineteenth Ward would certainly have provoked sexual attacks. Since Jewish girls brought a high price in the Chicago white-slave market, Hannah would have been in great danger.

Now that they were away from their parents, Hannah asked Josef the question she had not dared ask before. "Josef, do we really have enough money for the fair?"

Josef grinned and shook his head no.

"I *knew* you didn't!" Hannah laughed because she understood her brother so well. Josef took risks to get what he wanted. "Papa would be furious," she said, "but I don't care. Just as long as we can be near."

"We'll stand and look over the fence," he said. "That's better than not going at all."

"*Whatever* we see, it'll be worth it."

Josef was encouraged by her reaction. "Listen, Hannah," he said with great significance, "there's not just *one* show today.

There's two." He smiled mysteriously. "Personally I don't know which I want to see more."

Hannah stopped walking to watch him.

"Do you remember when I was teaching you to read Yiddish in Vilna?" he asked.

Hannah nodded. In the old country girls did not go to school.

"Do you remember a newspaper story about a famous show that was touring Europe? Remember? Called the Buffalo Bill Show? The paper said it was the best show on earth—with horses and real Indians and guns."

Hannah nodded again even though she had no recollection of this story.

Josef paused for dramatic effect. "Hannah, the Buffalo Bill Show is in Chicago right now! On a lot across the street from the fair."

"Oh, Josef." Hannah's disapproving tone made her suddenly sound very much like her mother. "We don't even have the money to go to one show—and now you're talking about two."

The truth of her comment embarrassed Josef. He'd get them in somehow. He knew he'd figure out a way.

A crowded streetcar heading toward the lake pulled up to the wooden sidewalk. Josef helped Hannah on board and handed two nickels to the conductor. In forty minutes the car reached South Halsted Street and stopped. The street was too crowded for it to go on.

"Might as well get off," the conductor called out. "End of the line."

The passengers on this streetcar from the West Side ghettos were mostly foreigners. They didn't understand what the conductor had said and continued to sit in the car. It always annoyed the conductor to deal with these people. He yelled angrily and jerked his thumb through the air to show them they should leave.

Josef and Hannah stepped off and were swept along in the crowd. In a few blocks Josef realized he had taken his sister into the worst part of town. They were surrounded by bars and gambling dens and whorehouses. As they crossed the street, he heard someone rapping from a window.

When he glanced up, he saw a whore sitting at a second-floor window, tapping a coin against the glass to get his attention. She had long frizzled hair and held a bed sheet in front of her chest, and when she caught his eye, she lowered the sheet to expose her bare breast. With her hand cupped under it, she offered it to him and winked.

Josef put his hand over Hannah's eyes and led her away. The last thing he wanted was to expose his sister to something like this.

Nearby, in a bar on State Street, another young whore was eating a hard-boiled egg. The politician who owned the saloon gave a free lunch to anyone who needed it. After all, many people were out of work these days. A favor like this was worth votes at election time.

Edna's nerves were jangled from all the beer last night. She figured she must have had every man on South Halsted. The number thirty stuck in her mind, but it had to be more than that because she had more than fifteen dollars. Christ, no wonder she was tired! She hadn't felt this weary since she got pregnant and her mother threw her out of the house.

A pink-faced Irishman reeking of stale beer came over to lean against the bar. He stuck his face close to hers and pinched her breast. Edna smacked him away. God, she hated this life!

Just then Mike Touhy strolled through the door, and Edna quickly hid her purse. Mike was a cop, and she expected him to hit her up for protection money, but if Mike saw her, he didn't seem to care. Instead, he slapped his meaty palm on the bar and barked at the bartender.

"Lissen, Nippy, I thought I told ye not to sell booze to the Indians."

"Come on, Mike, for Criminy sake. Their money's as good as anybody's."

"Fer yer information, President Cleveland's in town and the place is crawlin' with federal agents. If they see that drunk Indian out in front, they'll shut ye down and there won't be nothin' I can do about it."

While Nippy soothed Mike with a complimentary beer, Edna decided to find Phyllis. Phyllis had been her best chum ever since she got into this life. If they could work the parade

together, maybe they'd have a few laughs. Edna stretched her
stiff back and slipped out the side door.

Isabelle had been waiting for her husband for more than
an hour. She had opened the front door so she'd see him the
minute he arrived. The new carriage was waiting in front,
hitched with their loveliest horses. Once, when the horses
snorted and tossed their heads, she stuck her head outside, but
Phillip wasn't there. The driver leaned back against the carriage
and yawned.

All this delay made Isabelle nervous—not at all the way
she'd wanted to feel in the parade. She was also hurt, and with
every minute that passed she felt more distressed. She knew
Phillip didn't really care about her, but normally she tried not
to think much about it. Missing dinner and coming in late at
night—that was one thing. What Isabelle couldn't understand
was how he could be so cruel as to abandon her today. Today,
when they were going to ride in the parade.

Phillip knew how much being in the parade meant to her.
How could he not? She'd spent months helping Bertha Palmer
work on the Women's Pavilion for the fair. She had even gotten
involved in Mrs. Palmer's battle against that radical Susan B.
Anthony for control of the project. Miss Anthony wanted the
exhibit to make a statement about suffrage, but Mrs. Palmer
knew the world wasn't ready for an idea as advanced as women
getting the vote. And Isabelle had agreed with her. This was
the first major exhibit dedicated to women's accomplishments
that had ever been done. Better to have something for women
than nothing at all.

After all this work Isabelle feared that unless Phillip got
here soon, she was going to miss the biggest event of her life.
When she heard a messenger clattering up the driveway on
horseback, she hurried outside to meet him.

"Are you Mrs. Woodruff?" he asked.

Isabelle nodded nervously. Something must have happened or Phillip would have come himself.

"Mr. Woodruff says he's been delayed at work. He says you
should ride in the parade without him, and he'll meet you at
the speakers' stand in the fairground."

Isabelle felt so disappointed that she had to turn her face away. She went back into the house to get her son and compose herself. The idea that she would be the only woman in the parade to ride without her husband was deeply humiliating. People would talk. They would probably say that her husband was unhappy with her or that she wasn't good enough for him.

By the time Isabelle's carriage reached the Lexington Hotel, the President's cortege had already gone on, and the streets were full of people. Bert, her carriage driver, said he'd check inside, but Isabelle knew she was too late.

The parade was gone. She could hear the faint sounds of the band up ahead in the front of the crowd.

When Edna left the bar to avoid paying the cop her protection money, she went out the back door. She hadn't seen Phyllis around today, so she figured she'd be at her boyfriend's flat.

Tony Rinaldi was a gambler. Sometimes, after he'd hit Phyllis too hard, he promised that he'd stake her to a house so she could quit working and hire her a stable of whores to do the dirty work for her. But that was probably just talk. Edna stepped cautiously into the alley and headed toward the flat he kept behind his keno and poker establishment.

It was a nasty block. A gang of Irish thugs often hid there. Once one of them had threatened to cut her face when she refused to pay passage money. But today, as she hurried toward Rinaldi's flat, she saw no signs of them. They must be out in the crowd, she reasoned, taking advantage of the greater opportunity.

In the distance she could hear the band. The parade was getting near. If she and Phyllis were going to work the crowd, they'd better get moving.

"Phyllis," she called. "Phyll-is." From an open window on a second floor the sound of a baby crying floated over the alley.

Kee-rist, she thought. *She must already be gone! Why am I always the last one to get in on a good deal?*

As she approached a cluster of trash cans, she recognized a dirty yellow garment lying on the ground, puffed out as if something were under it. It was Phyllis's coat. Edna stepped nearer and saw the back of her friend's greasy dark hair. "Hey, whatcha doin' lyin' in the alley? You drunk or somethin'?"

Edna pulled her friend's shoulder to lift her head out of the dirt. The malnourished body offered little resistance. From the neck up, Phyllis looked the way she always did when she was unconscious from opium or strong drink. But below her bodice, her abdomen gaped open, awash in dark shiny gore. In horror, Edna released her friend's shoulder. As Phyllis's torso toppled over on its side, her bloody intestines oozed onto the pavement with a soft plop-plop.

Edna screamed uncontrollably just as a band a block away struck up a new tune. Her terrified shrieks were covered by the trumpets which were loudly tooting a zippy rendition of "Yankee Doodle."

When Isabelle Woodruff's carriage finally turned into the gates at the fair, she saw her husband standing on the speakers' stand chatting with George Pullman. Both men looked worried. For months now the nation had been sinking into a deep depression. Although the fair had stimulated train travel and Pullman was rehiring workers for his sleeper car company, they feared that Chicago's boom would be short lived.

Phillip finally noticed that Isabelle's carriage was blocked near the gate, and he pushed through the crowd to help her. While the driver lifted down little James, Phillip extended his hand to Isabelle. He could see that she was angry by the way she averted her eyes, but he took her hand anyway. He wanted onlookers to see that this beautiful woman belonged to him.

Phillip Woodruff had no illusions about himself. He was a gaunt, unattractive man, many years older than his wife. He knew that when people didn't immediately recognize his importance, they understood it soon enough when they saw the prize he had captured. Isabelle was a lovely ornament. That was all he expected from her these days, and he felt entitled to it.

Isabelle gazed past him, so angry and hurt that she couldn't make herself meet his eyes. Phillip patted her arm. "Sorry, I couldn't meet you, my dear. Business."

Her eyes burned with tears.

"Three more banks closed yesterday," he said. "I do have a lot on my mind."

* * *

Just before noon President Cleveland, followed by his Cabinet and the world's fair officials, climbed the stairs to the platform. Isabelle and Phillip stood behind them for a moment, looking out over the enormous crowd. Four hundred thousand people were packed between the speakers' stand and the pillared Administration Building across the concourse. Behind them was the magnificent jumble of gilded white buildings.

Pillars and domes and turrets spread across hundreds of acres of wooded parkland like a magnificent, strange fairyland. Huge man-made lagoons filled with gondolas shimmered in the sun.

When the crowd noticed that the presidential party was on the stand, they cheered and waved excitedly. On the platform Clarence Darrow whispered something to Governor Altgeld, and a short distance away, inside the Transportation Building he had helped design, the young architect Frank Lloyd Wright paced impatiently as he waited for the speeches to be over.

Across the concourse from the speakers' stand, Buffalo Bill Cody, flanked by seven of his Sioux braves in full ceremonial dress, looked down with excitement from the roof of the Administration Building. With the size of this crowd, he figured he'd draw the largest box office in the history of his show.

Outside the gates, jammed against the thousands who couldn't afford the fifty-cent admission fee, Josef perched Hannah on his shoulder so she could see. A woman on the stand in a beautiful green silk dress caught Hannah's eye.

Someday, Hannah promised herself, *I will have a dress as wonderful as that.*

Finally, with the speeches and musical pieces over, the sun burst through the clouds as President Cleveland rose to speak.

He announced that this was the beginning of the modern age, and he hailed Chicago as the most American of cities. He claimed that the fair was the stupendous result of American enterprise, and he urged everyone to look to the wonderful new beginning the new century would bring.

As the spectators cheered, he pressed a gold telegraph key. Instantly an electric circuit was opened, and the fair was set in motion.

The machinery beneath the ground emitted a loud, low rumble, and the crowd stirred in surprise. Suddenly water spewed high into the air from the Columbian Fountain. Hundreds of flags unfurled. Battleships on the lake fired their guns. Two hundred white doves were released into the air. And the orchestra played "America."

The crowd gazed in rapture at this breathtaking introduction to the twentieth century.

Yes, yes! Surely this *was* the modern age. Who could doubt it when they could feel the power of the electricity pulsing beneath their very feet? Who could doubt that, in a time like this, everything would be possible? This was the greatest land and the greatest time in the history of the world!

Thousands of eyes misted with a rush of patriotism. A murmur of "Oohh-hh-hh" went up from the multitude. And among them a hundred pickpockets made their grab.

2

_____

AS SOON AS THE PRESIDENT finished his speech, the multitude dispersed, surging toward the various exhibitions. Hannah and Josef hadn't heard a word of the speeches, but when the crowd began to move, they knew the ceremonies were over.

It wasn't much fun, standing there while everybody pushed to get past, so they strolled along the high fence, peeking through holes to get glimpses of the buildings inside. When they reached the Sixty-third Street entrance to the fair, they saw a huge tent the size of a city block. A sign in front of it read:

BUFFALO BILL'S WILD WEST AND ROUGH RIDERS SHOW
THE GREATEST SHOW ON EARTH

When Josef saw the buffaloes painted on the sign, he knew he'd finally found what he wanted to see. The newspaper story he'd read back in Lithuania had said that performers rode horseback while they shot real guns. This was why Josef was so eager to see it. Ever since he was a boy back in Svislovich, he'd been fascinated with guns. His stealing a gun was the reason the family had been forced to flee their home to begin with.

When Josef was only twelve, he and his chum Leivik had noticed a Russian soldier sleeping outside the town's only tavern. What attracted them was that the slumbering soldier was cradling a rifle in his arms. They had carefully slipped it away and hidden it in a hollow tree outside town. They couldn't fire it near town because of the noise. But every couple of days they walked four miles downriver to practice.

Josef had come to love the excitement of sighting a target, taking aim, and squeezing the trigger. He and Leivik knew that stealing the rifle was wrong, but they told themselves that they could use it to protect their mothers and sisters if there were another pogrom against the Jews. At least that was what they *told* themselves before all the trouble started.

Now, standing outside the gate to the Wild West Show, Josef knew he had to find a way to get in. As he watched, a tall, portly man with flowing white hair and a mustache emerged from the tent. The man took long steps and bent his knees deeply as he walked. Then he laughed and waved to the fairgoers.

"Right this way, ladies and gentlemen," he called. "Right this way."

When the crowd stopped to listen, the tall man continued. "Folks, I ain't sayin' that the exposition next door is secondrate—far from it. But if you want to see the *greatest* show on earth, the show that thrilled Queen Victoria and kings all over Europe, this one here is what you want to see."

As he turned back toward the tent, waving his western hat enticingly, Josef was thrilled to realize that the man was no other than Buffalo Bill Cody—the man whose drawing he had cut from the newspaper in Vilna.

Without wasting a moment, Josef grabbed Hannah and pulled her away from the entrance. They raced along the tent toward Sixty-fourth Street until he spotted a stretch of canvas that hadn't been staked to the ground. Without hesitation, he hurled himself toward the opening and struggled in the dirt under the tent.

Hannah stood, watching in astonishment until he whispered, "Hannah! Here! Quick!"

She crawled awkwardly under the tent flap, and when they were on the other side of the canvas, they heard a man's voice bellowing an announcement to the crowd.

Directly in front of them, silhouetted in front of an opening that led to the bright arena on the other side of the tent, was a woman. She was tiny—no larger than a child—and had long brown hair that flowed over her shoulders. She was dressed like a child, too, in a buff-colored skirt that ended in fringe just below her knees. High spats that tied under her dark, flat shoes covered her legs from view. A wide-brimmed hat topped off the curious costume.

The woman stood there waiting until a man's voice in the arena announced: ". . . the little lady who dazzled Queen Victoria, herself, the gal Sitting Bull called Little Sure Shot, Ann-i-e Oakl-e-y!"

Then, skipping and waving her small arms out at her side, the woman danced out to the arena.

Josef crept to the opening and peered out. He saw the woman curtsy to each section of the bleachers and skip over to a small oak table draped with a fringed golden cloth. There she picked up a rifle.

"Pull!" she shouted, and her light voice filled the arena. As a small round missile flew threw the air, she twirled, stopped, sighted the target and fired. The missile exploded and vanished in the air. A few women in the front row gasped at the noise. The crowd cheered enthusiastically.

Josef was thrilled. As he stood spellbound, watching the tiny woman shoot faultlessly again and again, a group of Indians, resplendent in feather headdresses, trudged past him into the room.

With a start, Josef realized that he was hiding in the performers' waiting room! The Indians stared at him sullenly and lowered themselves to sit on the floor. Finally, one of them leaned forward and grunted. He extended two playing cards in his hand. Josef took them and noticed that a bullet had been shot through them, leaving a round hole in the center of each.

Josef heard the crowd outside thunder with applause, and in moments the tiny woman skipped back into the room. When she noticed Josef, instead of throwing him out, she smiled and patted his shoulder familiarly. She was raucous and friendly. She was the only American who had ever touched him.

"Why, whatcha doin' watchin' the show from back here?" she asked.

Josef was awed by her presence. This woman was not only an American from the Wild West but a performer! His mouth refused to form words.

"Hey, fella." She pointed to the bullet-riddled cards he was holding. "These here passes will let you and your gal sit out there in the bleachers. You don't have to stay back here. Come on. I'll shove some people over and make room for you to sit."

While Josef and Hannah followed Annie Oakley to the bleachers, the Indians lumbered to an enclosure where horses were corralled. No sooner had Josef and Hannah been seated than Buffalo Bill strode to the center of the arena.

"Ladies and gentlemen," he declaimed loudly, "sittin' here in the shadow of the amazin' inventions over at the world's fair—the electric lights and such—it's easy to forget that it was only twenty years ago that the West was still being won by brave settlers.

"We will now illustrate that time, showin' an authentic prairie emigrant train an' what happened when settlers crossin' these plains were attacked by maraudin' Indians."

Buffalo Bill ended his introduction by firing a pistol into the air. In response, a covered wagon drawn by four horses clattered from behind a curtain of draped canvas toward the center of the arena. A man drove the team. A woman in a calico hat, holding a baby doll, sat beside him on the bench.

Suddenly a terrifying scream arose from the far side of the arena. The audience gasped. Josef and Hannah watched transfixed as three Indians on horseback shrieked and galloped at full pace from behind the draped canvas. Another followed, then another, and another until the far side of the arena was filled with savages. Some were crowned with a full band of feathers; others wore feathers stuck in their braided hair. Some were bare-legged; others wore buckskin pants. They carried bows and arrows—seventeen wild men screaming and galloping insanely.

They hurtled around the perimeter of the arena, so close to the bleachers that the crowd felt the Indian peril as if it were new today. Josef leaned forward, enthralled by the danger.

The woman on the wagon screamed in alarm. The man whipped the horses, and they lurched into motion, first run-

ning, then galloping as the wagon careened wildly, barely missing the bleachers. The woman took the reins, holding her baby
between her thighs. The man stood and turned, shouldering a
rifle. He fired at the Indians. An Indian fell to the dirt and
rolled quickly to avoid being trampled under the horses.

The noise that filled the staging area was tremendous. Hannah held her hands over her ears, amazed that women could
have endured such hardship.

Now shots rang out from the *far* side of the arena. Buffalo
Bill Cody, flanked by four cowboys, was riding into combat.

Cody was a big man, but he rode loosely, letting the movement of the horse flow through him. He put the horse's reins
in his teeth and pulled his rifle from the saddle. Still riding at
top speed, he sighted his rifle with both hands and fired it BOOM
and cocked it and fired it again BOOM and cocked it again. The
cowboys riding with him fired their six-shooters into the air.
They screamed HAIE HAIE HAIE.

The Indians stopped their pursuit of the carriage. They
turned in their tracks, reining in their horses so hard that the
startled animals reared on their hind legs and nearly fell back
onto the bleachers. Now, threatened with a new enemy, the
Indians charged the cowboys. Buffalo Bill and the cowboys
met them head-on, firing as they came. One by one the Indians
fell from their horses. Some were dragged along the ground.
The arena was filled with smoke and the pungent odor of gun-
powder.

With half the Indians lying on the ground, the others galloped away in retreat. Buffalo Bill, miraculously still on his
horse, pranced to the center of the arena, waving his hat.

The audience was overcome. They had never seen anything like this in their lives. They had heard about Indian attacks, of course, and read about them in dime novels. But they
had never dreamed how terrifying it had really been.

They leaped to their feet to salute the big man whose white
hair floated across his shoulders. His wave said, "Don't worry.
It's over now. Everything is fine." They were grateful to him.
Their applause cascaded down from the bleachers in a sound
so warm, so strong it felt like waves of love.

Josef was dazzled. He forgot that his family lived in a dark,
dirty tenement. He forgot about the drudgery and exhaustion

that usually hung over him like a heavy shroud. *This* was the America he had expected to find! A wide-open place where trouble could be handled easily BOOM instead of the close, cramped spaces that made discontent and unhappiness such quiet, constant companions.

Event after event flowed past him. The Pony Express demonstration. The capture of the Deadwood mail coach. The demonstration of the strange life customs of the Indians. The reenactment of the Battle of the Little Bighorn, which left the arena littered with the lifeless bodies of white men.

Then the moment he had not dared dream of actually happened. Buffalo Bill invited some brave person in the crowd to try his hand at shooting. He held up a five-dollar bill. Without thinking, Josef jumped into the arena before Hannah could stop him. Another boy took up the challenge, too.

As Josef moved to the center, he heard the crowd's applause. He saw, and would always remember, the event in small, isolated impressions. The ground in front of him as he walked forward. Buffalo Bill's mouth and cheeks as he spoke. His big extended hand. The sound of his name being announced to the crowd. The feel of the gun barrel, warm from all the shooting, and the sound of the gun as he fired it. The dark hole that formed in the center of the target where his bullet entered it. The woman, Annie Oakley, cheering and waving at him from the side. Then, watching with his heart pounding as the other boy shot. Seeing the boy's bullet darken the target farther from the center. Feeling the crisp crinkle of the money as he walked back to the bleacher. The roar of applause meant for him.

Later that day, having spent a dollar of his prize money for admission to the fair, Josef and Hannah gazed at the great buildings of modern commerce. They saw electric lights for the first time. They saw Edison's kinescope, a machine that made pictures of people move as if they were alive. They saw designs for alternating electrical current created by an immigrant from Croatia. Hannah marveled at displays of sewing and cooking at the Women's Pavilion. Josef studied the giant cogs that turned gears in the new electric locomotive in the Transportation Building.

And while he was there, Josef discovered a new dream. To

create something from his brain that would change the world. To be an inventor! That was the way he would succeed in America.

Then, as they were leaving the Transportation Building, he saw something that filled him with immense yearning. It was a fifty-foot model of a town called Pullman: an ideal community just twelve miles south of here that had been built by an inventor named George Pullman, the man who had created the sleeping car. It was a town built for the workers, with parks and flowers and trees and a little church and a school. A place where his mother might feel happy, where his sisters would be safe.

As he tucked a brochure about the town into his pocket, he overheard the incredible news that this same Pullman factory was hiring! Perhaps he could get a job there and find a home for his family.

Overwhelmed as he was by this momentous day, Josef did not know—or care—that the other boy who had entered the shooting contest, the one who had lost, was named Flo Ziegfeld and that this day—which had introduced Ziegfeld to the excitement of show business—would profoundly affect him as well. All Josef knew was that from now on, somehow, things were going to be different.

The front pages of the newspapers the next day were filled with the marvels of the fair. The story of a brutal slash murder of a whore was buried at the bottom of the third page.

One paragraph to summarize the life and death of Phyllis Conroy. And the reporter who wrote the story didn't think it was worth even that.

3

NO MATTER WHAT HANNAH and Josef said, Papa and Mama wouldn't even consider going to the exposition.

"Spend fifty cents to go to a fair! Your mother and me?" Yankel scoffed at such foolishness. But as he shook his head, he cast a sidelong look at his wife. How he would have loved to take her to such a fine event.

"Hannah, look," Rachel said, pointing to her youngest daughter's feet. "Frieda's toes are pushing through her shoes! If your sister is to go to school next fall, we must save for new ones."

Hannah and Josef exchanged glances. Until that moment the fair had seemed a bargain! The experience of a lifetime, two tickets for a dollar!

"I'm sorry, Mama," Hannah said. "I didn't think."

Yankel hated to crush his favorite daughter's spirits. "Pish. So you won some money, you spent some money. At least, you brought most of it back home to the family! I'd say you're both very good children."

"You're young," Rachel added. "You need to understand the future. It will help you get ahead in your life."

"But, Mama, it would help you, too!"

"So? You and Josef can tell us about it. You can describe everything exactly the way you saw it. It will be as good as being there ourselves, maybe better."

The stories Josef and Hannah told *were* good, so filled with wonderment and excitement that for weeks the family wanted to hear them again and again. A family ritual quickly developed. Each night by seven Frieda and Mashke would perch on the landing, waiting eagerly until Josef returned from the rawhide company. When his footsteps sounded on the steps below, they would rush back into the apartment, shrieking, "He's home. He's home!"

Inside the airless apartment Rachel would put her sewing aside, rub her eyes, straighten her back, and smile. *Tonight*, she would think, *we have something to look forward to!* By the time Josef had entered the apartment, Rachel would have the bread sliced for dinner.

Later, gathered around the light of a single candle in the front room, the younger sisters would ask Hannah to describe the beautiful dresses she'd seen at the fair that day. And Rachel and Yankel would listen in amazement as Josef tried to convey the stunning moment when, just as the twilight was deepening, the electric lights had suddenly come on, illuminating the fairgrounds in a blaze of light.

"Hannah," Josef said, unable to describe such a sight, "Hannah, *you* tell them."

And Hannah searched for the words that could re-create it—the words that would help them understand how it looked when more light than any of them had ever seen poured forth from the windows of those white buildings to reflect magically on the watery lagoons.

Over the ensuing weeks a dream was reignited in that tiny dark apartment. Without understanding what was happening to them, the Chernik family rekindled their sense of hope. They felt a lightness and joy that none of them had known since they had arrived in America. And in feeling the joy, Josef realized that the hard life in Chicago had all but deadened them to the dreams that had drawn them across the turbulent Atlantic in the first place.

They had come looking for freedom, and that they had

found. Here they were not trapped in overcrowded ghettos decreed by the czar. Here in America they could live anywhere they wanted! The fact that they continued to live in a ghetto was simply because they were too poor to live anywhere else.

The escape from oppressive fear—that, too, was behind them. No matter what else happened to them, Josef would not be arrested and tried in a false court for a crime he had not committed. But even with these blessings, there had been more to their American dream. So much more. Their dreams had included affluence and the joy of being able to have what they wanted. Their fantasies had nurtured shimmering images of wealth, visions of wonderful cities where ordinary people could become rich.

These were the visions that had sustained them through the poverty in the old country, through the years in the Vilna ghetto when even a satisfying meal was a rarity. Dinner in Vilna had meant Rachel closing the storefront where she sold her lace, tying her head in a kerchief, and hurrying to Mottye Kazar's little store to buy a small fish and a cup of fish brine. That night the family would share the tiny fish and dip their bread in the diluted brine.

Those nights in Vilna, while their stomachs growled with hunger, they would count the kopecks they were saving for their passage and dream of living in the country where a man— if he was willing to work hard enough—could have what he wanted.

But then they had arrived in Chicago, and life was the same hard struggle for survival, the same day-to-day battle to put bread on the table. Somewhere in that struggle, with starvation and death always so near, the light had gone out of the dream. They had come to accept a life of poverty and ugliness and sweatshops as natural. Living among impoverished immigrants exactly like themselves, they had never known anything else.

"And so, Josef. So tell us. Walking to the fair, you saw carriages? You saw people riding machines made from two wheels? So tell us."

As the mother in the family, Rachel's life was the most limited. Her existence was bounded by the tenement where she lived and the dirty, windowless room, a few buildings away, where she picked up her sewing. For a while she had gone to Sabbath services in a nearby storefront where a small congregation of Lithuanians held services. But it had been months since Rachel had even left the block. She spoke so little English, where was she to go?

Hannah, too, had rarely been farther from the tenement than the public school three blocks away. It was the fair that burst open the boundaries of her world, for it had allowed her to witness for herself the glittering world outside. Seeing ladies ride past in their beautiful carved carriages had filled her with the certainty of a life she had only imagined.

For Josef, it was the giant electric generator—an invention of an immigrant—that had most inspired him. Josef was painfully aware of his deficiencies. He was not a student. In Russia his performance in *cheder* had been disappointing. Here, of course, his situation was worse. Unlike Hannah who attended a free public school, Josef had immediately gone to work. He had learned to speak English, but he could read only a few words.

"So, Josef. Do people ever fall off these two-wheeled machines?"

"Sometimes. It's too hard to stop the bicycle. The person riding it has to jump off while it's still rolling. It's a good idea, but it could be better."

What Josef *could* do was tinker. He could understand the relationships between things. That was one reason he had taken a job at Illinois Rawhide.

His father said that touching the nasty leather skins with his hands was demeaning, that there was no future in factory work. But Josef couldn't make his clumsy fingers sew the small stitches needed to help with his mother's sewing. When he found a job making leather strips into giant pulleys, he took it.

Six days a week, for ten hours a day, Josef loaded the sticky, tanned leather strips onto a machine. It didn't seem so bad at first. Except for the stench of the tanning solution. Or the boredom and the low pay. Or the way the tanning fluid turned the skin on his fingers into hard sheets that cracked and bled. Of course, there was also the danger. One of the workers had caught his hand in the machine, and it had ripped off three of his fingers.

But somehow, none of it really touched him. He didn't even join the union as some of the workers had requested because Josef didn't think of this job as his life. To him it was temporary—only a way to keep bread on the table.

It wasn't his *own* future that concerned him. It was Hannah's. Every day, when school was over, the girl returned to the tenement to help her mother sew. But soon, when she had finished school once and for all, Josef feared that her part-time sewing would become her future. When Josef thought that his beautiful sister might be trapped in the life his mother lived, he felt crazy with desperation.

He knew there had to be some opportunity that would save her. He felt that if only something could be arranged, something that would put Hannah in just the right place at just the right moment, a good life would fall into place for her. His problem was that he had no idea what to do to make it happen.

His passion for this idea took root and grew. Now, during the warm nights when he took Hannah on walks to get her out of the apartment, he used his time alone with her to kindle her ambition. He felt that if he could impart his determination to her, she herself could somehow make that mysterious "something" happen.

"There aren't many opportunities for a girl, Hannah," he said fretfully, walking slowly. "Not many at all."

Hannah looked at her brother out of the corner of her eye. *He's starting again*, she thought.

"There aren't *many* good jobs," he continued, determined to finish, "but there must be one somewhere. A respectable job. Not a job in a sweatshop. A good job in a nice place where a rich man will see you and want to marry you."

"Imagine being married to a rich man." Hannah sighed, and for a moment she allowed herself the luxury of that dream. "Imagine having beautiful dresses and hats and never having to worry."

"Hannah, in this country you *can* have that, but not from thinking. You have to *do* something."

Hannah stopped and turned to her brother in exasperation. "But what, Josef? What can I do?"

Josef looked away. Without a solution he could offer no answer. But he did have news he felt he should tell her.

"Hannah, last week, Papa told me he's been talking to Samuel Nachman about a match."

"No!"

Hannah shuddered. Samuel Nachman's older son, Nathan, was ugly. He had stringy black hair that was already thinning and a long, scraggly beard that didn't hide the pimples on his face. Anyway, Samuel Nachman and his son were peddlers! If she married him, she would only be exchanging one tenement for another.

Hannah shook her head impatiently and walked ahead. Why was everyone in such a hurry to rush her into the future? This constant pressure to push her into the rest of her life was making her crazy. She was a good girl. What she needed was to be told what to do. Then she could do it.

One evening as Josef returned home from the factory in the late-summer twilight, he passed a group of children in the neighborhood playing a game. They were jumping into squares scratched on the wooden sidewalks, and as they jumped, they chanted a song over and over:

All the girls who wear high heels,
They trade down at Marshall Field's.
All the girls who scrub the floor,
They trade at the Boston Store.

That Friday Josef held back twenty cents when he gave his pay to his mother. The next day, wearing clean clothes, Josef and Hannah nervously stepped onto the streetcar and dropped five cents each into the change box. When they got within sight of the large buildings that marked the heart of the commercial district, they got off.

They had arrived at State Street.

"How beautiful." Hannah sighed. She was awed by the majesty of the shopping district. Palatial white buildings supported by pillars with ornate cornices faced each other across a wide, tidy street. Clean, paved sidewalks stretched grandly in front of them. Lacquered carriages raced by, barely avoiding the pedestrians who hurried across the street.

Just around the corner from State Street, at the side entrance to the magnificent Marshall Field store, Josef and Hannah watched as a carriage pulled up to the door. The coachman jumped down from the driver's seat and helped his lady step from the carriage. When she reached the entrance of the department store, a man in a blue uniform opened the door and greeted her by name.

The brother and sister stood where they were as if their feet were glued to the pavement. This opulence was more than they had expected. Even worse, the man at the door seemed to know all the shoppers. What if he noticed their shabby clothes and wouldn't let them in?

As they began to walk slowly along State Street, Josef kept his eyes fixed on the sidewalk in front of them. He had talked so bravely until then that he didn't want Hannah to see the intimidation on his face. When they reached the large doors of the main entrance a half block away, they noticed that there was no doorman. Shoppers were casually strolling in and out. After a quick glance at each other Josef and Hannah found the courage to enter.

Inside, the splendor was awe-inspiring. High, frescoed ceilings were emblazoned with clouds and angels. Soft carpets hushed the steps of shoppers as they moved past glass cases filled with sheer Belgian lace, French hats, and gleaming Bohemian glass trinkets.

In the center of the first floor, light glowed through a glass dome to illuminate bright Oriental silks and sparkling silver buckles that were strategically placed below. A grand staircase twenty-three feet wide led from the broad middle aisle to the second floor. Even from the first floor they could see a profusion of beautiful dresses hanging along the walls.

Hannah and Josef were anxious to avoid making a mistake, so when they saw several well-dressed women waiting in front of a large closed door, they waited with them. When the door opened, they followed the women inside a small room.

A Negro man, wearing a glove on his left hand, closed a metal door and said, "Floors, please." He pushed a lever with his right hand, and they felt a peculiar sensation in their stomachs. When the door opened, they were on another floor where carpets woven with large roses were piled high in a luxurious disarray.

The Negro man closed the door and moved the lever again. Once again they felt the strange sensation as they soared upward. When the door opened, they saw hundreds of women sitting at worktables stitching dresses. Everyone left the small room but Hannah and Josef and the elevator operator who did not speak to them or seem to notice them. When a woman entered and said, "Down, please," he closed the door and the elevator floated downward. When the door opened on the first floor, Hannah and Josef stepped out. Without speaking to each other, they left the store.

It was all just too much for Josef. He walked quickly to get away from the truth he had just seen. It was impossible. His little sister in her plain brown dress could never work in such glittering wealth. He was seized with shame that he had misled her so badly. He had encouraged Hannah to want what she could never have. What a terrible mistake!

For once Hannah didn't notice Josef's mood, for she was busy with her own thoughts. The opulence thrilled her. She had never believed such beauty could be so near at hand, so accessible. Now she understood the life Josef had described! Now she had a clearer idea of what she wanted.

She stopped walking and resolutely turned to her brother. "You were right, Josef. That is where I belong."

Josef's heart ached. He turned away gruffly. "Don't be ridiculous, Hannah. Don't be crazy."

While they were returning home on the streetcar, Hannah sat quietly. She was angry and confused by Josef's attitude. First he had nagged her to make her life different. Then he had told her to forget it. As far as Hannah was concerned, she had just discovered her dream.

In the privacy of her thoughts, she debated with Josef. She was pretty, wasn't she? People paid attention to her. She could do things other girls in her position might not be able to do. She *knew* she could. It was the first time Hannah had ever resented her brother's control. For the first time in her life Hannah made plans for herself.

Early on Monday morning, after Papa had taken his push-cart to the street and Josef had left for work, Hannah quickly finished the last jacket in Mama's pile. But instead of putting it with the others, she hid it under the dingy cloth she used for a sheet. After Mama left, carrying the heavy bag of clothes to the man who would pay her, Hannah sent her younger sisters outside to play.

Quickly, her heart racing, she splashed her face with water from the pump. Then she put on her brown dress and ran a broken comb through her hair. With trembling hands, she took ten cents from the coffee jar, carefully folded the new jacket, and went outside. When the streetcar arrived, she climbed aboard.

The car arrived at State Street and she knew just where to go. She walked to the main entrance at Marshall Field's, headed toward the back of the store, waited until the elevator door opened, and, with her heart pounding so hard she was sure the Negro would notice, said, "Up, please."

He looked at her with amusement. "Up? Up to where?"

Hannah panicked. She couldn't remember where she had seen the women sewing. "Up to—up to where the sewing happens."

The man shook his head. The store sure was attracting a low class of customers these days. "You mean five."

"Yes. Five."

When the elevator arrived, Hannah stepped out and asked one of the women for the boss.

A man wearing thick glasses low on his nose stepped forward. Without speaking, he examined the jacket she had brought as a sample of her work. Then he stared at her for a long moment.

"You an immigrant?"

Hannah swallowed and nodded yes. As she lowered her eyes nervously, he watched her. She was so beautiful, so incredibly desirable. When he handed her back the jacket, her hand trembled. Despite the compassion that her vulnerability stirred in him, he felt a rising of excitement.

He knew that the store tried to limit the foreign influence among its employees. Foreigners were usually the ones who instigated the wage strikes in the factories. But this one, he thought, this one might be worth the risk.

He cleared his throat. "All right, start tomorrow. Be here at seven-thirty and don't be late. You'll get four dollars a week— not a penny more. It's low, but you also get the prestige of working at Field's."

Hannah felt color rush to her face. She looked deeply into her new boss's eyes to make sure she really understand what he had said. She felt such joy and gratitude that she wanted to take this stranger's hand and kiss it. Tears filled her eyes, and she whispered, "Thank you, sir."

As she turned away from him to move toward the elevator, he stopped her dryly. "Take the back stairs, sister. You work here now."

Hannah emerged in the alley behind the store, jubilant over her good fortune. She wanted to jump up and down or laugh insanely. She had done it! And it had been so simple! Her mind raced as she hurried to the streetcar. Four dollars a week! Her mother earned only three. Of course, she *did* have to pay for the streetcar. Let's see, at five cents each way, six days a week, that was—her heart sank—sixty cents! No matter. She would pay her family two dollars. Out of the two dollars left, she'd pay the streetcar and have a dollar and forty cents left over. She would save and save, and someday she would buy a beautiful dress.

When she was a block from home, Hannah saw her mother standing on the front steps, waving her arms, talking loudly to several of the neighborhood women. When she got closer, she saw that her mother was crying.

Hannah ran to her, alarmed. "Mama! What's wrong?"

A neighbor named Etta shook her head in disgust. "You couldn't tell your mother you were leaving? Look at her! You frightened her to death!"

Sobbing, Rachel embraced her child. "My baby! What got into you to leave the house? I was so frightened."

Hannah's eyes glowed with pride. "I got a job, Mama. A job! At Marshall Field's big department store!"

The fear on Rachel's face shifted to fury. "To get a job, you leave your sisters outside, Hannah? And the door unlocked! How could you do such a thing?"

The joy Hannah had felt began to disappear. This was the first time she had ever disappointed her mother. She led her mother to the back stairs to get away from the neighbor's prying ears, and they walked wearily up to the apartment. Now that Hannah's enthusiasm was extinguished, she felt so tired.

Inside the apartment her mother paced back and forth, harsh words of blame flowing as easily as her tears a few minutes before. She was shocked, she said, shocked—as much that Hannah would take the family's money without asking as for the reckless will that her behavior demonstrated. Was this the sweet girl the family had trusted? What could have happened to change her?

When Yankel burst through the door, he was enraged. Etta had met him at the landing so she could be the first to give him the news about his errant daughter. For the first time in Hannah's life Yankel grabbed her roughly and shouted at her.

Hours later, just when Hannah had begun to feel so bad about going downtown that she was considering giving up the job, Josef arrived home. When he heard what she had done, pride shone in his eyes.

"Wonderful," he sighed to the astonishment of his parents. "It's wonderful."

For the rest of the evening Josef talked and cajoled his parents into accepting Hannah's new job. To his mother, he spoke of the opportunity and the healthy working conditions in the beautiful, clean store. To his father, he spoke of the money Hannah could bring to the family.

To conclude his argument, he added, "I'll walk Hannah to the streetcar every morning and meet her there every night. She'll be safe. Anyway, she's safer on State Street than around here, where the Irish stare at her and yell."

Yankel and Rachel looked at each other. It was true. They couldn't keep Hannah locked up in a tenement room forever. Someday she would have to go. Maybe this was the place for her to find a good life.

The next morning Hannah and Josef set off for the street-car at six-thirty to make sure she wouldn't be late. He waited at the stop until the car had arrived. Even after she had climbed on board, he stood watching and waving until it had disappeared.

Later, when Hannah recalled this period in her life, all the days blurred into one. She remembered climbing aboard the streetcar each morning and saying good-bye to her brother. She remembered the supervisor at the back door making a mark beside her name when she entered the store. She remembered walking up the back stairs to her floor, sitting at her table and pushing a silver needle through the exquisite fabrics, knowing there was a better life somewhere, downstairs, in the wide aisles filled with the dresses and lingerie and lace. And she remembered wondering how she would ever be able to get there from the sewing room on the fifth floor.

4

HELEN CLIMBED THE STAIRS to Isabelle's second-floor sitting room heavily. She wasn't used to delivering notes from fancy society ladies to her mistress, and she didn't like the idea one bit. One night, while old Phillip Woodruff was stripping off his trousers in her room, he had mentioned Isabelle's inability to make new friends. "A disappointment to me," he had said. "A severe disappointment."

Well, that was just what Helen wanted Isabelle to remain: a disappointment.

"This note was just brought here by Mrs. Potter Palmer's driver," Helen said. Even Helen knew that the Palmers owned the famous Palmer House, but she rolled her eyes to show how little she thought of the note. "I wonder what she wants?"

When Isabelle didn't answer, Helen continued. "If I was you, I wouldn't let that woman take advantage of me!"

Isabelle waited until Helen had left the room before she opened Bertha Palmer's letter.

"Please join me at my home," it said, "for a lecture I will be giving for the advancement of shopgirls. I think that, as an intelligent young woman, you might have much to contribute to the less fortunate of our sex."

Isabelle wrote the event in her calendar. Then she folded the invitation and tore it into small pieces. Lately she'd had a feeling that Helen looked through her things. There was no sense making it easy for her.

Isabelle leaned back in her chair and thought about the note. The phrase "the less fortunate of our sex" stuck in her mind. Isabelle had always believed herself to be one of the least fortunate women she knew. It was not because she had lived in fear of starvation or anything as serious as that. It was because she had always lived so close to wealth that she was aware of all the things she was missing.

Isabelle Chadwick had married Phillip Woodruff partly because he was the wealthiest man who seemed likely to ask and partly because her family insisted. They had been in debt to Woodruff for years—since just after the Chicago fire in 1871. Like thousands of other Chicagoans, her father had been devastated by the fire. Completely burned out. Not only was his barbed-wire factory lost, but the family's home had been reduced to ashes, too. All they had managed to save was a heavy chest filled with gold-rimmed china and some precious pieces of silver.

Her father had already lost the licensing rights to his process for making barbed wire, but he was sure that he could develop another process if he only had the funding. But the bankers in Chicago thought he was a bad risk for a loan. Only the stern Phillip Woodruff had agreed to help William Chadwick arrange the money to rebuild his business.

Unfortunately the other bankers were more correct in their estimate of Chadwick than the usually tightfisted Phillip Woodruff. Chadwick's weakness for strong drink had made a bad situation worse.

All Isabelle could remember about her childhood was her parents' bickering. Her mother endlessly lamented her father's bad luck, pointing out how Marshall Field, Cyrus McCormick, Philip D. Armour, Gustavus Swift, and Potter Palmer all had been burned out by the same fire. But while Chadwick Wire barely stayed in business, the rest had become wealthy—rich as kings. It seemed to Isabelle's mother that everyone had made a success but William Chadwick.

Isabelle's mother sent her to Miss Hopkins's School for

Young Ladies, but even as a child, she could feel the vast social distance that separated her from her wealthier schoolmates. As she grew up, she felt isolated and different. She shyly yearned to be accepted but, at the same time, feared she wasn't good enough.

It seemed to her that her father's drinking was *her* disgrace. The girls were civil to her, but she was rarely invited to their extravagant parties. Whenever she overheard them whispering about a glittering event she hadn't been invited to, she walked away, holding her head high as if she didn't care. But she did care. Being ignored made her feel ashamed. It always seemed to her that she was the only one in the school who was excluded.

It was a difficult way to grow up. She was shy and quiet all day at Miss Hopkins's, but when she returned home in the afternoon, she had to face her mother's questions. Did you speak to Sara Covington today? Isn't she having a party this weekend? Young lady, your father and I are sacrificing to send you to that school so you can make friends with the better people. Someday you'll regret not taking advantage of it.

With no one in the world she could talk to, Isabelle escaped into music. Every day she practiced on the old carved piano in the parlor. By playing the scales and arpeggios hard, she could pound out her anger at being trapped in an unhappy family at home and a sterile, lonely life at school. But when she played Chopin and the sad, haunting melodies by Schumann, she learned to let her fingers stroke the keys gently, coaxing all the sorrow from the music while she grieved silently for herself.

In her final year at Miss Hopkins's, Isabelle was introduced to Phillip Woodruff at a graduation party given for the entire school. Two evenings later Woodruff called at the Chadwick home.

Phillip Woodruff was a thin, angular man with a high forehead and dark eyes that lacked luster. His manner was stern and terse, and he had a way of pursing his lips in the silence that always hung in a room before he spoke. When Woodruff appeared at the front door, Isabelle's father first thought that the purpose of his call was to discuss the outstanding sum on the loan. But when Isabelle came into the living room to greet him, old Woodruff's deeply lined face had actually flushed. When he didn't even mention the loan and returned the following night, it became clear that he was courting Isabelle.

Phillip was not the handsome, young lover Isabelle had dreamed of, but he seemed to be the only way for her to come into her own. With Phillip, she hoped she could finally feel as good as everybody else—perhaps even develop the easy confidence she had envied in the richer girls. She thought that as his wife she would be accepted, and she eagerly anticipated invitations to the elite gatherings in the mansions on Prairie Avenue and Lake Shore Drive.

But that had not happened. Her mother had gone overboard planning an extravagant wedding. The tables at the reception had been heaped with enormous flower arrangements, and Isabelle was stunning in a luminous silk dress encrusted with embroidery and seed pearls. And as Isabelle's mother had hoped, the wedding was covered in the papers. But a small scandal sheet that pandered to the elite ran a peculiarly savage item:

CHADWICK-WOODRUFF NUPTIALS

Amid the orange blossoms and seed pearls at the Chadwick-Woodruff reception at the Palmer House were rumors that romance was only one of the bride's motives. After a short, three-month engagement it was said that the bridegroom, as a wedding present to his beloved, canceled the note her father had signed so many years ago. While this city is no stranger to weddings that are little more than commercial transactions, tongues are wagging.

When Isabelle read the item, she felt sick with shock. She knew, despite all the compliments at the wedding, that this nasty gossip would be savored and repeated. She had feared public embarrassment all her life, and now, just when she thought she was safe, it had finally happened.

Phillip was angry about the article—angry enough to have a severe talk with the publisher—but Isabelle could feel a subtle change in his feelings toward her. As a rich man he had looked forward to capturing a young prize and showing her off. Now

his prize had been publicly tarnished and was less valuable to
him.

In the first few months of their marriage Isabelle was too
humiliated to appear comfortably at social events. It was ironic.
She finally had everything her old classmates had, but nothing
had changed. She was still friendless and alone.

Two weeks after the arrival of Mrs. Palmer's invitation,
Isabelle knocked self-consciously on the door at the Palmer
mansion. When she was admitted into the massive stone house,
she looked about in awe. The hallway was three stories high!
It was hung profusely with exquisite tapestries and European
paintings.

Isabelle followed the maid, still aware that she didn't know
why she had been invited. It certainly was not because Mrs.
Palmer was impressed with her socially. On several occasions
when they had been in meetings for the Women's Pavilion,
Mrs. Palmer had been courteous, but she had never shown any
personal interest in her.

When Isabelle reached the ballroom, she stood by herself
for a few moments to survey the room before she entered. The
walls were covered with colorful, blurred paintings she had
heard about but never seen before. She assumed that they were
the strange Impressionist paintings Potter Palmer purchased
every year in Paris.

In the crowd Isabelle noticed that about two dozen of society's bright young members were chatting amiably with one
another. Standing around the room in small, self-conscious clusters, at least forty shopgirls awkwardly munched cookies and
sipped tea. It was obvious that they, too, felt uncomfortable and
out of place.

When Isabelle spotted Mrs. Palmer's shining gray hair, she
walked across the room to greet her. But before Isabelle could
get there, Mrs. Palmer stepped up onto the bandstand at the
front of the room.

Dominating the gathering with her powerful presence,
Bertha Palmer began. "I'm sure you all know, ladies, that this
city is filled with chivalrous men." She made her opening announcement ironically, casting her eyes over the crowd to bring

them into the joke. "Indeed, there are very many men who believe that women should never, ever work! Isn't that kind of them?"

Several women chuckled, and Mrs. Palmer paused so the irony would not escape the rest of the audience.

"Alas, these splendid fellows claim that when a woman becomes a breadwinner, it destroys their sense of chivalry."

She paused again, letting it sink in.

"Of course, we are told that chivalry is a higher sense and that we should feel lucky that it even exists. But ask yourself, my friends, does this higher sensitivity help widows survive? Does it enable the wives of drunkards to feed their children? Unfortunately what this so-called nobility of thought does is keep women from earning the same pay as their male counterparts!"

The women standing on the floor whispered among themselves. Many of them had heard Mrs. Palmer's chivalry speech before. But Isabelle was astonished to hear these notions spoken publicly. Phillip would not have tolerated such talk about work and equal pay.

"The shopgirls you meet here today," Mrs. Palmer continued, "exist on four to six dollars a week. Think of that! Yet many of them support children. Ladies, it is up to us to help them in every way that we can. To that end the first half of this meeting will be devoted to a new science called nutrition."

With that Mrs. Palmer introduced a young woman in round spectacles who began speaking about how the emerging concepts of dietetics would enable a woman to nourish her family on very little money.

As she left the platform, Mrs. Palmer noticed Isabelle and walked to her resolutely. When Isabelle extended her hand, she accepted it in her calm, regal way. "I'm so happy you could come, my dear," she said.

Isabelle nervously searched her mind for a charming response. She heard herself say, "I appreciate your invitation."

"Good. I invited you here because—" Mrs. Palmer paused for a moment, searching for the proper way to express her thought—"because I felt that *you* would be particularly sympathetic to undeserved pain."

This remark caught Isabelle by surprise. She felt embarrassed and violated, as if this stranger had suddenly lifted a lid to peer into her personal life. She met Mrs. Palmer's searching eyes for a second and then looked away to compose herself.

So Mrs. Palmer knew about her father! Of course, she did. His drinking, especially that terrible time at the Swifts' Christmas party, was probably well known in society. Perhaps she knew what was going on in her marriage, too. What if Phillip had told Mr. Palmer during one of their lunches that he didn't even like to come home!

Isabelle blushed a hot deep crimson. She was flattered by Mrs. Palmer's attention, yet she deeply resented this personal intrusion. She spoke carefully, ignoring Mrs. Palmer's meaning.

"My husband believes that women should not work," Isabelle said. "He believes that if men are robbed of their right to protect the weaker sex, they will become indifferent to women."

Mrs. Palmer surprised Isabelle by laughing. "Why, of course, he does. But, my dear, justice for all is more to be desired than pedestals for a few. Surely we can convince your husband of *that*."

As if she had been moved by a new idea, Mrs. Palmer continued with excitement. "Isabelle, have you heard of Hull House? It's the only settlement house in America, and it's right here in Chicago."

Isabelle looked at Mrs. Palmer curiously. Hull House? She had heard of that place. Apparently poor people were free to drop in there whenever they wanted. She had heard somewhere that Mrs. Palmer had taken to visiting there herself.

"We've all been busy getting the Women's Pavilion ready for the fair, but now that it's running smoothly, it's time to redirect our energies. Meet me at Hull House next week. I know you have much to contribute, and I'm sure that once you see it, you will be very impressed."

Isabelle realized that the invitation was more of a command than a request. She tried to appear interested, but inwardly wondered why anyone would want to go to the worst part of town to visit an old, run-down house full of poor people.

Before Mrs. Palmer walked away to greet the other guests, she smiled confidentially at Isabelle. "My dear," she said, "social involvement is not only a moral thing to do. I have found that the best way for a woman to handle an absentee husband is to become involved in fascinating things herself."

It took Isabelle three weeks before she was brave enough to go into that notorious neighborhood to visit Hull House. She arrived late for a meeting of the Italian Social Club, and now that it was finally over, she found herself waiting awkwardly in the doorway to speak to Mrs. Palmer.

A group of poor Italian women reeking of garlic and body odor shoved past her to get downstairs for coffee and cake. Isabelle moved out of their way into the hallway and asked herself for at least the tenth time this evening what she was doing here.

How silly she was to come! To sit through an interminable women's meeting spoken in a confusing argot of Italian and English—just because Mrs. Palmer had asked her.

And if that wasn't bad enough, the neighborhood around Hull House was so dangerous that even her coachman was afraid to wait outside. He had insisted on taking the carriage back to the safety of Michigan Avenue and wasn't due to pick her up for more than an hour.

When Mrs. Palmer finally emerged from the meeting room, it was obvious that she had completely forgotten that she had invited Isabelle. She was engrossed in conversation with a short woman who held her head awkwardly to one side and an old Italian woman in a worn black dress. The Italian woman was carrying a large cloth that was elaborately embroidered in bright red and blue thread.

Mrs. Palmer noticed Isabelle standing at the door. "Oh, Mrs. Woodruff, how nice that you could join us. May I present Jane Addams, the founder of Hull House?"

Isabelle extended her hand to the short woman and murmured a greeting. In the last few years everybody had heard of Jane Addams. The fact that she had created the first settlement house in America was said to be highly commendable.

Mrs. Palmer continued her introduction. "And this is Mrs. Giannelli. Ever since she started teaching embroidery here, her daughter has become proud of the beautiful handwork she did in the old country, isn't that right, Mrs. Giannelli?"

"*Sì*. Before the classes, my daughter, she not like the old ways."

Miss Addams smiled at the woman. "Your daughter liked only things that were American, isn't that right?"

The Italian woman was smiling and nodding. "Now she come to meetings, she believe my stitching is *bella*. She learn to stitch herself."

This comment prompted Mrs. Palmer to give Isabelle a look that said, "You see how much these people need!" But Isabelle felt baffled. She had no idea why this woman's stitchery was so important to Chicago's greatest lady, and she felt out of place. Even the old woman seemed more comfortable than she did.

When they got downstairs, Mrs. Palmer turned to Isabelle and extended her hand. "My dear, it was so nice to see you here, but forgive me, I must run. I promised my husband I would entertain friends from out of town, and I simply cannot be any later than I already am. I'm sure Miss Addams will be delighted to show you around. Send me a note, and we'll try to get together here next week."

Isabelle tried not to show her disappointment. What a ridiculous evening, she thought. The least Mrs. Palmer could do was offer her a ride! Now she was trapped here for more than an hour with a group of women she couldn't even understand. And she was supposed to come back next week!

As the large front door closed behind Mrs. Palmer, the tiny Miss Addams looked up at Isabelle. "Well," she said matter-of-factly, "might as well make the best of it."

Isabelle decided to acknowledge her disappointment honestly. She took a breath and nodded. "Yes, I suppose you're right."

"Well, then, why don't I show you the place and you can ask me whatever you want to know about our work here."

They moved down the hall until they were even with the reception room. Miss Addams stopped for a moment and looked in. "Well, things seem to be going well in here."

Inside, Italian women of all ages—some with small, wet-nosed children hoisted on their hips—were chattering loudly as they devoured cake. *This is just a party*, Isabelle thought. *How can they call this important social work?*

"I really don't think I understand what you do here."

"We do whatever needs doing," Miss Addams said. "To-night you saw women who had lost all sense of their worth in America even though they had brought wonderful skills from their homeland. We try to help them feel pride in their accomplishments."

"I see. Do you ever help Americans?" Isabelle asked.

"Native-born Americans? Oh, certainly. In this neighborhood everybody needs assistance. Lately there have been some horrible murders in the area—women being stabbed on their way home at night—and we're trying to organize neighborhood protection. Of course, our biggest challenge is the poverty."

Jane Addams hobbled upstairs as she talked. "So many of the people who come here have lost their jobs and can't find work. The situation is simply overwhelming. Even City Hall has run out of space."

"City Hall?"

"Heavens, don't you know?" Jane Addams stopped on the stairs to turn back to Isabelle. "Last winter hundreds of people slept in the halls and stairs at City Hall every night. I know of people who actually *begged* police officers to arrest them just so they could sleep on a dirty mattress in jail."

Isabelle was sorry for such people, but she wasn't sure why she should get involved. It seemed so obvious that anyone could get a job if he really wanted one. Her husband had told her that.

"Well, of course, most of them never dreamed it would happen to them," Miss Addams continued. "And now that it has, well, they're just very embarrassed about it. Imagine. Good, solid Americans in this kind of fix. Sometimes they won't even come for help."

Jane Addams turned to move down the hall toward the second-floor lecture room.

"Don't misunderstand me, Mrs. Woodruff," she said. "I myself firmly believe that people *should* work. I do think that indolence is bad for the human spirit. In my work here I've come to see an enormous difference between those who are *temporarily* embarrassed and those who have become accustomed to it."

"Miss Addams," Isabelle asked, "I can understand helping

people who need jobs, but ... I still don't understand what good a meeting like the one tonight accomplishes."

"What *good*—"

"Well—" Isabelle was at a loss for words—"it won't help them earn money for their families, will it?"

"Why, of course not." Miss Addams walked off down the hall. "It's not intended to. A good life is *more* than simple sustenance, my dear. For life to be good, people need laughter and society." With a gesture and spirit that seemed unfamiliar to her, Jane Addams gaily threw her small hands in the air. "They need to have fun—just the way you do."

Isabelle nodded. Yes, she knew how much she needed fun because she had so little of it. She still spent most of her time alone or with little James in the mansion. She couldn't even remember the last time Phillip had complimented her or danced with her or told her he was pleased to be married to her.

She did remember something Phillip had said before she had the baby. "You're not just *any* woman anymore," he had said. "You're special. You're going to be the mother of my child."

At first she had taken that as a compliment, but from that time on Phillip had stayed away from her. He had moved into another bedroom with the excuse that he didn't want to "bother her" when she was pregnant, and he had never touched her again.

Now, standing in the hallway at Hull House, Isabelle realized that Miss Addams was still talking about the needs of the poor. "Poor people are like anybody else," she said. "They need beauty and music like the rest of us."

Isabelle suddenly realized the absolute truth of what Miss Addams was saying. "Of course," she agreed. "Especially music. Everyone needs music."

"Ah!" Miss Addams said, looking at her with new interest. "So you play, do you?"

"Playing means a great deal to me."

"I see."

As Jane Addams led this young woman down the hall, she wondered about her. She felt sadness and longing in her, emotions quite different from the attitudes of the other rich women who came here to help. Those women were talkative and expressed themselves with ease and self-confidence. They exuded a sense of haste, the hurried pace of people who had other, more interesting things to do. Instead of enjoying a life that was full to bursting with parties and events, this Mrs. Woodruff seemed to be starving.

"Well, we could certainly use more music at Hull House," Jane Addams said. "These people would greatly appreciate it."

Isabelle didn't care two snaps about Hull House. Whether Jane Addams liked it or not, the idea of finding something worthwhile among poor people was puzzling to her. She had spent too much of her life looking up, always wanting to please people above her.

When they arrived at the end of the hall, they came to another meeting room. The door was open, and they could see a tall man with high, prominent cheekbones and straight dark hair lecturing at the front of the room. About a dozen men dressed in an astonishing assortment of rags were listening intently. The man was speaking calmly, almost quietly, yet the audience was transfixed, leaning forward to hear every word.

"That seems to be a successful lecture," said Isabelle.

"Oh, indeed. There's no one more compelling to listen to than Clarence Darrow," Miss Addams said. "The men he's addressing are tramps and hoboes. Some of them haven't worked in years."

As Isabelle turned her attention to the lecture, one of the Italian women hurried toward them. "Miss Addams," she said, "downstairs, please."

"Oh, dear, sounds like an emergency." Jane Addams winked at Isabelle. "They must have run out of cake or need me to find the cookies. Why don't you find a seat, Mrs. Woodruff? You might enjoy hearing Mr. Darrow yourself. He has quite a following."

Isabelle looked over the crowd of dirty spectators and carefully chose an isolated seat in the last row where she wouldn't have to sit next to anyone. As she focused on what Clarence Darrow was saying, she became increasingly perplexed. The tall man in the rumpled suit was actually encouraging the poor men in his audience not to work.

"Victims," he was saying. "You are all victims in a capitalist society that has shut you out. First they lock you out. Then they heap you with blame for being outside. The problem is—you believe them."

He paused and looked at them. "Yes, I know you believe them. You feel bad for being out of work—bad, as if the fault were with yourself. I expect, even now, you're sitting out there, foolishly dreaming about respectability and work. Well, gentlemen, I urge you to forget it. Don't tie yourself to someone else's dream. Follow your own hearts."

Isabelle could feel the power Darrow exerted over his audience. *What a shame*, she thought, *and what an outrage that he doesn't use his power to better use. How dare he encourage these men to distrust work and abandon their chances for a good life?*

When Darrow ended his speech and the men applauded, Isabelle fixed him with an angry stare.

Darrow had noticed the attractive young redhead with the serious face who had seated herself late. A rich woman, he thought. A spoiled rich woman. He stepped off his platform and strode slowly—almost insolently—toward her.

"Well," he said, grinning broadly, "enjoy the lecture?"

"If you mean, did I enjoy hearing you irresponsibly mislead those impoverished men, the answer is no."

Darrow tilted his head back and grinned down at the pretty woman. "No?"

Isabelle glared back defiantly. What was he doing here anyway? she wondered. Hadn't Miss Addams told her, less than twenty minutes ago, that she believed it was important for people to work?

"As a matter of fact, I plan to speak to Miss Addams about the subject of your lecture. I happen to know that she thinks it extremely important for people to improve themselves—not indulge in indolence, as you advocated."

"You 'happen to know'?" he mocked, smiling. "What you happen to know apparently does not include the fact that Miss Addams is nonpolitical, nonreligious, and nonsectarian."

My God, she's attractive, he thought. *How can anyone so serious and righteous be so attractive?*

Isabelle's eyes snapped. "What does that have to do with dangerously encouraging a crowd of unemployed hoboes to be irresponsible?"

"You see, Miss . . ." Darrow waited for Isabelle to give him her name. When she didn't, he continued. "You see, miss, Jane Addams believes that the free exchange of ideas is important— even when you don't agree with what's being said. She doesn't presume to control the discussions here. It's just another way of believing in our government's Constitution."

"I see." Isabelle felt irritated at being rebuked by this arrogant man. "And I suppose you are an expert on the Constitution?"

"Well, as a lawyer I've given it some thought now and then."

Isabelle's cheeks grew pink from being disparaged so rudely. "Nevertheless, I plan to discuss your lecture with Miss Addams."

"I hope you will." He smiled. "And I hope I see you again."

"You won't if I have some choice in the matter."

"Too bad," he said, enjoying her discomfort. "It would be fun to see you when you've become a little more human."

5

EVEN THIS EARLY IN the morning it was sweltering. The man sleeping in the alley stirred uncomfortably. Flies were buzzing madly at a pool of dried blood nearby. They were so agitated that they would drone furiously in the blood, then fly off in an arc to hurl themselves back at the feast that was hardening on the unpaved dirt. One of the flies buzzed near the sleeping man's ear, and when he turned, the sunlight exploded against his eyelids. His next sensation was the pain throbbing in his head.

He groaned and covered his eyes with his hand and tried to remember where he was. He remembered buying a bottle of whiskey in a bar and taking it outside. Even with the show in town, many bartenders didn't like having him inside. That was fine with him. He didn't like being in their bars, bumping up against the pale-faced men he hated. He preferred to do his drinking in private, where he could lose himself in his thoughts without the threat of interruption.

He sat up and glanced at the blood. For a moment he couldn't remember. Had he killed another woman last night? He felt a throb of anxiety. If he had and she was nearby, he had better get away from here fast. His eyes fell on the fur of a small animal, and he relaxed. As he waited for the thumping of his heart to subside, he remembered killing the cat.

He had found it devouring the remnants of a meal in a garbage can and had lifted it out. He hadn't planned to kill it, but when it scratched him, he had felt driven to hurt it. All in all, though, cutting it hadn't been that satisfactory, for the cat was a stray that nobody cared about.

He enjoyed killing city animals only when it was clear that they were cared for and fed by loving masters. Then, at least, he could imagine their horror when they came out, calling for their beloved pet, only to find it lying disemboweled on the ground. He liked to think about those people and how sick they felt when they turned their pet over and realized that all it was now was just a hollow dead thing with matted fur.

That scenario provided a grim enjoyment for the man when he needed it. But he knew that one of these days, when the fair and his show had closed, he'd have to eat those animals. Eating cats and dogs was nothing to him. He'd eaten worse things than that many a time. When it came right down to it, he figured he could survive in this city on his own pretty damn well.

A tiny, emaciated kitten stepped into the alley, meowing loudly. It walked nimbly to the lifeless cat and licked its fur tentatively. The man watched for a second before he pulled himself to his feet. First he had to do something to make his head stop hurting. Then he had to get to work. It wouldn't do for them to know he'd been drunk again.

He swooped up the kitten in one large hand and stuck it in his pouch. He'd either feed it later or put it out where the horses would run over it. It didn't really matter which. It would depend on how he felt.

Josef stepped to the edge of the stair landing and looked at the roof across the way. It was still hot this morning. The papers said it was the worst heat wave Chicago had seen in years. He knew that by noon hot air currents would ripple upward from the tarred roofs of the factories.

The air inside the family's tenement was so stifling that lately they'd slept on the landing outside, sharing it with three other families on the third floor. Since the toilets were in the backyard just below the stairs, the stench was almost nauseating. But Josef had found that after a while it was like working in the rawhide company. Somehow you lost your ability to smell.

Josef and Hannah climbed over the sleeping families on the lower landing and set off for work. She had been working at the department store for several months and was showing the influence of her new surroundings. Her new high-button shoes showed off the curve of her ankles, and she now walked erectly, with her shoulders back and her head up, to give herself an air of poise and assurance. Josef knew she must have seen this posture in the rich women who came for their fittings. He was pleased that she was picking up traits that might help her get out of the ghetto.

When they reached the streetcar stop, he waited until Hannah had gotten on the car. Then he walked east to the rawhide factory. When he arrived at the plant for work, the front door was still locked, and the foreman was standing outside, turning the workers away.

With nowhere to go, the men were hanging around uneasily in groups, shuffling their feet and talking in soft whispers. They looked frightened. Factories all over the city had been laying men off. As far as they knew, no one in the city was hiring.

Josef stepped up to the foreman. "What is happening here?" he asked.

"Go on home," answered the foreman. "You're laid off. A couple of factories that use pulleys have gone bust. Their orders have been canceled."

Josef saw a big man named Karl Lubek approach the yard. Lubek was muscular with dark, stringy hair and a long, drooping mustache. When the men saw him walking toward the guard, they nudged one another. They knew that when he found out, there was no telling what he'd do.

Karl Lubek took trouble with him wherever he went. Years before, in Warsaw, he had settled a labor dispute to his satisfaction by kicking in his employer's front door and nearly beating the man to death. With the police after him, Lubek had quickly set off for the shores of America and the reluctant arms of his relatives in Chicago.

Josef knew Lubek because they worked at machines that were no more than a few feet apart. Josef had tried to keep his distance because Lubek seemed like an angry, dangerous man, but Lubek had taken it upon himself to urge Josef to attend union meetings.

When Lubek heard about the layoff, he was furious.

"And so," he shouted angrily, "without conscience, you lay us off without pay!"

The foreman looked at the big Pole contemptuously. He had seen this type before. For the last decade the city had been ripped apart by strikes, and all of them had been started by these European anarchists.

"Hey, bud. There's no orders," said the foreman. "Figure it out! We're overstocked as it is."

"And you have no concern for anything but your damned profits! What about us? How are we to feed our families? This company owes us *something*!"

The foreman folded his arms with the attitude of a man in charge. "Give me your name."

Lubek answered immediately. "You want my name? You want to put me on report? Fine! I've done nothing wrong. I'm Karl Lubek, and—"

The foreman pulled a small notebook out of his jacket and jotted down Lubek's name. "Keep talkin', scum! Keep talkin' and I'll blacklist you! This company has every right to close its plant when there's no work. You turn this into a labor protest, and you'll not work in this city again."

The blacklist! Josef had heard what happened when such a list was circulated. Once you were on it, no one in town would hire you. He had heard of a man who spent two years going from place to place for work. He was in jail now for robbing a small dry goods store.

Josef saw the muscles in Lubek's shoulders tighten for a fight "Karl, don't!" he said. He pushed himself between Lubek and the foreman. "This man is upset," he said to the foreman. "He's worried about his family."

"Get him out of here!" the foreman shouted, shoving Josef away. "And you get the hell out, too. We don't need your kind here."

Lubek faced the foremen tensely for a few moments, hatred burning in his eyes. Then he turned abruptly and walked away.

Josef hurried to catch up with him, but Karl refused to

look at him. "Some fine Jew!" Karl lit a small black cigar as he walked. "Kissing the ass of a company man. And I thought you might be a good union man!"

"I've had trouble with the police before, and I don't want any more. Not here, in this country." Josef had another thought. "Why'd you give him your name? Don't you know what he'll do?"

"Ahhh! Who cares about a blacklist? If there's no work, what does it matter? You're out of a job, any way they slice it."

Josef suddenly had an idea. He stopped walking to get Lubek's attention. "Karl, I know of a place that's hiring. It's called the Pullman Palace Car Company."

Lubek stopped and turned, his face narrow with suspicion. "How do you know of this?"

"I got a brochure at the fair," Josef answered.

"Chssst." Lubek spit contemptuously and turned to walk on.

"You don't want to hear! Then good. Go on."

Lubek walked on a few steps. Then, reluctantly, he turned to wait for the rest of the information.

"Pullman makes special cars for trains," Josef said. "Sleeping cars, dining cars, parlor cars. They build beds into the ceilings and the walls that come down to—"

Lubek interrupted. "Can you explain to me why this company has work when others don't?"

In spite of himself, Josef always felt intimidated by Lubek. Lubek was his senior by twenty years and had been seasoning a foul temper all his life.

"Because of the *fair*, Karl," Josef answered. "The fair! Thousands—no *hundreds of thousands*—of people have been coming to Chicago for the fair. Railroad companies from all over America keep ordering Pullman cars. Most people don't want to ride a train unless they're in a Pullman car."

Josef pulled the Pullman brochure out of his pocket and carefully unfolded it. On the cover was a drawing of the town of Pullman. "Look, the company has even built a nice town for the workers to live in."

"Chssst!" Lubek's spittle flew inches above the brochure. "Whoever heard of a company doing anything decent for its workers?"

"No, you see, they *had* to. It's outside town, and the workers had to have somewhere to live. But see, they made it nice. The company thinks people will work better if they're living in a nice place. Look what it says."

Josef pointed to the opening words of the brochure. Hannah had read them to him so many times that he knew them by heart. "A community developed to eliminate all that is ugly, discordant and demoralizing."

Lubek laughed contemptuously. "I'm not going to live in a house owned by a railroad company. You want to live like a serf again? Once you put yourself in their power, they won't just own your work, they'll own you!"

Josef remembered what his father had always said about Russians—how they wouldn't let Jews own property to keep them powerless. But he didn't want to think about that now. He wanted to think about living in a nice town where his sisters would be safe.

"We have to go there to apply for the job anyway," Josef said. "Then we'll see the town and—who knows?"

After Lubek grudgingly agreed to check out the job situation in Pullman, he and Josef walked to the Illinois Central depot at Michigan Avenue and Twelfth Street.

A balding man with gold-rimmed glasses looked out at them from behind the bars at the ticket counter. "Pullman?" he repeated. He noticed Lubek's filthy face and took his time. Then he pointed in the general area of the tracks. "Train leaves on track three in twenty-three minutes. Round trip is fifty cents each."

Fifty cents! That was a princely sum for two men out of work. Lubek gave Josef a look that said it had better be worth it.

The train chugged out of the station, and as it headed south, the two men watched the soot-covered buildings rush by. For several blocks the train hugged the lake shore; then it raced on, picking up speed. Gradually the crowded city buildings became intermittent, and finally the tracks turned away from the lake and entered the open prairie. The men sat back, drinking in the sight of green fields and trees. Neither of them had seen a natural environment since they had arrived in Chicago. Under its influence they felt a sense of peace. They settled back on the rough, wooden benches and gazed thoughtfully out the window.

In twenty minutes the train slowed down, and the porter called out, "Pullman!" They came to a stop at a neat red-brick station trimmed in white limestone. Josef and Karl climbed down from the train and looked across the street toward the town.

What Josef saw made his heart light with joy. In front of the station was a broad stretch of freshly mown lawn. Acres of flower beds still glistened from being watered. In front of a large building a pretty little lake shimmered in the sun.

"What lake is that?" he asked the porter who was assisting passengers down the steep stairs.

"Lake Vista. Old Mr. Pullman put it there in front of the factory to make things look nice. The water comes from a pipe outta the factory. Kinda pretty, I'd say."

"So that's the factory there, is it? There, behind the lake?" Josef pointed at the large building that ran alongside a tall clock tower.

"Sure is. If you fellas are lookin' for work, they've got it. They been real busy lately."

Josef glanced at Lubek. Lubek was scowling. The pleasure Josef felt from seeing the clean, well-kept town was not enjoyed by a man who hated dirty capitalists. Without a word Karl Lubek stalked off the platform toward the factory. Josef had to hurry to catch up with him.

6

HOW THE MONTHS FLY BY, Hannah thought. It was October, and a chill had settled upon the city. She was stitching a rush order for a black funeral dress and feeling discontent.

The sewing job at Field's had lost its glamour, and the possibility of moving up in the company seemed less likely every day. It was true that she had moved away from the sweatshops in her neighborhood, but even so, she spent her days exactly like her mother—sewing in a room without windows. Only her brother with his new job at the Pullman Palace Car Company had made a change that seemed better.

Is this the way Mama and Papa feel, watching pointless days lengthen into meaningless years? she asked herself. *Is life always a matter of getting up, working all day, and going to bed—with every day exactly like every other? Here it is almost fall, and even though I'm working at Field's, I'm only a little better off than Mama.*

Hannah looked up to see her manager, Mr. Petersen, walking toward her, his jaw set in determination. He was followed by an even more serious-looking young man who was chewing his thin upper lip as he hurried forward in nervous, quick strides.

"Hannah," said her manager, "this is Mr. Harrison. He would like to know if you speak Yiddish."

Hannah blushed. She had tried to keep the staff at the store from knowing she was Jewish because she knew she'd be more likely to be promoted to a sales job downstairs if she were viewed as American.

"I . . . used to. But only a little."

Mr. Petersen turned to the young man. "You see. I told you she wouldn't be able to help you."

The young Mr. Harrison had managed to trap the scraggly end of his mustache over his bottom teeth and was chewing on it for all he was worth. "Too bad," he said. "We need someone to help us with an important Jewish customer at the wholesale house."

Hannah realized her mistake. "This customer—he speaks Yiddish?"

"He speaks English, too, of course," said the young Mr. Harrison. "At least I think he must. But Mr. Girard over in wholesale thought he'd feel more at home with a salesman who could speak to him in his own language. You know how it is."

Hannah did know, and she was determined that if anyone were going to sell to this Jewish merchant, it would be she.

"I'm sure I can handle the job, sir," she said, disregarding the frown from Mr. Petersen. "You can trust me."

"Hurry up then." Mr. Harrison was already heading toward the back stairs. "We don't keep our wholesale buyers waiting."

Petersen was furious. He didn't want to lose Hannah. She not only worked hard but was the prettiest girl in his department. Not that he had approached her, but it was nice to have someone around he could dream about.

He spoke to her severely. "I thought you understood when I hired you, Hannah, that I need you in *this* department."

Hannah dazzled him with a sudden smile before she turned to follow Harrison. "Don't worry, Mr. Petersen," she said. "I'll be back."

Hannah had heard all about Marshall Field's wholesale business. While it was well known that Mr. Field himself preferred the theatrical elegance of his retail store, the company depended heavily on the profits from the wholesale division. A wholesale buyer didn't spend all afternoon picking out *one* dress. When he walked through the big doors at the granite wholesale building, he was there to stock his store in Milwaukee or Des Moines or Gary with *hundreds* of dresses and shoes.

Those out-of-town merchants were so important that if one of them wanted a tour of the town, well, then, he was escorted wherever he wanted to go. If he came from a German community in Columbus, Ohio, and spoke no English, he was taken through the wholesale house by a salesman who could speak his language. If he was a Jew with a small dry goods store, the clerks suddenly became oblivious of their prejudice and treated him almost as nicely as any other customer.

Hannah followed Mr. Harrison to the alley where a carriage was waiting. After she was in the carriage, he closed the door. "His name is Meyer or Meyerson, I think," he said. "Good luck."

Sitting alone in the plush interior of the carriage, Hannah stroked the velvety smoothness of the seats with her fingertips. She inhaled deeply to catch the faint scent of lavender that clung to the upholstery and tried to imagine what it would be like to own such a wonderful carriage. When she reached the wholesale house, one of the official doormen ushered her to the second floor.

A trim man with pale blue eyes saw her and tossed his head back with a little cry of "Ah!" Stroking his short blond mustache, he walked toward her quickly. As he swept through the aisles, holding his head imperiously high, the gold chain from his pince-nez glasses swayed from side to side. He introduced himself as Roland Girard. Hannah had heard of him. Shopgirl gossip had it that he did twenty-one million dollars a year in silk stockings and lacy lingerie.

When Roland Girard led Hannah to Mr. Meyer, the old customer smiled to see such a lovely girl moving down the aisle toward him.

"Ah, a *shayner madel!*" he said, and even Mr. Girard knew that Mr. Meyer was calling her a beautiful girl.

Hannah noticed that Mr. Meyer was not at all embarrassed about speaking Yiddish, and he was delighted to have such a guide from so near his family's hometown in Pinsk. As Hannah translated Mr. Meyer's questions, Girard realized how much this girl already knew about the latest fashions.

Hours later, after Meyer had signed for a substantial order to be sent to his store in Milwaukee, Mr. Girard smiled at her and touched her slender arm gently with his soft hand. "Oh, yes, my dear. Oh, yes. You have much too much talent for that sewing room. I think we must find something else for you to do."

Girard was an innovative merchant. His flair for dramatic displays had transformed the wholesale division from a boring, dusty warehouse into a stylish store for executives. Girard knew, even in wholesale, that his ultimate customers were women, and he paid close attention to the whims of his wife and her friends. He had learned from his wife's rapturous visits to France that Chicago matrons had a fascination for all things European.

"I have an idea, my dear," he said politely. "And I would like to discuss it with you in private." Girard checked his gold pocket watch. "Let's adjourn across the street for a sip of tea."

A short while later, in an intimate tearoom, Hannah found herself seated at a small cloth-covered table, sipping tea and peering across the candlelight at one of the most powerful merchants in the city.

"I have a theory," Girard said as he stroked his blond mustache. "I have a theory that the department heads in retail are missing a very important boat."

Hannah watched the shadows the candle was casting on Girard's face. In the back of her mind she was wondering what it would be like to be married to such a powerful man.

"And I think I'm the one to catch it for them," he said.

Hannah's thoughts came back to the matter at hand. "Pardon me. What do you wish to catch?"

"That boat I was mentioning."

Girard smiled indulgently at Hannah's lack of understanding. He went on to explain that if he could create a truly theatrical presentation for the retail side of the business, he would expand his sphere of influence past the wholesale house. "They like to say that I only understand selling large orders to men." He stirred his tea impatiently. "You won't believe this, Miss Chernik, but the large sales in my department don't curry that much favor with Mr. Field. His only thoughts are on captivating women at the State Street store. Can you imagine?"

Hannah shook her head to show her disbelief that Mr. Field could be so blind to Mr. Girard's value.

"What do you think, Miss Chernik?" He smiled at Hannah and touched her hand. "Do you think I know how to influence women?"

Hannah's heart lightened, and she could feel her face color. Mr. Girard had an interest in her—that was clear—and it was becoming increasingly obvious that the interest was personal. If she admitted that he influenced her, wouldn't she be revealing that the attraction was mutual? On the other hand, if she denied that he was able to influence women, she might insult him and make him angry.

Hannah paused for a moment. "I think that the retail store would profit from your special touch." She was pleased with herself for her diplomacy. She smiled at him brightly. "Perhaps if you had a woman on your staff to help guide you . . ."

"I see." He was amused by her suggestion. "A woman on staff. Not to *guide* me, of course. But perhaps someone who might understand both the business side and the woman's point of view . . ."

He looked at Hannah appraisingly. There was an innocence about her which he found most attractive.

"Miss Chernik," he said thoughtfully, "you will forgive me if I offer a business observation? Being a Jewess doesn't really suit you. How would you like to be a countess? Perhaps a countess from . . . one of those countries over there?"

Be a countess? Hannah was thrilled by the thought. "But what would my name be?"

Roland Girard narrowed his eyes in thought. "Let's call you Maria. No, not Maria. That's too Catholic. Let's see. We'll call you . . . the countess Alexandria Nichelovich."

Three weeks later the same wealthy Chicago ladies who so avidly traveled to Europe each year gathered in the rotunda of the State Street store to view a private showing of America's first "fashion show." They sat on tufted straight-back chairs while they enjoyed lemonade and tiny cakes and watched an exclusive preview of the latest European styles, as modeled by "important" young women from Europe. Of the four models, the prettiest was a young countess with green eyes and soft dark hair. Her final costume, a gold silk dress, was topped with a deep green taffeta cape that tied under her slender chin. It set off her beauty so enchantingly that it seemed to have been made specially for her.

As she moved nervously down the grand staircase, the wonderful gold dress rustling luxuriously, Hannah trembled from the attention that made her feel so special. How exquisite that dress felt next to her skin. How splendidly the supple kid gloves snuggled into the curve of her hand. Later, in the dressing room, when Girard whispered to her that the dress had been sold, she felt bereft, as if something precious had been taken away.

"But not sold to the prettiest woman in the store," he said quietly. "That woman is with me now."

"The dress is so beautiful."

"The beauty that sold this dress is yours," he said softly. "My countess, you made this event a success for me."

Girard told her that Field had rewarded him with an advisory position in the retail store, and Hannah was pleased for him, for she knew it was important that Mr. Girard do well. But as for herself, it seemed so hard to take off the beautiful clothes and return home to her brother's worrisome concerns and the rancid smells in the tenement. It seemed so unfair that she had to lay her clean body down on soiled gray sheets in the ugly tenement when during the day she was surrounded by luxury and beauty.

That taste of luxury made Hannah determined to cling to everything Mr. Girard offered her. Was it really so important that he let his blue eyes rest on her breasts a moment too long? What was the harm, really, that when he touched her arm, she could feel the intensity of his desire? She knew what he wanted. Since the family's arrival in America, she and the girls slept in one room with Mother while Father and Josef slept in the other. But sometimes at night, after the children's breathing had become deep and regular, she could hear Papa slipping into bed beside Mama, and she would cover her ears with her hands to shut out the sound of her parents' bodies moving against each other.

Just because he wanted her—this prim, efficient man whose demeanor seemed to soften only around her—didn't mean she was tarnished by his *thoughts*, did it?

Wasn't she valuable to the company? Wasn't Mr. Girard putting her in lingerie sales, where she could charm the customers with her delightful accent? Why shouldn't she enjoy being an adviser to the boss just a little longer?

Several weeks after the fashion show Mr. Girard gave Hannah a pale blue silk dress to celebrate her seventeenth birthday. Of course, it wasn't really a gift from him. It was from the store. A matron had returned it, obviously worn, but since Field's had built its reputation on a money-back return with no questions asked, the store had to take the dress back. Since Field's couldn't sell it, Girard explained, giving it to Hannah was the clearly best thing to do with it.

Hannah was thrilled, and Girard's explanation seemed logical—so logical that she thought nothing about putting the old gray and pink dress she had made from fabric scraps into a bag and wearing the new dress home.

She was anticipating a happy evening in honor of her birthday, but when her mother caught sight of her, she was shocked. "That dress, Hannah! Where did you get it?"

"It was worn," Hannah answered, sliding over the truth only slightly. "The store gave it to me so I would look nice with the customers."

Her father exploded with anger. "Don't lie to us! Who gave you this? Who dared do such a thing?"

When Hannah hesitated to answer, he threw his hands in the air. "My God! Was there ever a man so unlucky? First, my son wants to leave our community to live in a town owned by a Gentile railroad car maker. Then my daughter comes home in clothes we cannot afford to buy. Gifts she accepts when they mean only one thing!"

The anger in his own voice inflamed Yankel's suspicions. In moments he was filled with rage. He grabbed Hannah by the shoulders and began shaking her violently.

"Take it off. Take it off! Do not insult this house by wearing this token of sin." And before Hannah could move, he had ripped it, ripped the bodice until it was hanging open. Then, incited again by his own fury, he ripped the beautiful skirt.

Hannah was stunned. She stood in the torn dress, her chest trembling, trying not to cry. The only beautiful thing she had ever owned was destroyed. And her father was so angry that his wrath made him seem a total stranger to her.

Except for the morning when she had slipped off to apply for her job, Hannah had never opposed the will of her parents. She had always thought of herself as a good, obedient daughter. But this anger and violence made her feel alienated, as if she were no longer a part of the family. In the disorienting emotions of the moment she did not notice that her soft, firm bosom had been exposed above her cotton corset or that the torn petticoat revealed a slender stretch of thigh above her stockings.

But Father did, and as he felt the disturbing sexual power his rough masculinity gave him over her, he became even more incensed. Josef, who had never seen his beautiful sister uncovered, found himself torn between sympathy for her and a mystifying physical attraction.

Instead of a joyous evening with her family, Hannah's birthday became a night in which everything was used to punish and blame her. Her mother had made *mandelbrod* cookies as special treat, but instead of giving them to her in a happy way, her father had thrown them on the table and yelled, "Here! You see what your mother did for you? And this is how you repay her kindness!"

That night Hannah fell asleep crying to herself.

The next morning she boarded the streetcar in a heavy daze. She knew from the emptiness she felt that some loving connection to her family had been irreparably broken. Only a year ago her love for the family had been so strong that she would have done anything for them. But after the outburst last night she found herself hating them for being so unfair.

By the time Hannah arrived at the store, her sadness had changed to rebellion. Rather than avoid this Mr. Girard who had so troubled her household, she sought him out. Her main concern now was explaining to him why she wasn't wearing the new dress. She decided to tell him that she had torn it getting off the streetcar.

"Then we will have to replace it," Girard had said, looking curiously at her puffy eyes. From his expression Hannah realized he probably could guess what had happened, but he continued, "And to celebrate, before you change back into *this* to go home"—he touched her homemade dress—"we will have a little dinner together."

That night, dreamily riding the streetcar back to the tenement after the most splendid evening of her life, Hannah rehearsed her lie. It was a simple story: She had worked late to inventory the stock. But when she finally stood before her father to tell him the story, she trembled so badly she was sure he would know the truth and beat her again. Her father noticed that Hannah's hands were shaking, but since he had spent the day agonizing over the memory of his violent outburst, he assumed that his favorite daughter had become afraid of him. Yankel was determined to win back her love. He quietly accepted the story without question.

The second time Mr. Girard took Hannah to dinner, she invented a new story to explain her late return. She had, she told her family, modeled in another "fashion show"—this time an evening presentation. After a question or two her father had accepted that story, too.

Each time after that it became easier, a game she played with an old man she loved but no longer admired. Roland Girard would present her with a new dress or a handsome shawl or a pair of stockings from Marshall Field's own stock, and afterward they would celebrate. And before she returned home, he would unlock the darkened store so that she could slip into his office to change back into her own clothes.

All this time he had treated her with respect, only pressing her hand at the end of each evening, and she had begun to imagine that he would marry her. Finally, one sweet evening after dinner in a private dining room at the Tremont House, Roland Girard gently led Hannah to the reclining couch and kissed her. She felt him slip his hand under her skirt and ever so gently stroke her thigh. Just when she thought she would faint from the dizzying sensation of his soft hand, she felt his mustache brush the inside of her knee, and when his lips moved higher on her thigh, just above her garter, she felt his tongue lightly touch and lick her skin. When he finally moved his body above hers, kissing her mouth and moving rapturously, Hannah lost herself, forgetting everything else in the world except the joy of inhaling his cologne and the racing of her heart until he overpowered her mild resistance and her body exploded with a shudder of swirling lights.

Soon, these thrilling assignations became a regular Tuesday night ritual. Hannah would enjoy delicious rich food she had never before tasted and give herself to the intoxicating passion afterward. It was all so wonderful, she told herself it would never end.

During dinner she would eagerly listen to Roland Girard's stories about his business triumphs, and she came to believe that she was the only one in the world who could understand the determination that drove him to such success.

"It was hard," he said one evening, leaning forward so that the candlelight made his features glow. "I worked so late at night that I was practically living at the warehouse. I knew I had to create a way to come to the attention of Mr. Field."

Hannah smiled. She was flattered that he was sharing these painful memories with her. "Were you ever discouraged?"

"Certainly," he said. "I had no one as wonderful as you to encourage me."

"Did you—did you have a sweetheart?" she asked.

For a moment he seemed more interested in answering her question accurately than flattering her. "No, not really," he said. "It was before I met my wife."

Hannah had never dared to ask Mr. Girard about his life away from the store, partly because she hadn't wanted to appear intrusive but also because she didn't really want to be faced with the truth if it turned out that he was married. She blinked and tried not to show her disappointment.

"Your wife?"

Girard glanced at her to read her face. He knew it was time to disabuse his delightful companion of any notions she might have about marriage. He lowered his eyes and flicked his mustache before he went on.

"Yes." He shrugged. "A nice woman. Heir to the Chicago and North Western Railway fortune. Formerly Diana Mortensen. Have you heard of her?"

Hannah, dazed, shook her head no.

"Oh, you haven't? I assumed you had. Quite a nice woman. Not exciting or as beautiful as you, of course, but a good match."

It was only a month after this conversation that Hannah first realized she was pregnant. When she finally told him, after enough troubled nights had passed that she was sure, Roland Girard looked at her searchingly.

It was a strange, appraising look, Hannah thought, with only the slightest trace of sympathy in it. It was a look she had seen on his face when he was evaluating a piece of merchandise before he decided to place an order. After commenting that she would have to make some decisions about it, he said that he had better get her home early tonight and walked her to the streetcar.

When Hannah arrived at the store the next day, queasy with morning sickness, she did not expect that she would be called to the personnel office on the top floor, where a man with ruddy cheeks would pay her three dollars for the days she had worked that week and fire her without telling her why. Nor did she expect that when she went to Girard's office in the wholesale building for help, she would be told by his imperious gray-haired secretary that he was busy and not to be disturbed.

When Hannah finally left the store, the three dollars in her pocket, she was numb with fear. The women passing in their carriages and the men walking to their appointments blended into a blur. After hours of walking in the December cold and trying to think, she finally became so overwhelmed with fatigue and nausea that she collapsed on a bench along the lake.

Sitting there, Hannah allowed herself to understand the full ramifications of her situation. The pregnancy had not seemed quite so bleak when she had believed that Girard would somehow save her. Even the effect of her disgrace on her family had seemed like a bad dream that she might be able to make go away.

But now she was alone, and she realized that there was no one to save her. She also knew that she could never return home again, ever. She remembered how Papa had flown into a rage over the dress. She knew that when he found out about her situation, he would have no compunction about throwing her out.

Hannah knew that—whether she returned home today or not—the time was rapidly coming when she would be dead to her family. That was what happened to Jewish girls who had so seriously broken the rules: They were declared dead. She knew that her parents would bitterly sit *shivah* for her. They would drape their one small mirror with black cloth, accept food and condolences from their friends at the synagogue, and they would intone the heartrending prayer for the dead for her.

As she shivered in the cold, the enormity of her betrayal came to her. She had lied to her family while she wantonly gave herself to a man who was married to another woman! She had rewarded her family for their love and care by disgracing them. She knew she could not bear to tell them. It was far kinder to let them believe that she was a good daughter who had died rather than make them live with the embarrassment of knowing she was a whore.

Tears flowed down her face, leaving warm, sticky rivulets on her cold cheeks. Her chest heaved in deep sobs, and her heart ached so painfully that she thought the misery would destroy her. She thought about her sweet brother who loved her and had tried so hard to protect her. She thought about Mama and how hard she worked and about her young, innocent sisters, who would suffer without her income. And she felt a more profound, wrenching sadness than she had ever known.

Hannah sat on the bench for the rest of the day, shivering and grieving for the life she had so foolishly thrown away. But as the dreary winter light began to fade into evening, she was confronted with the immediate needs of her situation. Despite her grief, she knew that if she could not find a warm place to stay and some food to eat, she would die in the penetrating cold of the Chicago winter.

7

———————

SERGEANT LANGAN WAS HAVING coffee in the operator's room when the message from the Thirty-third Street station came in. By the time he confirmed the information, he could see reporters from the *Daily News* and the *Tribune* running up the front steps at the South Court of City Hall.

Damnation, he thought. He pushed himself through the crowded corridor to inform the police chief of the latest disaster. Within two minutes of hearing the news, Chief Brennan had summoned Detective Wheeler to his office.

Wheeler, a tall, cocky man known around the patrol wagons as Big Wheel, was not Chief Brennan's favorite detective, but he knew the town and the dregs who lived in it. Wheeler might just come up with enough information to keep the reporters at bay.

Big Wheel strolled into Brennan's office, picking his teeth with a broom straw. "What's up?" he asked in a casual tone that aggravated both the weary chief and Sergeant Langan.

"*What's up*, Detective," Sergeant Langan said, "is that we seem to have a whore killer in the city."

Big Wheel grinned and flopped into a chair, slinging one

leg over the wooden arm. "So what? We've always had whore killers in this city."

"Not like this, Detective," cautioned Chief Brennan. Brennan spit a mouthful of slushy brown tobacco juice into the cuspidor at his feet. "Slit from belly to breast. Third one in six months."

"Third?"

"Yeah. The first was opening day of the fair," explained the chief. "The second one sometime in the summer—"

"August," Langan remembered ponderously. "Middle of—no, more toward the end of August."

"Yeah. I remember," said Wheeler, ignoring Langan and examining the meat loaf he had excavated from his teeth with the broom straw. "You mean the sarge here ain't done nothin' about that yet, Chief?"

"Maybe I'm waiting for a detective who'll finally do *his* job," the sergeant countered.

The chief ignored his men's bickering while he sliced into a new plug of tobacco. "Nobody paid much attention back then. Like you said, this city's always had its share of whores and some of them got killed. But now, with the fair closed down, there's not a lot of news to report. The papers will begin to think it's their duty to get the citizens all worked up about it."

Sergeant Langan confirmed this notion. "Reporters from two papers are here now."

"Yeah," said Big Wheel. "I seen 'em. And you'll have six papers on your ass tomorrow." Wheeler stretched his arms and thought for a moment. "You think the fair brought the killer to Chicago?"

The chief slipped the plug of tobacco between his cheek and his teeth. "Don't know. But wherever he came from, he's still here. Anyway, that's up to you to find out."

"Me! All by my lonesome?" Wheeler shrugged and gave the sergeant what he thought was an ingratiating smile.

"Isn't it about time you started earning your salary, Detective?" Sergeant Langan interjected.

The chief agreed impatiently. "Hell, yes. Whadda you think you're a detective for, dammit? You want the rest of the department to do your work?"

Wheeler grinned. It amused him to see his boss so uncomfortable. "Got any idea where I might start?"

"For openers," said Captain Brennan now red with irritation, "you might start hanging around some sporting houses."

"*Start* hanging around!" Sergeant Langan chortled.

"Langan," said the chief, missing his spittoon with a new missile of tobacco juice, "either you can shut your mouth or you can shut the door with you on the *other* side of it!"

Langan put his cigar in his mouth and glared.

"Like I was saying, Wheeler," continued the chief, "start hanging around the sporting houses. When you find someone there who carries a big carving knife, pick him up. That shouldn't be too hard, eh?"

Detective Wheeler smiled broadly. This was too good to be true!

"Wipe that grin off your face," the chief shouted, "and go figure out something to tell those GD newspaper reporters out there."

Hannah got up from the park bench, and a wave of nausea hit her. She stumbled over to a tree and leaned against it as her stomach heaved and contracted. She had not eaten all day, and the bitter taste of stomach bile filled her mouth. Weak from sickness and exhausted with the shock the day had brought, she rested against the tree.

When she was finished being sick, she wiped her mouth with the back of her hand and began walking away from the lake, aimlessly heading west along Washington Street. For the first time in her life Hannah thought seriously about dying. She had nothing to live for, that was clear. The man she loved had discarded her, had thrown her away like something vile and untouchable.

It was this shock of such callous treatment that hurt her most. As a delightful, beautiful child she had always been given special treatment and had grown up assuming that she deserved it. But now her lover's abrupt betrayal forced her to reconsider her assumptions about herself. What if she had gotten it all wrong? What if she had been adorable only to her family? What if she were not only poor but so degraded that there was nothing left for her? If this were true, wouldn't it be better to die?

As Hannah was formulating her thoughts about dying, a gust of wind from the lake slashed against her. Shivering, she put her icy fingers in her coat pockets and huddled against herself. The bite of the cold alarmed her and brought her again to the reality of her situation. As she was crossing near the Palmer House, she glanced up the street.

There, up ahead was the Tremont House, the warm, luxurious restaurant where only last night her lover had mesmerized her with his attention. It seemed a lifetime since she had been ushered courteously into the main lobby. Had that really been she, sitting inside, dressed in one of the store's shimmering silks, sipping champagne? As she neared the front of the Tremont, the doorman opened the door, and a well-dressed customer emerged from the rich interior.

For a moment Hannah's eyes met the doorman's. He nodded to her discreetly in recognition. She had walked a few feet past the Tremont House when another blast of wind drove the cold through her thin coat. As she turned her face away from the wind, she saw the customer get into his carriage, and she hurriedly moved back to the protective shelter of the awning.

"Can I help you, miss?" the doorman asked her formally.

"Could I come inside for a while? I'm so cold."

The doorman hesitated. "I haven't seen Mr. Girard tonight, miss."

"No," Hannah said quickly. "He wouldn't want—I mean, I wasn't looking for him."

The doorman understood. She was too vulnerable—too forlorn—to be anticipating another evening with Mr. Girard. *These shopgirls never get the picture,* he thought. *To a wealthy man, a shopgirl is as valuable as yesterday's newspaper.*

"I'm sorry, miss. But what would the gentleman say if he came in with a lady and found *you* standin' there? That wouldn't do at all now, would it? I mean, he's a customer. And a respectable one at that."

Hannah heard and understood. Without Girard she was *not* respectable. It occurred to her that perhaps even last night, while this doorman was doffing his cap courteously, he had viewed her with contempt.

The injustice of his attitude blazed inside her, and she lifted her shoulders with as much pride as the cold would allow. "How dare you?" she asked intensely, stirred with a sense of her own humanity. "How dare you?"

The doorman shrugged his big shoulders and stepped back into the warmth. He had seen girls like her before, and he would see them again. Sluts, they were. No concern of his.

Hannah continued down the street. She was furious to realize that just when she needed shelter most, she had been denied it. Her outrage swept away thoughts of suicide and filled her with determination.

There was a time, she thought, *when I belonged in that restaurant. Someday I will go back, and when I do, that doorman will respect me for who I am.*

But then the thought arose that she had been there *only* because she had been with Girard, and the despair started to grip her again. She realized that she would never be with him again and she wanted to cry like a baby and give up. As her emotions swayed back into helplessness, she stopped herself. "No!" she said out loud, not noticing that a man and woman walking ahead of her turned back to stare.

Then Hannah remembered something that had happened in Russia when she was a little girl. A rough peasant boy had called her a dirty name and thrown a rock at her. She had felt so hurt by his unprovoked meanness that she had run home, wailing loudly. Her mother had washed her face and *admonished* her, "Hush, Hannah. You mustn't cry about this. That boy doesn't care about you. Never let yourself be hurt by someone who doesn't care about you. What's the point, eh? It only lets them win."

When the memory of Girard's blue eyes and the sweet, intoxicating scent of his cologne came flooding back, Hannah reminded herself: *He doesn't care about me. I will not let myself be hurt anymore by someone who doesn't care.*

As she reached the corner, a gust of wind blew her coat open. She roused herself from her thoughts of Girard and forced herself into the clear, unsentimental thoughts of survival.

I will find no help in this part of town, she realized. *The people here are too rich or too pretentious. I might have a better chance farther south where the people are poor and more like me.*

While Hannah huddled in a doorway, a discarded newspaper blew past her, flapping and dancing up the street. Squinting into the wind, she saw a streetcar heading toward her on its way south. When it was within a hundred feet of her, she hurried to the center of the street, climbed on board, and dropped a nickel into the coin box. The conductor jingled a bell at his belt, and the car lurched forward. When it reached Thirty-third Street, she got off.

When Hannah had not returned home by eleven o'clock that night, her parents were frantic. Even Josef had trouble concealing his growing anxiety.

"She's stayed out late before," he said, pacing aimlessly in the small room. "Perhaps she had to work late again."

"But since that first time, when she scared us nearly half to death with that inventory business," Rachel insisted, "she always let us know the day before."

The reference to the "first time" brought back memories of the night Yankel had attacked Hannah because of the blue dress. Josef remembered and silently blamed his father, thinking that Hannah had stayed out late the next night to avoid him.

"But, Josef," Mama said, her voice breaking with tears, "she's never been out this late."

Josef was frightened, too, and knew he couldn't maintain a calm presence much longer. It seemed important to do something. Anything was better than sitting around.

"I'll go wait for her. Don't worry, Mama. She's probably all right, but it's dark outside. Better I should be there than here."

Josef ran to the streetcar stop. He waited in the dark for an hour, stamping his feet on the cold plank sidewalks. Each time a streetcar approached, he peered hopefully for a glimpse of Hannah's face. Once, when he thought he had spotted her, he felt himself become angry. How could she scare him this way? Had she no regard for his feelings? But when the car went by and Hannah wasn't on board, his anger subsided to fear.

Finally, when the last car had come and gone, Josef told himself that Hannah must have worked late and was trapped in the city without a ride home. Alternately running and walking, he covered the three miles from the Jewish section on Western Avenue to the downtown Loop on State Street.

When he arrived, he found the city's powerful center of commerce so deserted that his footsteps echoed eerily against the stone buildings. The large white department stores stared out at him blankly from dark, sightless windows.

Desperately Josef raced toward every lighted, open building. He pushed past doormen into the Palmer House and the Tremont House, startling the few well-dressed women still sipping champagne in the lobbies with his intense, searching stare. When he had checked every open hotel and restaurant in the Loop, he headed south, barging into the lowlife bars and gambling dens he had never before entered.

By the time the uniformed security guard arrived to unlock the department store the next morning, Josef had been waiting behind the store for nearly an hour. He watched, driven with feverish hope, as clerks and seamstresses and maintenance people arrived. When the store was finally opened at 8:00 A.M., he was allowed inside.

Standing under the lighted dome in front of rich, glittering merchandise, Josef became intensely aware of his poverty. His tattered clothes clearly marked him as an outsider who was someone to be suspected and dispensed with. As he went from clerk to clerk, asking about a pretty girl named Hannah, what he saw in their faces was not compassion but the hope that this embarrassing outsider would not be near when customers arrived at their counters.

He ran to the back of the store, pounded impatiently on the elevator doors, and was lifted slowly to the sewing floor. A man named Mr. Petersen gruffly told him that the girl named Hannah had not worked in custom sewing for several months and that he should use the back stairs to check at the employment office. His cheeks stinging with humiliation, Josef ran up the stairs, taking two at a time until he arrived at the seventh floor. He shoved the door open with a bang.

His presence created such consternation that he was quickly led to a man in a brown suit who checked the personnel ledger. "Ah," he said, his index finger finding the information in a list of names. "Well, it would seem that Miss Hannah Chernik was fired yesterday morning, so you certainly won't find her in the store today. You sure she's not at home?"

The news hit Josef with a jolt. Fired? But she'd been doing so well! After the shock wore off, Josef gratefully accepted the suggestion that she might be home. Yes! Surely she was home by now. He hadn't been there himself since eleven o'clock the night before. He turned abruptly, ran down the stairs, and jumped on a streetcar with renewed hope. After a long, slow ride with endless stops, he reached his neighborhood. When he opened the door of the apartment, the looks on his parents' faces told him Hannah had not returned.

"Is Hannah at work?" his father asked hopefully.

"No," Josef said. "Not today."

"Oh, God," his mother sobbed. "My beautiful girl. What has happened to my beautiful girl?"

Josef watched Yankel desperately create another story to explain her absence. "Maybe they made her work late and since it was cold, she went to sleep at a girl's house who lives near the store. Josef, did you ask the boss if she had worked late?"

Josef shook his head. His father was pleading with him for comfort, for something that would explain why Hannah was safe. But his own heart was so leaden that he could not create the lie they wanted to hear. Nor could he bring himself to tell them the truth. If they knew Hannah had left work after being fired, they would be forced to wonder why, of all days, she had not returned home to her family.

There was only one reason Josef could imagine that did explain her absence: Hannah was *unable* to return.

With a start he knew that he needed help from the police. He decided to go to the main police station at City Hall, thinking it would be the best place to go. He told his parents he was returning to the store to check for Hannah again. When he found no streetcar in sight, he walked briskly until one finally overtook him.

He stood outside City Hall until he had summoned courage to overcome his ingrained fear of the police. A Sergeant Langan was sitting at the tall desk, reading a newspaper. Josef waited politely for a few moments until it was clear to him that he would have to interrupt to be noticed.

"Excuse me, sir," Josef said deferentially. "I need help."

Sergeant Langan reluctantly lowered the newspaper. "What's the problem?"

"My sister . . ." began Josef haltingly before his voice broke. The fear he had denied all night, the fatigue, and the realization that his sister's fate was in all likelihood a police matter overwhelmed him. He struggled to calm himself so he could speak.

"What's up, buddy? I don't have all day."

Josef gave the sergeant a description of Hannah, a short-ened version of her disappearance, and the family's address. When the sergeant asked where he worked, Josef told him that he worked in the shop at the Pullman Palace Car Company. When the sergeant had finished with his questioning, he checked the police docket for murders and then looked at the list of hookers who had been brought in.

"Nope. No sign of her here."

"But you will look for her, yes?"

"Buddy, I can't even submit this report today. For a person to be considered officially missing, we have to wait at least twenty-four hours. Get a grip on yourself. She's only been missing overnight."

Josef fought to control his impatience before his voice loudly escaped his control. "Can't you see?" he said hoarsely. "This is my sister!"

"Listen, kid," said the sergeant somewhat reassuringly, "this kind of thing happens all the time. A girl gets involved with the wrong people, you know what I mean, or maybe she decides to run away. If you could prove there was foul play, I'd submit it. But we're too busy with real problems to worry because some guy comes in here pissin' his pants about his sister."

Josef returned home slowly. He dreaded the inevitable encounter with his anguished parents. When he arrived, he found his mother lying weakly in bed, too exhausted with grief to sit up. Yankel was rocking in his wooden chair, staring at the wall. Neither seemed to notice Josef's presence. Mashke and Frieda huddled quietly in the corner, their faces white with shock. They had resigned themselves to the worst, and no one asked Josef what he had learned. That, at least, was a blessing.

After sitting numbly in the apartment for a few minutes, Josef pulled himself to his feet. No matter what had happened, *someone* had to bring money into the household. If he didn't work today, there would be no money for food tomorrow. Sadly he left for the train that would take him to his job in Pullman.

By the following morning, when Hannah had still not returned home, it was clear that she was gone. A neighbor heard Rachel weeping and came to investigate. Within a few hours the news had spread throughout the neighborhood. It was cause for general concern and grief. Most agreed that Hannah had been abducted. After all, if she were able to return home, would she not have returned? The suspicion they would not let themselves discuss hung over them bleakly.

Friends began to drop in, bringing food for the family. Yankel rocked in his chair in the back room, his head turned to the wall. Listlessly Rachel washed the faces and hands of her remaining daughters so that their appearance would not shame her in front of her friends from the synagogue.

When Etta and her husband, Avrum, arrived, Rachel went into the other room to get Yankel. "Please," she pleaded, "please, for appearance sake, get up, Yankel. Our friends are here."

Yankel stood weakly and went into the front room. Etta had her arm around Rachel. Avrum stepped forward to shake his hand grimly.

Yankel gestured to a couple of chairs away from the women so that he and Avrum could discuss important matters without being interrupted. As the women began putting out the food, Etta asked Rachel, "So, where is Josef on such a sad occasion?"

Rachel glanced at Yankel before she admitted that Josef had gone to work.

"During this sorrow he goes to work?" asked Etta. "What kind of son and brother is this?"

Yankel heard Etta's comment and was annoyed by it. Ignoring her, he directed his answer to Avrum. "It is well and good to say what things should be, but were the boy to lose his job, it would be a disaster for the family."

This flexible approach to tragedy irritated Etta almost as much as having Yankel ignore her. She turned to Rachel again. "So, your Josef, he still works for the *goyish* company then?"

Yankel and Rachel both recognized the criticism in Etta's reference to Pullman. It was no secret that Josef's work in the factory puzzled the community. Here a man was expected to work in his own community or start a business of his own. Struck by the meddling bitterness in Etta's tongue, Yankel did not answer. Avrum glared at his wife furiously.

After a few seconds, to ease the tension in the room, Rachel quietly answered, "He earns a good wage."

"Hmm," said Etta, ignoring Avrum's look. "Those young

people and their work! I myself knew it was a mistake for Hannah to go downtown to work. And you see what has happened! She should have stayed with her own people."

At the mention of her eldest daughter Rachel began to weep.

"Let us not distress Rachel with talk about Hannah," Avrum said pointedly as Rachel wiped her eyes. "Let us talk about other things."

Etta was known for being difficult, and being rebuffed a second time rankled her more than she could tolerate. She sat for a moment in silence, resenting her friends' refusal to deal with the truth she was so anxious to dispense.

"Ah, well," she said after a pause, "she would have come to trouble anyway. My son, Leonard, told me he saw her coming out of a restaurant late one night with a blond man. God only knows what terrible things she did to disgrace this family."

Immediately Yankel was on his feet. He was outraged. No one in the family had dared mention their dark fear that perhaps Hannah—for God knows what terrible reason—had *decided* not to return.

Such an idea was too dreadful to be spoken. It sullied the memory of their lovely daughter. Now Etta had removed the doubt. Her words had disgraced the whole family.

"How dare you?" he roared. "How dare you say such a thing to my face?"

"You don't fool me, Yankel. You don't fool me," Etta continued, egged on by his response. "Remember, I was *here* when she sneaked downtown without telling anyone. If you hadn't been such a fool, you could have seen what kind of girl she was."

Yankel hurled himself across the room, exploding with rage. His intention was only to quiet this meddling little woman, but when he got close enough to touch her, he grabbed her by the shoulders and shook her violently. Etta screamed, and Avrum lunged between them to defend his wife. Rachel burst into loud, sobbing wails, and the girls cried noisily.

Serious, unforgivable improprieties had been committed—first by Etta, who had voiced the unspeakable, and then by Yankel, who, in touching another man's wife, had crossed a more serious line. "How dare you dishonor my family?" Yankel shouted hoarsely, aware of his error. "How dare you?"

"How dare you touch my wife?" Avrum shouted.

Outside on the stairs, two other couples had just arrived at the landing with covered dishes of bread and food when they heard Yankel shouting, "Get out! Get out!"

A few seconds later Yankel threw open the door and stared into the astonished faces of Rachel's friends from the synagogue.

"We'll go," said Etta, conveniently including the others in her remark. "And we won't come back. When you decide you want to do the prayer for the dead, when you decide you must have a *minyan*, believe me, you won't even be able to get one together."

Rachel rushed to Yankel with her arms outstretched. "Yankel, please. Don't do this! They're our friends. We need them."

Yankel stopped. He was ashamed now, ashamed of his violent outburst. He might have been able to apologize if only Etta had not dishonored his daughter. But that could not accept.

Now this issue of the *minyan*, this necessity to bring together ten men in order to sit *shivah* or conduct services for the dead, brought him up short. Yankel had spent his childhood studying the Talmud and his adult life being a good Jew. No matter how hard the persecution, he had always *believed* in the rightness of the rules. The rules meant something to him. They had been hammered into his head since he was a five-year-old boy.

Now his grief shattered even that. The idea of needing to have a group of people who didn't share the pain that was burning his chest—just to be able to say services for his daughter—intensified his rage.

"I don't need people who tell stories about my girl to help me grieve," he said hoarsely. "Get out. This is my home. Get out."

Etta looked pointedly at the neighbors standing in the doorway. Yankel had now so disgraced himself that any blame that could have been leveled at her was forgotten.

"Listen to him," she said to the neighbors. "Could you have imagined this? We come to help. We bring food. And he throws us out!"

Etta swept through the door, but before disappearing down the stairs, turned back to the room. Rachel's face was gray with shock. Seeing this, she said condescendingly, "I'm sorry for you, Rachel. First your daughter and now this. May God help you."

When the door closed behind them, Rachel buried her head in her hands. "Yankel! Please . . . go after them."

"How can you ask such a thing?" he said through clenched teeth. "The woman dishonored us."

"Throwing her out will make it worse," Rachel said disconsolately. "She will tell stories. She will poison the air. Believe me, I won't be able to go to synagogue with my head up."

"The synagogue," Yankel cried. His throat was tight with pain. "Go to the synagogue and pray to a God who has deserted us! What kind of God is this that you pray to, Rachel? A God who would let our girl become so willful that she would become a whore?"

Rachel backed away from her husband in a daze. For the children she had tried to stay a little calm, but now she lost control of herself. "She's my child, too, Yankel," she screamed, her tears flowing. "She is my child, too. Oh, God, you are breaking my heart with this."

Rachel collapsed into a chair, sobbing. Little Mashke, subdued by the power of her parents' emotions, crept to her mother. "Leave me something, Yankel," Rachel wept. "I need something to hold on to."

"False friends you never need, Rachel," he said. And in the heat of the moment, in the midst of pain that kept him from thinking clearly, Yankel made a decision that would alter their lives more than he could imagine.

"If you're so worried about Etta's mouth, we'll leave this street. Bad enough that we should suffer so. But I will not be blamed and hounded and censured by the self-righteous babbling of false friends. We will leave this hellhole of a city. We will go where they won't bother us again."

When Josef finally returned home from his job in the Pullman factory, his father met him with the news. "I have made a decision," Yankel said. "We will move to this Gentile town you have told us about and get away from here. It is time we thought about protecting the young girls."

"But what about Hannah?" Josef asked. "If she returns, how will she find us?"

Yankel's face was stern with determination. "It would appear that your sister was lying to us. She has done something shameful. She is no longer a daughter of mine."

Josef looked at his father in confusion as Rachel began to scream, "No, Yankel. Please. Don't do this."

"I am the head of this household," Yankel said, raising his voice authoritatively. "The girl is no longer a member of this family. From this day forward I want that her name never be mentioned again."

"What is he saying?" Josef asked, looking to his mother for understanding. "Hannah is—"

Yankel roared, "Never, never mention her name in my presence again."

Josef's face blanched with understanding. As he had never done before, Yankel had spoken the law that the family would live by from that time on.

"We will say Kaddish," he said, "just among ourselves. Just with those who share our pain. From this day forward the girl is dead. She does not exist. Do you hear me?"

As Rachel slipped weakly into a chair, Yankel walked into the next room to get his tallith. When he returned, he kissed the fringes on both ends of the prayer shawl, then swept it around his shoulders and over his head. When he was ready, he pointed at the floor beside him.

"Here," he said to his son.

Josef reluctantly took his place beside his father and, against his will, joined him. Outside, on the wooden stairs, their voices could be heard mournfully chanting the most melancholy words in the language, the prayer for the dead. *"Ysgadal v'ysgadash shmae rabah."*

8

AFTER HANNAH GOT OFF the streetcar, she walked until she saw a sign on a building that read, WHISKEY. BEER. ROOMS UPSTAIRS. The paint on the sign was peeling, and the building was dilapidated, but she headed toward it anyway.

She hesitated for a moment before she went in. She had never been in a place like this and didn't know what to expect. Once inside, she looked around but couldn't see much more than a dim light behind the bar. In the semidarkness a hand reached out and grabbed her elbow.

"Over here, honey," said a voice belonging to the hand.

When Hannah spun around, she found herself looking into the absurd leer of a toothless man who appeared to be sixty years old. He was wearing a blue cap on his head as if, even inside, his old body needed help to stay warm. When Hannah tried to jerk her arm away, he held on tight.

"Come on, gal," he said. "I got a seat right here with your name on it." He slapped his free hand against his lap.

In the dim light his leering face seemed like a vision of hell. "Let go of me," she cried. When the old man tightened his grip, she called out to the shadowy room, "Help!"

"I'll give ye some help, lady," drawled a male voice from the far end of the room. "That is, if old Wendell won't give ye what yer cravin'."

As if in response to this remark, another male voice chortled. "She-it, ye can put me down fer a little of that stuff, too."

When her eyes adjusted to the light, Hannah saw three men lined up at the far end of the bar. They grinned at her senselessly. Hannah blanched. She had no idea what kind of place this was or what these men might do to her. Nor did she know what she could do to discourage them. She instinctively squared her shoulders and assumed the mantle of dignity she had learned to affect at the department store.

"How dare you?" she demanded, pushing the old man away. "Let go of me!"

"Oh, oh. Don't wanna be dippin' into that, Wendell," said one of the men down the bar. "She sounds like a foreigner."

"I am the Countess Alexandria Nichelovich," Hannah said as impressively as she could.

In the darkness Wendell and another man jeered and hooted.

In response to the noise of the catcalls a woman appeared in a doorway at the other side of the room. She was wearing an apron smeared with food stains.

"Clam up," she said to the men. She swaggered toward Hannah aggressively. "Yeah? Whaddaya want?"

Hannah was relieved to see a woman and pulled her aside to speak privately. "How much are your rooms?" she asked quietly.

"Watch out, Maggie," called the man at the end of the bar, sarcastically. "She says she's royalty. You don't want to displease her none."

"If you're lookin' to take men upstairs, you'll have to pay double," Maggie announced.

"Take men upstairs?" For an insane moment Hannah thought the woman was talking about the awful-looking men at the bar. "What I want is a warm place to sleep where I won't be disturbed."

The woman stared at Hannah appraisingly. She had half a mind to throw her out. Hannah stared back. As awful as this place was, it was cold outside, and she had no idea where else she could go. "Please," she said earnestly. "Please. I need help."

Something about Hannah's urgency reminded the woman of when she had been down on her luck herself. "Well, I guess it's all right," she said. "But no trouble. And I mean it about having visitors upstairs."

The man with the blue cap called out, "Hey, Maggie, send 'er upsteers for me!"

"Shut it up, you old fool," said Maggie, suddenly protective of the girl. "Didn't you hear the lady? She's royalty." When Maggie turned back to Hannah, she gave her a look that said she knew the countess story wasn't for real but that, by God, she wasn't going let those fools at the bar take advantage of her.

She led Hannah up the worn wooden stairs and lit a kerosene lamp in a chilly room with a torn curtain. "This here's the bed," she said. Then she lifted the worn bedspread and pointed to the basin under the bed. "And here's the potty."

"Thank you."

In the glare of the lamp Maggie noticed Hannah's pallor. "You ain't gonna be sick, are you?" she asked. "If you are, try to hit the potty instead of pukin' all over the floor."

Hannah nodded.

"That'll be fifty cents. But I'm telling you, if I find a man creepin' up here . . ."

"If you do," said Hannah, "I want you to throw him out."

"You said it," said Maggie.

Hannah carefully pulled her three dollars from her pocket and handed Maggie one of the bills. "I don't have change."

Maggie took the money and shrugged her shoulders. "I didn't bring no money with me," she said. "An' I don't want to have to run up and down these stairs. You can git it tomorrow." Then she turned and left.

Alone in the room Hannah sank onto the bed. Once she was seated, exhaustion overwhelmed her. She lay there, still but awake, until weariness overcame her fear of being in this rough place. In a while she escaped blessedly into sleep.

Carrie Watson strode impatiently to the bottom of her mahogany staircase. Last night the girls had taken in a higher sum than usual, and she wanted to make a deposit at the bank before the weather turned bad. It looked as if it were going to snow.

"Are you ready, Zorrine?" Carrie called up to the prettiest of the harem upstairs.

Twenty women had rooms on the upper three floors of Carrie Watson's large stone mansion, but Zorrine was by far the best one to take downtown. When she was dressed up, she never failed to attract attention.

"Just a minute!" Zorrine called down crossly. "Jeez, it's only one o'clock in the afternoon."

"Don't forget your hat, Zorrine," called Carrie Watson. "And clean gloves."

Carrie folded her arms and squinted at her thoughts. She was getting tired of Zorrine's attitude. Zorrine was pretty, and she sure had learned the tricks that would tantalize the richest men in the city. But sometimes she acted like she was getting too big for her britches.

Zorrine appeared at the top of the landing and flounced down the stairs. "Jesus, Carrie!" she said. "Can't you make a bank deposit without having to drag me along?"

"Nope," said Carrie. "Not when you can sit out there in the carriage and remind Chicago which sporting house has the loveliest facilities and the prettiest girls."

"The champagne must be getting to your head," Zorrine complained, "if you expect me to sit outside and wait for you in weather like this."

By early the next afternoon Hannah had been wandering the cold Chicago streets for hours. She had fled the awful room as soon as she woke up, but since Maggie had not returned her fifty cents, Hannah had been forced to bang on every door in the building before she had found her. Hannah's demand for her money irritated Maggie no end. Having held on to it all night, she had come to believe that she deserved it. After all, she had given a complete stranger a break out of the kindness of her heart.

"Be advised not to come back," ordered Maggie, slamming the door to her room. "Royalty!" she sputtered to her sleeping companion. "Ain't it just like a rich person to rob a working girl of a few cents rightfully earned."

Maggie wasn't the only person that day who told Hannah not to come back. Hannah was turned down for a job at every dry goods and apparel store in Chicago. "We're letting people go as it is," one small store owner commented. Another turned her away angrily: "Young woman, can you give me one good reason why I should give a job to a foreigner when there are thousands of trustworthy Americans who need work?"

By early afternoon Hannah was discouraged and alarmed at her lack of prospects. She was also getting weak. She realized that she had not eaten anything since her fancy dinner at the Tremont, and that had been two days ago.

Hannah was standing on the curb at Randolph Street when a marvelous coach carrying a pair of attractive women rounded the corner in front of her. She was transfixed. This was not the sort of carriage she had seen parked in front of Marshall Field's. This was a carriage that belonged in a fairy tale! It was snow white with shining yellow wheels, and the two women in it were dressed elaborately, like storybook princesses. The driver smartly reined in the two horses and brought them to a stop in front of the South Side Bank and Trust. Hannah watched as the driver removed a soft fur blanket from the laps of the two women and helped them out of the carriage.

One of the women carried a large tapestry bag and walked efficiently into the bank. The other walked behind her slowly and voluptuously, looking about until she caught the eye of a dapper man standing nearby. When the second woman had disappeared into the building, a pair of poorly dressed men strolled up to the carriage and stopped.

"This here is Carrie Watson's carriage," said the older one, trying to impress his nephew with his knowledge of Chicago.

"Who's Carrie Watson?"

"When you've been in town a little longer, nephew, you'll find out," the older man said. "Carrie runs the best sporting house in the city."

"A whoor!" said the second man incredulously. "Come on, Cal! You don't mean those rich-looking ladies wuz whoors?"

"You heard it right, Henry."

"Which un wuz Carrie Watson?"

"The one carryin' the bag of money. The other one, she's the show whoor."

"She's pretty all right."

"You got fifty bucks and you can have 'er."

"Fifty!"

"Yup. Carrie Watson's girls don't come cheap."

"No thanks. I'll just keep porkin' my wife for free. Hell, I don't earn fifty dollars in two months!"

Hannah crossed the street and wistfully looked inside the coach at the plush interior. A moment later she felt her head spin and her body become heavy. Before she lost consciousness, she reached out to grab the yellow wheel to keep from falling.

The men who had been discussing Carrie Watson's establishment saw Hannah fall and stepped closer.

"What do you 'spect is wrong with the girl, Cal?"

"Maybe she's sick. Maybe not enough to eat lately."

"Well, she wouldn't be the first."

Cal and Henry were still standing beside the coach, observing the unconscious girl, when Carrie Watson and Zorrine emerged from the bank.

"Looks like the carriage has drawn a small crowd," Carrie said to Zorrine.

Zorrine snorted. "Good. Next time I'll stay home and let the carriage do your advertising for you."

As Carrie neared the carriage, she called out cheerfully, " 'Scuse me, gentlemen." When the two parted, she realized that they were staring at a beautiful young girl who was lying unconscious on the sidewalk. With the certainty of having seen hungry, outcast girls before, Carrie briskly called up to her coachman.

"Whatsa matta with ya, Joe? Ya blind? Didn't ya see the girl faint? Get her in the carriage. I've got to get her home."

At Miss Watson's command the coachman leaped from his box and lifted the slender girl. " 'Scuse me, gentlemen," Miss Watson said again, and the men stepped back at her command. As they watched, Carrie lifted her dress daintily, exposing an ankle as she climbed into the carriage. A moment later the show whore joined Carrie and the unconscious girl.

As the coachman applied his whip and the carriage pulled away from the curb, a thought occurred to the younger man. "Cal, I don't think that gal came here with those whoors!"

"Don't matter none," the other responded. "She's a whoor now."

When Hannah regained consciousness, the first thing she saw was the dark face of Miss Watson's upstairs maid, hovering about twelve inches above her. The maid was busily shaking her shoulder to bring her around.

"Oh, you awake now?" the woman said as if she had found Hannah awake and was not responsible for rousing her to consciousness.

"Who are you?" asked Hannah with some alarm. She had no idea where she was or how she had gotten there.

"Hush, child, I'm Vina. But don't you worry about me. You just rest, and I'll go tell Miss Carrie you're still among the living." Vina handed Hannah a cocktail made from bourbon and sugar. "Drink this, honey. It always makes the girls feel better."

When the maid left the room, Hannah lifted her head to examine her surroundings. In the back of her mind she was somewhat expecting to see the dreary little room she had rented the night before. That made the sight that met her eyes all the more remarkable.

Hannah was lying in a round bed under a soft white cashmere coverlet. A brass floor lamp towered beside the bed, and the walls of the room glowed a deep Chinese red. In the corner, a large Oriental folding screen covered with white translucent paper had been painted with men and women in a variety of close embraces.

Hannah had never seen anything remotely like it. For a fleeting moment the thought crossed her mind that maybe this was what the Christians called heaven.

She brought Vina's drink to her lips, and as she sipped the strong amber fluid, she studied the curious positions of the figures on the screen. It took her a few moments to notice the giant pink members that protruded strangely from the abdomens of the males and realize what they were. As she was adjusting herself to the notion of this peculiar art, Vina opened the door, and Miss Carrie Watson herself stepped into the room.

At the age of forty-one Carrie Watson was an amply built woman with rich chestnut-colored hair. She had become famous throughout the Midwest as the owner of the best sporting house in America. The city of Chicago appreciated her success as a businesswoman for the simple fact that she paid one of the highest property taxes in the entire city.

Carrie had arrived, an eighteen-year-old virgin from St. Louis, just after the Chicago fire in 1871. A smart girl with limited means and no connections, she had examined the professions available to an attractive young woman. After a cursory study she rejected the positions of shopgirl and sweatshop drudge and became an apprentice whore in Lou Harper's rowdy establishment. In two years she had saved enough to leave Lou Harper and buy the bordello at 441 South Clark Street, which she had been operating successfully ever since.

"I'm Carrie Watson," she said in a commanding but friendly voice. When Hannah struggled to pull herself up from the bed, Carrie dismissed her effort. "Keep your seat, honey, keep your seat."

In Hannah's attempt to rise, the cashmere coverlet had fallen back. Now she noticed with surprise that she was wearing a glossy satin gown. When she touched it, Miss Watson commented, "We thought you'd like to sleep in something a little less confining."

Hannah stared at Miss Watson, still wondering what she was doing here. Realizing that she had to say *something*, she finally whispered, "Thank you. I'm Hannah."

"Green eyes," Carrie Watson noted out loud to Vina, who was hovering in the background.

"Yes, ma'am," said Vina cheerfully. "Be real nice around here."

Hannah continued to stare until Miss Watson matter-of-factly sat on the side of the bed. "All right, Hannah," she said. "Let's talk. First, tell us how long it's been since you had anything to eat. Second, how long have you been pregnant?"

Hannah gasped. "How did you know?"

"It's my business to know," said Carrie Watson. "Are you sick?"

"Not right now."

"Good. Vina, go downstairs and get Hannah here something to eat."

As soon as the maid left and the door was closed, Hannah looked at Carrie Watson beseechingly. "Miss Watson," she asked, "where *am* I?"

"Hannah, you're in my house. And the way you look, I think you could fit in here and make a good bit of money with no problem at all. But that depends on you, of course."

"I don't understand."

"Hannah," Miss Watson said, "I didn't get rich by mincing

words. You just spent the last day of your life sleeping in a whorehouse."

Hannah fell back onto the pillow too stunned to respond. She had heard of such places. They were the dreaded last stop where women of bad character wound up and were never heard from again! Her eyes filled with tears.

Miss Watson waited until Hannah had somewhat adjusted to the impact of her announcement. Then she tried to reassure her by appealing to her sense of reason. "Honey, are you married?" she asked Hannah.

"No, I'm not."

"Well, then, you can relax. Whatever you did that got you pregnant is no different from what we do here that gets us rich. Honey, it's all the same."

Carrie Watson hung around for a while to give the girl a chance to adjust. When Hannah had eaten some food, her color came back enough that Carrie allowed herself to continue. "Hannah, nobody ever accused me of running a charity here, but I sure ain't no white slaver. If I was, you'd have been drugged, raped, and sold by now. So, if you want to leave, I won't stop you. Now, I can't be more fair than that, can I?"

Hannah sighed. This information did make her feel better.

"I don't know what you got waitin' for you out there," Miss Watson said, "and if it's better than this, go to it. But if it ain't, why don't you hang around for a few days, get your strength back, and see how things work out? You know, honey," she continued, "compared to 'most everything else, this ain't so bad."

"Isn't," interrupted Vina at the door, a tray of wake-up cocktails in her hand. " 'Isn't,' not 'ain't.' "

When Carrie looked around annoyed, Vina said, "Don't you be mad at me, Miss Watson. You done tole me to correct you."

"Stick around a few days," Carrie continued to Hannah, "and if you want to stay, we'll teach you the ropes. You know, there ain't—there *isn't*—a better house anywhere. It says so right in this book."

Miss Watson pulled a guidebook from her pocket and held it up. The title across the book said *The Sporting & Club House Directory.* "You could'a picked a lot worse places to wake up in."

* * *

Hannah spent the remainder of the afternoon resting. At five o'clock Vina knocked on her door and stuck her head inside. "Miss Carrie says come on down for dinner. She wants you to meet the other girls."

Hannah got up and pulled on a robe. She followed Vina downstairs into a large room at the back of the building. At least fifteen women were seated at long tables, helping themselves to food heaped on platters. Miss Watson was presiding at the head of one of the tables. When she noticed Hannah, she stood and hit her fork against one of the water goblets.

"All right, girls, calm down. I want you to meet our new roomer. She calls herself Hannah, and I want you to be nice to her."

A woman with bright carrot-red curls and even brighter lips waggled her fingers in Hannah's direction. "Hello, Hannah," she called in a singsong voice. "Welcome aboard."

Miss Watson remained on her feet at the head of the table. "Hannah's new, and since a few of you lately seem to have forgot your proper behavior, I'm going to take this opportunity to review the rules of the establishment. I want you all to pay attention. It won't hurt none of you to hear them again."

Miss Watson surveyed the room with the air of a schoolteacher cracking down on miscreant behavior. "Now the first rule here," she said, "is that this is a class place. You don't run around in your underwear or your nightclothes."

Hannah drew her robe around her, and Carrie clarified. "Not you, Hannah. Your robe is all right tonight because you're still under the weather."

This handled, Miss Watson resumed her lesson. "Now, when the men come into the entrance hall, you don't yell, 'They're here!' and run down the stairs like a herd of elephants. You walk sedately, and you talk to them in a cultured way."

Hannah heard a voice near her whisper, "The only culture Carrie understands is in a glass of buttermilk."

Miss Watson continued, "And if I *ever* see or hear of any of you mixing morphine in a gent's drink, you can pack your bags. It's too easy to kill a man that way, and if you ask me, the only reason for doing it is to knock him out so you can steal from him—and that is *definitely* against the rules."

Carrie looked around the room until she saw something

that drew her disapproval. "Kitty, is that tobacco in your mouth?"

A thin woman with beautiful black hair made a face and shifted the contents of a full mouth to one cheek. "Food," she said.

"Oh, yeah? Then swallow it."

Kitty looked like a little deer caught in a bright light. With an attempt at nonchalance, she unconvincingly wiggled her Adam's apple to simulate swallowing.

"Just as I suspected," said Miss Watson. "Kitty, if I find that you've been spitting on the rugs again, you're out! You understand?"

With the threat of swallowing the tobacco juice now past, Kitty resumed chewing with elaborate boredom.

Miss Watson sat down in defeat. "I swear, Hannah, some of them try me so. I'm going to my office. As soon as you finish your dinner, I'd like you to join me in there. We have some things to talk about."

In a short while Hannah joined Miss Watson in her office. She was relieved to get away from the girls at the table. A very pretty woman named Zorrine had insisted that Hannah try a vile-tasting food called an oyster. "Get you used to some other things you'll have to swallow," she had announced to the table, and the other girls had laughed raucously.

Carrie Watson was sitting at a small desk, adding up a column of numbers. The desk was disorderly. Three rows of tiny drawers at the back of the desk were overflowing with slips of paper. The winter afternoon had deepened into night, and the draped room was dark except for the glow from a lamp with a bottle green shade.

"Sit down," Carrie said. She looked at the new girl appraisingly and lit a small cigar. "Hannah, there is no question but that you're one of the prettiest girls I've had in here in a long time. You got a nice, quiet manner, and I think the customers will like you."

"But Miss Watson," said Hannah, "I thought you said I could look around for a few days before I decided—"

"Sure. But in the meantime, you can talk to my customers, can't you? To pay me back for my kindness to you?"

Hannah thought for a moment. She didn't want to talk to

anybody, especially a "customer" who might think she was there for other reasons.

"But what if they want to—"

"Want to take you upstairs?"

Hannah nodded.

"If they want to take you upstairs, you blush and smile and tell them, 'I have to get to know you better.' Think you can handle that?"

"Can you do that here? I mean, will they let me?"

"Let you? First thing for you to learn is that *you're* the one who decides what you're gonna do. If you don't get that straight, you'll wind up doing a lot more than you should! See, the main thing, Hannah, is always to avoid unnecessary wear and tear."

Miss Watson leaned forward to point to a framed piece of embroidery. "Always keep these words in mind."

Hannah strained forward to read the embroidery in the darkened room. "Pleasure is like certain drugs."

"Right!" said Miss Watson. "Balzac said that. He was from Europe—you didn't happen to know him, did you?" Carrie searched Hannah's face for a sign of recognition. She seemed to expect that Hannah might have stumbled across Balzac in her travels. Hannah shook her head.

"No?" Miss Watson confirmed, a little disappointed. "Well, the saying was too long for the girl to get it all on the embroidery, but I memorized the rest. It goes: 'Pleasure is like certain drugs. To continue to obtain the same results, one must double the dose, and death or brutalization is contained in the last.'"

"What does that mean?" Hannah asked. She was exceedingly uneasy about the direction the conversation was taking.

"What it means is conserve your energy. See, the first thing you gotta understand is what the customers are really buying, and it ain't necessarily sex. Think of it this way: If you were rich and old and could do anything in this city you wanted except make your bean hard, wouldn't you rather dream about doing naughty things to a young beauty than be embarrassed when she finds out you can't?"

Hannah was finding the subject of the conversation completely bewildering. "I suppose so," she said.

"Good. And whether you say yes or no to those fellas, Hannah, there's another thing you should understand."

"Yes, Miss Watson?"

Carrie Watson got up and walked over to point at a little floor safe. "Never forget that this is a whorehouse. In a whorehouse, nothing—and I do mean nothing—is free."

9

AT 6:30 A.M. JOSEF and his father stepped from the Illinois Central onto the platform at Pullman. It was a half hour before Josef was due at work, and the wind off the lake made the damp cold all the more bitter. The town was still dozing in the early-morning darkness, but the streets were brilliantly lit with gas-lamps.

Yankel looked about him appreciatively. Last night, in the middle of the night, he had awakened, his mind spinning sorrowfully about Hannah. The move to America, a journey that was supposed to bring such safety and comfort, now seemed regrettably stupid, all the sacrifice and effort in that journey so futile.

As he lay there in the overcrowded rooms that without Hannah, felt so empty, it had occurred to him that perhaps he was making another mistake. What if moving the family away from the city would prove as pointless as the pilgrimage from Russia? Yankel's troubled mind slipped irresolutely from one point of view to the next. To find support for his decision, he reassured himself with the thought that Josef worked in Pullman and had begged him to see it. It was inconceivable that his own son with firsthand knowledge would mislead them.

Now, surveying the little town, Yankel was pleased. Yes, this was better. Everything he could see—the neatly paved street and the buildings along the main road—was made from clean red brick. As he drank in the sight, a woman wrapped in a shawl hurried inside a long V-shaped building across the street.

"Is that the factory?" Yankel asked his son.

"No. The factories are back there." Josef turned to point directly behind him. "The one I work in is under the clock tower. That place across the street," he continued, "that's the arcade. The shops on the first floor have everything you could dream of: groceries, furniture, clothes, paper for writing letters. There's even a pharmacy with an ice-cream parlor."

"Ah, your mother and the girls will like that!" The smile Yankel allowed himself was followed by a pang of regret. The great pleasure of ice cream would not be enjoyed by his missing daughter.

As they walked down the platform steps from the train station, Josef continued. "Up on the second floor in the arcade, that's where we have to see the agent about renting a house. There's a library up there and some meeting rooms." Josef paused briefly before he continued. "There's even a a barbershop."

Yankel understood his son's unspoken suggestion. Like many of his friends, Josef had shaved his young, thin stubble soon after he arrived in America. But Yankel still wore a full beard. With his black hat and clothes, Yankel bore the unmistakable look of an Eastern European Jew.

"Josef, I'm still a Jew," he said. "I will not shave." His tone told Josef that his father's mind was firmly set on this issue.

Josef stopped walking and glanced up the street before he met his father's eyes. Now that Papa had decided to move to Pullman, Josef had hoped he wouldn't insist on making it so obvious that they were *different*. After all, there was only one other Jewish family in the entire town. Josef thought it was important to get along, to blend in.

"Papa," he finally said, "I'm a Jew, too. But I don't have to wear a beard to be who I am in my heart. This isn't a Jewish community, you know that. And if you're going to live here—"

"A man must be what he is," Yankel said.

Josef decided to drop the subject. This was an old argument. They were merely saying the same things to each other they had said before. "Let me show you the town," he said, anxious to get around their impasse.

But his father was annoyed about Josef's insistence on blending in. Now he wanted to show Josef he distrusted his information. "Have you been *inside* these houses?"

"Of course not, Papa," Josef answered. "I don't live here, do I? I've never even walked more than a few feet up this street here, but I know where the houses are."

They began walking briskly in the cold. They explored one street to the end of the block, then turned right for another before they headed back to the center of the town. The houses were laid out neatly in blocks that formed perfect grids. Each little bungalow looked exactly like the next, fronted with Romanesque arched windows trimmed in white.

Yankel had never seen anything like it. There was no paper, no cigarette butts, no dirt anywhere. It seemed to Yankel that it was too perfect, almost as if human beings didn't really live there.

"How can this be?" asked Yankel, astonished at the picture book quality of the neighborhood.

"It's the way it is here, Papa. The company takes care of everything."

"But why all this?" Yankel gestured toward the little park with its trees and bushes. Even in its barren winter condition, it was a triumph of civilized planning. "I don't understand why a company would do all this for its workers."

"I am told it is to make us better workers."

As Josef and Yankel made their way back to the main square, doors up and down the streets began to open. Men and women looking quite normal in dirty, rough jackets noisily filed out onto the pavement to head toward the factory.

"Wait for me in the arcade," Josef said to his father. "I should tell my foreman I'll be late."

Although Josef had been concerned about his father and mother's fitting into this regimented little town, he had to admit that the family's move to Pullman was coming at a good time. The fair had closed in October and, with train travel down, Pullman had been laying off workers. Josef's foreman, Rufus McFarr, had dropped strong hints that soon only those who rented Pullman's housing would be kept on.

Rufus McFarr was a short, strong-muscled man given to abusive language and explosive outbursts of temper. Josef worked in the body shop, assembling the axles and spring suspension that gave the cars their smooth ride. In his first week on the job Josef had seen the foreman lift a worker off the floor and slam him against a wall. From that moment on Josef had worked as quickly and quietly as he could. Calling unnecessary attention to yourself seemed foolhardy.

This morning in the shop Josef found Rufus drinking coffee from a large mug, talking loudly to another foreman.

"Excuse me, sir," Josef said politely.

"What is it?" Rufus asked brusquely, annoyed by the intrusion.

"My family is moving to Pullman, and I have to see the rental agent. I will be a little late today."

"Then you'll make it up at the end of the day or I'll dock you. I won't have my shop thrown off schedule."

Josef hurried back to the arcade, muttering to himself. Dock his pay indeed. Unlike the women who upholstered the cars' seats and were paid by the piece, Josef and the other workers in the body shop were paid by the day. But Rufus had already offered them a "take it or leave it" deal and had lowered their $2.20-a-day wages to $1.80. Everyone took it because nobody was hiring outside.

When he got there, Josef and his father walked up to the second floor. They found the rental agent unlocking the door to his office.

"Come in, come in," he said abruptly, not so much out of courtesy as to keep the cold air out of his office. Before he took off his overcoat, he knelt at a small gas burner, turned on the gas, and lit it. When he was sure it had caught, he stood and used the same match to light the lamp on his desk.

"All right," he said, settling himself behind his desk, "What can I do for you folks?"

"I work in the body shop here at Pullman," Josef began, "and I want to move my family to live in the town."

"That's not a bad idea, these days," the agent said. He glanced at Yankel momentarily, taking in his hat and beard. "Is this man coming with you?"

"This is my father." Josef noticed that his discomfort was

making him sweat. "My father and mother and two sisters will be moving with me."

"So there'll be five of you altogether?"

"Yes. What do you have available?"

"Oh, lots of things available," the agent said. "First thing, though, is to determine if you're the type Mr. Pullman wants living in his village."

"Well, like I said," Josef stammered, watching his father react to words and attitudes he didn't like, "I work here—"

"When did you start?" The agent dipped his pen in a bottle of ink.

"Several months ago, in early fall."

"I see," the agent said dryly. "You made it in before the fair closed, did you?"

"Yes, sir, I did."

"Do you use tobacco or strong drink?" Josef had just started to shake his head no when the agent continued. " 'Cause if you do, you won't want to live here. There's no liquor to be had in the entire town except at the Florence Hotel, and most men don't like paying a day's wages for a drink."

Josef assured the agent that he wasn't a drinking man.

"Well, if you're single and looking for the coarser element of women"—he paused, raising one eyebrow until he was sure that Josef understood that he was speaking of whores—"you won't find that here neither. The company disapproves of workers carousing until late of the night and coming in not fit to work."

Yankel had understood most of what this man had said, and he impatiently addressed Josef in Yiddish. He wanted his son to explain to this representative of the company that the reason they were moving to Pullman was to get *away* from the bad element. After Josef had presented this thought, the agent nodded.

"Well then, I'll mark you down as a man of good character." He made a note about the older man's foreign language. "We do have a large foreign element here, so you'll likely feel at home. Though most of 'em are Irish and Swedes."

The agent laid his pen on the table and moved to the next phase of the negotiation. "You asked about the houses, so let's get that issue handled right now. The houses will run you at least twenty-five dollars a month. They're expensive, and they're reserved for managers and foremen anyway. So why don't we just rule the houses out right now?"

This announcement dashed Josef's dreams of living in a modest house. Twenty-five dollars a month! He had always assumed the houses were for ordinary workers, but no worker could afford such exorbitant rent.

"Where do the workers live?" he finally asked.

"Tenements are our most popular housing and where most of the foreign workers live. Course, if you're bent on living in a separate residence, there are also the shacks."

The agent checked his list of availabilities. "We've got a tenement over in Building B on the third floor. It's got two rooms, and it'll run you twelve dollars a month. South of town behind the brickyard we've got some wooden shacks. They'll run you eight bucks a month."

Josef was still disappointed about the brick houses. But surely, he thought, in a town like Pullman, the tenements would be nice. "Can we see them before we choose?" he asked.

"Well, I'm not supposed to do this, but . . ." The agent pulled a long skeleton key off a ring. "There's three blocks of tenements on Fulton Street at the edge of town. Just head east, and you'll find it. This key opens all the tenements so be sure you unlock the right door."

"What about the shack? Can we see that, too?"

"Head south and go past the brickyards. Shack eight is available. You'll find it unlocked."

Josef and his father left the arcade and headed toward the tenements. Josef walked silently, blaming himself for misleading the family about the housing in Pullman. It was obvious to him that he should have asked the people who lived there.

They had to walk several blocks before they could even see the large tenements. Josef realized that the town had been laid out so that they were hidden from view.

Yes, there they were. Three dismal blocks loomed ahead, each packed with three large tenements. From the outside it looked very much like the building Mama and the girls were sitting in right now. Once they got inside, he realized they would have less space, not more. At least the water faucet was in the hallway inside, but it had to be shared with five families.

The shack was equally bad—a cold wooden lean-to with a soot-covered fireplace at one end. Somehow a space that measured no more than sixteen by twenty feet had been divided into two bedrooms and a sitting room and a kitchen. The seven-foot-high ceilings made the rooms seem even smaller than they were.

Before they returned to the rental agent, Josef and his father stood silently in the shack. Josef was aching with disappointment.

"I'm sorry, Papa. I heard the American men complaining about the rent, but I thought they were talking about the brick houses."

Yankel listened grimly. There were so many harsh things he wanted to say to his thoughtless son, so many things that his chest ached with the effort of controlling himself. He yearned to remind him of the years of trouble he had caused the family. He was the one who had persuaded them to let Hannah work in the city. And now this! He was convinced that he would never have yelled at Etta if he hadn't believed Josef's tales about this place.

"You did it again," he said bitterly. "This is a shit hole!"

"We don't have to take it, Papa," Josef said. "But I'm worried because the workers who don't live in the town are being fired."

Yankel walked slowly, the hard soles of his shoes banging on the plank floor. This consideration made these homes more palatable. "Is it at least true," he said finally, "that this town would be safer for Mama and the girls?"

"That is definitely true, Papa. You heard the agent yourself. There are no bars and no brothels. Only a good influence."

"Then this may be better than where we are now." His father was grateful for an excuse to leave the West Side, where the neighbors were talking about him. "This may be better after all."

Before Josef signed the lease, he complained to the agent, "Why are the rents so expensive? There's less space than we have in Chicago, yet it's two dollars more a week."

"Mr. Pullman didn't have charity in mind when he built this town," the agent said as he filled out the lease form. "This beautiful little village was built to elevate the workers who live here, maybe even create a feeling of gratitude. But that don't mean you won't pay for what you get.

"By the way," the agent said, "you're expected to open a savings account in the company bank. That's where residents pick up their paychecks. When they cash your check, they'll deduct your rent from it right then."

"They deduct it?"

"Don't worry about it," said the agent. "It's a convenience you'll grow to appreciate."

When Josef awoke early the following Sunday, his mother was already busy. She was wrapping an old Yiddish newspaper around their dishes and packing them in a vegetable crate.

Josef pulled his pants and sweater over his long underwear and walked to the other room. His mother's face was calm, but there was no life in it either. Josef was aware that she had already suffered too much, and he feared what another shock would do to her. Neither he nor his father had exaggerated the size or condition of the shack once they had actually seen it. All Yankel had said was "It's a decent place to start a new life." But Josef worried that his mother was counting on the grandiose living quarters he had talked about when he first started work at Pullman.

He smiled at Mashke and Frieda and kissed his mother gently on the cheek. Rachel gave him a sidelong look with weary eyes. She had always had a soft spot in her heart for her irresponsible firstborn.

"The coffee's hot," she said to him as she carefully handed Frieda a wrapped plate to put in the crate.

Josef poured coffee into a cracked cup and began to pace back and forth. He wanted to prepare her for what lay ahead, but then he didn't want to make it sound too bad either. At least the girls would be safer in Pullman than in Chicago, of that he was sure.

"I hope you like the new place," he said.

"Sit," Rachel said. His pacing annoyed her. She put a slice of bread on the table and pointed to it with a small knife. "Eat."

"About the house, Mama . . ." Josef didn't know exactly what to say.

His mother looked at him for a moment before she spoke. "I take it it's not so great."

Josef nodded. His mother had always been able to read him.

"So answer me this question, Josef. Is it worse than this?"

"No, Mama. No, it's not worse."

"This I can take. Worse, I don't know." She gave him a sharp look. "Answer me this, Josef," she said. "Are there any Jews in this town?"

"Yes. A few."

"A few but not many?"

"One family."

"So how does this one family get food to eat that is not *traife*?"

Rachel knew that approved kosher foods could be found only in a Jewish community large enough to provide such necessities. When Josef didn't answer, Rachel shrugged. "So am I to serve my family nonkosher food, is that it?"

"There is a grocery store, right in the square—"

"Tell me, Josef, is there a church there?" she continued relentlessly.

"Yes, but—"

"Then how does this one Jewish family protect itself at Easter?"

Rachel had always been uneasy about churches. There had been ugly episodes in Russian villages, where, following observances of Good Friday, peasants had left their churches intent on burning Jewish homes. She had never gotten over the fear.

"It's a church *building*," Josef said to reassure her.

"So? A church building means a church."

"No, Mama." Josef was so happy to give her this good news that he failed to see how peculiar the situation was. "There's no church in the building because no church can afford the rent."

Rachel had never heard of such a thing. "Josef, son, you must learn to think," she said. "This cannot be true. Ask yourself, why would the church building be there if it were not used?"

"From what I understand, Mr. Pullman didn't think it would look good if the town didn't have a church. Visitors don't know it's not used."

Rachel shook her head at this craziness. Either her son had misunderstood again or this new town made no sense at all.

Yankel lay in bed listening. He knew Josef wanted to warn Rachel about the new home, but she knew what was facing her. The woman was no fool. The one thing no one had brought up was the likelihood that she would have to return to the city by train in order to pick up and deliver her sewing. Yankel knew he had made a mistake, and he dreaded the look he would find on his wife's face.

After he finally forced himself to get up, the family began packing in earnest. Rachel had refused to work on the Sabbath, and that meant that between Friday and Saturday evenings, all preparations had ceased. But ready or not, Sunday was moving day. Any other day Josef would be at work, and Josef's help was essential.

The plan was that Yankel, Rachel, and the girls would take the train to Pullman and carry whatever they could. Josef would load the rag-stuffed mattresses, the chairs, and the kitchen table onto his father's pushcart and walk it out there. His journey was sure to take at least six hours. Since darkness came as early as four-thirty these winter days, it was important that he be on his way before noon. But what with Rachel's friends coming to the door to say good-bye, the preparations were slowed down. At the rate they were going, Josef figured he wouldn't arrive until well after dark.

Before the family closed the door to the tenement for the last time, each looked around, lost in private thoughts. No wealthy landowner ever felt more despair at leaving a beautiful home than Rachel felt at this moment. For her, this dark, squalid place held memories of her sweet daughter. The walls themselves felt special, having surrounded, and perhaps still retaining in some magic way, Hannah's essence. At the door Rachel had told her friends, over and over, that if the girl returned, to tell her that she loved her. She wasn't allowed to speak her name, but her friends understood whom she meant and promised.

For Yankel, the pain of departure was different. This wretched tenement had been the place where he had finally been forced to face his failure as a good provider.

Even the girls felt sad. This time they were not leaving in triumph to go to a new home with boundless possibilities. They all knew that they were trying to escape fear and poverty, but this time they had no hope that their new home would be better.

For Josef, it was a reminder of the time when as a boy he had stolen the rifle from the soldier. Once again he was caught up in events that he himself had set in motion and that had led to events he hadn't counted on. Josef remembered the afternoon in Svislovich when he discovered that his stolen gun was missing from its hiding place. By the time he returned home, a soldier had been found shot to death. Then things had gotten crazy. Somehow the military knew that he and Leivik had taken the gun.

When the constable had knocked on the door of the family's little wooden house, Josef had climbed through the back window and raced through the yard to get away. By the time he plunged into the Berenisa River to reach the forest on the other side, his heart was pounding. There he had hidden on a large branch in a tall tree until so much time had gone by that he thought he would die of thirst if he couldn't come down.

From his perch in the tree Josef had seen Leivik being led off the next morning, bound with ropes like an ox being led to slaughter. Several nights later, under cover of darkness, Josef's family had left the little town for the ghetto in Vilna.

Now, as the family headed for the train, carrying their clothes and a little food, Josef set off with his father's pushcart. He trudged down the icy street, waving to the neighbors who knocked on windows and shouted good-bye.

During his solitary journey he had much to think about. His mother's comments were still in his mind. She and Hannah had always been his allies, staunchly defending him against his father's criticism. Yet despite the help he had tried to give the family, the outcome of his efforts was seriously inadequate. Josef told himself that he had to be more careful, that he couldn't go on making these mistakes. But since he had been unaware that he was being careless, he didn't know what to do to improve.

Pushing the heavy cart was tiring, and Josef slowed his pace. He was barely south of the Loop when the winter sun was setting. He was turning a corner when a man on a bicycle abruptly cut across his path.

"Hey!" Josef yelled. "Watch it!"

The cyclist's carelessness annoyed him, but before he started walking again, another body careened into the wooden bars of the cart. It was a young man running fast, and the impact made Josef lose his footing on the ice. He slid to the ground beside the man who had run into him.

"Outta me way," yelled the man, roughly pushing himself away from Josef and giving him a kick for good measure. Three more thugs rushed past, yelling, "Come on, Paulie! Come on!" Paulie clambered to his feet and kicked Josef again before he rushed on to join his pals.

Josef was furious. When he sat up, he saw that the first three had caught the cyclist and knocked him off the bicycle. One of the roughnecks had pinned his arms while another was hitting him in the abdomen. Josef saw the third thug pull out a knife and move toward the struggling man.

Josef's first impulse was to get away from there as fast as he could. The last thing he needed was to be involved in a crime. But as he got up, his side hurt and his anger returned. Without thinking, he ran after Paulie, who was hurrying to join his gang for the kill.

It happened fast. Josef leaped forward, hurtling himself through the space between them, and knocked the thug to the ground.

"Jesus, Mary, and . . ." Paulie sputtered. Before he could twist himself loose, Josef hit him as hard as he could in the side of the face. Then Josef hit him again in the back of the neck and knocked him out.

Josef heard someone yell, "Look! Somebody's got Paulie."

The man with the knife turned toward Josef, brandishing the weapon. "This ain't your fight, mister," he yelled. "Git away."

As the man with the knife approached, Josef slipped his hands under Paulie's unconscious body and hoisted it in front of him. The man who had been hitting the cyclist shouted, "Jesus, Tim, look! What's he doing with Paulie?"

With his attackers distracted, the cyclist leaned back against the man who was holding him and brought his foot into the belly of the man who was punching him. There was a groan as the hoodlum doubled up in pain.

Then the man holding the cyclist tumbled backward over the bicycle. While the hoodlum was tangled in the spokes, the cyclist was able to roll sideways and drive his elbow so hard into the thug's ribs that he could hear them crack.

The cyclist could see that the hoodlum with the knife was advancing toward the stranger who had helped him. The young man was holding one of the hoodlums up, trying to keep the limp body between himself and the knife. The cyclist freed himself from the bicycle and lunged forward. He punched the knifer in the back near his kidneys, and when the knifer arched his back in pain, the cyclist threw his forearm around the man's neck in a hammerlock and tightened it.

Josef dropped Paulie. The knifer, unable to escape from the cyclist, made one clumsy pass at Josef with his weapon, but Josef grabbed his wrist with one hand, and smashed him in the gut with the other. Then another punch. And another.

Josef later would not know how many times he hit the man, but suddenly all his anger and frustration became focused on the ugly, violent person in front of him. Finally, when the thug was unconscious, the cyclist let him slip to the ground.

The two men stared at each other for a moment, gulping air and trying to calm themselves. "Thanks," the cyclist said. He was a tall man, and he sported a thick dark mustache over a heavy jaw. He appeared to be well into his forties.

After he had scrutinized Josef, he looked around. Four men lay on the ground, groaning or unconscious.

"Wish there was a cop around here," he said.

"I don't," said Josef, worried about his part in the fight. "We were fighting, too."

"They were attacking me, and you stopped them. I'd say that makes you a hero—not a subject for arrest." He looked around for a moment. "I bet I can find a cop in that bar."

The cyclist went into the tavern and returned a minute or two later with two police officers. One of the policemen pulled a napkin from around his neck. He was still chewing a mouthful of food. "That's one of them lying on my bicycle," the cyclist said. "And there's the rest of them."

The policemen roughly pulled the hoodlums to their feet and led them away, cuffed together. When they were gone, the cyclist righted his bike and examined it under a light post. The metal wheel was bent.

"I'll never be able to ride this thing home," he said ruefully. "But I suppose I should consider myself a lucky man. I'm pretty sure they would have killed me."

"Why?" Josef asked. "Do you know them?"

"Nah. They just wanted to steal the bicycle or take my money. I sure wouldn't have made it without you, son. What's your name?"

"Josef. Josef Chernik."

"I'm Frank Swift."

"Swift? Are you the man who owns the meat-packing company?"

" 'Fraid not. He's my old uncle, though it doesn't help me a lot when it comes to money. By the time Uncle Gustavus finishes pinching a nickel, the buffalo squeals as loud as those cows he slaughters."

When Josef laughed, the middle-aged relative of Gustavus Swift continued. "Well, you're one hell of a fighter, Josef. You saved me. How's about I give you the cycle? It's worth about a hundred dollars—at least, that's what it cost when I bought it."

"A hundred dollars!" Josef had never had that much money at one time in his life.

"Yep. Take it. Every time I get on the doggoned thing, I get myself in trouble one way or another."

Josef was delighted with this expensive show of gratitude. "Could you show me how to ride it?"

"You may be asking the wrong man about that. I don't have any special advice. Just get on and let 'er roll. If you think you've got to stop, though, jump off. The way you're supposed to stop it is by jamming your foot against the wheel. Myself, I've never been real good at that."

Frank Swift helped Josef lift the bicycle onto the top of the family's furnishings on the pushcart. Then he shook his hand and disappeared into the night.

10

PHILLIP WOODRUFF FROWNED STERNLY at little James. The boy
was sitting opposite him in the carriage, kicking his heels against
the mahogany paneling under the seats. It seemed to Phillip
that raising a child was sheer aggravation. He glanced at his
wife beside him. *No help there,* he thought. She hadn't even
noticed the boy's behavior.

Isabelle was lost in her thoughts. They were on their way to
an important social event, and she was especially delighted because she knew that this time the invitation was a tribute to her.

In the last couple of months she and Bertha Palmer had
actually become friends. After that first unsatisfactory evening
at Hull House Mrs. Palmer had sent Isabelle a note inviting her
to come again. Isabelle had accepted reluctantly—really only
because her son had started a new year at school and his studies
kept him so occupied that she had nothing else to do.

That second visit to Hull House had taken place during
the morning, and she and Mrs. Palmer had found themselves
playing with squealing toddlers. It was an informal way to get
to know the great lady, and by the end of the morning they had
actually begun to enjoy each other and talk about their own

families. Even more important was the feeling Isabelle developed for the children she was taking care of.

She began to forget her social interest in Mrs. Palmer, and she returned again simply because she cared about the children. She discovered that reading to the children or cooking macaroni or soup in the kitchen with Jane Addams gave her a feeling of being needed and loved that she had long been missing.

Now, glancing at Phillip's face, she could see that he was not enthusiastic about the party this afternoon. He saw it only as another one of those extravagant theme parties that the wives of his wealthy associates seemed intent on giving. He was going only because the other guests would be wealthy and he hoped to pick up some new banking customers.

When they arrived, they were met outside on the front steps by Potter Palmer's "greeter." The short, wiry Irishman flashed them a large, toothy smile and said, "Good afternoon, Mr. Woodruff, Mrs. Woodruff, Master James." He nodded to each separately. "Welcome to 'Circus in the Snow.' "

Phillip knew that this personal attentiveness from the servants was one of the Palmers' special touches. The Palmers had been fortunate enough to find a man—acceptable, though Irish—who had a perfect memory for names. This gnomelike character could always be counted on to remember you even if he'd met you only once years ago. It was a trick to make each guest feel special.

Phillip followed the greeter up the front steps to the door. Inside Bertha Palmer was standing in a receiving line, flanked by her sister Honoré and Honoré's husband, Frederick Dent Grant. Frederick Grant still went by the title Lieutenant though he hadn't seen any real duty since he had left the Custer encampment to return for the birth of his first child. His timing had been impeccable. He had been home only one day when word about the Custer massacre reached Chicago.

The invitation had stipulated that the party was a "circus" for her friend's children, but Phillip couldn't help noticing that Bertha Palmer was dressed elaborately. Although it was frosty outside, she had managed to acquire fresh pink roses, which she wore intertwined with a strand of diamonds in her hair.

Previous to this occasion Phillip had never seen more than a polite nod pass between Mrs. Palmer and his wife, so he assumed that Bertha would not remember her. He stepped forward and bowed courteously. "Bertha, you remember my wife, Isabelle?"

Mrs. Palmer immediately turned her attention to Isabelle and clasped her hand warmly between both of hers. "Why, of course! We've become good friends. How are you, my dear?"

To Phillip's surprise, Isabelle answered without a hint of her usual shyness. "Mrs. Palmer," she said with genuine affection, "it's wonderful to see you. The children told me to say hello to you."

Mrs. Palmer glanced at Phillip. "Your wife has become invaluable to us at Hull House," she said. "I'm sure you must be very proud of her."

Phillip looked at Isabelle with barely concealed surprise. He had never heard anyone talk about Isabelle this way—certainly nobody important. Of all the words that might be applied to this sorry excuse for a wife, "invaluable" would be the last one he'd think of.

He could recall nothing about Isabelle's going to Hull House. If she *had* told him, he had dismissed the notion as frivolous, an unimportant passing fancy. But it was interesting. Somehow his wife had managed to make social inroads by pretending to be concerned about the poor.

"Isabelle," Mrs. Palmer said, "I want you to meet my sister Honoré and her husband, Lieutenant Frederick Dent Grant. Frederick's father, you'll recall, was General Grant."

Phillip was pleased that his wife had finally made wealthy friends, but he was vaguely annoyed that she was getting all the attention.

"Well, Bertha," he broke in, "where is our host?"

"Oh, Potter's probably out in back feeding the elephants."

"Elephants!" said little James in an amazed voice.

Mrs. Palmer turned her beautifully coiffed head toward the boy. "This must be the darling child I've heard so much about."

Phillip looked again at Isabelle quizzically. Heard so much about? These revelations about his wife's association with Bertha Palmer were becoming irritating. He had the unpleasant feeling that while he was not being ignored, he was certainly not being properly acknowledged by his hostess.

"So, Potter's outside?" he repeated.

"Oh, no, not outside. In the tent. Potter thought that the best way to brighten up this cold, dull winter was to create a summer circus for our friends' children. A nice idea, don't you think?"

"Very innovative," Phillip said, and despite himself, he frowned. Phillip believed in keeping up appearances, but the outrageous sums expended on some of the parties given by his friends seemed to him nothing short of ludicrous. The Mikado Ball that Marshall Field had given a few years ago had run him seventy-five thousand dollars by the time the New York decorators had been paid. Of course, they had changed the whole house into a replica of a Japanese tea garden.

"Oh, you know Potter," Bertha said gaily. "When I wanted to give a party, naturally he went all out."

"Is it cold in the tent?" asked little James, wide-eyed with the idea of animals outside in the snow.

"No, no dear," answered Mrs. Palmer indulgently. "It's quite well heated."

A servant led Isabelle, Phillip, and little James through the enormous rooms to the back of the house. An awning that protected the back stairs and the connecting walkway from the cold had been painted with life-size animals so that to reach the tent, partygoers walked past monkeys, zebras, and tigers. They arrived in the main tent just in time to see a real tiger leap through a burning rim.

Black servants dressed in maroon uniforms decorated with gold braid stood around the tent, holding torches that lighted the gigantic enclosure. Large cages filled with lions and bears and other wild animals lined the tent. A white dog with a tail that stood straight up over its back raced through a crowd of strolling guests toward Phillip. Phillip was startled to see the animal hurtling toward him, but at the sound of its trainer's whistle, the dog stopped in its tracks and leaped backward in a full *aerial* somersault.

Phillip was in no mood for this nonsense. The depression was severely affecting his bank's reserves, and a frightening number of the businesses and houses purchased with loans from his bank had gone into default. While it was true that the bank could repossess them—and in some cases it had done so—the face value of those properties had declined significantly. What he needed now was cash. Lots of it. And here today thousands of dollars were being wasted on this silliness.

If business worries weren't enough, last night he had crept downstairs for a midnight cozy with Helen and she had rebuffed him abruptly. "You got a wife sleepin' in this house," she had said, "Try slippin' it to her once in a while 'stead of always being after an underpaid servant girl." The only thing that had kept him from firing her on the spot was the fear that she might tell Isabelle what had been going on in the back rooms of her own home.

When a waiter arrived with a tray of champagne, Phillip accepted a glass. In the light of one of the torches, he caught a glimpse of George Pullman deep in conversation with John DeKoven, a director of several banks and railroads. "Watch the boy," he said dryly to Isabelle, and headed toward the businessmen.

DeKoven greeted him with bad news. "George here says that damn socialist paper the *Alarm* just published another letter on the subject of dynamite." DeKoven was famous for a foul temper when his opinions were questioned.

"Damnation!" said Phillip. "Another one?"

Phillip looked at George Pullman for confirmation. Pullman had a round face with intensely bright brown eyes. Years ago he had grown a chin beard in an attempt to look more mature. Phillip observed that these days his face had grown so severe that facial hair was hardly necessary.

"Same damned kind of thing," Pullman confirmed sourly. "The letter recommends that its readers stuff several pounds of dynamite into a pipe, plug both ends of it, and light the fuse in the neighborhood of rich men. It goes on to say that in giving dynamite to the 'downtrodden millions,' science has done its best work."

"Hard to imagine a decent paper printing something like that," commented Phillip.

"The *Alarm* isn't a decent paper," said Pullman. "The editors of that damn rag should be strung up from the nearest lamppost."

"If I had money lent out to an outfit like that, I'd call the loan right now and put those bastards out of business," DeKoven said vehemently. The idea of his neighborhood being blown up was not appealing.

Phillip turned his attention to George Pullman. "Any more trouble with the workers out in Pullman?"

Pullman frowned, causing the ends of his chin whiskers to jut forward. When his model community had been built, journalists and dignitaries from all over the world had traveled to Pullman to see it firsthand, and he had been universally acclaimed as a great humanitarian. He had a lot at stake, personally and professionally, in his community's success.

"Well, yes and no," Pullman answered. "There are always those few malcontents who aren't grateful for what we do. But we keep an eye on them."

"How's that?" asked Phillip.

"I have spotters placed anywhere those people congregate, including the churches and saloons in the neighboring communities. Spies," he added matter-of-factly. "These days an employer can't be too careful."

For a moment Isabelle watched Phillip converse with Pullman before she turned away. Her husband's bad humor was not lost on her, but she was accustomed to overlooking it. The only way she had endured being ignored by him for these several years was by detaching herself. She was not about to be distressed by one of his bad moods—especially not at a wonderful party where Mrs. Palmer had so clearly shown affection for her.

She stood in the tent with her son, enjoying his delight in the animals and their trainers. When a young boy from the Latin School took him off to see some new thrilling sight, Isabelle wandered back into the mansion. She found Bertha Palmer in the drawing room, and for the first time Mrs. Palmer invited her upstairs to see her private quarters.

Mrs. Palmer's Moorish bedroom had been done in ebony and gold. Light streamed through arched windows copied from a Cairo palace onto an original Louis XVI bed. Mrs. Palmer sat in front of a carved mirror and smoothed her hair with a silver-handle brush. She smiled at Isabelle. "I understand that the Polish Club is going to have quite a treat tonight."

Isabelle hadn't played the piano in front of a gathering

since her school days, and she was nervous about her performance tonight. She hoped there would be no illustrious guests
at Hull House who would listen with a critical ear. "If they still
want me," she replied.

Mrs. Palmer smiled. "I hear the way you work with the
kindergarten children is quite wonderful. You must be liking
the settlement house better than you did at first."

Isabelle blushed. She realized that her earlier discomfort
in Hull House had been obvious.

"I do like it," she answered honestly. "I confess I still don't
really understand the adults there—they seem to be from another world—but the children . . . well, children are the same
everywhere, aren't they?"

"Indeed, they are."

As they stepped out into the anteroom on their way downstairs, Mrs. Palmer indulged herself with another question.

"Isabelle," she said, turning to face her again, "does your
husband resent the time you spend at your charitable activities?"

If Phillip had been aware of her activities or objected to them,
he had given Isabelle no indication of it. "I don't think so."

Mrs. Palmer fixed Isabelle with her dark brown eyes. "Well,
if he does, you be sure to tell me about it."

Several hours later Isabelle was standing at the back of Hull
House's large parlor with Jane Addams. She watched as the
members of the Wednesday night Polish Club filed past her.
She never felt comfortable with the adults who met in these
rooms. Right now they were speaking to one another in an
angry-sounding language, and they looked so unappealing, so
different from everyone else she knew. The men were big and
rough, their burly bodies cloaked in shapeless, dirty trousers
and large, heavy sweaters.

The women were equally alien to her. With hair tied back
from their faces, the wrinkles around their eyes and the dryness
of their skin gave them a look of experience that Isabelle could
only guess about. Once, when she had been staring at an older
woman across the room, it had dawned on Isabelle that the
woman was not old at all but probably her own age.

Tonight Isabelle was feeling uneasy. She was getting more
nervous by the minute, and the harsh tone Phillip had used
with her before she left home still troubled her. When she had

told Phillip that she needed transportation to Hull House, he had irritably commented that he had a meeting downtown and that the butler would have to drive her.

"If you have to go to that place during the day, that's one thing," he had said, "but I don't understand you riding an hour across town in the dead of night."

When the audience had assembled, Jane Addams walked to the front of the room.

"I am delighted to present Isabelle Woodruff. Mrs. Woodruff will entertain you with some selections from the great Polish composer Frédéric Chopin."

Then she clapped her small hands together and was joined in polite applause from the audience.

When Isabelle heard her introduction, her heart began to race. She couldn't believe she was playing before a crowd of this size. In her mind the audience, which moments before had seemed of no consequence, was transformed into a panel of Polish judges who would hear their own music.

As if she were being controlled by strings, she walked unwillingly to the front of the room. She felt disconnected from herself, aware of what she was doing but as if she were seeing herself and the room through a thick layer of glass: the images of a few upturned faces as she walked past them, the rough feeling of the piano bench as she pulled it out to sit on it, the slight tremble in her hands as she placed them above the keys.

She began with a polonaise. When she had planned this program, it seemed to her that Chopin's dances would be perfect for this audience since he had written them in memory of the Polish folklore he wanted to preserve. For a few seconds she was too aware of the audience to feel the music, and her playing seemed artificial and emotionless. Then, as she continued to play, she forgot herself and became more in touch with the rhythms and harmonies in the piece. When she finished, bringing the sprightly dance to a vigorous conclusion, she remained seated.

Barely pausing until the audience's applause had died down, Isabelle began the next piece. This was a slower, sadder dance, and as she drew out the haunting melody, she felt herself move into the music, the way she had so often done at home by herself. It was as if the audience weren't even there.

By the time she started the third piece, Isabelle had begun

to become aware of the listeners again. But this time it was different. It wasn't as if they were outside her. Instead, she was aware of their responding and connecting with her through the music. When she began a musical phrase, she sensed their tension until she had finished it. As she played on through the slow, mournful theme, she felt the people as a warm presence that touched her and surrounded her.

Then, from a place somewhere outside herself, Isabelle saw a mountain covered in snow. It seemed like springtime because the snow was melting and running off the hillside into a stream. As she played, she felt such an intense longing that it hurt her. She began to see and feel a homeland she had never known, yearn for people she had never met. She saw them dancing in colorful costumes. She felt their grief as they left their homes and family, and as she felt the loneliness and sadness of their lives, the dance slowed and changed to a haunting, aching melody.

When she finished the piece, not a sound could be heard.

The room was hushed. The audience was leaning forward, barely breathing. Then the dancing and the landscapes in her mind vanished, and she felt stripped bare. She looked out at the audience. Tears flowed down the wrinkled face of an old man close to her. The people in the room had their arms across their chests, as if they were holding themselves together.

Standing in the back of the room, Jane Addams could feel the emotional power in the room. To break the long silence, she began to applaud. Gradually the audience began to applaud with her.

As the sound built, Isabelle stood beside the piano to take a bow. She looked out at the people she had touched, saw them cheering for her, and knew how intimately they had touched *her*. Suddenly feeling them, understanding them, caring for them, she was flooded with the realization that her life had expanded to encompass people she had never before known. As she looked out at their faces, her own cheeks were shining with tears.

11

CARRIE WATSON'S PARTING COMMENT stuck firmly in Hannah's mind. "Nothing is free in a whorehouse," she had said, and the *way* she had said it was so loaded with meaning that Hannah knew she was also referring to her room and board. This realization distressed her profoundly.

Miss Watson's gentle invitation to think things over had advanced rapidly to discussions of handling customers. As Hannah climbed the stairs, the weakness she had felt out on the street returned. Being light-headed made her all the more desperate. If she was too sick to survive out on the streets, then her only alternative was to accept the conditions of living here. Sooner or later she'd have to earn her keep.

Halfway up to the second floor Hannah stopped to rest. Three women that she didn't remember seeing in the dining room were on their way downstairs. Hannah glanced at them as they passed, but when one of them smiled at her, Hannah quickly averted her eyes. It troubled her, being surrounded by women known to be evil, dreadful creatures. It was even worse somehow when she had to confront their pleasant smiles and hellos.

Nothing in her background had prepared her for such moral ambivalence. It seemed to Hannah that whores simply had to be a different type of woman altogether, a type inherently wicked or nasty. But some of them confused her. Not only were they pretty in an untouched kind of way, but some actually showed her signs of kindness.

When she reached her room on the third floor, she was so dizzy that she barely made it to the bed. Lying on top of the coverlet, she pulled a corner of it over her and rested there, trying to force her mind deal with her situation.

Her alternatives were clear: She could go back out in the cold or she could stay. But both choices were so unacceptable that her mind balked at thinking them through. It seemed to Hannah that she needed to find some unthought-of alternative, but aside from a yearning to fly magically out the window and land safely back in her childhood, she couldn't think of a thing.

Hannah was unaware that she had fallen asleep until she was startled awake by the sound of a woman's voice. The room was dark now, and the voice was in the hallway just outside her door. It was laughing in a low, sultry kind of way Hannah had never heard before. The laugh was followed by a man's voice, teasing and playful. Hannah lay still, listening tensely. It frightened her to think that the man and woman might be planning to come into her room. As the voices continued on down the hallway, she relaxed.

She became aware that she was cold. The coal burner in the room had stopped putting out heat. She pulled the blanket around her shoulders and walked across the room to poke the coals. When she straightened up, she realized that the dizzy feeling was gone. She felt better than she had before her nap. Standing there in the dark, she heard a door open somewhere downstairs, and the faint sound of piano music floated into the room. A man was singing with the piano, a plaintive song she had never heard before. It surprised her that something as pleasant as music would be enjoyed in a place as bad as this.

As she continued to listen, she began to isolate different sounds: men and women talking; glasses tinkling. Somewhere in the house other music was being played—music different from the popular tune on the piano. She had heard a violin and a cello once in Russia, and she was sure she was hearing those instruments now. It was such formal, polite music that it made her feel less frightened.

As the coals glowed with more heat, Hannah remembered that she had promised Carrie Watson she would talk to her guests. She wasn't sure how to light the gas lamp, so she felt around for her dress in the armoire and put it on in the semi-darkness. Before she opened her door, she paused for a moment to collect herself.

When she finally did open the door, she was relieved to see that the hallway was empty. There were two stairways, one at either end. Torn by her desire to satisfy Miss Watson's request to meet the guests and her own wish to stay hidden, she quietly walked the length of the third-floor passageway to the rear staircase.

The back stairs were steep and dimly lit. In the dark it was difficult to manage her skirts and hold on to the banister at the same time. When she reached the second floor, she looked down the hallway. It was wider than the floor above, and though the brass wall sconces were larger than those upstairs, they were turned discreetly low. When she stepped onto the stairs that led to the first floor, she bumped headlong into a young woman who was standing in the shadows.

"Oh, excuse me!" said Hannah, startled.

The woman silenced her with an intense "Shh." Then, grasping Hannah by the wrist, she pushed her back up the step to the second floor and into the last room in the hallway.

"I'm hiding," the girl said, as if nothing were unusual. Then she squinted at her with recognition. "You're new, ain't you?"

Hannah nodded and stepped back to distance herself from the girl.

The woman was young, perhaps even younger than Hannah, with straight brown hair that was clean and shining. It was drawn back at her neck in a mode that struck Hannah as too simple for a woman in this profession. Her skin was pale and, except for a splash of freckles across her nose, perfectly clear and smooth.

"I'm Ermintrude," she said. "But here everyone calls me Marie. What's your name?"

"Hannah."

"What are you doing up here alone?" asked Marie.

"Just looking. What's it like downstairs?" Hannah asked, probing for information. "I mean, what do they do down there?"

"Is this your first night?" Marie asked.

Hannah nodded.

"Well, downstairs it's just beautiful." The girl sought for ways to describe the marvels of the first floor. "The hallway is just blazing with lights, and they're serving iced wine out of silver buckets. A three-piece orchestra is playing in the Mikado Room—that's the room where the walls and ceiling are covered with mirrors. There's five parlor rooms down there, you know—all different. That's where the girls meet the gents and talk to them."

Hannah didn't know how to respond to Marie's enthusiastic description. The whole situation was so odd she hardly knew what to ask first. "Why are *you* hiding?" she finally asked.

"Well, I'm kinda new, too," Marie confessed. "And some-times . . . well, there's just a lot to learn around here."

Hannah waited, hoping for the rest of the explanation.

"See, last week this gentleman got carried away and was carrying on something awful, wantin' me to dance with a mask on, and . . . oh, lordy, he just scared me something awful. So I bit him."

Hannah reacted to this peculiar story with a start. Although the music and the pretty gaslights had been a calming influence, it now seemed that lurking beneath the luxury of these rooms were dark, unsavory impulses—much worse than she had feared.

"Well," the girl continued, "Carrie said that wasn't the way to handle a man and told me to stay away from the gentlemen until I picked up a few pointers. Zorrine—you know her, the real pretty one?"

Hannah nodded. She remembered Zorrine from supper.

"Carrie told me Zorrine has some tricks I should learn. And Zorrine said I could watch, only the gent mustn't know. She's going to drop her handkerchief at the bottom of the stairs as a signal. Then I'll go hide. See, there's a tiny little room right next to Zorrine's, but there's no door except through the bedroom. So I have to be in there when she shows up with her gent."

"Why don't you just go in there and wait?"

" 'Cause it's cold and dark and it gives me the creeps sitting in there all alone." Marie's eyes brightened with sudden inspiration. "I've got an idea. Why don't you watch with me?"

Hannah drew back. Watch what these women did with their men? It was a shocking notion. Hannah knew what she had done with Roland Girard, and in those private, intensely personal moments she certainly would not have wanted other people to watch. Yet that had been love—at least, *she* had thought it of as love—and this was something different altogether. This was a place where men got carried away and could require her to do all sorts of dreadful things if she lacked the proper skill.

Marie smiled and took Hannah's hand. "Come on," she said, glowing with conspiratorial pleasure. "There's lots you should learn, too. Anyway, I'll be with you."

Hannah followed Marie down the hall, and when they reached the room, Marie softly pushed the door open and peeked inside just to make sure it was empty. The bedroom was large, and its walls were covered in green silk moiré. A large bed with tall carved posts dominated the room. Under the windows a reclining couch stretched languorously on the floor. A light was burning inside a Turkish brass lamp studded with tiny holes, and it cast mysterious shadows on the walls and ceiling. A cone-shaped mound of ashes glowing on a brass plate emitted a pungent odor that smelled floral and harsh at the same time.

Marie walked directly to the wall where a rectangular shape was outlined by woodwork on the wall. When she pushed on it, it opened like a door.

"In here," Marie whispered. "Behind this panel."

Hannah crawled in behind Marie and waited a moment to let her eyes adjust to the dark. Marie felt along the floor. "Here it is," she said, and with a loud pop a match flared. As Marie touched the match to a candle, Hannah surveyed the small hiding area. It was only about three feet wide, but it was as long as the large bedroom on the other side of the wall. There were no chairs in the little room, and Marie was already kneeling on the floor.

"Before Carrie bought this place, it used to be a panel house," Marie said.

"What's that?" asked Hannah.

"A house where they'd steal from the customers. They'd put one chair in the room for the gent to hang his pants on, and they'd put that chair right in front of this panel. While the man was busy with one of the women, the one hiding in here would open the panel and take his money."

"Didn't the men complain?"

"Sure, but they couldn't prove nothing. See, nobody ever *saw* the woman take the money. Plus, if the man was from around here, he wouldn't want to make a stink or his wife would find out."

"Is that what *you* do in here?" Hannah asked.

"Gosh, no. Carrie'd skin us alive if she caught us stealing. This is a respectable house. That's why she's so successful."

Marie's posture stiffened as she heard a sound. "Shh," she said. "I think that's them out in the hallway." She quickly blew out the candle and struggled to reach a wooden handle nailed to the back of the panel door. She managed to get the door closed just as the main door to the bedroom opened and the voice of Zorrine was heard in the room.

"Here we are," the woman said. "In the king's private sanctuary. You didn't peek, did you?"

The man's voice was slurred as if from too much alcohol. "Wouldn't dream of such a thing," he answered.

"Good. Stand here while your servant places your champagne on the serving table."

Marie, who had been leaning forward with her ear pressed to the panel, pushed it open a couple of inches to peek out. She closed it quickly. "My gosh," she whispered, "she's got him blindfolded!"

Marie gently pulled Hannah in front of her and then sat up on her knees so she could see over Hannah's head. When they were settled, Marie reached past Hannah and pushed the panel open a few inches again. A plump man dressed in a black evening suit was standing unsteadily beside Zorrine. When his body swayed into her line of vision, Hannah saw that a silk handkerchief had been tied around his head to blindfold him.

"My mighty king," said Zorrine. Beneath the scarf the bottom half of the man's face widened into a foolish smile.

"Ahh," he said, inhaling loudly. "Zanzibar. The scent of Araby's incense . . ."

The man stumbled, and Zorrine led him to the reclining couch, where she helped him lower his ample posterior onto the cushion.

"The mighty king should rest himself, in preparation for a night of pleasure," she said.

"Umm," he said, settling himself on the couch. Although his trousers fit his heavy legs tightly and his protruding stomach would surely have been more comfortable had he leaned back, the man sat forward in a posture of alertness.

"Which story from your collection of *Arabian Nights* will your king hear tonight?" he asked.

"I was thinking that my royal highness might be pleasured to hear about the night I was so cruelly stolen from my palace by the big Nubian slaves," Zorrine answered.

"Yes, yes," he said, sitting more erect than ever, still staring blindly into the handkerchief.

"But would my king first enjoy more champagne?"

"A good idea," he said. "Yes. Yes. Good idea!"

As if using his legs for support, Zorrine ran her hands down his stocky thighs and then lowered herself onto her knees in front of him. Then she filled his glass with champagne and lifted it to his lips.

"My king," she said.

"Umm," he said, extending his pink lips forward to reach the glass. As he slurped enthusiastically, Zorrine took one of his hands and held it until she was sure he had control of his glass.

Hannah could see that Zorrine was nestled alongside the man's leg so that as she moved, her bosom rubbed against it. Each of her moves was performed to enhance his excitement. Zorrine deliberately ran her hands up the inside of the man's thighs, eliciting a deep sigh from him.

"My king should lean back . . . and relax," she said. "My story is about to begin." She moved her hand over his stomach and chest and gently pushed his shoulders back against the chaise. The man leaned back without resisting.

In his new semireclining position, Zorrine skillfully unbuttoned his fly. When she drew a bright pink, semiturgid member from his pants, Hannah hid her face in shame.

"Please," she whispered to Marie, "get me out of here."

Marie was suddenly aware that she was in a bad situation.

This new girl was distressed and had started to breathe rapidly as if she were ready to burst into tears. Marie knew she had to do something to calm her. If Hannah cried out, the wealthy client would realize he was being watched, and that would get her in terrible trouble with Zorrine and Carrie Watson.

Marie knew she was stuck. There was no way she could get Hannah out of there before the performance in the next room had been concluded to the customer's satisfaction. But there was another side to it, too. Marie knew that for all of Hannah's shock, they were *privileged* to be observing an expert storyteller. After all, they were watching the house's leading earner, and it was obvious that both of them had much to learn. Marie wanted to see every moment of it.

To calm Hannah, Marie found Hannah's right hand with her own and squeezed it. Just to make sure she could cover Hannah's mouth in case Hannah decided to scream, she also slipped her left arm over Hannah's shoulder.

Hannah accepted Marie's hand and arm as a much-needed kindness. There in the dark the closeness reminded her of her mother's arms during the fearful times in the old country. Hannah squeezed Marie's hand in return. The protection she sensed made the scene in front of them more bearable for her to watch.

From the next room they heard a delicate musical ching. When they peeked back into the bedroom, they saw that Zorrine had picked up a tiny pair of circular brass cymbals and had brushed them together to create an atmospheric chime.

She raised up a little on her knees to put the cymbals back on the brass table and stretched forward to untie the silk hand-kerchief from the fat man's head. Then she raked it, ever so gently, across his face and head. He smiled as if in ecstasy, and the look in his eyes revealed that he was already transfixed by the scene he was seeing in his imagination. As Zorrine rose from her kneeling position in the floor, the man took his stubby pink member in his hand and toyed with it gently.

When Zorrine reached the bed, she began to unfasten the buttons on the front of her bodice. "I was only fourteen," she said in a voice modulated to suggest a scene long ago and far away. "It was the darkest of nights in my castle, and I undressed to get ready for sleep."

Zorrine paused in the narrative to lift her elaborate dress over her head. As she revealed the flimsy violet-tinted silk drawers she was wearing under her dress, the man sucked in his breath noisily.

"I knelt at my bed to say my prayers," she said, kneeling in her underwear to act out this fantasy of schoolgirl purity. She had turned her rear to the man so he could be treated to the sight of her full buttocks straining against her drawers. "When I had finished my prayers," she continued, "I heard something in the hallway."

Zorrine lifted her head up in a pose that suggested listening. Hannah, sure that she had been detected, squeezed Marie's hand again. But after a moment Zorrine continued.

"When I heard nothing else, I was sure I had made a mistake. Surely I could not be harmed in the home of my dear parents, the king and queen of Araby. They only had one enemy, an evil king named Naballazar, who ruled the adjoining kingdom."

She turned her head and looked up at the windows above the customer's head as if in great agitation. "They burst in through the windows. Big black men carrying cruel scimitars. They were bare-chested, and their thighs were cloaked in shiny, golden pants."

Hannah had become fascinated with the story in spite of herself. She leaned forward, aware that Marie had not released the pressure on her hand. The man on the couch whispered hoarsely, "How many of them were there?"

Zorrine rose dramatically and answered, "Four. Four men the size of stallions. And when they tore off those gold pants, they had organs larger than cucumbers."

Then Zorrine did something that Hannah remembered for a long time. She looked right at the fat man's stubby member and recoiled as if in great fear. "Such a huge organ," she said, raising her hand to her face as if her fear were now directed at her customer's awesome sex.

"They stripped me," she said in a desperate tone, and began to unlace her corset. Her breasts fell free from the undergarment, and she dropped her corset on the floor. "And they put their big hands on my breasts to excite me."

As Zorrine began to caress her breasts to demonstrate the

technique the marauding rapists had used, Hannah, who had experience being inflamed when Roland Girard's hands had touched her breasts, felt herself growing excited. Without intending to, she squeezed Marie's hand. When Marie returned Hannah's squeeze, Hannah leaned back against Marie's chest.

Zorrine continued with her scene. When she described how the Nubians had ripped off her drawers, she took them off. When she described how they tied her to the bedpost to beat her, she wrapped her fingers around the bedpost and wriggled for dear life. When she described how they forced her and forced her and forced her, she lifted one of her legs so that, still facing the customer, she straddled the bedpost. And when she described how they raped her until she screamed with pleasure, she wildly thrust her pelvis against the bedpost.

She began to make small crying sounds as she moved with greater abandon against the bedpost. Through her own growing astonishment and excitement, Hannah realized that Zorrine was timing her cries so that they seemed to answer the moans she was eliciting from the fat customer.

As if in a perfectly performed dance, Zorrine's cries reached their peak in time to elicit an orgasmic groan from the customer. Just when his cries marked his emission, Zorrine turned her face to the crack in the panel, looked directly into Hannah's eyes, and winked.

Hannah looked away just in time to see a spray of jism arch from the fat man onto the floor.

After the man's orgasm Marie silently closed the panel door. The two girls sat in the dark, still holding each other's hands. Hannah was numb with what she had seen and ashamed that she had allowed it to excite her.

Later, when they were finally back in Hannah's room, she looked at Marie despondently. "Why do men come here?" she asked. "Why do they do this?"

"Carrie says it's to get what they can't get at home," Marie answered.

"Why did *you* come here?" Hannah asked sorrowfully, staring at her new friend through tears. "I don't understand. Why would a girl like you—"

"Probably the same reason as you." The girl had started to

respond to Hannah's sadness and was beginning to feel despondent herself.

Hannah looked at her through tears. "Were you pregnant?"

"Naw. I'd been working over at a print factory painting etchings. One night my back was hurting me so bad from sitting hunched over all day that I stopped in for a drink at Mike Murphy's bar. Somebody must have put powders in my drink 'cause the next thing I know, it's morning and I'm waking up in a room up over the bar. Somebody had took all my clothes off."

"How awful!" said Hannah sadly. "And you knew nothing about what had happened to you?"

"No," said Marie, starting to cry a little. "And when I went home and told my mother and daddy where I'd been, my pa said it killed him to see how bad I'd turned out. He threw my clothes out on the street and told me I'd have to leave. Ma cried, but she said it was better that way; otherwise I'd be a bad influence on my sisters."

"And then you came here?" Hannah asked.

"Not directly. At first I stayed with a girl from the paint shop. But it was so dreary, coloring in between the lines every day and then going back to her little room at night, that I couldn't stand it anymore. So one day I decided that if I was going to live the life of a bad girl, I'd make dern sure I'd get the good that went with it. So I come here, and Miss Carrie has been like a mother to me ever since."

"How long ago was that?" Hannah asked.

"Two months," she said. "The longest two months of my life. Every night, I swear to God, every night I go to sleep thinking of my ma and my sisters. Sometimes," she said, her voice breaking into a high-pitched whisper, "sometimes I feel so lonely I don't think I can stand it."

The girl started to cry, and Hannah slipped her arm around her and wept with her. Hannah missed her family, too, and ached when she thought of them. At least knowing that someone else felt this way offered some consolation. Hannah patted Marie gently.

"Do you ever try to see them?" she whispered.

"Once I did," Marie said, wiping her tears away with the

back of her hand. "but Mother wouldn't even talk to me. That's the worst part of it. Nobody on the outside ever wants to have anything to do with you. It's like you died or something."

Marie and Hannah cried for a little while, and then Marie curled over onto her side. Hannah couldn't think of anything to say that might comfort her for she was in the same distress herself. She covered Marie silently with the cashmere blanket and gently stroked her shoulder.

After Marie had stopped crying and gone to sleep, Hannah got up and changed into her nightgown. She slipped under the covers and lay staring into the darkness, and she thought about Roland Girard.

She knew he had hurt her as deliberately as those bad men who had drugged Marie. Rage surfaced in her for the first time since she had been fired at the department store. She realized that Girard must have known she would die—either die or wind up homeless in a place like this.

Hannah lay for a while letting herself understand Roland Girard's callousness. *I don't know how*, she finally promised herself, *but someday I will hurt him. No matter what I have to do, I will make him feel as bad as I do right now.*

Her anger strengthened her and crowded out her sadness. She rolled closer to Marie and slipped her arm around her sleeping friend before she herself sank into sleep.

12

___

DETECTIVE WHEELER STOOD ON the front porch of Carrie Watson's establishment and rang the bell. A maid wearing a uniform with a little white apron opened the door. Big Wheel smiled expansively. He appreciated the class and respectability Carrie had created here. As he removed his hat and stepped into the entranceway, Carrie's green parrot squawked, "Carrie Watson. Come in, gentlemen."

The detective stuck his finger in the parrot cage to tease the bird. During the warm weather Carrie kept her parrot on the front porch so that its loud squawk would advertise the premises to prospective customers as they walked by. It was a darn sight more dignified, the detective thought, than those places that put their whores in the window, winking and shaking their titties at everyone who passed. Then he painfully pried his finger out of the bird's beak.

Big Wheel gave the maid his coat and hat and strolled into the crowded front parlor. He found an empty place to sit and stretched his lanky legs across one of Carrie Watson's love seats to make himself comfortable. This was not the kind of duty a policeman could object to. No, indeed. Imagine getting paid to visit the whorehouses! It was a dream job. And there were so many of them in the city that Wheeler figured he might as well check out the good ones before he sullied himself with the others.

Not that being a member of Chicago's finest would keep a policeman from visiting a sporting house. Not at all. The police and the whores had long ago worked out relationships that benefited each other quite profitably. So it wasn't a matter of suddenly finding a legitimate reason to frequent the bordellos that was making Big Wheel smile.

Nor was it because the privileges administered to him during this assignment would, in all likelihood, be "on the house." The free gratification of pleasure was an everyday occurrence for policemen anyway. Few whorehouses were so foolish as to charge a man wearing the uniform, although ordinary coppers rarely got the *best* girls. No, Big Wheel was grinning all over because his assignment to find the whore slasher would probably mean he'd have his pick of the best girls in the city for as long as his investigation continued.

Carrie Watson stepped warily into the front parlor. In her earlier days she had decided not to pay police bribes, and the force had retaliated by arresting some of her girls and customers with "John Doe" arrest warrants. When Carrie found out that carrying blank warrants was against the law, she had taken her case to court and, much to the surprise of the police, had won.

Though Carrie drew the line at bribing the police, she was always generous to a man wearing a shield. When the door maid had told her that a detective was waiting in the front parlor, she headed there right away.

"Good evening, Detective," she said. "Is this a social call or are you on business?"

"Oh, maybe a little bit of both, Carrie," he said. He lifted one bushy eyebrow, and his lean face broke into a provocative grin. "You had any trouble around here?"

"I run a clean place, Detective. You know that."

"A damn fine place." Detective Wheeler agreed, nodding. "And you always have such good oysters."

Carrie Watson could recognize a request when she heard one. She leaned toward one of the nearby whores who was hanging around without a customer.

"Clara," she said, "go tell Millie to come in here and take the detective's order for some supper."

Wheeler made a grand gesture of clearing his throat and rubbing his hands together as if trying to warm them up. Carrie got that message, too. "Oh, yes. Tell her to bring out some of that good whiskey that come in from Tennessee the other day."

Wheeler leaned back again and smiled. He loved dealing with a professional.

"What kind of trouble are you concerned about, Detective?"

"A whore killer."

Carrie frowned. She hadn't heard about anything like that lately. Once, a few years back, a crazy man inspired by religious fervor had gotten into a whorehouse and strangled some girls before they caught him. She didn't want to see anything like that happen here.

"He kills girls *in* the bordellos?" she asked.

"Well, no . . . at least, not yet. Usually he gets 'em when they're walking around on the street."

"Ah," said Carrie, trying to evaluate the danger. "My girls don't walk the streets. Are all the victims in the profession?"

Detective Wheeler stuck a well-bitten fingernail under his collar to loosen it. He was embarrassed to realize how little he actually knew about the killer outside on the streets. "Well, there's been three so far. Two of them definitely prostitutes. One of them, we're not sure. But I figured it'd be a good idea to check with the local houses to see if anyone carrying a big knife had been in lately."

"A big knife? Detective, this place don't normally attract the type of man who walks around with knives. We get a lot of bankers and businessmen and such."

A young girl with the most beautiful eyes he had ever seen entered the room and walked directly toward him. The detective was so stunned that he stopped listening and stared. Carrie became aware that the detective was mesmerized by something behind her back and turned. It was Hannah.

"Excuse me, Miss Watson, where is the banker you wanted me to have supper with this evening?"

This girl is so darn green, thought Carrie. *The least she could do is say hello to a man sitting with me.* "Hannah," Carrie said pointedly, "meet Detective Wheeler."

Hannah, who had some of her brother's fear of the police,

stiffened and lowered her eyes. "How do you do, Detective?"
she asked quietly.

Carrie noticed Hannah's reaction. She knew Hannah was
worried about being called upon to favor the customers with
more than conversation, and she figured Hannah thought
Wheeler might be the one. Of course, Carrie had more important clientele to reward with a plum as perfect as Hannah.
That was why she had decided not to push her too fast.

"Mr. Cudahy is in the Mikado Room listening to the orchestra," Carrie said in answer to Hannah's question. "Why don't
you go introduce yourself?"

"Yes, ma'am."

"And, Hannah, dear, unless you *know* someone has died,
won't you try to brighten up and smile?"

Hannah gave Carrie a small smile and left the room. When
Carrie turned back to Detective Wheeler, his eyes were alive
with pleasure.

He gave a long, low whistle. "Who was that?" he asked.

"Hannah Chernik," Carrie answered. "A new girl."

"Carrie, you old fox," Wheeler joked, hoping she would
pick up on this hint as quickly as his bid for oysters, "for a
second I thought you were makin' me a peace offering with
that gal."

Carrie looked at the lanky policeman severely. "Detective,
I don't have nothing to give you a peace offering *for*. You can
eat my food and you can drink my whiskey, and maybe, if one
of my girls is free . . ."

Carrie noticed that the detective was frowning. She drew
in her horns. After all, there was no sense making an enemy
out of a cop.

"What I mean is . . . if I put you with that girl, I probably
would owe you a peace offering. She's so new there's no telling
what she'd do. A new girl here bit one of my customers a few
weeks ago."

But Carrie had misunderstood the detective's frown. Something about the name Hannah Chernik had jogged his memory.
He knew he had seen or heard it fairly recently, but he couldn't
remember where. Since he prided himself on his recollection
of names, not being able to place it was bothersome to him.

Carrie's story about a whore's biting a customer did distract
him from his thoughtfulness. Just the image of *where* that new

gal might have bitten the customer amused him mightily. He
leaned back in the love seat and guffawed as Millie arrived with
his Tennessee whiskey.

That little green-eyed girl had aroused him, and since it
was clear that he wasn't going to have her tonight, he figured
that after his oysters, he'd meander over to Kitty Plant's Circus
House. Kitty's place didn't have the class of the Watson establishment, but her exhibitions of women and animals were always
fun to watch.

It was certainly difficult to have a conversation in the Mikado Room without being distracted, Hannah thought. With
mirrors covering all four walls as well as the ceiling, she practically had to keep her eyes glued on Mr. Cudahy. If they wa-
vered, no matter where she was sitting, the chances were that
she would find herself gazing directly at her own face.

In fact, Hannah could see that Mr. Cudahy himself often
shifted his focus from her to the far wall. When Hannah turned
her head to join him in a peek, she could understand why. The
old man was enjoying the sight of the two of them. From across
the room he appeared an elegantly dressed man in black evening clothes with an attractive young girl who seemed to be
hanging on his every word.

"We're a handsome couple together, my dear," Mr. Cudahy
said, turning his head back to her and leaning forward to pat
her hand. "It's a pleasure to look at us."

Hannah smiled. In a way, she realized, that was true. The
image of herself in the beautiful pink velvet dress Carrie had
given her, in a room shimmering with candlelight—yes, it was
a lovely sight to behold. And the three-piece orchestra that was
playing over in the far corner of the huge parlor made the scene
as impressive as anything Hannah could ever have imagined.

"It must look like this in that French palace with all the
mirrors," Hannah said.

"Yes," the old man conceded, though he was not nearly as
interested in the room as he was by how it always made him
look so much younger. "If I were a little less advanced in age,
my dear, I'd take you upstairs for a romp that would have made
the king of France envious."

Hannah was sorry he had said that. It brought her back to

the fact that she was, after all, in a house of prostitution, and that took some of the fun out of it.

Miss Watson had explained to Hannah that she wouldn't have to be worried about any physical demands from old Mr. Cudahy. Mostly he just liked to talk.

"That's just the way it is sometimes," Carrie had explained, and then she had told Hannah about another old customer who liked to hire three or four of the girls for an evening. He'd laugh and buy champagne as if there were no tomorrow, and when he was good and drunk, the old guy would take take off his shoes and socks and plunge his feet in the ice in one of the silver wine buckets and yell like crazy. There was just no accounting for it, Carrie said. But he was harmless, and what with her champagne going for twelve dollars a bottle, who was she to object to a little harmless fun?

Mr. Cudahy didn't put his feet in ice or carry on in a way likely to scare a young girl off, she said, but he did like to share his thoughts with a pretty young woman. "So just pretend like you're one of them geisha girls over in Japan and be pretty and listen. I hope that's not too hard for you, is it?"

Hannah had heard the sarcasm in Miss Watson's tone and agreed that it didn't sound too hard.

Now, in the Mikado Room, the old man indeed looked as if he needed to talk. "I'm so worried, my dear," he said, turning his attention from the mirror to the soft, compassionate look in the young girl's eyes.

"Why would a man like you be worried?" Hannah asked in her most polite manner.

"Oh, dear. You women never do understand the financial problems a man has to face, do you?"

Hannah thought about this for a moment before she answered. The financial problems she had known were serious but not hard to understand. They had involved avoiding starvation and eviction. The idea that there were complex types of money problems intrigued her.

"I would be honored if you would explain them to me," she answered demurely. "In a way I can understand."

"Well, my dear, being a banker is not without its risks. You see, customers bring money to us so we can deposit it in our vaults for safety. But the bank doesn't make money on that deposit until we lend the money out to someone else. We make our money when we charge the borrower interest. Does that make sense to you?"

"Yes, it does," said Hannah.

"Well, my dear, right now, with the country in a depression, factories and farms are closing. If you happen to own property, you can't sell it, and even if you could, nothing today is worth nearly what it was just a year or two ago."

"But how does that affect you?" Hannah asked.

The old man took another sip of champagne. "I have lent out a large amount of our customers' deposits to businesses that have since failed," he said. "Obviously they can't pay me back my money; they can't even pay me interest. While it's true that I can repossess those businesses . . ."

Hannah eagerly finished the old man's sentence for him. ". . . they're worth less now than they were when you lent the borrower the money!"

"Yes," he said, mildly surprised at her keen understanding. "A grave problem even if I were lucky enough to *find* a buyer."

"You mean," Hannah asked, "if you could find a buyer, you'd sell those businesses and houses—even if you had to accept a lower price than the value of the loan?"

"I'm afraid so," he replied. "A bank has to have money in its vaults. If customers suspect that the bank is out of money, they panic. And next morning you see long lines outside the bank, and before you know it, the bank has failed."

"Would you go to jail?"

"Oh, certainly not. Be jailed because my bank had failed? Never. But I would be out of business."

Hannah felt an eagerness that surprised her. There was something in what this man had just told her that she knew— she just knew—was valuable. What it was, she hadn't figured out, but she believed that if she put her mind to it, she might be able to work it out. She felt a little the way she had before she had gotten the job at Marshall Field's. She hadn't known what to do to make things better for herself; she had just believed that there had to be a way.

Hannah became aware that the old man had noticed her excitement and was looking at her peculiarly. "The way you explain the banking business is so fascinating," she said, "so very fascinating."

She lifted the champagne glass to her lips and took a tiny

sip. "But you are such an intelligent man," she said, probing for more information. "If *your* bank has made loans to those businesses, many other banks must be in even more danger."

"Of course, they are!" The banker was relieved that this notion would keep this bright young thing from thinking—or telling someone—that his bank was in trouble. "There are *many* banks in worse shape than mine."

When the old banker had consumed so much wine that he no longer made much sense, Hannah got bored. She wanted him to leave so she could go up to her room and think. She stifled a yawn and told the old gentleman that his financial instruction had been so fascinating that she found herself quite exhausted. The old man looked at his watch, surprised. He had been with this lovely young thing only an hour and a half. Carrie had promised him an entire evening. She would have to make an adjustment on his bill.

When Miss Watson saw Hannah leading the old man through the front hallway, she gave her an angry look. If little Miss Hannah Chernik thought her responsibilities to the house stopped with an hour's chat, she had another think coming. Carrie made a mental note to have a serious talk with the girl sometime in the near future.

13

ISABELLE LOOKED DOWN FROM her chair and smiled. A group of children were sitting around her in various positions on the floor. The Hull House nursery was still draped with the red and green paper chains the children had made before Christmas. It was time to get rid of them, but the color added so much cheer that Isabelle hated to take them down.

She was just finishing a Grimm's fairy tale about dogs with eyes the size of saucers, and the children were rapt with attention. The little boy the children called Goosie was listening so intently that his mouth was open. *It's either suspense or adenoids*, she thought, and made a mental note to share that humorous notion with Jane Addams.

Since she'd been coming to Hull House, Isabelle had discovered that she had a natural sense of humor. And she found that when she made a little joke, Jane Addams was always an appreciative audience. Of course, these days, with the strain of the depression, Jane needed a good laugh.

More than a hundred thousand jobless men were shivering on street corners in Chicago. The city was filled with ragged people who slept in hallways and stood in long lines for an occasional bowl of thin, charity soup. With no government agencies to assist the poor, Jane was working desperately to create relief stations and temporary lodging houses in various parts of the city. She had opened Hull House to homeless women who could find shelter nowhere else.

When Isabelle finished reading the story, the children noisily got up from the floor and ran into the kitchen for milk and cookies. Only Goosie remained. The children had given Goosie his nickname because he often arrived with goose feathers stuck to his clothes and hair. His mother stuffed down pillows in a factory, and to keep her son warm on his way to the settlement house, she would wrap him in her shawl. The feathers that stuck to her shawl usually resulted in Goosie's picking up a few feathers, too.

"Don't you want a cookie, Goosie?" Isabelle asked.

By way of an answer, Goosie walked over and, without a word, flopped against her knee. When he stuck his finger in his mouth and stared at her, Isabelle smiled. Of all the children at the settlement house, Goosie was Isabelle's favorite.

The thin little boy had alarmingly pale skin, but he had the sweetest disposition Isabelle had ever known. His mother, a woman named Sara Shaw, had another baby who was too young to be left at the kindergarten. Every day, before she dropped off Goosie and went to the factory, Sara Shaw carried the baby and his little crib to a neighbor's kitchen where she left him during the day.

Isabelle removed a bit of white down from Goosie's hair and stroked his head. "Would you drink some milk if I went with you?" she asked.

When the child nodded, Isabelle felt warm and appreciated.

The next day the weather turned bad. Strong gusts of cold wind blew up Halsted Street with such force that Isabelle could hear the children shrieking as the cold wind battered them up the street.

Isabelle was hanging one of the children's coats on a hook in the hallway when she heard such a terrible scream that she thought her heart would stop. She looked up from the coat hook in time to see Goosie's mother pushing past two of the children in the hallway. Tears were streaming down her face, and her breath was coming in jerky spasms.

"Come quick," she cried hoarsely. "Something's happened to my boy."

Isabelle threw on her cloak and ran after the woman all the way to her tenement. She could hear Sara Shaw ahead of her, making those terrible, frightened sounds.

"Back there," Sara Shaw yelled, pointing and running toward the rear of the building.

When they reached the backyard, Isabelle followed her to a wooden shed. A clothesline had been rigged on the roof of the shed, and clothes were flapping high above them in the strong wind.

When they got within a few feet of the shed, Isabelle saw little Goosie lying in the rubble. He was very still. She knelt beside him and touched his tiny shoulder.

"Goosie," she said to rouse him. The child didn't move. His face was whiter than she had ever seen it, and his eyes stared blankly at the clothes hanging above them. The realization struck Isabelle that he wasn't seeing her through his eyes, and for an instant she wanted to pull away from him.

"Goosie," Isabelle called louder, her voice trembling in a higher pitch. She shook him harder. "Come on now. Look at me."

When Isabelle slipped her arm under the boy and tried to lift him, his head fell back strangely, and Sara started to scream in that awful way again. The way he looked was so odd—not like a child at all. His head flopped from one side to the next as if it weren't attached to his body. Isabelle felt sick with fear. Carefully supporting his head in her arms, she lifted his face next to hers. She felt no breath or signs of life.

With the little boy's face so close to hers, Isabelle started to cry. She struggled to her feet to take him inside.

They went up the stairs as fast as Isabelle could make it with the lifeless weight in her arms. The poor mother followed, sobbing. She alternately called to Goosie, pleading with him to live, and to Isabelle about how the accident had happened. "Oh, don't die, son! Please, son, don't die. Oh, God, ma'am, I was hanging my washing out on the shed roof, and the boy was up there with me, handin' me the clothespins. Next minute I look around and he was lyin' on the ground. I guess the wind must have blowed him off the roof. Oh, son! My little boy. I didn't even know you was hurted."

When Isabelle got him upstairs, she carefully held the boy's head and laid him on his pallet on the floor. Inside, away from the noise of the wind, Isabelle had hoped to be able to hear a heartbeat, and she desperately felt the little boy's wrists and chest for a sign of life. He was strangely still.

Not knowing what to do, she rubbed his little wrists to put life back into him. But his hands were already cold. The child was dead. A doctor later informed them that his neck must have been broken in the fall.

They laid the little boy out in a room upstairs at Hull House, away from where the other nursery children would see him. It was such a tiny wooden coffin that Isabelle knew it was the saddest thing she had ever seen. The boy's mother clung to the little casket all day, looking down at her child. She was hollow-eyed with grief. Even when a few friends came by that evening to pay their respects, the woman was barely able to tear herself away from her boy to greet them.

The next morning a Baptist minister read the funeral service over the little casket, and when he was finished, Jane and Isabelle rode with Mrs. Shaw to the cemetery in the undertaker's carriage. The little coffin trailed behind them on a small cart.

At the cold, windy graveside, the minister hurried through the final service. He read a few words from the Bible. "In my house there are many mansions. If it were not so, I would not tell you." And then he closed his Bible and said, "Suffer the little children to come unto me."

The gravediggers loosened the rope and easily lowered the small casket into the ground. The minister picked up a handful of dry clods and put them in the hand of the boy's mother.

"Dust to dust. Ashes to ashes. I commit this child to the everlasting care of the Almighty. In the name of the Father and the Son and the Holy Ghost."

Sara Shaw stood still. The dirt sifted slowly from her hand. She stared ahead numbly, tears streaming out of her eyes. She looked like a woman who had lost her connection to this world.

"Dust to dust," said the minister, nudging her to remind her of her part of the ceremony.

For another long moment Sara Shaw could not move. When the minister touched her again, she came to herself and, reluctantly performing this one last service for her son, dropped her handful of dirt onto the little wooden box.

Sara Shaw returned to Hull House after the burial and sat wordlessly as people came and went. Jane left her to take care of events that were happening in other rooms. But Isabelle never left her side. Without looking at Isabelle, Sara Shaw repeated again and again, "I didn't even knew he had hurted hisself. I said, 'Get up, son. You're all right. Climb up again, son!' Oh, my poor baby. You was lying there dead, and I didn't even know!"

Isabelle sat quietly, feeling that all this was somehow her fault. It was true that after the accident she had made sure that Sara's younger baby was being taken care of by a neighbor, but she wished she had done more *before* the accident. She was tormented by the thought that she had missed some opportunity that might have saved the little boy. She didn't know what she could have done, but she feared that her failure had killed him.

It was ten o'clock that night when the last visitor had left the settlement house. Sara Shaw was still sitting in the nursery, trying to postpone the moment when she would have to go back to her lonely rooms. Jane came into the nursery and gently took the woman's hand in hers. "I know that we can't take away your sorrow," she said, her blue eyes bright with sadness, "but is there anything at all that we can do for you?"

The pale, overworked woman thought for a moment. "I can't afford to miss another day in the factory," she said. "But, oh, miss, if you could just give me my wages for tomorrow, I would have one day when I could stay at home and hold the baby." The woman broke down in sobs. "The boy was always asking me to take him, but I never had the time."

"Let me," Isabelle said to Jane. "Please. It would mean a lot to me."

Isabelle gave Sara Shaw all the money she had in her purse and helped her outside to the carriage that was waiting to take Isabelle back to Michigan Avenue. She left the grieving mother at her small apartment and went home, as sad and disconsolate as she had ever been.

No one opened the front door for Isabelle when she arrived

home. Isabelle had to ring the doorbell several times before Helen finally opened the door.

"Is my husband home, Helen?" she asked, taking off her hat in the front hallway.

"No, ma'am," Helen answered stiffly. "A man don't have much reason to sit home with his wife out and about, now does he?"

Isabelle looked at Helen and shook her head. She was too stricken to accept such audacity without comment. "Really, Helen," she said, "after all the nights I have spent here alone, I don't think that comment even deserves an answer."

Helen knew her mistress was right, of course, but that didn't improve her disposition at having been disturbed by the doorbell. She sniffed loudly and turned away. As she walked down the hallway, her skirt switched back and forth like the tail of an angry cat.

Isabelle climbed the stairs and felt a dark dread rise in her. After a day like today she didn't want to face the empty second floor alone. She realized that Sara Shaw must be feeling this same dread. Without anyone there to love or talk to, she didn't want to go home. Isabelle walked down the hall and quietly opened the door to her son's bedroom. The light from the hallway fell across his face.

Isabelle looked tenderly at James. He looked so small and vulnerable lying there asleep. She didn't want to wake him, but she needed to hold him close. She took her son in her arms and held him gently, noticing how sweet and warm his hair and face were. When she felt his breath against her cheek, Isabelle knew she had never felt anything as wonderful as those fragile signs of life.

Huddled in the dark there, holding her son, Isabelle was struck with how precious and momentary life is. She began to weep softly, thanking God that her child was alive. The thought occurred to her that the only reason Goosie had died was that his mother was poor. Otherwise he wouldn't have been on the roof of the shed to begin with.

Why? she asked herself, stricken with this realization. Did God really mean for that sweet little child and his mother to suffer because they were poor? How could that be God's way? Holding James in her arms, she wondered again, *Why did this happen? What is the purpose of all this?*

As she rocked him softly, James stirred and, irritated with being awakened, pushed her away roughly. "Stop!" he cried out in his sleep. When Isabelle tried to move him in her arms to make him more comfortable, he shoved her again. "Leave me alone," he said, and turned over in his sleep.

Isabelle got up from the bed quietly and stood looking at her son. She hated to admit it to herself, but the boy was beginning to resemble his father.

The next afternoon after school James didn't know his mother was waiting in the carriage until he had climbed in.

"What are you doing here, Mother?"

"I'm going to take you somewhere special," she said. "It's where I help out every day." She rapped on the ceiling of the carriage to tell the driver to go on.

James looked at her curiously. His mother had mentioned this place often when the two of them had dinner together, but it hadn't sounded very special to him. From what she told him, it was a sad place, filled with pitiful people. Certainly not his idea of a fun afternoon.

"You mean, the place where the poor people go?" he asked.

"Well, yes," she said. Isabelle was suddenly aware that she hadn't had anything specific in mind. When she had decided to take her son there, she hadn't thought about what he would do or how he would fit in. It was just that last night it had seemed important to expose him to the people she had come to understand. She didn't want him to grow up as she had, thinking that there was something inherently "different" or "inferior" about them. They were just people, but it had taken her months to feel comfortable with them.

"Don't worry, darling. I wouldn't take you if you weren't going to enjoy it, now would I?"

James sat up straight so he could see out the window. When they arrived at the curb in front of the old Hull mansion, he looked around in dismay. Dirt and clutter were everywhere. Across the street, junk and half-burned planks were piled high in disorderly mounds. Lines heavy with clothes were hanging between buildings. A hungry dog was digging through the rubbish for food. Men with pushcarts, food vendors, and ragmen were vying with one another for a place in the street. He felt frightened.

"What is this place, Mother?" he asked.

Isabelle remembered her first impression of the neighborhood. She patted her son to reassure him. "People are very poor
here, son. But inside, there are nice children to play with. Won't
that be more fun than just sitting at home alone?"

This argument had merit for the boy, and he timidly followed Isabelle up the walk. Once inside, he was relieved to find
that the nursery looked cheerful after all. Isabelle led him over
to a group of boys who were playing paper, scissors, stone, but
as soon as he arrived the boys stopped playing. They lowered
their heads and looked at one another sideways to read the
others' impressions of this new boy. Everything about him
seemed suspicious. In the midst of children who were tattered
and uncombed, he was neat and clean.

Finally one of them shoved him. When he shoved back
harder, they got the idea that he was just a regular boy after
all. After the story hour Isabelle was happy to see that James
had fit in and was playing happily. She had a notion that it was
important for her son to see past the grime and tatters and
accept these companions as just "friends."

When Isabelle and James arrived home that evening for
dinner, Phillip was waiting. As soon as she saw him, she felt a
sudden uneasiness.

"Oh, hello, Phillip," she said. "Are you having dinner with
us this evening?"

For the first time it occurred to Isabelle that if Phillip heard
about her son's afternoon, he would disapprove. She was relieved that they were eating their meal in silence. Finally Phillip
addressed James.

"Tell me about your day, son."

The boy was accustomed to sitting still in the presence of
his father. Being asked a direct, open-ended question was like
opening a floodgate during a wet spring. James recounted at
great length the story from *The Young Heroes* that had been read
to the children that afternoon. He concluded by saying that
when Prince Roland died, Guido had cried.

"Guido?" said his father, repeating the strange name. He
seemed vaguely perplexed. "Italians at the Latin School? I don't
remember a child named Guido on the school roster."

James laughed loudly. Even James knew there were no

Guidos at the prestigious Latin School. "Not at Latin," he said. "At Mother's place. At Hull House."

Phillip stopped chewing his apple torte and wiped his lips. "*You* went to Hull House, son?" Though he spoke to James, Phillip was looking intently at his wife. When he saw her face color, he didn't need to hear the boy's response.

"Mother took me," James continued. "The neighborhood was scary—filled with old junk and things."

"Yes, I imagine it would be," Phillip said.

Phillip didn't really hear his son when the boy went on about how nice things were inside Hull House because he was distracted by his own thoughts. Phillip knew there was no love between him and his wife, but that in itself did not disturb him. A few months before James's birth he had told her not to expect those kind of feelings from him, and the declaration had given him a pleasant sense of freedom. Once he had told her of his lack of affection, his conscience was clear. He could spend his evenings however he chose, without the irritation of an occasional pang of guilt.

But while he knew they did not love each other, he at least had assumed that they supported each other's values. Isabelle had been raised in a family that, although financially insecure, at least had pretensions to gentility. How could his wife have forgotten herself to the extent that she would expose his son to the human trash down on South Halsted? He had never specifically forbidden such a thing, but he had expected her to be smart enough to know better.

"That's fine, son," he said, interrupting James. "Your mother and I have something to talk about. Will you excuse yourself?"

The boy had enjoyed his little talk and now was puzzled. "But I haven't finished my dinner, Father."

Phillip had a short fuse when it came to children, and he had suddenly heard all he cared to from this child. "You heard me," Phillip said, his voice at the level of a roar. "Leave the room, dammit!"

James got up from the table and walked to the large closed doors. "I can't get out," he said, reaching up and ineptly turning the ornate brass door knob. It was obvious to Phillip that the child was resisting following orders.

"If I have to tell you one more time . . ." Phillip threatened.

"But I can't," the boy protested, still twisting the knob back and forth.

Isabelle watched nervously. It seemed clear that the child couldn't open the door by himself, and she was concerned that her husband might lose his temper and beat him.

"He's too small, Phillip," she said, getting up from the table. "Let me help—"

"You'll do nothing of the kind," Phillip thundered. "We need less pampering and more discipline in this house. James," he ordered one last time, "leave the room!"

The boy awkwardly turned the oval knob, and with his weight against it, the door flew open, throwing him into the hallway.

"Now close it," Phillip ordered.

James looked at his mother for support. When he saw none coming, a look of rebellion flashed in his eye, and he slammed the door.

Now that they were alone in the dining room, Isabelle sat quietly, staring down at her plate. It was clear that Phillip was upset. He seemed dangerous, as if he might strike her. When she finally met his eyes, he was looking at her with an expression akin to contempt.

"Isabelle," he said after the silence had lasted several seconds, "it is one thing for you to waste your days at that place. But it is quite another for you to contaminate my son there."

"Oh, Phillip," she replied in a tone that she hoped would placate him, "I didn't contaminate him. I just—I just wanted him to meet those people and see that—that they're like us."

"Like us! Have you lost your senses?" He looked at her as if she had suddenly become quite mad. "There's not a thing about those people that's like us. Or have you become so acclimated to them that you can't see the difference?"

This comment stopped Isabelle because she knew that was, in effect, what had happened. She *had* become used to them, and in that process she had come to see their similarities as human beings rather than the uncomfortable differences she had felt in the beginning.

"There are differences, of course," she said, searching for

the way to teach her husband this important lesson. "But when you see the suffering and feel the sadness, they're—they're the way we would be in those circumstances."

"Yes, but, Isabelle, we will never *be* in those circumstances. Don't you see that? There is a reason for why they're *there* and we're *here*! They're as different from us as the day from the night."

This point of view was not unfamiliar to Isabelle. She had heard such ideas all her life. She was so confused by Phillip's belief in the correctness of his thinking that she fell silent, a sign that he interpreted as acquiescence. For a moment Phillip relaxed his intensity.

"Isabelle," he said as if to a small child, "it is not for people of our class to go down there and mix with these people." As Phillip spoke, he noticed that a tear had escaped from Isabelle's eye and was slowly streaking in the direction of her chin.

"I'm all for helping them," he said in a gentler tone, "but there are other channels. There are legions of people out there who do this sort of thing quite well."

This notion about the other people gave Isabelle renewed strength. She knew full well that there were not many people concerned enough to help.

"But who, Phillip? Who are they?"

"Well . . . that Jane Addams woman," he answered.

"Yes, Phillip. But there's only one Jane Addams for thousands of people!"

"Isabelle, that doesn't mean *you* should go down there."

"But if not me, then who?"

Phillip abruptly pushed his chair back from the table and threw his napkin onto his plate. He felt intensely frustrated by her insistence on an answer. The conversation had not taken the direction he had assumed it would when Isabelle had started to cry.

"Very well, Isabelle. Let's leave it at this. You can do whatever you want with your days, but I forbid you to take my son with you again."

"But why, Phillip? I want to expose him to a different side of life."

"Why? Do you want your son to be a bricklayer? To work in a sweatshop? If not, why expose him to this?"

"I'm not teaching him to be a bricklayer! I'm teaching him to care about people."

Phillip looked at his wife with growing anger. He had never had such a stupid, irritating argument in his life. "What do you want him to know, Isabelle? That these people don't work? That they don't care for their children?"

Much to Phillip's disgust, his wife started to weep again. She began sobbing some incoherent babble about how the woman was working and how it wasn't her fault that the boy died.

"This is insanity!" he shouted. "I never want to discuss this subject with you again. But I am giving you fair warning, Isabelle. You can waste your time at that place if you want to, but if you *ever* take my son with you again, I swear, Isabelle, I swear . . . I will divorce you!"

Phillip stormed out of the dining room, grabbed his hat and coat, and left the house, slamming the front door noisily. Isabelle sat at the dining table, stunned. Divorce? She had *heard* of people getting divorced but had never personally known anyone who had actually done it. Divorce simply wasn't done, especially among the upper classes.

When a marriage fell apart, outsiders might suspect a problem, but usually the couple lived with their unhappiness and kept their differences quiet. Unless, of course—and this was the *only* reason Isabelle had ever heard of that justified a divorce—unless the wife had behaved so shamelessly and blatantly that she had disgraced her husband.

Isabelle didn't know whether to take Phillip at his word or not. But the fact that he had even threatened divorce shocked her. She felt she had already given everything she could to keep this dry shell of a marriage together, and she hoped he wouldn't demand that she give up her work. Divorce was unthinkable. But without Hull House she knew her life would be unbearable.

14

CORLISS SCANLON WAS PUTTING the last few stitches in the upholstery of a Pullman cushion when her cousin Bessie O'Doud
walked by and playfully pinched her shoulder.

"Time to call it a day," Bessie said. Bessie was a short, little
woman in her late thirties with large breasts that stuck straight
out like a shelf. Her lusty reputation for enjoying strong drink
and younger men had made her about as popular in some
circles as it had made her avoided in others. "Why don't you
and me walk over to Kensington for a nip or two?"

Bessie's pinch had startled Corliss, causing her to prick her
finger with the needle. She saw a drop of her blood ooze onto
the pale gray fabric and quickly pulled her hand away to stop
the stain from spreading.

"Darn!" Corliss said, sucking the end of her finger. "I wish
you'd be more careful."

"It's just like you, Corliss," Bessie said, "to get so concerned
about a tiny prick when you could be enjoying the pleasures of
a larger one."

Corliss shook her head at her cousin's language and turned
her attention back to the stain. "I hope Mildred doesn't see this
or she'll whup me good."

163

The forewoman of the upholstery room was an unkempt giant of a woman named Mildred Beale. Mildred kept her girls in awe of the strength in her massive forearms by knocking them around every now and then. No one dared confront her even though over the last few months she had cut their pay by almost a third—a take-it-or-leave-it order each time. Since the girls were paid by the piece, a lower rate meant that they had to complete more work or try to live on less pay.

Corliss stretched her shoulders and arms. "Anyway, if I'm going to make my money today, I'll have to do two more cushions before the night is over. Otherwise I've got to get in early tomorrow."

Corliss was at least seven or eight years younger than her cousin, and her thin body had a certain grace. Her long brown hair had red glints, and her pale blue eyes were pretty enough to attract casual attention—though she was so shy she usually failed to hold it for very long.

"I didn't mean that just the *two* of us was going to hang around together," Bessie said, tying her head up in a bright orange kerchief. "I invited somebody else."

"Who?" Corliss asked carefully. Although her husband had died, she had little desire to replace him with one of Bessie's picks. Corliss had already spent one evening trying to avoid the grabbing hands of a worker Bessie had selected for her.

"The good-looking one from the machine shop."

"You mean that Quincey O'Hare?"

"Not him," said Bessie, turning up her nose. "He's too old. I like 'em young and tender. The younger the meat, the firmer the bone, I always say."

Bessie liked to make a dirty comment now and then. With a reputation as bad as hers, she figured she might as well enjoy herself. "I'm referring to that darlin' lad with the slanty eyes, Josef Chernik."

Corliss had noticed Josef a couple of times herself when she walked through the machine shop. She had also seen him looking at her. His high cheekbones gave such a nice shape to his face that she might have been interested, even though he never seemed to smile and his eyes were so hungry that she wondered if she could handle him if they were ever alone.

"Why do you want me along?" Corliss asked. She had no

desire to taint her reputation by being seen out with her black sheep cousin.

"He didn't seem too interested in coming until I told him you was going, too," Bessie said.

"Well, isn't that the lowliest lie!" Corliss was greatly aggrieved at being associated with her cousin. "Anyhow, isn't he Polish or Russian or something?"

"A Hebrew, I think, if you can judge from his old man."

Corliss shook her head again. The notion of fraternizing with a Jew, while not repulsive to her, was confusing. The young man was attractive, but she didn't know how to feel about someone from the race that had killed her Lord. She knew her mother would take a dim view of it, too, but then she didn't know how much her mother's opinion should matter about such things.

Bessie saw a tall figure heading their way. She leaned down and whispered urgently in Corliss's ear. "Come on, now, dearie, he's here. Surely you owe me a little something for looking after your ma when your father passed."

Corliss reluctantly stuck her needle in a small piece of leather and put it back on her work area. Bessie's argument was irrefutable. She *had* helped out when her pa had gotten the injuries that killed him. She just wished she could pay the debt once and for all. Her cousin always seemed to be finding new ways to pay her back again.

"All right," she whispered angrily. "But I'll only walk with you until we get to One Hundred Fourteenth Street. Then I'm heading home, and you're on your own. I'll have to be in here darned early tomorrow to make up for this."

When Josef got near the two women, he could tell that the pretty one was angry. He had been wanting to meet her since the first time he laid eyes on her, but he had never been able to think of a plausible reason to speak to her. When the one with the big breasts had approached him in the machine shop, Josef had thought the idea of going out for beer with her was ridiculous. But when she included her cousin in the evening, he had accepted readily.

"Here he is!" Bessie sang out gaily, as if she hadn't seen him coming "Now I guess we'll find us a good time."

Josef nodded and tried to smile. When no one said anything, Bessie introduced him to Corliss.

"Josef, say hello to my cousin Corliss here."

"Hello," Josef said.

When Corliss glanced up at him for a moment to acknowledge the introduction, he got a glimpse of the blue in her eyes. "Hello," she said quietly before lowering her lids and turning away to get her coat.

"Well, now that's over, why don't we move on?" Bessie said. With no further ado, she swept toward the door, leaving Josef and Corliss to risk colliding into each other in their shy attempts to avoid looking at the other's face. When they got outside, it was already dark, and Bessie slipped her arm through Josef's.

"It's about a mile and a half to the nearest tavern in the next town. You don't mind if I hold on to you in case I slip on a patch of ice, do you?"

"No," Josef said, not knowing what else to say. He wanted to offer his arm to Corliss, but she had turned her head away and, though she was walking with them, stayed several feet to the side.

Josef searched his mind for a bit of conversation to engage her attention. "I believe this is the coldest winter I've seen here so far," he said.

Though Corliss did not answer his opening sally, Bessie did. She responded to the notion of cold by hugging his arm close to her bosom.

"Lord, yes," she clucked. "It makes my nipples hard just to think about it."

Corliss and Josef were so embarrassed they practically stopped in their tracks. Bessie, sensing her impropriety, tried to smooth the situation over gracefully.

"I mean hard from the *cold*," she corrected, as if that would remove any disturbing sexual connotations from the comment.

After this Josef had no idea what to say that wouldn't alienate Corliss even more. He certainly didn't want her to think that *he* had started all that talk about nipples. The idea was so awful that he decided to keep quiet until after they all had had a glass of beer. Perhaps by that time the nipple comment would be so distant that he could engage her in a regular conversation.

With all his hopes pinned on a little talk in the bar, he was dashed when they approached Fulton Street and Corliss announced, "I'm going home. You two have a nice evening."

Under the streetlight Josef caught another glimpse of her blue eyes before she turned up the street. "But I thought we were all . . ." he started to say, but she was gone.

Bessie pulled his arm so close to her bosom that for an instant Josef thought he actually *could* feel the hard nub of a nipple even through her cloak and his coat sleeve. "She's a nice girl," Bessie said, continuing to lead him up the street toward the tavern. "Spends all her time looking after her mother."

Corliss could hear Bessie's comments about her as she plodded home. She was happy that the good-looking stranger was hearing things about her that would keep her from seeming like a barfly. But as she moved farther from them, she caught one last comment: "Too serious to have a good time, if you know what I mean. If you want a bit of fun, you'll not be finding it with Corliss."

With still almost a mile to walk, Bessie hoped to relax Josef with a jot of conversational banter. "Well, then," she began, "I hear you just moved to Pullman. Do you hate it as much as the rest of us?"

"Yes," he said simply. Since Josef's arrival he had learned how many of the residents detested living in the town. "The change has been hard."

"It's tough to live with Pullman's rules, ain't it?"

"It certainly is. Guards came to the shack to explain the rules the night we moved in. I hadn't arrived yet, but when I got home, my parents were upset."

"Oh, they shouldn't let those bums bother 'em," Bessie said.

She didn't want the conversation to depress her date, but she hated the company inspectors as much as anyone. "Just be sure to tell your folks not to throw down any paper outside. Those bastards fired Mick Guinn and evicted his family the same day because they caught him tossing a bit of rubbish in the street."

"They won't let my mother put a nail in the wall," Josef said. "Told her decorating is against the rules."

"Ah, well," Bessie said with a philosophical tone, "surely she can live without hittin' nails."

"I don't know," he said. "It's awfully important to my parents to put the mezuzah on the doorpost."

"The what?" said Bessie.

"Oh, it's just a little thing—a religious thing—that some people put on their door." Josef didn't want to get into details that concerned his parents' Jewish observances.

"I see," said Bessie. Though she really had no idea what he was talking about, she figured it had to do with being a Jew. "Is that your father I seen the other day, walking around with that cart?"

Josef shuddered. The pushcart. It had been another source of trouble. The day after they moved in, his father had taken his cart out onto Florence Avenue to peddle the wares he bought wholesale back in the old neighborhood. Within minutes two policemen on horseback had galloped up to arrest him. He managed to take them to the shack to prove that he lived there, but still, they gave him warning. Mr. Pullman would not tolerate a peddler on the street, they said. Finally they had worked out an agreement. If the old man got his cart into the next town before the sun came up the next day, they'd leave him alone. Otherwise the cart had to go.

When Josef didn't answer Bessie, she straightened his arm so that his hand would come in contact with her thigh as she walked. "Ah, well," she said with a sigh, "there's no point in going out for a good time and then dwelling on the bad, now is there?"

When Josef realized that his hand was making contact with her leg, he held it very still. He didn't necessarily want to encourage her because there seemed no end to what she might be expecting of him. He did wish he had known this was coming, though. If he had, he would have left his gloves off so he could get a better feel without seeming to want it.

With Bessie swinging her hips mightily and Josef dangling his arm rigidly the way she was holding it, they continued walking until they got to the Hard Day Tavern. By this time Josef was so excited that he hardly knew what to think about all this.

On the one hand, he would have liked to get away from this woman, but on the other, it seemed like a unique opportunity to explore the feminine body while getting acquainted with a nearby watering hole. Living so close to the factory in a town where nothing happened after dark had already started to make Josef feel closed in. He needed a little excitement.

When Bessie released his arm and opened the door, Josef followed her in.

The Hard Day was dimly lit and noisy with the sound of men drinking and arguing. It was about half full, mostly with men, but there were also a few women standing about. Josef recognized some of the men from the machine shop. The Hard Day apparently catered to locals and the Pullman workers who wanted to escape their perfect town for a normal rowdy conversation and a bucket of beer.

"Why, hello there, Bessie," a grizzled old bartender lisped as Bessie pushed her way between two customers who were bellied up to the bar.

"Hello there yourself, Gummy," she answered. "Set me and my friend here up with two mugs of your finest."

As the toothless bartender filled the mugs, Bessie stepped back and made room at the bar for Josef. The way she looked at him made it clear that she expected him to pay for the beer, so he pulled a quarter from his trousers and put it on the counter. The bartender took it and casually put it in his pocket.

"Oh, no, you don't." Bessie challenged noisily. "Give the man his change."

Josef was grateful for the return of his fifteen cents but wished Bessie hadn't demanded it so loudly. Several of the men from his shop were looking at him suspiciously. He nodded in their direction, but when he didn't get a friendly response, he handed Bessie her beer. She noticed the men's looks, too, and led him away from the bar.

"Don't worry about it," she said. "They haven't seen you around here before, so they probably think you're one of Pullman's spies."

Josef had heard that Pullman paid people to hang around the workers and pick up information. Lately, with wages being slashed, the union had become more active. Secret meetings were rumored to be held several times a month, though Josef didn't know where. Employees reported as union sympathizers were fired immediately.

"Come on over this way," she said, threading her way through the crowd. "This table back here is where I always like to sit."

Bessie planted her short little frame on a chair that faced the corner, leaving Josef no choice but to climb over her to get to his seat. As he lifted his legs to clear her knees, he felt her hand slip up the back of his thigh to an area very near his crotch. He jerked uncontrollably from the surprise of it and spilled a good amount of his beer in the floor. Much to his embarrassment, Bessie laughed gaily at his mistake.

When he had recovered his composure and was seated, Bessie looked at him closely. "Josef," she said, and her eyes narrowed to an evaluative stare, "do you know what it means to love a woman?"

Though Josef certainly knew what she meant, it was such a forward question that he decided to act as if he had misunderstood her. "Why, certainly," he said. "I love my mother and sisters very much."

"Oh, Josef," she said, shaking her head as if he had just said something very silly.

"Well, my sisters are . . . I mean, they're not really women, you know. Just girls. Two of them anyway."

"Why, Josef! No wonder you always seem so down-in-the-mouth. To stay in a good state of mind, a man needs a little recreation with the female half of the race."

Bessie took a big swallow of beer and wiped the foam off her lip. Then she grinned at him knowingly. "You ain't going to pretend you don't understand me, are you?"

Josef felt extremely agitated about this turn of events. He hadn't known exactly what to expect, but the last thing he had imagined was this kind of offer. At least it *seemed* to him she might be making an offer.

"No, ma'am." Josef was in such a quandary that he didn't know what to make of any of it.

"I'll tell you what," she said. "Your family is at your home, and my brother and his family are at mine. Lord knows it's hard to find a little privacy these days. But there's a nice warm room in the back where we can be cozy and get away from the crowd. What do you say?"

Before he could answer, Bessie stood up and took the beer from his hand as if that were the lure that would make him follow her. "Come on," she said. "It's just back here."

Bessie opened a door beside their corner table and led him through it. The room was warm, but its comfort was certainly debatable. It was filled with wooden boxes, heaps of newspapers, and some old empty beer casks. Bessie made herself at home, stacking a pair of wooden boxes together and pushing them against a wall. Then she covered them with some newspapers.

"Sit yourself right here," she said, slapping one of the boxes with her hand.

As soon as Josef sat down, she stepped forward and straddled his legs. His face was so near her billowy breasts that when she leaned forward, he had no choice but to lean back against the wall. While Josef was thus occupied, fascinated by the big breasts moving around in front of him, she managed to unbutton his fly. Suddenly she reached in and hauled his pole right out from his pants.

Josef was so shocked that he hardly knew what to do. It had never entered his mind that a woman would behave in such a way. He had always been told that girls wanted to be married before giving themselves such private moments. It was also amazing to him that despite his confusion, his pole was busy proving that it had a mind of its own.

"Oh, you're a regular post digger," she said, responding to what her fingers told her. But when she took a look at the unhooded crest of his circumcised member, her face showed as much surprise as it had probably registered in a long time. "Good Lord, Josef," she said. "Someone's gone and whacked the end of it clean off!"

In response to this surprising challenge, Josef's post started to weaken, but before things had gone too far downhill, Bessie regained her composure, lifted her skirts, and climbed on. "Don't worry," she whispered. "Whoever done this to you left us more than enough for a good time."

In a short while Josef felt his pole quiver like an umbrella in a windstorm. A few seconds later Bessie must have felt the force of the storm, too, because Josef heard her make a funny grunt. A few moments later she stopped moving on him and gazed at him contentedly.

"Well," she said after she had rested herself, "I guess you Hebrews do it pretty much the same way most everyone else does."

"I guess so," Josef said.

Now that Josef had started to enjoy Bessie's company and would have talked volubly if she had wanted to listen, she seemed interested in other activities.

"Are you thirsty for another beer?" she asked, climbing off him. Bessie wasn't too keen on spending the rest of the night trying to talk to a man who didn't enjoy a good laugh. "Or are your folks waitin' for you at home?"

Josef's reclining position against the wall had been forcing his neck forward into a strange cramp. Now that he had nothing to look at but his withering organ, he discovered that his main concern was straightening his neck. He might have enjoyed having a beer with the men in the tavern, but they had acted so suspicious that it didn't seem like much fun. He was also a little concerned that they would know what he had done in the back room with Bessie and laugh at him.

"I guess my folks *are* waiting for me at home," he answered. He wasn't sure of the etiquette involved, but suddenly it seemed like a nice idea to be able to leave the woman without having to make strained conversation or apologies.

"Well," she said, smiling brightly, "I don't want to keep you, but if you're ever looking for a good laugh and then some, you can usually find me here at the Hard Day."

Josef stepped outside the tavern, still in a daze of postcoital bliss. Even though the sensations Bessie had given him were enough to give him a twinge of gratitude, he preferred her cousin Corliss. He even allowed himself the pleasure of imagining that his experience had been with *her*. Maybe it wasn't really fair to enjoy Corliss this way without her knowing about it, but it did make his memories all the more entertaining.

With all this going on in Josef's mind, he didn't pay much attention to where he was going and lost his bearings. He had walked about five blocks the wrong way, deep into the scruffy community of Kensington, when he realized that he had made a wrong turn somewhere. It didn't seem sensible to retrace his steps exactly—that would be the long way to get home—so he turned south. He was walking toward what he hoped was Pullman when he turned a corner and saw another tavern just up the street. Josef figured he'd go inside and ask for directions.

A second later he saw something that stopped him in his tracks. Just outside the tavern a man was weaving and stumbling and singing what appeared to be a dance. Josef wasn't particularly afraid of the Indian—after all, he had seen the Indians performing with Buffalo Bill and had every reason to believe that the Indians and white men in America had made their peace—so he stepped closer to watch.

The Indian was dancing, picking his feet up and down in a funny kind of shuffle. But it wasn't the footwork that was interesting since he was so drunk he could barely move his feet at all. What captured Josef's attention was the way he moved his arms—in large, swinging motions that a person might use if he were in the middle of a river and trying to push a wall of water upstream. While the Indian was trying to move the river, he was singing a combination of the most eerie moans and sobs Josef had ever heard.

Josef walked unnoticed toward the Indian; he had to pass him to get inside the tavern to ask for directions. When he was about thirty feet away, the door to the tavern opened, and a woman stepped outside with a shawl around her shoulders and a broom in her hand.

"You git away from here," she yelled, thrusting the broom at him. "You git."

The Indian stopped singing the mournful sound and stared at her. He would have stopped moving his feet, too, if he had been sober enough to stand up without pitching back and forth.

"You git home now!" she ordered. "You sound like a tom chasin' a cat in heat, caterwauling like that. I won't have the police on my backside 'cause of a drunk Indian."

Josef noticed that the Indian looked at her for a moment in docile surprise. Then he bared his teeth, the way a mountain lion might before he decided to spring, and the expression on his face changed to rage and fury. The Indian reached back with his right hand and suddenly pulled a knife from a sheath at his hip.

The woman saw all this, too, and quickly shoved her broom into his chest, sending him sprawling backward against the un-painted wood siding of the tavern. It took the Indian a moment to regain his composure and by this time Josef was near enough to be in the Indian's line of vision.

The Indian looked sullenly from Josef to the woman and back again to Josef. Two against one. He was drunk enough that Josef could almost see the thought pass through his mind.

The Indian put the knife back in his sheath and, using the wall for support, regained his balance.

"You go on," the woman yelled again, gesturing with her broom. "And don't come back again, you hear? Drinkin' and pullin' a knife on me like that."

The Indian looked at her long and hard for a moment and glanced again at Josef. Then he turned away with as much dignity as his drunkenness would allow. As he staggered up the street, he promised himself that one of these nights he'd catch her alone. When he did, he'd slash her open from belly to neck.

The woman didn't thank Josef because she didn't think she had been in danger. She had handled drunks before, and would again, she reckoned.

"Well," she said to Josef, still feeling angry from the fight, "you gonna come in or what?"

Buffalo Bill Cody was drunk that night. Seemed like drinking was all he did when he was home, and his wife was sick and tired of it. Ever since he had closed his show in Chicago for the winter, he'd been back in the house she had built in North Platte, Nebraska. Bill claimed he didn't feel comfortable sleeping indoors, and after all these years of watching him stay away for just any pretense, Louisa felt as if she had an intruder in her home. In fact, she didn't know how she was going to hold her head up in the community if he didn't set out on another tour soon.

"I swear, Bill," she said with exasperation, "this is my town and this is my house. And I am not going to allow you to disgrace me in either of them."

Bill Cody prided himself on being a polite man. It seemed to him that every woman he had ever met but his wife had found his courtesy quite charming.

"My dear," he said, trying to perform a sweeping bow from his chair in the living room, "first you tell me not to drink in town—"

"Yes," she snapped, "so I wouldn't be disgraced in front of my friends when you go falling out of the tavern."

"But in response to your requests," he continued, ignoring her interruption, "I have taken to staying home. Surely a man can enjoy one drink—"

"One drink!" she mocked. "I've seen what you call one drink. You fill a big washbasin practically full of that old whiskey so you can call it one drink. Ha! You may have been able to fool your show manager that way, but you're not fooling me. You hear me, Bill? You're not fooling me!"

Cody sighed as Louisa stomped upstairs. What an old, ugly warrior of a woman she had turned into. Lord, how he would love to divorce her. He'd given it quite a lot of thought. The only thing that held him back was that the publicity would surely give him and his show a black eye in the press.

Now it seemed that he might be in for bad publicity anyway. Just when things had been going so well. He had made eighty thousand dollars this past year in Chicago, more than his show had ever cleared before. Of course, he'd done pretty well in spurts when he hit the big cities in Europe on a tour. But he had always been dogged by troubles that ate up his cash.

During one of those European tours a boat carrying his authentic Pony Express coach had sunk, and he had been forced to make a costly reproduction. The program billed it an "exact replica" and that was what it was, but Cody had always preferred using the real thing.

Using the real thing was partly why the Indians in his show were often warriors from the very tribes he had fought. If a battle had ended in the capture of the tribe and Cody stuck around long enough to get to know the Indians, he usually found a lot to admire in those fellows. They were like him after all. They loved riding the plains and testing their skill against each other. Usually they wound up liking him, too. They knew he was fair and told them the truth. That was why he and Sitting Bull had become such good friends.

Poor old Sitting Bull. It was awful the way the Bureau of Indian Affairs had killed him. There he was, a grand old warrior, minding his own business—just sitting in his tepee on a reservation. They had barged in there, wanting him to get the Indians to stop doing the ghost dance. Damned fools! They acted as if they really believed that the ghost dance would roll back the land and bury the white men while it unearthed the dead Indians. It was hard to understand how they could take such a notion seriously. Yet when Sitting Bull had refused to stop the dance, they had shot him dead.

Cody shook his head at the memory. He had been on

his way there himself because the bureau had sent him. Maybe if he had arrived earlier, he could have prevented the murder.

It was this kind of memory that often made him want to take a drink.

Cody got up unsteadily from his chair. He did feel like another drink, but he was darned if he was going to listen to Louisa yell at him all night for it. If she wasn't nice to him at home, he'd could always find a welcome ear down in North Platte at the Mumbelty Peg.

Cody put on his coat and stepped out the back door of the gray frame house. It was curious the way Louisa had built that place. It was a narrow structure and stood three stories tall, kind of the way a house might be built in a large city where there was no land. But land spread out from the house in all directions—flat, lonely land with only two or three fully grown trees within sight.

At least the air was warmer tonight. He figured spring would be along in a month or two, but it looked as if he might have to leave and handle a certain nagging problem before then. He hated confinement anyway.

Cody walked out back to the horse barn and lovingly saddled his golden palomino, Gypsy. He thrust his boot into the stirrup, laboriously pulled himself up with the saddle horn, and swung his leg over the horse's back. It was getting tougher every year, but by God, he and Gypsy here could still ride better than most of the young ones. City living made people soft.

His arrival at the saloon was greeted by the usual enthusiasm from the locals. Bill Cody was a man who could always be counted on for a few rounds. After the drinks had been served up, a wiry man with straggly whiskers and bowed legs walked in. Cody immediately recognized him as John Elkins. They had been best buddies until one unsuccessful season when Cody had brought him in as a partner in the show.

"John!" Cody called, delighted to see him. Cody graciously strode down to the end of the bar and threw his arm around his friend's shoulders. Whatever differences they'd had as partners were over as far as he was concerned.

John Elkins accepted a shot of whiskey, tossed it back, and looked at his old buddy. He felt a stab of jealousy. He had been an Indian fighter in the Fifth Cavalry, too, but had never been able to capitalize on his name the way Bill had. Just looking at Bill Cody now made it clear why.

Even in a local tavern Bill Cody had a remarkable presence. His long dark hair had turned white, giving him a radiance that attracted attention and set him apart. And of course, there was his name. Buffalo Bill had been legendary since the Pony Express days back in the sixties.

Elkins shook his head at his own foolishness. He should have known he'd never make a go of show business on his own without Bill Cody.

The two theatrical entrepreneurs walked back to a table and sat down. "How's it going, John?" Cody asked, settling in for a chat.

"Not bad, not bad. I finally got the old show debts paid off. . . ."

"I was sorry you had such a bad time of it."

"No, no, it's all right, Bill. Live and learn, live and learn. I'm farming now and—"

"Farming!" Cody exclaimed. Bill had never understood how someone who had slept outside and been free to ride off at the drop of a hat could tolerate the same roof over his head for long.

John Elkins squared his shoulders and drew his dignity around him. "I've made peace with it," he said firmly. He certainly didn't want Bill Cody to get the impression that during those wild years when they were raising hell on the prairie, he had been a farmer at heart.

He shrugged. "There was nothing else left to do."

The two men stared at their shot glasses for a few moments. Elkins knew it was his turn to ask about Cody, but he already knew the answer. Bill Cody had made a dag-blasted fortune in Chicago last summer, and Elkins didn't much want to hear about it.

"What about you?" he finally asked, staring straight ahead.

"I've got myself a wee bit of trouble," Bill answered. "Indian trouble."

"Indian trouble? Why, hell, those rascals are all on reservations now—except them that travel with you."

"Yep, they're supposed to be." Cody grinned and shook his

head. "I guess handling Indian troubles will be something I'll always be slaked by."

While Cody called for another round, Elkins waited to hear his problems, but Cody didn't resume his story until he had tossed back his shot and called for yet another.

"Were you and me together back when the Bureau of Indian Affairs decided I had to be officially commissioned?" Cody asked Elkins.

"I don't remember that."

"Well, the way those fellows figured it was, since it was illegal for the Indians to be off the reservation, traveling with my show would be contrary to the law. The thing was, the bureau *wanted* the Indians to be in the show because it exposed them to the white man's ways and all."

Elkins nodded, understanding the logic of the situation. "So?"

"So they made me an official of the department to make it legal. That way, even though the Indians are off the reservation, they're still in the charge of a U.S. official when they're with me. You understand?"

"What's wrong?"

"Well, when I shut down a show, I have to send the Indians back to the reservation—that or at least keep an eye on 'em."

Cody paused and stared out into space as if he were trying to remember exactly how he could have made the mistake he had.

"Last November, when I closed the show in Chicago, I sent them back the way I was supposed to. Why, hell, most of them *wanted* to go back. I didn't have to corral them and follow them there! They wanted to go see their families."

"Then what's the problem?"

"One of them didn't go. A peculiar Indian by the name of Running Wolf. He was just a kid when I first met him."

John Elkins sat up straight. "I remember him! A strange little kid, wasn't he? Son of a chief?"

Cody nodded glumly. "Yep. He was Yellow Hand's kid."

"Why, hell," Elkins said slapping his thigh, "I remember when you killed Yellow Hand! His braves had stole two or three white women from a settlement and killed 'em. I remember the damn ambush they set for us. That red bastard came riding down a hill to beat all hell with his braves behind him. You rode right up to him with the reins in your mouth and shot him point-blank just as he was taking aim to shoot you."

Cody gazed into space, remembering. It was funny how you could feel good and bad about something at the same time. He liked remembering that battle. That was the skirmish that had made him a legend. But he remembered how bad he felt when his men shot the women in the tribe to revenge the dead white women.

It was pitiful to see how that kind of thing affected the little kids. He could see even then that Running Wolf was messed up about it. That was when he had started taking care of him.

"Them were good days, Bill," said John Elkins fondly.

Cody nodded. Despite the killing and bad things, they *had* been the happiest days of his life. There was nothing better than riding around on the wide open plains, feeling the wind blow through his hair, knowing he was important because he was needed. These days about the only thing that kept him going was that his show let him pretend that he was still on the plains, doing what he had done before.

"Well," Cody said, referring to his troubles, "the other day I got a letter from the government about Running Wolf. Seems he didn't go back to the reservation."

"What'll they do?"

"The government? Oh, they're threatening to not let me take the Indians out this spring. But I don't think they'll go that far. I reckon if I can find Running Wolf and get him back, things will shake out all right."

"Where do you think he is?"

"I don't know," said Cody, shaking his head. "Chicago maybe. But what he's doing there or why he's doing it, I just can't figure." Buffalo Bill stretched his legs out in front of him and thoughtfully took a tiny sip from his jigger. "John, if you was a half-crazy Indian, hating the white man and still troubled about your dead parents, what would *you* be doing in Chicago?"

15

"WE NEED TO TALK," Carrie Watson said.

She leaned forward at her desk to turn up the gas under the green lampshade. It was time to get down to brass tacks with her newest boarder. Hannah sat down primly on the horsehair love seat and folded her hands. She was so caught up in her own plans that she didn't notice the glint in Carrie's eyes.

"I've about had it with you," Carrie said with vehemence. "I pick your pretty little ass off the street when you faint and bring you in here until you get well. And I'm patient—"

"But, Miss Watson—" Hannah flushed a dark red. She had been so involved thinking about her proposal that it hadn't occurred to her that Miss Watson might have some strong feelings about the meeting herself.

"Don't interrupt me when I'm talking to you!" Carrie said. She tried to slam one of the little drawers in her desk for emphasis, but it was too filled with receipts and notes on the customers to close. She smacked the drawer again for good measure before she turned back to Hannah.

"I have fed you and clothed you and, courtesy of Zorrine, even gave you a lesson on first-class sporting. I haven't even pressured you to let a customer plug you yet. But when I put you with an old harmless banker who just wants to talk, and you cut off his conversation after an hour . . ."

Carrie got angrier as she talked. Just thinking about how her good nature had been abused put her almost into a frenzy. She rose from her chair and walked back and forth for a minute.

"When you cut off Mr. Cudahy, you cut off the free ride, girlie. Yes, sir-ee. You done cut off the free ride."

"Wait, Miss Watson," said Hannah. She knew an ultimatum was coming, and she wanted to change the stakes before Carrie laid down the law. If Miss Watson went that far, Hannah was afraid she wouldn't be able to reverse Carrie's demands. "Miss Watson, I know what you're thinking. You told me that nothing in a whorehouse is free. And I *agree*. If I'm staying here, I *should* be earning money for you. And I will."

This acknowledgment took a little of the wind out of Carrie's sails. "Well, if you know that, you sure picked a fine way to show it."

"It's just that I've figured out a way to earn more money for you using my head than I could by . . ." Hannah paused, looking for a polite way to finish her thought.

"By lettin' a man play with your parsley? That's a laugh. Don't you think we'd all be bankers if we had the choice?"

"Yes, ma'am," Hannah said quietly. It was awful that she had to present her idea to Miss Watson while she was this angry. It certainly was going to make it harder to sell her proposition. "It's just . . . what if I figured out a way so we *could* be bankers?"

"The Lord have mercy!" Carrie exclaimed, looking at Hannah as if she had lost her mind. She sat down abruptly, her green and black taffeta ruffles sending up fine particles of dust. "All right," she said. "Let's hear it."

Hannah was so excited that she actually got up and paced the room. "Miss Watson, Mr. Cudahy told me his bank has lent money to businesses that have gone under."

"Why, heck, all the banks have! But they don't care. They just repossess the business or the building, and then they *own* it. That ain't much to complain about!"

"Yes, but the buildings aren't worth as much now as the banks already lent out on them. Mr. Cudahy says if he could find a buyer, he'd sell those buildings for even less than he's got in them. For *far* less!"

"So what are you getting at?"

"Why, Miss Watson, you have cash. Why don't we buy some of the buildings?"

Miss Watson looked at the girl seriously for a second. "*We!* What part would you have in this?"

"I'd manage everything for you. I mean, you're about as busy as you can be now, running this business. But I could select the buildings, and buy them, and rent them out. I could handle everything *for* you."

Miss Watson shook her head at the foolishness of the idea. "What would I want with a bunch of old buildings nobody's using?"

"I was thinking," Hannah said, ready to present one of her main arguments. "What happens if the laws change and you have to close?"

"That'll be a cold day in hell."

"But there's that English newspaper reporter in town. He's giving reform speeches and turning the whole town against us."

"Look, Hannah," said Carrie Watson firmly, "I give money—lots of money—to the Catholic church in the next block, and the Presbyterian church and the Jewish synagogue nearby. You don't really think *those* people are going to shut me down, do you?"

Hannah thought for a moment. This discussion wasn't going the way she had hoped. "Well, what if the depression gets worse? What if people can't afford to come here anymore? Then what will you do?"

Carrie thought for a moment. Her sales *were* down lately. There was definitely less money coming in. "I'll figure out something," she answered.

Hannah sat down. She had not counted on Miss Watson's attitude, and she was afraid she was running out of ways to convince her.

"Miss Watson, you own this building, don't you?"

"You bet I do. Free and clear. You don't have control unless you own your business."

"My father always said that land and property are the key to wealth and power." Hannah blushed to be using her father as a source of wisdom.

"Hannah, forget it. I wouldn't know what to do with other property."

"But that could be *my* job," Hannah said earnestly. "This depression isn't going to last forever, is it?"

"Well, they never have before."

"If you could buy some buildings and wait to sell them when the depression is over, wouldn't you make a lot of money then?"

"I suppose so."

"In fact, Miss Watson, your money might be *safer* in buildings than in the bank. I know Mr. Cudahy is worried that his bank might go under."

Carrie Watson needed time to think. Maybe the girl was right. It had happened before. Banks had failed, and the do-gooders had shut down the town before—though never for long. What the hell, if she owned a lot of property, she'd be as hard to push around as Marshall Field.

But when she saw the girl's hopeful smile, she got angry again. She hadn't finished with Miss Hannah Chernick yet. She had two very important issues she wanted to discuss.

"All right," she said. "You had your turn, and now it's time for mine."

Hannah smiled again and nodded.

"Whether I go with your plan or not, do not think it will excuse you from your primary duty here. Because it won't."

Hannah felt crushed with disappointment. So that was it. If she was going to stay here where the rooms were clean and warm and the food was good, she had to be a whore. Hannah vividly remembered trying to rent a bed in the awful tavern and find a job. These days it seemed that there was no other way to survive.

Her expression was not lost on Carrie Watson, who was irritated enough with Hannah not to care about the girl's feelings. She had invested in this girl, and it was time to get a return on her investment.

"In the second place," Carrie said, as if explaining something very elementary to a child, "this is a bordello. When men come here, they don't want to be reminded of hearth and home. I've taken great care and gone to great expense to make this a pleasure palace—not a playground for children."

"Yes?"

"When you came in here," Carrie said, "you said you were pregnant. The other thing I wanted to tell you is that I've got the doctor coming here in a few days to take care of that little problem."

Hannah left Carrie Watson's office feeling depressed and hopeless. She went to her room and sat there for a while, thinking about how foolish she had been.

How could she have believed that she could sell Miss Watson on a business scheme different from the one that had made her rich? Why, Carrie Watson was the most successful businesswoman the city of Chicago had ever known! It was going to take more than a little talk about buying repossessed properties to keep her from whipping a new girl into line.

Carrie had made herself clear: Get busy or get out. And now there was nothing for Hannah to do but get started. Hannah wished prostituting were something she could do once and get over with—like taking a bad-tasting dose of medicine. That would be one thing. But this was forever. She was going to have to learn to let strange men stick her with their ugly red pokers. And that would go on until *they* stopped wanting *her*. Even if she could learn to keep them at arm's length sometimes, she always had to be prepared to accept them.

She was involved in these thoughts when she heard a light knock on her door. For a second Hannah didn't answer because her spirits were so low she didn't want to talk to anyone. Except for Marie, who had held her hand while they watched Zorrine, Hannah mostly didn't talk to the girls at all. She spoke politely, of course, when she had to. But as long as she wasn't prostituting herself, she had been able to hold on to the notion that she was different from the rest. Now that illusion was about to be destroyed.

The knock came again, this time only as a warning, and the door flew open as Marie hurled herself into the room, breathless with excitement. She was wearing only her petticoats and a chemise. Above that scanty attire a large piece of jewelry hung around her neck. Her mood was as jubilant as Hannah's was low.

"Hannah, look!" she said. She touched her neck to call Hannah's attention to the necklace she was wearing. "It just come by messenger! It's from my customer last night. Oh, I just can't believe it! I've never seen nothing so beautiful."

Hannah didn't want to offend her only friend in the world so she looked admiringly at the jewelry. It was a large, ornate piece made of numerous small red stones. It was set in gold in such a way to suggest clusters of flowers.

"I never dreamed I could own something like *this!*" she said. "And from a real gentleman." She was practically dancing around in the room. Then another thought replaced Marie's joy. "Do you think, if he changes his mind about me, he'll make me give it back?"

Hannah looked up at Marie from where she was sitting on the bed. "I don't know." In Hannah's one experience with a man, he had been able to take back everything he had conferred on her. "I suppose he could. Especially if Miss Watson wanted you to."

"What's Carrie got to do with this?" Marie said indignantly. "It wasn't her he stuck it to."

"But if he's a good customer here . . ." Hannah didn't need to finish her sentence. Neither of the girls was under any illusion about Carrie Watson. It was true that she was kind to her girls and never had been known to hire men to rape new recruits to break them in as other madams did. But it was also true that she was hard as nails when it came to business.

"Oh, he's a good customer, all right," said Marie. "Carrie said he was very important at Marshall Field's. In the wholesale division."

Hannah's breath caught, and she looked at Marie closely. "What is his name?" she said.

When Marie answered, Hannah was hit with a flash of nostalgia and pain and anger unlike anything she had ever felt before. Roland Girard. The name aroused such a quick succession of conflicting emotions that she felt dizzy.

Her thoughts began to spin, too. So Roland was a customer here. Had he been buying girls here, she wondered, when she was trusting him, thinking he wanted her because of love? That was a bitter idea. And the necklace! Hannah looked at it more closely. He had never given her jewelry. Just dresses and underwear.

None of this was Marie's fault, she knew. It was just Roland Girard being the way he had always been. The fact that he came here offered opportunities for revenge she hadn't counted on. Still, she didn't want him to see her here. How awful it would be if he tried to buy her from Miss Watson! Hannah knew she had to make sure that when he was in one part of the house, she was somewhere else.

Marie stopped dancing and plopped down on the bed beside Hannah. Now that she had calmed down a bit, she noticed Hannah's mood.

"What's wrong?" she said. "You seem downcast."

There was no sense in telling Marie about Girard. What was the point in spoiling her happiness? Hannah's most pressing problem was that Miss Watson was going to force her to start prostituting. Somehow she didn't know how to explain her dread of this activity to a girl who was already plying the trade.

"Was Miss Watson angry with you when you bit that customer awhile back?" she asked Marie.

"Angry! Lord, I thought she was going to tear my head off! She said she'd throw me out."

"Did she get over being mad?"

"After a while. Why? Did *you* make Carrie mad?"

"Yes. She says I have to go to work."

"Well, of course! What'd you expect?"

Hannah shrugged her shoulders, wondering again how she could have deluded herself so badly.

"Oh, Hannah. Cheer up," said Marie to lift her spirits. "It ain't so bad. The gents here are usually clean. And Carrie don't like it if they hurt you. The main thing, of course, is not to get pregnant."

Hannah looked at Marie blankly. "I am pregnant. Didn't you know?"

"Ohh!" Marie was struck with how silly it was that she *hadn't* realized it. Maybe she really had known but had simply put it out of her mind. She chewed over this news for a few moments. "You know, Hannah, I don't want to give you no bad news right now, but the last girl who had an abortion here died."

"Died?" The news hit Hannah with all the force of a death sentence. For a moment she thought her heart would stop beating.

"It wasn't too long ago neither," Marie went on. "She bled a whole lot and then got fever. Wasn't but a couple of days before she was gone. Carrie was furious at the doctor for doing such a bad job, but he said there wasn't nothing he could do.

Said the girls should take more care and not get with child in the first place."

Hannah was silent for a moment, taking all this in. Then she looked deep in Marie's eyes to share her dreadful news. "Miss Watson is having the doctor come first thing next week."

"For you?"

Hannah nodded. "But I think she wants me to prove myself, first, to see if I'm worth the expense."

"Oh, Lord," Marie said as tears suddenly filled her eyes. "Oh, Lord." She put her arm around Hannah and held her.

They sat in this state for a few moments, each thinking her own thoughts. Marie's joy about her necklace was long forgotten, for neither of them could see any other way for Hannah. She was going to have to play things Miss Carrie Watson's way or she'd have to leave the house and starve.

"There's one good thing about it," Marie said after a while. "That doc ain't going to take no chances with you. Carrie said she'd get him in big trouble if he *ever* killed another one of her girls."

That night Hannah appeared downstairs at eight o'clock sharp. She had spent extra time on her hair, pinning it up elegantly with combs to make sure she looked especially nice. All afternoon she had fought off her depression, but she finally made peace with herself and came to a decision: She would do whatever it took to stay in the house. The fact that she might die with the doctor still wasn't as bad as her certainty that she *would* die outside.

Many of the girls were still upstairs lolling around or getting dressed. Since their night wouldn't end until 5:00 A.M., nobody was in much hurry to get started. But tonight, Hannah figured, it didn't matter what the others did. This was no time for *her* to show any signs of reluctance. She had noticed Miss Watson staring at her during dinner, and she didn't know if that was a bad sign. Hannah knew she had to prove that she was going to pull her weight.

By the time the first doorbell rang, Hannah was waiting in the front parlor with only two other girls for company. She saw the maid open the door and two men step into the hallway. They were as different from each other as two men could be.

One of them was a gaunt little man with a wide mustache that sat squarely in the center of his woebegone face. The other man was tall and fat, and his face was florid. Even if she had wanted to look at the little man, Hannah thought, her eyes would have been drawn to the big one.

As soon as the big man took off his top hat, swung it around in a wide arc, and bowed to the maid, one of the girls sitting near Hannah whispered, "It's Bath House! It's Bath House John Coughlin!"

Bath House John had cloaked his large frame with a Prince Albert coat that was striped bright green. Under that, his large belly strained against a plaid vest and overhung a matching pair of plaid trousers. His feet were sparkling in yellow patent-leather pumps.

Bath House John strutted a few steps down the hall until he stood beside the door to the parlor. When he saw the girls inside, he swung his hand through the air again and made a deep, courteous bow.

Almost immediately Hannah heard Carrie Watson hurrying down the hallway. "Aldermen!" she said robustly, as if seeing them were the biggest thrill she had ever had. "What a pleasure!"

She beamed at them for a few moments while the big man bowed again. This time he continued to shift his weight from one foot to the next, bouncing his girth up and down until the muse inspired him to create a poem.

Oh, Carrie Watson, my lady fair,
You're a beautiful woman, standing there.

Having concluded his outburst of poesy, he stood back and beamed.

"A poem for me, Bath House!" said Carrie. "How wonderful." Then she turned to Hannah and the two girls watching from the parlor. "Girls," she said, "say hello to the distinguished aldermen from our First Ward, Hinky Dink Michael Kenna and Bath House John Coughlin."

The two girls enthusiastically sang out, "Hello, Hinky Dink! Hello, Bath House!" and Hannah joined them as best she could, not being as familiar with the men's names.

"Well," said Carrie, "I guess there ain't no mistaking why

you gentlemen have done me the honor. Unless I mistake my calendar, you've come to talk about the annual party for Lame Jimmy."

"You got it right, Carrie," Bath House beamed. "The finest, most proper orgy in this Protestant satrapy." He cleared his throat before he continued. "Of course, a little contribution to the First Ward Defense Fund would not be amiss."

Hannah noticed that Carrie's face fell a little bit when she heard "defense fund," but Carrie recovered her graciousness quickly. "Of course, Bath House. Right you are! But why not mix a little pleasure with our business?"

"Delighted," he said.

Although Carrie tried to include the little man named Hinky Dink in her beaming smiles, he seemed oblivious of her charm. He kept his eyes cast down as if studying the roses in the carpet were the most important thing in his life.

"Let's go back to the Scarlet Room," said Carrie, "and we'll get Lame Jimmy to play us a tune or two."

Carrie gestured broadly to point them in the direction of the Scarlet Room, and Bath House once again bent his large girth in a bow. As he waddled out of sight ahead of the others, Carrie looked intensely at the girls in the parlor.

"Girls," she said, smiling in a phony way to make them understand that she thought they were as dumb as posts, "won't you join us?"

As Hannah and the girls followed Carrie down the hall, one of them whispered, "Them two are the most important men on the city council. They could shut Carrie down like that." She snapped her fingers to emphasize how fast *that* could be.

When Hannah got to the Scarlet Room, Hinky Dink and Bath House were already shaking hands with Lame Jimmy, though Jimmy had remained seated on his piano bench. Jimmy was a cripple, and he played piano and fiddle and often sang sad songs for the patrons who liked a good cry.

"Jimmy, the aldermen are here to talk about the annual party in your honor."

"Thank ye, gentlemen," said Lame Jimmy, bobbing his thin head up and down. "It always means a lot to me."

"It's mutual," said Bath House, inclining his head pompously. "The funds from the ticket sales mean a lot for the Democratic party in this here ward, too."

"I think it's a wonderful occasion when police captains and patrolmen can set down with the girls and the gamblers and just have a good time," said Carrie to show her sentiment about such democratizing.

As the men nodded in agreement, Carrie looked over at Hannah. "Hannah here is new and don't know nothing about all this. Why don't you come on over here and sit with the aldermen, Hannah?"

Hannah pulled a chair closer and sat down with the men. She could see that now that she was on Miss Watson's bad side, she was going to be put to a test.

"It's a pleasure," Hannah said charmingly. "I've never met an alderman before."

Bath House preened and fidgeted with his tight collar. "We do a lot of good for the city," he said. "Why, we was the ones that started the defense fund to provide protection for you."

At the repeated mention of the fund Carrie again looked grim. It was clear that a larger contribution from her was indeed an expected part of the evening.

"We've done many a fine thing for the brothels," he said imperiously. "As Carrie will tell ya, we been with ya from soda to hock."

"Indeed, you have, Bath House. And you, too, Hinky Dink," Carrie said to include the small, sallow-faced man in her praise.

"Let no man say we have ever shirked our duties," Bath House said. Then he turned to Hannah. "An' you'll be happy to know, my girl, that our fund will send any of you ladies who get TB to a sanitarium in Denver. An' if you get in trouble with the law, we have a lawyer ready to take care of you."

"How reassuring," said Hannah, trying to seem admiring and enthusiastic.

Carrie gave her newest boarder a wicked look. "Hannah, Alderman Coughlin normally don't take a drink. But being as how you're new here, he probably would like to see your new room."

Hannah felt her spirits fall. This wasn't fair! Usually a girl could sit downstairs with a gent for hours before she had to take him upstairs. She could see from Miss Watson's expression that this was indeed a test.

"I'd be delighted, Alderman," said Hannah, getting up as if she really wanted to. As she left the room, she gave her madam a look that said Carrie Watson could not throw anything her way that Hannah Chernik could not catch.

As they were approaching her room in the third-floor hallway, Hannah turned to Bath House. His big stomach was bobbing up and down, the buttons straining against his vest.

"You dress very fashionably, Alderman," she said.

"Thank you, my dear, thank you," he answered. "You know, the prince of Wales is held by some to be sartorially splendid. But personally I think the prince of Wales is a lobster in his tastes. He's simply a faded two-spot in the big deck of fashion."

Hannah was mildly impressed. "You know the prince of Wales?" she asked as she opened the door to her room.

"Not in person but in reputation." The alderman seemed unabashed that he had never even seen the person he was criticizing.

As they entered her room, he looked around as if he were indeed there to see its decor. "Very nice," he said. "I see you have a flair for color."

Hannah didn't explain that the room was exactly the way she had found it, but she did want to prolong the conversation. She didn't want Miss Carrie Watson to fault her for shortchanging a customer again.

"You must know many important people," she said engagingly.

"Yes, indeed. I was speaking with the ma'ar just the other day."

"The mayor?" said Hannah, feeling somewhat confused. From what she could see, the man was a buffoon. But he seemed to have such power.

"Indeed, yes. You know my partner downstairs may not be no bigger than a hinky dink, but his bar gives out more free lunches than anyone else in this here city. I estimate that in the past months he has cared for eight thousand destitute men."

"How kind!" she said, still confused. "So you help the poor then?"

"The poor. The rich." He sawed his hand through the air to show the equality of the two. "There're all the same. I formed this philosophy while studyin' the types who patronize the bath-houses where I began as a rubber. Believe me, I have done met 'em all, big an' little, from La Salle Street to Armour Avenue. And I learnt from every one of 'em."

"What a marvelous opportunity," Hannah murmured.

"Yep. There ain't no difference between the big man and the little man. One's lucky, that's all." He paused for a moment to reflect. "But as much good as we do, the reformers allus attack us. Ridiculous, ain't it? I only does what I thinks is right."

Hannah gave him a sympathetic look. "Of course, you do."

"Course, if thems that are helped by my work think I'm owed something, who am I to argue? The reformers call it boodle, but you know what I say?"

"What?"

"I say a man's gotta live. As long as you stay away from the big stuff, they'll leave you alone."

He was watching for agreement from Hannah, and she thoughtfully nodded again. "That's true, Alderman. We all have to live."

"Live and let live, I allus say," he said. Then he smiled and leaned forward and put his big, beefy hand on Hannah's knee.

Hannah looked at him and tried to smile. It was time. She knew she could no longer hold him off.

When Bath House had finished with her and was snapping his garters back on his bulging calves, he looked at Hannah with admiration.

"I think I'll write a poem to you," he said. "To guarantee you immortality in this vale of tears."

Hannah was feeling very close to tears herself. She was a whore now. It had been terrible to have this fat, repulsive man touch her and breathe hard on her, but she had shut her eyes and steeled herself.

"How wonderful," she said finally.

"Yas. Your very own tribute from the poet laureate of Chicago." He stood up to declaim, cutting such a foolish figure in his underwear and socks and garters that Hannah almost lost her melancholy.

"Here's one of my favorites. It's a little couplet that leads off a large poem on the glories of Lake Michigan:

Oh, why is the lovely lake . . . so near the ugly shore?
When I but see this ill combine, it always makes me
   sore.

Hannah congratulated him on his poetry and quickly finished dressing. It embarrassed her almost as much to be half
clothed and in the compromising activity of dressing as it had
when she was nude and could decorously hide herself under
the sheets. Much to her embarrassment, she was unable to button her dress and had to ask him for help.

As his big, clumsy hands dealt with the buttons, Hannah
tried to distract him from thinking about her by engaging him
in conversation.

"I've never heard the word . . . what is it you said that the
reformers accuse you of . . . 'boodle'?"

"Ah, boodle it is," he answered, clumsily pulling her dress
together at the waistline in back.

"But what—"

"Hold your breath, my dear," he said before he answered
her question. "What is boodle? Well, let's say Mr. Yerkes wants
to lay railroad track through a new part of the city's streets. Or
let's say the gas trust wants to raise rates."

"Yes?"

"Us aldermen are the ones that give the go-ahead. That
means a lot to someone who owns a utility."

"Do aldermen ever own railroads or utilities?" she asked.

"Ho, that would be the life!" he said, joyous with the
thought."An alderman own a railroad? Hmm." He considered
this for a moment before deciding. "Too dangerous," he said.
"Too big. The reformers *could* get you for that 'cause you'd be
voting for something you own."

"I see," she said, but she wasn't really paying much attention.

"Course, if it wasn't in your name, I suppose . . ." He was
thinking to himself now and trailed off. There was no point in
discussing it. "Naw. You'd never find someone to buy a utility
for you in their name."

Something about this twist in the conversation alerted Hannah. "Why not?" she asked.

He had finished buttoning her now and turned her to look

at her. "Ah, lovely as usual," he said with a clumsy bow. Then he set himself to the task of buttoning his own vest.

Hannah stepped close to him and smiled. "Let me. Turnabout is fair play." She pretended to flirt with him, and as she stroked his big belly and gently buttoned his vest, she continued the conversation that had become so engrossing to her. "But if you could find someone you could trust, why couldn't you have someone buy *for* you in their name?"

" 'Twould be a dream come true," he said. His tone told her that he was through discussing this remote possibility, so Hannah stopped her questioning. She figured she could reopen the subject sometime in the future if it seemed worthwhile.

When they both were presentable, she followed him downstairs, noticing how his large hams bobbed up and down as he walked.

The first floor was doing a rollicking business. The parlors and hallway were filled with customers talking and drinking with the girls. Carrie Watson had been trying to make conversation with Hinky Dink the whole time, and she looked a little put out. She was more than anxious to see the aldermen leave.

"Well, Bath," she said, looking him straight in the eye, "how did you like Hannah's room?"

"Very lovely," he said. "Very lovely. And you have a wonderously charming young girl in Hannah, too. No room, no matter how lovely, could do her justice enough."

"So you think I should keep her, eh?" said Miss Watson. She said it as if she were kidding, but Hannah, and perhaps Bath House as well, knew better.

"If you're *smart*, you will," he said, and gallantly bowed to Hannah and kissed her hand. "Wait," he said, suddenly standing up ramrod straight, "the muse of poesy is suddenly upon me."

The little group got quiet, accustomed to the verse outbursts of the city's poet laureate:

I love her more than I can say,
This woman of the hour named Hannah.
I'll love her more and more each day
Now that she's knowed my banana.

16

WHEN ISABELLE SAW CLARENCE Darrow walking directly toward
her on State Street, she was so wrapped up in her thoughts that
her eyes met his before she turned her head away. This amused
him. It always amused him to see fools who were stuck in their
belief of their importance. There was nothing he enjoyed more
than pricking the balloon of their self-righteousness.

Darrow stepped right into Isabelle's path and doffed his
hat to her.

"Well, well," he said, "it's the rich lady from Hull House."

Isabelle was not in the mood for teasing. Everything she
had heard about this notorious lawyer had turned her more
against him than he, himself, had the night they met. He was a
public supporter of "free love" and apparently had been able
to attract a number of women who embraced not only his political views but himself as well. He was a radical, it seemed, who
made no bones about flouting normal decency.

Isabelle simply lowered her eyes and did not respond. She
couldn't walk on because he was standing in front of her. Although she didn't want to speak to him, she also didn't want to
be openly hostile. The result was that Clarence Darrow stood

there, not two feet in front of her, smiling and waiting. He figured this tactic would force her to speak to him.

But finally he had to break the silence himself. "I guess a spoiled, pretty woman feels it's her right to disregard the social niceties, Mrs. Woodruff. But I do wish *you* a fine afternoon."

At the sound of his rudeness, anger flashed through her. After the disquieting scene with her husband the night before, Isabelle was not in any mood to accept insults from strangers.

"Social niceties!" she said. "That from *you*—you who are notorious for doing all manner of things to outrage decent people. Leaving women's rooms at dawn and . . ."

Darrow smiled. He had managed to cut through her ice.

"You mean to tell me people think I get up that *early*?" he said as if in amazement. "Why, I'm surprised anyone would seriously believe anything that good about me."

Isabelle shook her head with impatience. The man was impossible. She resumed her walk up the street and was chagrined to realize that he had fallen in step beside her. Since it seemed that his intention was to stay with her, she said coldly, "Please, Mr. Darrow. I am rather upset today."

Her hat somewhat impeded his view, so Darrow tipped his head forward to get a better look at her face. She *did* seem upset, and he was curious to find out what a privileged woman would find so unsettling. Instead of being encouraged to leave, Darrow decided to stay with her.

"I'm sorry to hear that," he said, sounding as if he cared. "I'm very sorry. Is it anything I can do something about?"

The concern in Darrow's voice touched Isabelle strangely. The sadness she had been feeling since little Goosie's death suddenly surged inside her until she thought the pain would take her breath away. She certainly didn't want to give in and cry in front of this man she disliked so intensely, yet she found herself unable to stop.

"A poor little boy died," she said, and her voice broke into a strange uncontrolled sound.

"Oh, my, I am so sorry," he said, feeling sympathy for her. As a man and woman walked past them, he became more concerned about the propriety of her weeping in public than she was. To cloak her from the view of people who had begun to stare, he protectively drew his arm across her shoulder and turned her in the direction he had been heading.

"Come along," he said to soothe her. "Let's go to my office."

When they reached his building at Randolph and Dearborn, Darrow led her up the stairs past an empty desk in the hallway into his private office. His desk was piled high with papers, and lawbooks were stacked like chimneys all over the floor. He led her to the leather chair across from his desk and removed some papers so she could sit down. For the first time in a long time he felt uncomfortable. Now that he had this pretty woman in his office, he wasn't sure what he should do with her.

"Would you like some tea? . . . Or coffee?"

Since her outburst on the street, Isabelle had kept her face turned away from him. Now she laid her head back against the high back of the chair. The motion tipped her hat up, and Darrow could see that her face was streaked with tears.

"Yes, please," she said quietly. "That would be nice."

Darrow walked out to the hallway. Mrs. Hastings was not at the reception desk, and there was no sign of his law clerk. Darn. The boy was probably picking up papers at the courthouse. Although it was conceivable that there was tea or coffee in the office, he had no idea where he might find it.

He made a mental note that he would have to buy one of those new telephone machines. With a telephone he might be able to contact someone outside for coffee or tea, though at the moment he had no idea how all that would work.

Darrow returned to the office, his tall form hunched in failure. He sat down at his desk and ran his fingers through the straight lock of hair that had fallen across his forehead.

"You know, my dear, sometimes I wish I paid more attention to how this office is run."

Isabelle looked at him without saying anything. Darrow noticed that she had removed her hat and placed it on her lap. Through the window the late-afternoon sun cast a golden light across her lovely face.

"What I'm trying to say is that I don't think we have any coffee." He began to move the pile of papers on his desk and in a few seconds withdrew a small paper bag. "But I'll tell you what! I didn't get around to eating my lunch yesterday. How would you like a nice apple?"

His demeanor was so appealing that Isabelle laughed through her tears. The tall, formidable lawyer suddenly didn't

seem so threatening after all. Darrow saw her smile and was
warmed by it.

"Now this won't do," he said, and stood up behind his desk.
"You sitting way over there, and me way back here hiding
behind these weighty legal matters."

Darrow dragged his large swivel chair over near Isabelle.
When the base of the chair ran afoul of a stack of books, he
commented, "Mrs. Hastings always chastises me about the condition of this office. Now I finally understand her concern."

The twinkle in his eye made Isabelle feel relaxed and
friendly, and she was surprised at how human he seemed. Darrow pulled his chair in front of her, so close that their knees
touched. Then he leaned forward and took her hands in his.

"Now, tell me about this terrible thing that happened," he
said gently.

As Isabelle told him about the death of the little boy, the
closeness of this large, gentle man encouraged her to relax her
rein on her emotions. With her control gone, tears sprang to
her eyes and flowed down her cheeks, and she heard herself
telling about her grief in short, childish gasps.

"I never really *thought* about how poor people feel about
their children," she said haltingly. "I suppose I must have
known that they would have the same feelings as we do—but I
never really knew it until now."

Darrow's dark eyes smiled at her proudly. "I knew you'd
be a hell of a woman when you put a few miles behind you."

Isabelle smiled as more tears wet her face. The powerful
warmth of this lawyer made her feel so good. She had never
felt so connected with a man in her life. Darrow leaned forward
and pulled a clean handkerchief from his breast pocket.

"May I?" he asked graciously, and dabbed her cheeks. Isabelle didn't resist his ministrations and sat still while he dried
her face. When he had finished, he took her hands again and
looked deep into her eyes, "You're beautiful, Isabelle," he said.
"And you're even more beautiful inside than you are on the
surface. No matter what happens, you always remember that."

Isabelle looked back at Darrow for a long moment before
she lowered her eyes. "When you were taunting me, I knew
what you thought about me: that I was spoiled and social. But
you were wrong." She hesitated before she revealed her darkest

secret. "I don't think most people approve of me. I don't know why, really. But they never have."

"Let me congratulate you on that," he said softly. "I have always found that when someone I like draws the disapproval of others, I like them all the more." Darrow smiled his slow, easy smile. "Listen, Isabelle, those people you've been worrying about, they're just sheep. I don't care about sheep, and I suggest it's time you forgot about them yourself."

Isabelle had never heard such an idea before. "I don't know what to say."

Without letting go of her hands Darrow replied, "Well, if you want to make a country lawyer very happy, you'll say you'll have dinner with me tonight."

As soon as Darrow had finished some paper work, he and Isabelle walked to Kinsley's restaurant. Kinsley's was not fancy, but it was a favorite among the town's political reformers. The Sunset Club met there on Thursday nights, and Darrow had seen Jane Addams herself give a speech at one of its meetings. Darrow liked the restaurant because it gave him an opportunity to see and needle the reformers. He also liked it because he could get a nice slice of pot roast with potatoes, bread and butter, and coffee for fifty cents. Isabelle didn't mention this, but she felt reassured when she saw its homely decor. It was not the kind of restaurant her husband would patronize.

When they had finished dinner and were returning across the bridge at State Street, Darrow unexpectedly took Isabelle's hand and pulled off her glove. Still clasping her hand warmly, he slipped it into his overcoat pocket and squeezed it.

Isabelle was by now completely charmed by the man. In the hours they had spent together, she had cried, talked openly to him, and felt his sympathy. He impressed her as such a deep, powerful man that she was a little afraid where all this would lead. But at the moment the invigoration she felt made the risk seem worthwhile.

"Isabelle," he said, smiling enchantingly, "you are such a bright, wonderful woman that I want to discuss something with you right now.

"Yes, Clarence," she said, smiling. "What is it?"

"I want to make it clear to you from the start that I don't

believe in marriage. I'm married now, and that's been a mistake for quite a while. But you must understand that I will never marry again, no matter what. Now, without any pretense between us, I want us to become very, very good friends."

"Why, Mr. Darrow," Isabelle said, pretending to be shocked, "I don't know why you think I'd want to marry you. I'm a married woman myself."

Darrow smiled. He was aware that over the last few hours she had lost most of the stiffness he had seen in her before.

"I was aware that you had the marriage affliction," he said. "That being the case, what are you doing here with me tonight?"

She shook her head. "One of the misfortunes of my life, Clarence, is that I married for money and wound up alone and unhappy."

"Well, did you get the money you wanted?"

"Yes. The money and a big house, too."

"Sounds to me like you made a deal and got what you wanted. Tell me, did you ever stipulate to the gentleman that he was supposed to love you, too?"

Isabelle smiled. "Of course not," she said. "That would have scared him away completely."

"Why's that?"

Isabelle thought for a moment before she answered.

"I'm not sure Phillip knows how to love."

Darrow nodded, "I think you may be right. I hope you won't mind my saying this, but I have met your husband, and I think he's a self-righteous, overblown bully. I don't trust him, and I don't like him."

Isabelle didn't answer. She felt slightly offended. For all his faults Phillip *was* her husband. It didn't seem appropriate that Clarence would attack him in her presence.

As they walked across the State Street Bridge, the wind blowing up the Chicago River caught Isabelle's hat and swept it into the air.

"My hat!" she cried, reaching after it.

"Just let it go, Isabelle," he said. They watched it float down onto the darkened water. "Try to think of it as a symbol of your old life. You didn't care much about it anyway. Now it's gone."

"Clarence," Isabelle said in a mocking tone but with a little concern, "it sounds like you're intent on having me give up a whole life without offering me anything in return."

"*Anything* in return?" he said. "Isabelle, I want to give you everything—everything but marriage: the stimulation of fascinating ideas, the warmth and companionship of a gentleman who admires you. It's obvious that you don't like your old life anyway. Why not just let it blow away?"

"It's not that easy, Mr. Darrow. You know that. What am I to do for money? Or for my child? Or for a roof over my head?"

"Aw, a smart woman can always think of something. Saint Jane has women living there in Hull House. From what I hear, you're there every day as it is."

"You know that?"

"Sure. I've been keeping about half an eye on you for some time now."

Isabelle smiled to herself as they walked on in a comfortable silence. "Tell me something, Clarence," she finally said. "How can a man like you live without ideals?"

Darrow was taken aback. "Why, what on earth would make you think I don't have ideals?"

"I suppose I'm confused about you. You seem concerned about poor people; then again, you work for the Chicago and North Western Railway. Surely, you don't respect what *that* company stands for?"

"Well, you got me there, Isabelle," he said. "I confess, you got me there. No, I don't think highly of the company at all."

"Then why do you do it?"

"It doesn't take a lot of time, and it pays me a lot of money. It also allows me to do work for folks who really need it without having to charge them a lot."

Darrow walked in silence for a moment. When he spoke again, his voice was different, more sincere. "You know, Isabelle, I'm afraid my real reasons stink to high heaven. And I thank you for reminding me that I'm sometimes as selfish a hypocrite as those phonies you socialize with."

He stopped walking and looked at her gently. "It's true, Isabelle. I am selfish. And that makes me want to take you back to my office with me."

Isabelle flushed. She had anticipated such a maneuver but not so soon.

"Clarence, please," she said.

"Don't worry, Isabelle, I'm too selfish to scare you away by being so impatient."

While Isabelle watched in surprise, Darrow waved down a hansom cab that was heading their way. "I'm going to send you home," he said as the horse drew near. "When you want to see me again, I hope you'll come by the office. You don't need to worry about my discretion. I promise, I'll never trouble you at home."

17

IT WAS ONLY 10:00 A.M. when Miss Watson knocked loudly on Hannah's door. Without waiting or pausing for an answer, she marched into the room, Vina close on her heels. Finding Hannah asleep, Carrie slammed the door to wake her up.

Today Carrie didn't want to touch the girl, not even to wake her up. On the one hand, she didn't want to shake her roughly because treating her mean was uncalled for. On the other hand, she liked Hannah far too much to touch her gently, the way the lonely girl would have liked. Carrie feared that the contact would soften her as well as the girl. And she knew that today was not the time to let her feelings get in the way of what they had to do.

The girl opened her bleary eyes and looked at Carrie through a haze of too much champagne and not enough sleep.

"Umm. Good morning," Hannah tried to say, and then flopped her head back on the pillow.

"The doctor'll be here in a little while," said Carrie. "You'd best be waking up now."

Hannah's eyes registered fear, and then she closed them with the dread of what was coming.

Carrie looked at the girl and tried to harden her feelings. She had been impressed with Hannah this week. In the last few days she had watched the girl stifle her reluctance and work as many customers as the best of her boarders. Carrie knew it had been difficult for her—God knows, she had tried hard enough to avoid it—but when the cards were laid out on the table, the girl had shown that she was no shirker.

In a way Carrie wished she hadn't been so tough on her, but it was important to let the girls know who was boss. Besides, it was bad for the house. Letting one girl lallygag gave the others ideas. But now that Hannah was in line, Carrie had to admit to herself that she liked her more than any of the others.

"Come on, Hannah," Carrie said bluntly. "It won't do for you to be asleep when the doctor gets here. He has other patients to attend to."

Hannah lay still for a moment. Then she tossed off the covers and sat up. "Do I have to get dressed . . . or what?" she asked, looking from Vina to Carrie.

"Lawd, no, child, you can stay in your nightclothes," Vina said kindly. "You jest be comfortable. But if you need to go to relieve your bladder, now's as good a time as any."

Hannah dragged herself to her feet and disappeared behind the folding screen in the corner. Carrie could see from the stiff way she carried her shoulders that the girl was scared. Vina could see it, too, and she looked at Carrie and shook her head in sympathy.

"This is a bad business," Vina said softly, "a bad business."

Carrie turned away impatiently to ward off her emotions. She had felt terrible when the other girl died a few months back, just terrible. And she hadn't even been particularly partial to that poor thing. Her biggest problem today was that she really liked Hannah.

Hannah was certainly the prettiest girl she had added in quite a while. But what struck Carrie as more important was that the girl was ambitious—just as she herself had been at that age. Carrie remembered that ridiculous meeting when Hannah had tried to talk her into letting her buy properties and shook her head. It may have been a good idea, but it was most certainly a boondoggle to keep her from spreading her legs for the customers.

It also touched Carrie's heart that the girl was so . . . well, *sweet*. This one had never made a mouth at her or snapped back with a flighty remark. It would be too bad if the life changed her disposition.

When Hannah returned from behind the screen, her face was drawn with fear. "Is this going to hurt?" she asked.

"A little, child," said Vina, "but we'll give you liquor enough to dull it."

Hannah nodded and sat back down on the bed. Her head hurt now from all the liquor she'd had the night before. Carrie looked at Hannah and could see the signs of a hangover. She made a mental note that when this was over, she should talk to Hannah about not drinking so much. Maybe it dulled her feelings, but it would turn her pretty features soft in no time at all.

Hannah looked at Carrie for a minute before she spoke. "I'm scared," she said softly.

"You'll be all right," said Vina, putting her arm around the girl's shoulders. "Miss Carrie'll make sure of that."

"You bet I will," said Carrie grimly. She promised herself that she'd kill that old quack if Hannah died.

Hannah looked at Carrie with one last appeal. "Could Marie be here with me?" she asked.

"Of course," said Carrie. "Vina, yell down the hall and have someone get Marie."

By the time Marie dressed herself and arrived at Hannah's room, the doctor was there. Dr. Marsh was a short man with a swayed back and a high, elongated forehead. He carried his eyebrows in a high arch as if he were too smart to be bothered with silly questions. When Marie came in, Hannah was sitting up on the bed and the doctor was feeling her abdomen with his hand.

"And you're not precisely sure when you conceived this child?" he was asking disdainfully.

"No," Hannah said softly, somewhat cowed by the presence of this exacting professional man. "But I think it had to be sometime in November."

"Hmm. November," he said, and then he began counting on his fingers. "Let's see. November, December, January, February . . . You don't know when in November?"

"I think it was early, sir," answered Hannah.

The doctor looked at Carrie with an expression that said, "I don't know how you expect me to work with *this*." Carrie shrugged as if to tell him that it was his problem.

"All right," he said as if he wanted to get it over with. "Lie back."

Before Hannah put her head on the pillow, Vina held a large drink of whiskey to her lips. Hannah choked as much of the nasty stuff down as she could, and then she felt her stomach lurch with nausea. She lay back and, while the doctor stood up and removed his cuff links, Vina pulled Hannah's nightgown up and got her situated in the proper position.

"Here, honey," she said, "just put your knees way out to the side. Doctor needs to see inside of you."

Even though Hannah could feel the effects of the whiskey almost immediately, she was mortified. She reached her hand out for Marie, and Marie immediately came across the room to sit at the head of the bed and hold Hannah's hand. Marie had never attended an operation before, and she was so scared she was whimpering. The doctor gave her an impatient look.

Carrie was upset herself. She was standing across the room beside the heavy draperies. Even from that distance she could see how embarrassed Hannah was to have the doctor look at her.

"It's all right, Hannah," she said. "This man's looked up more hind ends than you can shake a stick at."

Annoyed at having his professional credentials summarized in this manner, the doctor lowered his chin to give Carrie a dour look over his glasses. Then he pulled a chair close to the foot of the bed and began to examine Hannah.

Hannah felt his hands touch her, and she shuddered when the cold steel instrument was inserted. To make herself brave, she tried to imagine what her mother had done when she had to go to the *mikvah*, the women's public bath, so that her prospective mother-in-law could evaluate her suitability before her wedding. That had been the custom in Russia when her mother got married. The mother-in-law had to see for herself. Hannah didn't know if it had been like this, but she knew it had been humiliating because Mama had mentioned it once as an example of the things women have to endure.

Hannah felt a sharp pain as the doctor pushed something against her cervix. In a moment her stomach went into a spasm, and she uncontrollably began to vomit the whiskey Vina had given her.

"Stop, stop!" Marie yelled to the doctor. "She'll choke. She's sick."

Hannah continued to heave. First she emptied her stomach of whatever whiskey was there, and then her stomach continued in spasms until she thought she would vomit her insides out. As nasty as the whiskey had tasted going down, it was nothing compared with how it smelled now.

In disgust, the doctor gave her swollen uterus one last probe and withdrew his hand. "This is impossible," he said. "The girl is simply too far gone to perform this operation safely."

"I warned you," said Carrie, misunderstanding. "I warned you what I'd do if you killed this girl."

"I am not going to 'kill' this girl, as you put it, because I am not going to perform the curettage on her. It is too dangerous. I will not accept responsibility."

Carrie looked at the doctor with blood in her eye. "You little banty rooster! You mean you didn't even try?"

"No, I did not," he said, his eyebrows arching. "I've done girls this late on a few occasions, but since you insist on holding me accountable, I must refuse. As I said, it is too dangerous. She is too far gone. Of course, if you wish, I could leave a bottle of formaldehyde for her to take."

"I don't know why the hell I ever used you," said Carrie. "You know formaldehyde would kill her for sure."

As much as Carrie had feared the operation for Hannah, she was now mightily torn. She certainly did not want to wind up with an infant in her house. There was surely no better way to turn off her trade than with the sound of babies screaming. Plus it was a lousy example for the other girls.

"Madam," the doctor said as he packed his medical instruments, "if you truly want to avoid this in the future, instruct your girls to douche with a tincture of vitriol. If nothing else, the alum in the solution will have the astringent effect of tightening their organ of pleasure. That in itself should be good for business."

Carrie glowered at him maliciously.

When he was near the door, he turned back in a final

attempt to recover his dignity. "And my dear madam, I can only say that the stench in this room is truly a reflection of yourself. I wish you a good day."

When the door had closed behind the doctor, Carrie turned her attention back to Hannah. The girl had collapsed back on the pillow, and her face was so white that Carrie was afraid she might die no matter what. But the doctor had been right. What with the whiskey and the vomit, the room smelled simply awful.

"Vina," she said, "git someone to help you clean up this mess."

Before Carrie left the room, she turned to Hannah. "What in hell am I going to do with you now?"

Hannah suddenly burst into loud, tearful wails. "Oh, please, Miss Watson," she sobbed, "I was going to do it for you. I really was! Please don't turn me out." The girl reached out imploringly and tried to raise her head from the pillow. It was such a pitiful sight that Carrie Watson was almost moved to tears.

"Don't be worrying about the future just yet, Hannah," she said. "I'll do the worrying for both of us." And with that she left the sickroom.

When Carrie got downstairs, she went into her office and closed the door. She started to light the lamp, but then she thought she'd feel better just sitting in the dark.

It bothered her that she had become so attached to this girl—partly because she couldn't understand it. She had built a remarkably successful business on the hides of young women, and she had never kidded herself about being their friend. They were simply the commodity she had to trade. This approach didn't make her cruel to the girls, although it often had that effect in other houses. Cruelty—rapings, perverted beatings, and the like—she couldn't stomach that sort of thing. Anyway, Carrie knew that having the girls' respect and trust was an essential part in running the most expensive bordello in America.

Fair but firm. That was the way she handled her harem. And anybody who didn't like it was always free to leave. That was certainly the way Carrie had treated herself. Perhaps, in dealing with herself, she had been firmer than she had been fair.

When she first entered the trade and was saving money for her own establishment, she had driven herself mercilessly, forcing herself to work long, lonely nights even when she was feverish with illness. In those days she never once indulged herself in a pretty trinket or a bite of fancy food. She was hard on herself and put aside every penny that wasn't directly involved in her trade.

As Carrie sat in that darkened room, she thought about the girl she had been when she left home back in St. Louis. Something about Hannah made her lonesome for that innocent girl, almost as if her young self were someone she had deliberately smothered. At the time it had seemed so important to put her innocence—what remained of it—aside. She had already had too many years of fighting off her father whenever he was drunk and wanted to plug her and too many years of watching her mother slide into the gutter with him. Her mother didn't think she had a choice, and maybe, with nine kids, she didn't.

But even as a dirty-nosed little kid Carrie was determined that she *would* have a choice. As far as she was concerned, this was America. "The land of opportunity" they called it. And the way she had it figured was that all you had to do was decide what you wanted and then do whatever you had to do to get it. Even if you were a girl, that was what you had to do.

The night before Carrie ran away to Chicago, she wanted to say good-bye to her mother. She knew she had to handle the farewell in an offhand way because if her mother had thought she was leaving her with all those kids to raise, she would have stopped her. But Carrie wanted to leave her ma with some happy thought that she could perhaps remember her by, something that would give her ma a little cheer when she thought of it.

When Carrie came into the family's shack, carrying a bucket of water from the pump out in back, her mother had one of the babies at her breast.

"You have gave a lot of yourself to the family, Ma," Carrie said appreciatively.

"A lot of good it's done me, ain't it?" replied her ma.

Carrie was so struck by the statement that she was unable to lie. "That's true, Ma. You spoke right," she said. "I doubt it will ever come back to you."

Carrie's intention had been for her mother to know of Carrie's appreciation for her sacrifice. Instead, the surprised woman looked at her with a wild, startled hurt in her eyes. In that instant it seemed she saw that her whole life had been dedicated to raising kids who would grow up to be poor and sickly and start the process all over again. The look had been full of sadness and despair, her wasted dreams etched across her face like grief.

That look in her ma's eyes haunted Carrie for years. Even after all this time, she was surprised to feel the fresh sorrow it brought her. Many times she had wanted to go back, dressed in her finery, and say, "Look, Ma, look what your kid done." But her ma would not have had the sense to appreciate it. She would not have understood that Carrie had taken the only path she could to do it. She would just have felt shamed.

Her pain from that memory was what kept her walled up, away from risking closeness with anybody. She had enjoyed a boyfriend for a few years, and he had helped her set her house up. But then it seemed that his main interest in her was a return on his investment, which he wanted to take out in cash as well as in free samples of the girls. It left a sour taste in her mouth to be crazy with jealousy about the girls she hired to be alluring. It just didn't work. So when Carrie paid him off, she showed him the door and closed it on men forever.

Now, after all the determination and loneliness it had taken to reach her dream, Carrie was discomfited to realize that this new girl, this Hannah Chernik, had somehow gotten to her. Carrie knew she should tell her to leave—she had done it with others without much problem—but this time she couldn't. Carrie feared that the girl would die from exposure or a random attack or that she would wind up in another whorehouse where she might encounter brutality or cruelty.

Carrie heard a sound out in the hall. She leaned forward and struck a match to light her lamp. What if someone came in and found her sitting here in the dark? She had indulged herself in these soft feelings long enough. The issue she had to decide now was what to do with Hannah. The pregnancy wasn't showing much yet, and with a little luck the girl might be able to work for another month. That would leave four months, four long months, during which she would have to eat without earning her keep. That would never do, Carrie thought. That was stupid.

Maybe this scheme Hannah had dreamed up about real estate would work. She could start the girl off slowly, let her have a little bit of cash and see what she could do. It surely would beat letting her soak up money without paying her way.

When the baby came, if it lived, Hannah would just have to send it away to be raised. One thing Carrie knew for sure: Hannah was going to have to pick up *that* cost herself. There was no way Carrie Watson was going to pay to raise some woman's kid.

Carrie felt better now that she had worked out her solution. She looked at the papers overflowing the little drawers on her desk and planned to get Hannah busy organizing this establishment in a more businesslike fashion. When the girl was back on her feet tomorrow, she could start by straightening up this desk.

18

JOSEF WAS CERTAIN HE cut a dashing figure on his bicycle. Now that winter was melting into spring, the milder weather gave him the opportunity to take his bicycle out for a spin every now and then. When he did, he always looked for Corliss Scanlon. She'd been on his mind ever since the night he had met her with her cousin Bessie.

He didn't know exactly where Corliss lived, so to make sure she'd see him, he rode up and down the three-block section of tenements. Even though bicycles had been the rage for several years now, there were only a few in Pullman. At one hundred dollars each, a bicycle would have cost an average worker four months' wages. Josef hoped that seeing him perched on something so rare and expensive would impress her greatly.

He rode back and forth on Fulton Street several times before he gave up on seeing her. Then he returned to Florence Avenue, the main street of the town, and was whizzing along when he saw Corliss coming out of the Pullman Bank. He had picked up speed on the main thoroughfare, and although he'd been warned about the problems of stopping the bicycle, Josef jammed his foot as hard as he could against the front wheel.

The impact almost broke his ankle, and the fast deceleration nearly pitched him over the top of the handlebars. When he eased his foot back from the wheel, the contact made a loud embarrassing noise. Corliss was startled by the sound and looked up just in time to see Josef fly off the cycle onto the ground. The bicycle crashed onto its side, its wheels still spinning wildly. Josef was about as humiliated as he had ever been in his life.

"Are you all right?" Corliss asked in her small, thin voice. She hung back from him as if she were afraid to come closer.

Although Josef's right ankle and knee were starting to throb, he got up as quickly as he could and tried to pretend nothing was out of the ordinary.

"No brakes," he announced cheerfully as if hurling himself from the bicycle were his usual method of dismounting.

"Why don'tcha fix 'em?" she asked. "You could hurt yourself."

"Bicycles don't come with brakes." He tried to speak as if that particular hazard were part of the thrill. Then, in a show of courtesy and generosity, he offered her a turn. "Want to try it?"

"Without no brakes? No, thank you! If I was you, I'd be careful."

Josef didn't know whether to feel complimented that Corliss had shown concern about his safety or belittled that she had mentioned his fall. He was not the dashing figure he had hoped to dazzle her with.

"Where you heading?" he asked. "Home?"

"I guess," she said, looking glum. "As long as I've got one, I might as well."

Josef leaned down to pick up his bicycle. "I'll go with you."

"Not on that thing, you ain't," she said. "I got problems enough without you falling on me."

Josef felt chastened by Corliss's lack of appreciation, but he fell in step with her, pushing his bike with the handlebars. As he began walking, his knee hurt, and he slowed to a limp, using the bicycle as a crutch.

"Wis't I had the money to buy something nice like that," she said, sounding spiteful that he did while she didn't.

"Oh, I didn't *buy* it." Josef wished he could think of some reason to get her to cross the street and sit down in the park. His leg was hurting badly. "There's other ways to get the things you want."

His intention had been to convey the notion that he was smart and had finagled the bicycle by using his wits. This would have allowed him to brag about how he had saved the meat-packer's nephew from a gang of hoodlums. But she misunderstood.

"Well, if you think I'm going to walk around with a thief, you're mistaken! If I approved of thievery, I wouldn't be in the fix I'm in now."

To Josef's surprise, Corliss suddenly burst into tears. She started sobbing so hard that she had to hunch over and cover her face with her hands.

"Corliss!" he said, alarmed that she might be crying because she suspected him of thievery. "I didn't steal it. I swear."

His announcement didn't seem to calm her a bit. The girl looked so pitiful standing there all bent over that Josef wanted to put his arms around her to comfort her. He didn't, though, because he was afraid that if he let go of the handlebars, he would drop the bicycle on her. With his leg hurting this way, Josef was having a hard enough time without taking on other burdens.

"Let's go sit down, Corliss. Over there in the park." When Corliss didn't move, Josef repeated softly, "Come on, Corliss. I'm hurting. I need to sit. Please."

When Corliss pulled her hands down from her face, Josef led her across the avenue. After they had settled themselves on a bench, he turned to her earnestly. "I'm not a thief, Corliss. You don't have to worry about that. I swear!"

"It's not you, silly!" she answered. Then she started crying again. "Oh, Lord, I just don't know how I'm going to make it anymore. We'll starve. I know we will."

"Corliss, what's happened?" A sudden fear gripped Josef that Corliss had been fired.

"Look," she said, opening her drawstring purse and dumping the contents in her lap, "this is my pay. This is what them bitches in the bank just gave me for two weeks' work. And there won't be more for another two weeks. I can't live on this!"

Josef looked down in her lap. There were only $2.33 in change.

"Two dollars and thirty-three cents?" Josef asked. "How can that be?"

Corliss got so angry talking about it that she stopped crying. "It's easy—when you first consider that my forewoman, Mildred Beale, has cut my pay back by almost a third and sometimes even lays me off for a day or two at a time. No matter how much extra work I try to do, I can't earn more than a dollar a day."

"But still . . . two dollars and thirty-three cents! For two weeks' work?"

"You know how the bank deducts your rent from your paycheck when they cash it?"

"Yes."

"My ma got behind in her rent when my dad died. That was before I moved in, but the bank claims I have to pay them for the back rent. They're taking it out of my check." Corliss started to cry again. "I don't know what to *do*. They say I still owe them twenty-six dollars and eighty-four cents, but I don't know how much longer I can work and not take anything home for food."

Josef sat silently while Corliss rubbed her sleeve across her face. "When did your father die, Corliss?"

"Oh, only about eight months ago, but he lay dying for a long time. He was a watchman here. One night, when a man was stealing a box of tools, my dad tried to stop him. The bastard struck him in the face with a hatchet, and my poor pa fell and hit the back of his head."

"My God, Corliss." It distressed Josef to think of the violence and ugliness of it all. "Did the company doctor take care of him?"

"Yes. But not before they made Ma sign a paper that Pullman would be free of responsibility for the accident if the company provided medical care."

"You mean, when your father died, they did nothing for you?"

"It would seem not. My ma thought it would be useless for a poor widow to try to sue a corporation like the Pullman Company, so she wrote a letter to Mr. Pullman asking him to forgive the rent those months while my father lay unconscious.

"Anyway, that was before I began work here, and I don't think it should be my responsibility. But today they told me that if I didn't let them deduct what they did from my pay, they would put our furniture out on the street."

Josef wanted to comfort Corliss, but he could think of nothing to say that wouldn't blatantly gloss over the seriousness of her situation.

"You could go to Mr. Wickes," he said finally. "He's in charge of the works, and they say he's a fair man."

"Ha!" Corliss said bitterly. "I just told them that very thing at the bank. The manager flew into a rage and said if I dared go to Mr. Wickes, I would suffer for it."

At the mention of suffering, Corliss started crying again. "As if I haven't suffered enough!" she sobbed. "First my husband dies from the flu. Then I wind up taking care of my mother. And to make things worse, I have to pay off my pa's debts, which weren't rightly his anyway! It ain't fair!"

The sight of her crying touched Josef's heart, and he felt the first poignant stirrings of love. He wanted to save this pretty woman who was so frightened and sad, and he resolved that he'd fight for her. What he had been unable to do for his family, he thought, he would accomplish for her. He would make things right.

"Corliss," he said, taking her dusty hand in his, "we've let ourselves be walked over long enough. It's time we stopped worrying about Mr. Pullman's cars and started doing something for ourselves."

"But what can we do?" she asked in a small, choked voice. "What can we do?"

He answered her all of a sudden without thinking about it. The answer was so clear that he didn't know why he hadn't understood it before.

"We'll join the union." He realized that he was whispering even though there was no one near. "That way we might be able to do something that can help you. But we've got to keep this quiet, Corliss. Real quiet. Otherwise the company will find out and fire us."

"I don't see that I'd have much to lose even if they did fire me," she said petulantly. "I'd sooner quit and get another job than work myself to death without enough money to eat."

"But, Corliss," he said, trying to get through to her, "don't you see? There *aren't* any other jobs out there. We can't quit.

Our families depend on us for a living. Whatever we do, we've got to keep this quiet."

Two days later Corliss and Josef arrived at an old, unpainted building that had been designated as the site of the union meeting. They both were out of breath. The walk between Pullman and 115th Street in Kensington took almost forty minutes. Even so, Josef was afraid they might have been followed. As an extra precaution, they walked around the block twice before they finally felt safe.

As they were climbing the stairs to the front door, Josef was struck with the immensity of what he was doing. Corliss was opening the door when he stopped her.

"What's the matter?" she said.

"Wait," he answered, inhaling nervously. "Wait a minute."

He was frightened. Now that they were here, he was torn with doubt. He wondered if this was really what he should be doing. If he went into this meeting, would it really help anything? Or would it merely jeopardize his job and cause more problems for his family?

"Are you sick, Josef?" she whined. She was chilled and sweating. When he shook his head, she tugged on his sleeve. "Well, come on then. We're late enough as it is!"

Earlier, in the safety of the shop, Josef had been eager to get to the meeting. Eugene Debs, the man who had formed the American Railway Union, was going to be there. Debs was the only man in America who had been able to forge all the different trade brotherhoods into one large organization. If anyone knew how to help the workers, Debs was surely that person.

But standing outside the hall, Josef was worried. What if there were company spies inside the hall? If he were reported, he'd be fired and blacklisted; the family would be put out on the street! Such a thing had happened to eight men last week. That was why the union hall had been moved all the way to Kensington—to get as far from Pullman as the workers could.

It was terrifying. Being fired in these hard times was almost like a death sentence. Lately he'd heard about entire families dying from hunger in Chicago.

"Josef!" said Corliss anxiously. "What are you waiting for? Ain't we going in?"

He felt pressured by her insistence. All the same, he knew *something* had to be done. It almost seemed that the company was intentionally starving the workers to death. Though his wages had been cut, rent on the housing was as high as it had always been. There was so little left to live on that Josef sometimes didn't eat to save food for his sisters. He had come close to passing out several times.

A voice broke the night air. Someone louder than the rest was shouting. "This is a slave pen without an equal in the United States!"

"You hear?" Corliss said. "Is that what you came to this country for? To be a slave?"

Josef was moved by her argument. It was true. They were living like serfs: drinking the landlord's water, eating the food they bought on credit in his shops, living in his property, and paying for the privilege with whatever money he saw fit to give them. The longer they worked, the deeper they got in debt. Though the threat of being fired was terrifying, it was essential to do something.

"Let's go," he said.

Inside the hall the crowd was so large that all the benches were filled. People lined the sides and back of the room. A stocky, powerful-looking man with intensely blue eyes and a bristling red mustache was standing behind a table at the front of the room.

"I believe," said the redheaded man, "that Mr. Pullman doesn't understand the situation here. It seems likely that the new plant manager is not telling him the truth about what's going on."

A thin woman with stringy graying hair stood up, waving a socialist newspaper. "Is that so, Mr. Heathcoate? Then why is the old bastard selling us gas—the same gas he gets for thirty-three cents—for two dollars and twenty-five cents for the same measure?"

Several men and women yelled in agreement. "The old bastard!"

Mr. Heathcoate raised his voice to be heard. He had been appointed to head the union meetings, and he wanted to maintain order. "Could we stick to the subject, please?" he said. "We're trying to apprise Mr. Debs, here, about the abuses at the workplace." Heathcoate gestured to a man sitting at the table. Debs had calm, gentle eyes and a high, balding forehead.

A large man in his forties stood to his feet respectfully. His hair was so blond that it seemed to have no color at all. "If I may speak, Thomas?" he asked respectfully of Heathcoate. Thomas Heathcoate nodded, giving the tall man a go-ahead.

"Mr. Debs, sir, each step in making a car is done by four or five men plus a straw boss."

Lubek, Josef's old work companion, interrupted. He had developed a notorious reputation at the union meetings, and when he stepped forward, it was clear that he was irritated with the blond man's halting description.

"Mr. Debs, the friggin' straw boss is *supposed* to divide the rate among the men according to skill and performance. But what does he do? He pays his *friends* more than the others."

Men shouted in agreement, and another worker rose to his feet. "The foremen and the managers in the Pullman Palace Car Company have not yet had one cutback in their wages!" he yelled. "Not one penny! Yet we have been docked and docked repeatedly."

The room fell into disorder as men shouted in agreement.

"Sir. Sir." A woman near Josef was calling to the men at the front of the room. Josef realized with a start that it was Corliss. Gradually the room grew still to hear what she had to say.

"Mr. Eugene, sir," she said. A few of the men laughed when they heard her addressing the head of the ARU in such a simple way. After they had again become quiet, she continued.

"Mr. Eugene Debs, sir, the company has established some very mean policies when it comes to injury. In the last couple of years many workers have been hurt so bad that they have to go on leave. Yet the company says it won't pay for sick leave unless the men can *prove* the injury was not due to their negligence."

Debs sat forward. "They deny the workers pay after an injury?" he repeated.

Corliss nodded her head and took a few steps toward the front of the room. "Yes, sir. But while they're waitin' for the proof they want, the rent and gas and water meter keeps running."

Women in the crowd, responding to a woman in trouble, cried out in support. Corliss took another step down the center aisle closer to the front. She was now near the center of the room. All eyes were upon her as Debs stood to hear her and waved the room quiet.

"Sir," she said her voice breaking with the fear and injustice of her lot, "last week, when I picked up my check for two weeks' hard work, they had deducted so much for my dead father's back rent that all I had left was two dollars and thirty-three cents. My mother and I, we can't live for two weeks on that." Tears ran down Corliss's face. "Mr. Debs, we'll die soon, unless you do something."

The meeting erupted into uproar. In the middle of the pandemonium Lubek brandished his fist. "I say we strike!" he shouted.

Though the fomenting anger pointed in the direction of a strike, the mention of the word settled the hall down. As the crowd watched, Mr. Debs sat down thoughtfully. Thomas Heathcoate raised his arms even though there was now no need to quiet the crowd. The mention of a strike was terrifying to contemplate.

"All right," Heathcoate said, his voice tense and hushed. "A strike has been proposed. As you will recall, in December the steam fitters and blacksmiths went on strike, but most went back a few days later. The ones that didn't were fired and blacklisted. The point is that we can't fight this company if only one department or trade strikes. If we're going to succeed, we'll have to close *all* the shops."

Debs got back to his feet. "Wait. Wait," he said. "Hold it. You're not *ready* to strike. As I understand it, you have no all-inclusive union."

Josef, inspired by Corliss's contribution to the meeting, spoke up. "Why can't we join your union, sir? Wouldn't the American Railway Union take us?"

A Pullman carpenter replied, "Because we're not railroad workers. We're Pullman workers."

"Hell, yes, we're railroad workers," said another worker. "We operate twenty-odd miles of rails just between the buildings and the plants here. I'd say that every damned one of us works for a railroad!"

The crowd cheered at this notion, and Thomas Heathcoate agreed. "That's a point, Mr. Debs," he said. "I think that the track does, in fact, make us ARU workers."

"That's fine," said Debs, "but you still have to sign up enough workers to make a strike meaningful. You shouldn't even consider it until you've got at least a third of the employees."

This was a discouraging thought, and the audience grumbled quietly. How could they ever get a third of the workers to sign—what with spies and foremen rooting out the union sympathizers? In Chicago there were thousands of people without jobs who'd be thrilled to replace them—at least until they discovered they couldn't make anything working at Pullman.

"Let's look at alternatives," said Debs quietly. "Do you think Mr. Pullman knows of your grievances?"

"No. Not Pullman nor Mr. Wickes neither," answered a worker. "Their office is downtown in the Loop. I believe that the new general manager, Middleton, keeps the truth from them."

Debs rapped to get their attention. "All right," he said, "before you strike, you should appoint a committee—a sizable committee—and ask for a meeting with Pullman to discuss your grievances. This will give him a chance to hear what's going on and respond. While you're there, you should be prepared to tell him what you want."

Debs took out a notebook and a pencil so he could write down the workers' requests. "Let's discuss this now. What *do* you want?"

The man with the wispy blond hair stood to answer. "I think our pay should be brought back up to the old 1893 rates *or* the rent should be lowered."

"That's fair," said Debs. "Is that what everyone wants?"

The workers discussing the request filled the hall with the rumble of their voices. Debs had to quiet them. "What else?" he said.

A woman stood. "We want the foremen—the ones who are mean and abusive—brought up on charges."

"Hell, yes!" a man yelled angrily. "My foreman knocked me across the room last week. A more hateful bastard there never was!"

"All right," said Debs. "You'll tell Pullman about it. If he doesn't respond, then we'll come up with a different plan. Does that make sense?"

Suddenly Lubek voiced what many were thinking. "We came here to get ARU support for a *strike!*" he yelled. His face was red with his fury. *"We want to close down that friggin' plant. We want to close it down or burn it down!"*

The crowd was roused by his passion. The workers cheered, and some shouted agreement.

"You did *not* come here to close the plant," Thomas Heathcoate shouted. "You came here to get help so you can feed your families. What good will it do to tear everything down?"

When the crowd was quiet again, one of the women asked hopefully, "Will you go with the committee, Mr. Debs?"

"Not now," he answered. "I'm too well known. My presence would be sure to create distrust. Maybe I'll send an ARU representative, but I think it best for your committee to handle it. Just make sure that every trade in the company is represented on the committee. Also, have a member from each nationality. That's important. It will show the company the depth of your unity and commitment."

Within the next hour it was decided that Heathcoate would telegraph the head office in Chicago and ask for a meeting with Pullman. A committee composed of forty-five representatives had been appointed when Debs asked, "Now are you sure every group in the company is represented?"

Corliss stood to her feet. "There's no Russians on the committee," she said, "and we got one right here."

Corliss pointed at Josef. He winced. Being singled out for the committee was not something he had counted on, but since he was the only Russian in attendance, he felt he had to accept.

When the meeting broke up, the crowd left in small groups, each taking a different route back to Pullman. Corliss and Josef walked together. She was invigorated by the meeting, and Josef was hopeful about the plans. When she took his hand in hers, he forgot his concerns. He was impressed with her strength and how convincingly she had spoken.

"You were wonderful tonight, Corliss," he said. "I was so proud."

"I'm proud of *you*," she said. "Just think of it! Imagine

going to see Mr. Pullman yourself. I hope you say something that will really make him sit back and take notice."

"Just as long as it doesn't make him remember me," he said, knowing the danger of his situation. "I'll be better off if he forgets about me entirely."

19
_____

"ALL THIS MALARKEY ABOUT a group of illiterate foreigners dictating how I should run my company—why, it's outrageous. If I give in to this kind of extortion, it will mean the end of American business."

George Pullman had called a meeting with Mr. Wickes, his second vice-president, and Mr. Middleton, the new manager of his plant in Pullman. The delegation of the workers was due to arrive at his Chicago office in less than an hour.

"I agree, sir," said Middleton. "And most are anarchists. They've done nothing but grumble and complain ever since I took over the plant."

"That's because your job was to cut costs, Mr. Middleton, and keep the plant open," Pullman said. "The workers would certainly have no appreciation of that." He made a face as if he had tasted something bad. "When is your meeting?"

"The telegram said they wanted to send a delegation at ten o'clock, sir," answered Wickes. "In my reply I instructed them to meet us in the large meeting room on the fourth floor."

"Fine," said Pullman. "Just make sure you keep 'em away from *my* office. I'll join you men later."

Pullman fixed each man with a stare before he continued. Both men cringed. George Pullman was known for his violent temper. It was common knowledge that any man in his employ who failed to follow his instructions perfectly would feel the full fury of his displeasure.

His thick white goatee twitched as he formed his thoughts. "Be aware," he said, "that my position is firm. As managers of capital we must set salaries however we wish to protect our investments. That is our charge. We must protect our investors' trust."

"I agree with you completely, sir," said Middleton, stroking his dark hair to make sure it was plastered to the top of his head. Middleton was a stocky man who controlled his thick hair by combing large quantities of grease into it.

Pullman ignored Middleton's interruption. "You tell those men that they're free men, that they have a choice. You tell them they can labor for the company at the wages we have set, or they can go work somewhere else. But by no means will we discuss policy with them. It is not their right to turn commerce topsy-turvy."

"I believe the workers simply wanted to make you aware of their problems, sir," said Wickes. "They have every trust in you." He winced slightly as if he expected to be slapped with a reprimand.

"And so they should," said Pullman. "No businessman has ever done more for his employees. My God, the very idea of those men showing this kind of ingratitude cuts me to the quick."

Wickes paused a moment to give Mr. Pullman time to nurse his wounded feelings. When he was sure the old man had indulged himself sufficiently, he continued. "Sir, in their telegram, they asked that the workers in their delegation not be punished for coming. In my return telegram I assured them that there would be no reprisals."

George Pullman stared hard at Wickes for a few long seconds. Though Wickes was a tall graying man well into his fifties and had given the company many years of excellent service, he felt the threat in that stare.

"That was surprisingly ill advised of you, Mr. Wickes," Pullman said slowly. "Surprisingly so. Typically we give agitators what they deserve."

With that Pullman removed a gold watch from his pocket

and glanced at it. "Gentlemen, I have important work to do, as do you. Deal with those men as best you can. Remember, I will not give in to extortion. Nor will I tolerate a strike. I will join you later."

Josef and the forty-five other members of the delegation met promptly at eight-thirty at the Pullman train depot. Mr. Debs had been good to his word. He had sent along George Howard, an ARU representative, to help Heathcoate lead the committee.

Both Howard and Heathcoate had been anxious that the Pullman leaders be impressed by the responsible attitude of the workers. They had insisted that they should not be late under any circumstances and that they should look clean and behave respectfully.

Josef had taken extra pains to shave carefully, and he'd cleaned the oil and grime out from under his nails. His mother, though terrified that he was meeting with an owner known to be a tyrant, had trimmed his hair and mended and ironed his clothes. She didn't want him to go, but since there was no dissuading him from it, she was anxious that the men downtown be impressed with her son. "Who knows," she said to Yankel, "maybe they will offer Josef a better job." When Yankel scoffed, she insisted, "Who knows? Stranger things have happened."

The delegation, a herd of heavily muscled men dressed in brown and black suits, boarded the train for the city. Those who owned dark bowler hats were wearing them. When they were seated, one of the men joked, "If they ain't impressed by all this finery, to hell with 'em!"

"To hell with 'em is right!" agreed Lubek.

Josef winced. He hoped Lubek had enough sense to keep his temper today.

Heathcoate immediately turned to Lubek to chastise him. "I'll thank you to keep a watchful tongue in your head, sir. Disrespectful remarks such as those will lose our cause, sure as anything."

The men, aware that their lives depended on this meeting, mumbled in agreement.

Josef swallowed hard. He was very nervous, but he was thrilled by the realization that he was going to sit in the presence of great men. Powerful representatives of industry had actually agreed to meet with a delegation or workers. It was a tremendous feeling. He believed that the outcome of the meeting might even affect other workers elsewhere. His heart quickened when he thought about the responsibility on his shoulders.

At first he had been frightened that the company might be angry or retaliate, but Mr. Wickes had given his word that reprisals would not be taken. This meant that he could clear his mind of this fear and concentrate on the meeting. How could they best make the officials understand their situation? He thought about how beautifully Corliss had spoken to Debs at the meeting. He wanted so much to be that effective.

When the train finally stopped at the depot downtown, Heathcoate held his hand in the air to get their attention. He announced that they should follow him to the main offices at Michigan and Adams. It was a little embarrassing to be shepherded in this manner, but as he trudged along in the middle of the crowd, Josef was aware that he felt confident only when he could see Mr. Heathcoate's hand waving along, high above the heads of the men.

They arrived at the building and found no one to meet them on the first floor. Josef noticed for the first time that Mr. Heathcoate seemed insecure himself. To cover his uncertainty, he checked his telegram again though by now he certainly must have memorized its contents.

"Let's see," he said, adjusting his glasses to read the telegram. "Our instructions said . . . fourth floor. Well, I expect they'll meet us up there."

After the elevator had made its first trip to the fourth floor, Josef packed into the elevator with the second load of men. It took several trips before the entire delegation was on the proper floor. As he waited in the corridor while the rest of the men rode up, he felt concerned and out of place.

Finally, after a short wait, the elevator door opened again, and two men stepped into the hallway. The tall gray-haired man looked around him. "I'm Thomas Wickes," he said. "Which of you men is the head of this delegation?"

It seemed clear to Josef that Heathcoate must not have personally met Wickes before today, though it was obvious Heathcoate expected him to be sympathetic to the cause. He pushed forward through the crowd and pumped Wickes's hand in an awkward display of friendliness.

"Mr. Wickes, sir. My pleasure. I'm Thomas Heathcoate, the leader of this here delegation."

Wickes took in the Scotsman's red hair and mustache. "Yes, Mr. Heathcoate. It was you who sent the telegram, I believe."

"Indeed, it was, sir."

"Of course, you know Mr. Middleton," said Wickes to introduce the new plant manager.

Josef stood high on the toes of one foot to see Middleton. He had heard that most of their problems were the fault of Middleton's ruthless cost programs. Middleton was shorter and younger than Wickes, and his thick brown hair was shiny. Josef could see the marks his comb had made in it.

Heathcoate nodded formally to the new plant manager. "Mr. Middleton," he said, in a brisk, businesslike way. "Gentlemen, may I present Mr. Howard?"

"Howard?" said Middleton. "I don't recall your name on our employee roster, sir."

"I'm a representative from the ARU," said Howard.

Josef stood on his toes again in time to see Middleton raise his eyebrows and give Wickes a significant look. "The ARU?" Middleton repeated for Wickes's benefit. "And what might that be?"

"The American Railway Union is a federation of railroad brotherhoods," Howard answered.

"You're a representative from a *union?*" Middleton repeated for effect, looking nervously at Wickes. He remembered this morning's meeting with Pullman very clearly. "We have no union in this company, and we will talk to no union," he said emphatically.

In an attempt to smooth things over, Heathcoate explained. "You're not really talking to the union, sir. It's just that we have no experience in this sort of thing. Mr. Howard is here merely to make sure we handle things properly, sir."

"You are quite sure?" asked Wickes.

Josef could feel the chill in the managers' mood. He wondered if the other workers could feel it, too.

"Very well," said Wickes coolly. "We will go inside so long as unionizing is never mentioned."

Josef waited with the rest of the workers until the leaders were in the room. Then they shuffled in respectfully. Several of the men who had failed to remove their bowlers received nudges from those who knew better, and they quickly took off their hats.

"Unless all of you hope to participate in these discussions," said Middleton, "why don't those of you who are the spokesmen sit up here at the table? The rest of you can stand."

After they had taken their places at the back of the room, Josef found that he was behind two rows of men. He had to stretch his neck to see, but he could hear everything that went on.

"All right," said Wickes. "What's all this about?"

There was something in the man's voice that surprised and disturbed Josef. Wickes was not the sympathetic person he had expected. Heathcoate seemed surprised at the hardness in his tone, too, and for a few seconds he stammered. Josef was happy he was not in Heathcoate's place.

"What this is about, sir," said Heathcoate with great dignity, "is that the workers are suffering greatly. They have been cut down from a decent living wage to very low piecework rates. The new rates have reduced their income by as much as one half."

"I have something to say about that," said Middleton, breaking in. "Indeed, I do. Gentlemen, our goal in Pullman has been to keep the plant open. In order to do that, we have been taking repair jobs and contracts at rates that amount to a loss."

Heathcoate looked astonished. "But this is not what your own spokesmen have said in public statements."

The union representative, Mr. Howard, pulled a sheaf of papers from his reticule. Mr. Howard seemed much less nervous than Heathcoate, and his voice was stronger. "It is certainly not what Mr. Pullman himself has stated," Howard said, supporting Heathcoate's contention. "Here, in one article, Mr. Pullman is quoted on the soundness and continuing profits from the car operation."

Howard handed the article to Middleton. When the plant manager had it in hand, he glanced at it and dropped it on the table as if it were of no consequence. "That statement was issued because our stock had dropped ten points. If you men understood business, you'd know how important it is to reassure our investors. I'm telling you, most of our work has been taken simply to keep the workers on the job."

A man directly behind Josef could no longer contain himself. Josef flinched from the surprise of the noisy outburst. Without turning around, he knew from the voice that it was Lubek. "If that's true," Lubek said, almost shouting, "then it's only so you can keep people living in the Pullman houses so the company can keep on gettin' its rent money."

The men around Josef muttered their agreement. As the noise in the room started up, Heathcoate's face flushed in panic.

Heathcoate believed that when the company leaders understood the workers' problems, they would do something to correct them. He had cautioned the men that a respectful attitude was important for a good outcome, yet now the meeting suddenly seemed in danger of erupting into the kind of shouting customary at the union meetings.

"I'll handle this if you please, sir," Heathcoate said, trying to maintain control. "Please forgive the outburst, sir," he said to Wickes. "The men are justifiably very upset."

"Justifiably?" said Middleton, raising his eyebrows. "That has yet to be determined."

The room suddenly grew quiet. Josef noticed that Wickes and Middleton had stopped listening and were staring, not at Heathcoate but at someone in the doorway.

Josef turned to see a plump old man with a thick white goatee standing in the doorway, listening. Something about his bearing was so imperious that without being told, Josef immediately knew the man was George Pullman himself.

Pullman walked slowly into the room. "So," he said without passion, "you men feel that your wage cuts have been unfair, do you? Have you considered how the investors in the company feel, knowing that the dividends on their investments could fall to nothing? Have you men considered how industry would cease to exist without investors?"

No one said anything. Josef stretched his neck so he could see the man better. Pullman's effect on the room was electrifying. No one had courage enough to speak.

"No," he said, answering for the men. "You haven't considered that at all, have you? You're so busy worrying about your pay, you haven't considered American industry for one minute. Well, let me tell you men this: It's been hard to keep the plant open. Damnably hard. But we've done it—and we've done it for you."

George Pullman continued talking as he walked to the head of the room. "Yes, we've taken our cuts. We've taken jobs at less than break-even. And it was for you."

There was an awkward pause as Pullman sat down at the table. Heathcoate was clearly at a disadvantage. He looked like a child caught tattling about a parent. He finally recovered enough to clear his throat respectfully.

"Sir, if the company is hurting, we are indeed sympathetic. Times are hard. But with the rents so high and the pay so low, our people are in terrible straits. If it's necessary to keep the pay so low, we would respectfully like to request that the rents be lowered as well."

Pullman's eyebrows converged into one angry line across his forehead. He slapped his open hand repeatedly on the table to punctuate his words. "Do not confuse the company's roles of landlord and employer. One has nothing to do with the other. I didn't raise rents during prosperous times, did I? No. And I see no reason why I should lower them now."

When Pullman raised his voice, the first effect it had on Josef was to make him feel the way he had as a child when his father had threatened punishment. But as the seconds went by, the old man's anger lowered Pullman in his eyes. Josef began to see the tycoon less as an invincible patriarch than as a grouchy old skinflint.

"Sir," said the ARU representative, Mr. Howard, "let me point out that although the skilled workers' pay has been slashed by as much as one half, the foremen and officers still draw the same salaries as before."

Pullman frowned as if he had bitten something sour. "What I pay management is no concern of yours."

Josef cringed as Lubek spoke up again. "The foremen are the ones makin' the trouble," he said. "They pay their friends more than other men who deserve it. They even hit the women."

Wickes interrupted. "If this is true, provide us a list of names and specific offenses. We'll investigate and get to the bottom of this charge."

"Anything else?" asked Middleton, as if this promise had solved everything.

Josef was afraid the meeting was going to end without a

discussion about sick pay. That was the root of Corliss's problem and the anguish of so many others. He would have felt very guilty if no one brought it up.

"Sir," he said, his voice sounding strangely loud and high-pitched, "when men are injured, the company refuses to give them sick pay while they're recovering. It makes life terribly hard on their families—what with the rents continuing all that time and being so high and all."

Middleton looked from Josef to Pullman. It was clear that Middleton's desire was less to appease his workers than his boss.

"This company has always provided physicians for the injured," Middleton said, as if speaking to a child. "However, with four thousand one hundred fifty-five injuries on the job in two years, it was obvious we were being taken advantage of! It was no longer a question of the men's health. We had to consider the health of the company."

Pullman nodded irritably as if this explanation made sense to him.

"Men," he said impatiently, "this little discussion has already taken up too much of my time. I simply cannot lower rents, as it would be unfair to the investors in the company. Nor can I, at present, see a way clear to raise your wages. However, we will investigate these charges of foreman abuses. I'd like all of you to sign your names before you leave so that we're sure you represent the entire company—rather than just a few malcontents."

As Pullman stood up, Howard rose to his feet as well. "Sir, before the men sign your ledger, I wish you to reaffirm an earlier promise by Mr. Wickes that there will be no retaliation against any of these committeemen. These gentlemen have come here to represent the other workers in an act of good faith."

Pullman looked at Howard sourly for a moment. "That's fine," he said. Then he looked around the room. "Surely you men must understand by now that the town's well-being is very important to me. I want you men to know that I think of all you workers as my children."

He walked rigidly to the door and turned back to the room. "You should understand, however, that I will not tolerate any attempt to dictate how the Pullman Palace Car Company is run.

I will consider any organized disruption of work extortion and deal with it as such."

Pullman turned and passed through the door as quietly as he had entered. For a few seconds the room remained silent as if there were nothing more to be said. Middleton was the first to speak.

"That should take care of it."

"But it doesn't, Mr. Middleton," said Thomas Heathcoate. "It doesn't take care of anything."

"We have *begun* a dialogue," said Mr. Wickes, raising one eyebrow. It seemed to Josef that Mr. Wickes was trying to tell the men that their objections had been heard and would be dealt with later in private discussions.

Heathcoate turned red and sputtered. "We at least want to begin a list of the foremen who have been most abusive," he said. "We at least want to be free of that unbearable tyranny."

"Fine," said Middleton, smoothing his greasy hair again. "I shall leave two pieces of paper. On one, you men can list the foremen's names. On the other kindly list your own."

On the train back to Pullman, Josef felt letdown, and he could sense disappointment among the men. Thomas Heathcoate seemed especially unhappy with his weak accomplishments. Josef wondered what he would say to Corliss when she asked him about the meeting. He felt he had failed.

One of the men on the train finally said in a loud voice, "I still don't see why we have to suffer wage cuts without rent reduction if the bloomin' company is so damned healthy."

Heathcoate answered. "You heard Mr. Pullman. He says he's taking jobs at a loss."

Lubek responded. "Sounds to me like he says whatever suits him at the moment."

"I'm not satisfied with the meeting myself," said Heathcoate to cover his frustration. "But I counsel you to have patience. It's a beginning."

A thought crossed Josef's mind just before a machinist said what he was thinking.

"If this is the beginning," the machinist said, "what is it the beginning of?"

20

CLARENCE DARROW FLUNG OPEN the front door at Hull House and hustled his long legs awkwardly down the hall. He was so anxious to see Isabelle that he was as keyed up as a schoolboy.

"Is she here? Did she answer my note?"

A tall, thin woman with white skin and dark hair looked up from she napkins she was folding and shook her head no. Sybil Thatcher was one of the few live-in volunteers at Hull House. She vigorously pulled out a hairpin and tried to skewer a stringy wisp of hair in place. Darrow had bothered her about Isabelle so many times in the last few days that she was sorry she'd agreed to help him.

"*Your* note?" she asked, her eyebrows raising in indignation.

"The note you wrote for me."

"Hmph," said Sybil. "No, she most certainly did not respond, and I think it's rude. Even if she knew it was from you, it had my signature on it. What's more, it's been over a week since she showed up for the nursery school."

Sybil bustled around the table and vigorously flapped a tablecloth in the air. "If you ask me, Clarence Darrow," she said, "that woman is either plain irresponsible or she's trying to avoid *you*."

Darrow grinned. He liked Sybil. The way she made a point of disapproving of him amused him greatly. Of course, he almost always enjoyed people who disapproved of him. It made life interesting to watch them waver between their desire to insult him and their belief that they should adhere to a code of politeness.

Sybil interested Darrow because she was the only conventional woman he knew who had actually left her husband. In his crowd a "new woman" might shock her friends by filing a noisy divorce, but usually such women were financially secure in their own right. This drab, morally upright woman was poor as a church mouse. Yet one morning six months ago she had surprised her husband by dressing her two children, packing up most of their household possessions, and leaving.

Jane Addams took Sybil in because she had been volunteering at the settlement house for several months. Still, Jane was concerned that the husband might bring suit against Hull House for the goods she had brought with her. Jane quietly asked Darrow to offer Sybil legal counsel. When he tactfully asked the woman if her husband's behavior was such that a jury might understand her leaving him, she had looked at Darrow as if she could spit in his eye.

"Mr. Darrow, the man came home drunk and attempted to switch the back of my shins with a branch of forsythia to get me to bare more of my anatomy to him. Now, if that isn't the kind of behavior a God-fearing jury would accept as grounds for divorce, then your lawyering isn't as fancy as you think it is."

Darrow was highly amused by Sybil's confession. He grinned and asked her what had become of the forsythia switch.

"That, Mr. Lawyer," she said, "is none of your business. But I will tell you this. That man won't so much as *see* a forsythia bush without a strong stinging recollection of Sybil Thatcher."

Sybil smoothed the tablecloth and piled plates on the table. "If Isabelle is irresponsible," she continued, "I recommend you tell her that we prefer flighty women to stay away."

A troubling thought crossed Darrow's mind. Isabelle *wasn't* flighty or irresponsible. She was so dedicated to the nursery children that he had teased her about her large family. He suddenly became concerned that something had happened to her.

Sybil read his look and, despite herself, wanted to calm his fear. "For heaven's sake," she said, "she's probably just avoiding *you*—which is my stronger suspicion, Mr. Lawyer—and if so, she's an intelligent woman in my book." Sybil put some forks out on the table and tried to arrange them in a straight line. "It's harder to replace a woman who likes children than it is to find a profligate attorney—who shall remain unnamed."

Sybil gave Clarence a little look that showed she expected him to laugh at her disrespectful sally, but Clarence didn't even have the heart to smile. There was nothing funny to him about missing Isabelle, nothing at all. The only thing remotely amusing was remembering his chivalrous promise that he wouldn't trouble her at home.

Days had passed since their romantic evening, and he hungered for her. When he closed his eyes at night, he could see her pretty, slender face and her gleaming hair. He could almost remember how her soft, long fingers had felt in his hand when he told her that he would never marry again. He vacillated between thinking that particular speech had been ridiculous—for it had surely driven her away—and thinking that it had shown her his high-principled honor. With all the women in Chicago out to capture his attention, why, he wondered, did he feel so heartsick about a woman who wouldn't answer his messages?

"What did your note say?" Darrow suddenly asked Sybil.

"It said what you wanted it to say," she snapped. She was getting tired of this whole business. "It said, 'My dear Isabelle. A person important in the reform movement has requested a meeting with you. Please respond. Your friend, Sybil.' "

"Well, that seems safe enough," he said. "I wonder why she hasn't replied."

"Because, Clarence Darrow," replied Sybil, raising her eyebrows before she turned and left the room, "she knows that *you're* the person—and a scamp at that."

Isabelle paced across the floor in her sitting room again and stopped to stare out the window. A couple of carriages rumbled along Michigan Avenue. They distracted her for a moment until she turned back to her writing table. The fourth note from Sybil lay crumpled on her leather desk set. She knew the note was really another plea from Clarence, disguised so that her servants and husband wouldn't discover that a man was sending her notes. Even though she was grateful for his discretion, Isabelle was disturbed that anyone from Hull House knew that Clarence was trying to reach her.

Ever since her romantic dinner with him, she had wondered what on earth had possessed her to go to a public restaurant with that man. She had been indiscreet and silly. Clarence Darrow was certainly not admired by people in her husband's circle, and to make matters worse, any number of people might have seen her. If one of them told her husband, then where would she be?

When the cab had pulled up in front of her home that night a week ago, Isabelle's mouth was dry with fear. On the way home she had been struck by the foolishness of what she had done. Phillip could be inside waiting for her, and if he asked what she had been doing, she had no idea what she would tell him. She had not only been indiscreet, she had been alone with Clarence Darrow, and that was something Phillip would never understand.

Thankful that she had her key and could get inside without ringing for Helen, Isabelle had quietly tiptoed upstairs to her room. When she was safely in bed, she lay in the dark, staring at the ceiling and thinking about her evening with Clarence Darrow.

Isabelle realized that she would never have been so foolish if her husband hadn't somehow pushed her to it by bringing up divorce. That threat, for a trivial action regarding their child, had created a reckless distance in her. Up until then she had assumed that Phillip had turned against her because of some serious flaw in *her*. But the scene at the dinner table had shown her something about him she hadn't really understood: Phillip had a cruel, hateful heart. She didn't know why she hadn't seen it before.

She had spent years building walls to protect herself from his neglect, but that neglect had made her dangerously vulnerable to Darrow's kindness. Now, having been out with him publicly, she was dismayed at her boldness. Surely a man as quick to *threaten* divorce as Phillip would stand by his threat if she committed a true indiscretion.

Isabelle knew a divorce for sexual misconduct would mean the end of her. Phillip would certainly evict her from his house and take her son away from her. And she would be entirely without money. Even her parents were not likely to let her into their home after such a disgrace. She even doubted that she could live at Hull House because the scandal would keep away decent women—even poor women who needed help.

Although her mind was filled with romantic memories about Darrow, she promised herself she would never see him again. It was too dangerous. She knew he would charm her and captivate her again. If he did, she had no idea what foolish thing she would do.

Now that a week had passed, she felt trapped at home. She had stayed away from Hull House because she knew Darrow would come there to see her. But staying away was so painful. Her work there had given meaning to her days, and it was a place where she could enjoy human contact. With neither kindness nor a purpose in her life, she felt so lonely and adrift that she thought she'd die from the isolation.

Little James hadn't yet returned from school, and Isabelle felt she had to talk to someone. Impulsively she pulled the tapestry cord in her sitting room to ring for Helen. Helen had been even more unpleasant lately, and Isabelle didn't know if a decent conversation with her was possible. But she was the only person available in the house.

Downstairs Helen heard the bell and heaved an irritable sigh. *What now?* she wondered, and she pounded her feet heavily as she climbed the stairs. She certainly wished her mistress hadn't stopped going to that settlement house. With the missus away, she had very little to do but tidy up the upstairs bedrooms and sit in the kitchen with Cook and talk. For some reason Mrs. Woodruff hadn't been out of the house all week, and this annoyed Helen greatly.

When she got to the writing room, she found Isabelle looking out the window at the traffic on Michigan Avenue.

"Yes, ma'am," Helen said, standing in her most formal maid posture. Her back was arched, and her large buttocks stuck out behind her like a billowy cushion.

"Oh, there you are, Helen," Isabelle said smiling tentatively to test Helen's mood. "I'd like a cup of tea, please."

"As you wish, ma'am," said Helen.

As she was leaving the room, Isabelle asked tentatively, "How are you today, Helen?"

"Just running this household, ma'am." Helen folded her arms and looked at Isabelle. Her tone clearly said that she was too busy to be interrupted.

Helen had become impossible. Isabelle took a deep breath and matched her maid's curt tone. "Well, I would hope so, Helen. That is, after all, what my husband pays you for, is it not?"

Though Helen knew she had been asking for trouble with her attitude, Isabelle's comment griped her no end. "You wanted tea, ma'am?" she said, coldly but a bit more politely.

"Yes," Isabelle answered. "I'll take it in my room here."

"Here?" asked Helen. She made sure that her tone would make Mrs. Woodruff understand that in her opinion, this business of having afternoon tea upstairs should be reserved for days when a woman was ill or having her miseries.

"In my room," reaffirmed Isabelle.

"As you wish, ma'am," said Helen. She made a quick nod of her head and went downstairs. She was miffed that Isabelle had dared make that snotty comment about what her husband paid her for. Ha! If she only knew. Making beds and sweeping dust kitties out from under the furniture weren't the half of it.

When little James got home, Isabelle helped him with his lessons and, after an early supper together, put him to bed. As the evening grew dark, she felt so closed in that she didn't think she could stand it. A notion occurred to her that made her smile wryly to herself. She was miserably unhappy because of two men: one who didn't care about her and one who did. But this thought made her suddenly realize how wrong it was for her to give up her life for either one of them.

There were people who *needed* her, and they were at Hull House. It was also clear to her that she needed *them*.

This idea gave Isabelle a burst of determination. She quickly changed her dress and combed her hair and rang for Helen. Helen trudged up the stairs just as Isabelle was putting on her hat and cloak.

"I'm going to Hull House for a program tonight," she told Helen. "I will be requiring the carriage."

Helen let her mouth fall open in astonishment. "Why, it's evening," she said. "Bert'll have to hitch up the horses in the dark."

Isabelle looked at her levelly. "Then you'd better tell him to get busy," she said.

"As you wish, ma'am."

An hour later Phillip Woodward's elegantly lacquered carriage clattered down the dirty streets in the worst section of the city. As they passed the ugly tenements, Isabelle saw that the stoops were crowded with people sitting outside in the spring evening. Instead of the dread she had felt her first trip down here, she felt nothing short of elation. She was returning to Hull House.

Isabelle told the driver to wait outside with the carriage— it wasn't safe to leave it unguarded—and she walked to the porch and opened the front door. The Polish Club was meeting inside, and a party was in full swing. Barrel-shaped women and men were swigging coffee and eating. As she stepped into the hallway, Jane Addams saw her and came toward her.

"Isabelle," Jane said, looking at her closely, "I've been so worried. I do hope you haven't been ill."

"No," Isabelle said before she thought about how she was going to explain her absence. "Not really ill. But I missed you and the children."

"Well, we missed you, too. The children asked for you every day."

"Oh, my," said Isabelle, smiling. She was so pleased that she couldn't think of anything to say until she heard a voice behind her.

"The children aren't the only ones."

Isabelle turned and looked into the face of Clarence Darrow.

At the sight of him, her heart began to race, yet she felt despair at seeing him there. This was *her* place, not his. He had a life of his own apart from here, but she didn't, and she was afraid he was going to ruin it for her. All the same, when he grinned at her, she felt very pleased.

"Why, Mr. Darrow," she said, sounding calmer than she felt, "how nice to see you again." Isabelle turned to Miss Addams. "Jane, I met Mr. Darrow here one night when he gave a speech."

"Yes." Jane said. "I remember it well. You couldn't stand the sight of him."

"Well, that's true," said Isabelle, beginning to blush.

Miss Addams looked at Darrow, who was still grinning, and Isabelle, who was still nodding her head, and she realized that whatever it was these people had to say to each other would be better said if she was somewhere else.

"I have something to attend to," said Jane. "You'll excuse me, I'm sure." And she headed toward the second parlor, her head tilted awkwardly to one side.

Clarence stood there, smiling reproachfully at Isabelle. "You didn't answer my messages," he said.

"Clarence, no—no, I didn't. You promised you wouldn't try to see me."

"I had to," he said. "I missed you terribly. Isabelle, don't you want to see me?"

"No, I—Clarence, we can't—let's not talk about this now. Let's talk about something else."

"Fine," he said, smiling but not as much as before. He could see that Isabelle looked as if she had been under a strain, but God, he was happy to see her. "What would you like to talk about?" he asked.

"Well, what did you do today?" she said, glancing around the hallway, trying to appear casual.

"I came here to look for you. Before then I was in court."

"Were you in a trial?" Isabelle had never been to court, and the whole idea of it fascinated her. In the past week she had spent a fair amount of time imagining what Clarence would look like standing in front of a judge, arguing an important case.

"Yes, surely," he said.

"Oh? Were you successful?"

"Well," he said, grinning and smoothing back the lock of straight hair that always tended to fall in front of his eyes, "I must have made a good speech because the jury was in tears. Even the judge turned his face to the wall."

Isabelle heard the tease in his voice. "You're joking, aren't you, Clarence?"

"Of course I am," he said, taking her slender arm in his big, soft hand. "But I'm also telling you the truth."

Isabelle looked up into his eyes and felt herself melt in his warm smile. "Let's step out of this crowd," he said.

"I can't."

"You have to," he said."It's obvious that we have to talk. And this hallway is a terrible place to say honest things to each other."

She paused for a moment before she nodded, and when he walked across the hall, she followed him. He opened a door into an empty small parlor and waited there until she had stepped into the room. As he closed the door, he enfolded her in his big arms. Isabelle felt her heart race. Being this close to him was overwhelming. She felt soothed—the way a parched little plant might during a summer rain. In a moment she lifted her head to him, and he kissed her on the lips.

They stood there in the little room, holding each other, almost gasping from the joy of it. But the happiness Isabelle felt was mixed with stinging regret that this wonderful moment should never happen again. When she felt stronger, she pulled herself away and stepped back.

"You do know that this will destroy me if we allow it to continue, don't you?"

"Isabelle . . . destroy you?" He smiled before he saw how serious she was.

"I'm helpless around you, Clarence. I'm tied up in knots. I can't say no to you, so I have to stay away from you. But don't you see, it breaks my heart to stay away from *here*. This is the only place where I feel I belong. Don't you understand?"

"And I'm keeping you away?"

"Yes!" She whispered intensely, and tears were in her eyes now.

"And your 'virtue' is this important to you?"

"Clarence, don't you see? It has nothing to do with virtue. Where would I go if I were disgraced? I couldn't even come here."

"Oh, Isabelle," he said, and he held her in his arms again, only this time differently, this time like a friend who sympathized. "Oh, Isabelle," he repeated like a regretful chant. "I like you far too much to see you hurting this way."

He thought for a long moment before he continued. "Well, I won't hurt you any more than I already have. If this is what you want, I'll leave you alone, and I'll stay away from here. I promise. Even though that will hurt me a great deal."

Isabelle tried to smile. "You promised before."

"I was just being heroic. This time I'll try harder."

Isabelle nodded, but she felt sad. The nice sensation of being swept along in a rushing river had gone. Now she felt that she was being separated from her heart. It was a dreadful, numbing feeling. Clarence Darrow was going out of her life. She had asked him, and now he was going away.

"If you change your mind, Isabelle," he said softly, "all you have to do is let me know."

She turned away. There was really nothing else to say now that he had agreed to her request. She could return to her life at Hull House, and things would be the way they had been before their evening together had changed everything. But there was still so much to say. She wanted to tell him about her life. She wanted to amuse him and entertain him—shock him if she could. But she would never have a chance. There was nothing more to say, and that was the saddest thought of all.

"Which of us should leave the room first?" he asked.

"You." She didn't look at him. She knew she had to compose herself before she went outside where the party was going on.

Clarence turned and opened the door, the sounds of the party drifted in, and he left.

When the door closed and the room grew still again, Isabelle breathed deeply and wiped her eyes. She stood near the door until her hands had stopped shaking and her emotions had calmed. Then she went into the hallway.

"Oh, there you are," Jane said when Isabelle approached her.

"I must leave," said Isabelle. "My carriage is waiting. I really came because . . . I missed being here."

"Will we see you tomorrow?" Jane Addams looked at her earnestly. She had seen the tall lawyer leave, looking somber, and Isabelle had a look of deep sadness in her eyes, too. But now Isabelle smiled wistfully.

"Yes," she said. "You will see me tomorrow."

Forty-five minutes later, the driver eased the horses into the coach house and held out his big arm to help Isabelle down from the carriage.

"Sorry it's so dark, missus," Bert said. "I don't favor leaving the light burning in the carriage house while I'm away because

I'm always worried about setting a fire back here, near the horses. If you'll wait a minute, I'll light the lamp for you."

"I'm all right, Bert," she said. "By the way, thank you for harnessing the carriage on such short notice. It was very kind of you."

Bert smiled. Although he had complained mightily to Helen when she informed him of the request from "Miss High and Mighty," he had to admit that Mrs. Woodruff wasn't so bad. At least the lady knew how to show a little appreciation.

"You're welcome, ma'am," he said, opening the door to the backyard. "It's dark, ma'am. I'll help you to the back door."

Isabelle thanked him and touched his arm lightly. They walked carefully to the back of the house, using the illumination from the moon and the lights in the house to guide them.

"Do you suppose Mr. Woodruff is home?" she asked.

"Don't know, ma'am," he said. Bert coughed. He didn't figure the mister *was* home. As his driver he had often taken Mr. Woodruff to strange places at late hours. It didn't seem right to him, the things the mister did, but of course, it was none of his business.

"He *could* be home, though," Bert said. He didn't know how much Mrs. Woodruff knew about her husband's goings-on, and he didn't want to spill the beans, so he talked in circles. "Sometimes, if he has to . . . ah, work late and I'm not there with the carriage, sometimes he comes home in a hansom cab."

"I see," Isabelle said without thinking much about it.

They climbed the back stairs carefully and in silence. Bert took his key from his pocket and unlocked the back door. As the door opened, Isabelle stiffened. A strange sound was coming from one of the rooms. It sounded like a human voice, but it was different from anything she had ever heard before. It was deep and primitive—the sound of something raw and un-censored.

She grabbed Bert's arm. "What in God's name is that?" she whispered.

Bert listened for a moment before he recognized the sound. "Oh, Jesus, missus!" he said. "Don't pay no attention to that. You just hurry on up to bed."

She turned and searched his face. "Bert! What is it?"

The driver looked away and shook his head.

Isabelle listened again. This time she heard a woman laughing. This sound was odd, too, not at all the way a woman laughs when she's amused. It was almost angry and sinister. Then the male voice groaned again.

"It's coming from down there," she said, looking down the hallway.

Bert grabbed her arm and held it tightly. He hissed, "Missus, stay away from that room."

She was stunned by his behavior. "Bert! Let me go!"

"Missus, please," he said. Bert was torn. He didn't want to be rough with his employer's wife, but he couldn't let her see what was going on in Helen's room. He was scuffling, pulling on her arm to keep her back and trying not to hurt her.

"Bert," she whispered fiercely, "you let me go this instant!"

Isabelle wrenched her arm free. When she got to the door down the hall, she heard the groaning and the strange laughter again. Bert was behind her, urgently whispering in her ear. "Please, missus. Don't open the door."

It had not occurred to Isabelle to open the door, but now it did. After all, this was her home and something very strange was going on in it. As Bert reached out to grab her wrist, she jerked away and turned the knob. The door swung open.

The scene in that room was a sight Isabelle would never forget.

Across from her with his back to the door a man was standing nude. His arms were tied to the wooden cornices on top of Helen's armoire, and he was stretched tall. For a moment Isabelle didn't recognize him, but when he turned his head to the side, she realized with a horrifying jolt that it was Phillip. His thin, sinewy body was covered with angry red welts.

Helen was standing behind him, twirling a razor strop in her hand. She was wearing one of Isabelle's old robes. It was unfastened, and as she stepped forward to strike Phillip, the robe opened. Isabelle saw Helen's large, rippled thighs, her pendulous breasts and private hairs.

Isabelle screamed before she could stop herself. What were they doing? She had never seen or imagined anything like this. She heard herself scream, and once she had started, the sound seemed to be drawn from her without her will. She screamed and screamed as thoughts crowded in on her. In her house! Her husband and her maid! What ungodly things were going on?

Phillip heard screaming. What was happening? His arms

were bound, and he couldn't pull loose! With effort, he turned his head to see.

Jesus, it was his wife! It was his wife screaming. He pulled against the cords that bound his hands. "Stop it, Isabelle. Stop it," he shouted hoarsely. "Stop it and get out of here!"

Now Isabelle could finally speak words. "You monster! You disgusting monster. And you!" she yelled to Helen. "How dare you behave this way in my home!"

Bert was pulling on her arm, gently now to comfort her. "Come on, missus. A lady like you. You shouldn't be here. Come on, missus."

Isabelle stopped screaming, but she could not and would not be moved. She swayed forward. Her stomach was churning, and she bent over to vomit. When she had finished, she gave in to deep, luxuriant sobs. "This filth. In my home . . . in my own home."

"Come on, missus. Come on now." Bert felt dazed. This scene was strange even to him. But for the missus . . . why, this was an awful thing for her to see.

She was still hunched over when he put his arm around her to lead her away. She leaned against him and let the coachman direct her, She was so hurt, so bewildered that she was sobbing like a child.

In her house, this madness, in her home.

She was so weak she was almost unable to walk, but Bert helped her up the stairs, his arm around her shoulder, talking to her, giving her support. "Come on, missus. A lady like you don't understand such things. You'll be all right, missus. Just four more steps. Come on now."

Bert led her into her room and helped her sit back on the bed.

"Lie back, missus," he said. "Just lie back." He took his jacket off and put it over her and stood in the darkness with the light spilling in from the hallway. He took her hand in his big, rough palm and patted her, feeling strange to be here in the missus's bedroom, but giving her something to hold on to anyway.

"It's quite a jolt, missus. But it ain't no different from what's going on all over town. Believe me, they do this and worse downtown. Don't let it hurt you none. It's got nothing to do with you. You remember that. It's got nothing to do with you."

*   *   *

Phillip thrashed impatiently. "Untie me, you bitch! Hurry!" Helen was unknotting the rope, and when one of his arms was free, he swung it in a wild, dangerous arc. Helen dodged the blow. She was standing on a chair to reach the knots, and every time he lunged, she was afraid he would knock her down. The mood in which her dominance had excited him was over, and she felt exposed. She wished she could take a moment to close her robe.

"Stop pulling!" she said. "It slows me down."

Phillip glared at her as she untied him. As soon as he was free, he grabbed her forearm and yanked her off the chair.

"You bitch!" he hissed furiously. "You said she had gone out for the evening."

He held her arm tight and slapped her hard in the face. She tried to pull away from him, but when she couldn't, she made an attempt to return to the situation where she had been in charge. She tried to slap him.

"Don't you dare," Woodruff said as he hit her in her belly with his fist. When she doubled over, he swung his arm and hit her hard in the breasts.

"Ow, Jesus," she screamed. "Don't hit me no more."

He stared at her for a moment, disgusted by the rippled flesh that had so recently excited him. "Get out of here," he said. "Get out of this house now and don't come back."

Helen looked up at him, stunned. "No. That ain't fair."

His fury erupted fresh. "I said get out!" He wanted to strike her again. His hand itched to hit her until she screamed in pain. It was with great difficulty that he restrained himself.

"I don't have nowhere to go."

"I'll give you ten minutes to pack up," he said coldly. "No more."

Helen realized that nothing she could say would change his mind. She had to leave. She figured that even if he relented, Mrs. Woodruff would insist on it. "Surely you're not going to toss me out without no money," she said, whining. "Not after what we've meant to each other."

He made a disgusted sound in the back of his throat. *God, women are stupid,* he thought. Then he repeated her phrase contemptuously. "After what we've meant to each other!"

He pulled on his trousers and reached into one of the pockets. "Here," he said. "Here's fifty dollars. Take it and get out."

Helen reached greedily for the money. "That's all?" she said. "That ain't enough to get started again."

"That's your problem," he said coldly, opening the door to leave. "If I see you around here again, I'll have you arrested as a thief."

Phillip Woodruff left his maid's room and walked slowly to the front parlor. He didn't know what he could say to Isabelle to make this better. Nothing, he knew, would remove the memory of what she had seen. Not that he cared about how she felt—he didn't—but he had to keep her from doing something that would make his situation in Chicago even worse than it was now. Many of his bank's loans had gone bad. If word got out about this damned thing and some big depositor's wife forced a withdrawal of funds, the bank would collapse. He would lose everything he'd spent his life building.

A disturbing thought crossed his mind. He had threatened Isabelle with divorce only a few weeks ago. He himself had opened that subject. Unless he did something to stop her, Isabelle just might file against *him* first. A scandal like this, even in Chicago, would be sensational. If Isabelle described in a court of law what she had witnessed tonight, he would be censured and laughed at. Not so much for what he had done but because he had taken his desires *home*. He would be seen as a fool.

Well, the only thing to do now was to swallow his regrets and take charge again. He could not come to her apologetically. Best thing was to intimidate her—make sure she knew she'd better keep quiet about this. Although he felt uneasy about approaching her, he knew he'd better deal with her now. It wouldn't do to let her think about it all night and come up with some harebrained ideas.

Phillip climbed the stairs quietly. The door to Isabelle's room was open and Bert was standing, hunched over his wife's bed, talking to her.

"Leave my wife's room immediately." Phillip said forcefully.

Bert was surprised by Mr. Woodruff's commanding tone. He stood up and bobbed his head apologetically as if he had been caught in an impropriety. He suddenly felt frightened for the lady.

"Will you be all right, Mrs. Woodruff?" he said, turning back to her.

After a moment she answered him. "Yes, Bert. Thank you."

When Bert reached the top of the stairs, he stopped for a moment. He could hear Mr. Woodruff speaking. "All right, my dear. It's time we lay our cards on the table."

In the darkened bedroom Isabelle heard the arrogance in Phillip's voice. It was incredible! The shock she felt turned to ice inside her. She suddenly realized how much she hated him. Without bothering to answer him, she sat up and lit a lamp beside her bed. Then she looked at Phillip coldly. Her disgust and hatred made her feel strong.

The contempt on Isabelle's face alarmed Phillip. He had never seen her this way. Always before she had been anxious to please—at least anxious to avoid censure. Now she wasn't even trying to hide her anger. He realized he'd have to take a much firmer hand here.

"Isabelle, your situation here is very precarious," he said. "Very precarious indeed."

Isabelle continued to stare at him icily. She made no comment.

"If you dare repeat this or try to bring any action against me, I assure you I will deny everything. And as the man I will be believed. Should you attempt such a thing, I will divorce *you*—and you will go back to being nothing."

Isabelle watched Phillip's face closely in the lamplight. Not speaking gave her a chance to think and evaluate. She could feel that behind the strong words, he was frightened. She understood that if this got out, he'd be a laughingstock. But then Isabelle knew that people would laugh at her, too.

She also realized that he meant what he said. If she sued him and went public with the story, he would fight her with everything he had. She would wind up with nothing—not even her son.

All right, she thought, feeding on his unspoken fear. *All right. I will be smart this time. I will let him keep his nasty little secret quiet, and I will stay in this ugly marriage. That's the best solution for me and for my son. But from this day forward I will do whatever I want to do. And if Phillip ever threatens me again, I'll go directly to Bertha Palmer with this appalling story. Mrs. Palmer won't let him destroy me.*

Phillip was disconcerted at the way this encounter was going. His wife showed no signs of fear, nor was she telling him what she intended to do. He had expected her to be upset and cry. She would have been easy to dominate in that state, but she just kept staring at him coldly. It was unsettling.

"I'm sorry I had to be firm with you, my dear, but if you behave, we can go back to the way we've always been. That's the best course for everyone concerned."

Phillip looked at her for a few more moments and, getting no response, turned to leave. When he was closing the door behind him, he heard her say something, almost to herself. "No, Phillip. We will not go back to the way we've always been. You will live your life, and I shall certainly live mine."

Phillip glanced back at her, but she said nothing more. She was still staring straight ahead when he closed the door.

21

_____

THERE WAS NO QUESTION about it. Hannah's waist was growing. She didn't look pregnant exactly, but it seemed to her that every single day she got a little larger.

She was standing in her room in her petticoats. Her waist had been cinched in by a whalebone corset as tight as she could stand it, but even so, the dress refused to fasten. Vina had tried to button it, pulling the luxurious fabric as hard as she could. But it was no use. She just couldn't make the edges meet.

"I wore this a week ago!" Hannah said. "How could I have changed this much so fast?"

"That's the way it is when you got a baby inside of you," Vina answered. "It's not just you growin'. That baby growing, too."

"But, Vina, what am I going to do? I've got to get downstairs."

Hannah had every reason to be alarmed. Carrie Watson had been kind to her after the doctor refused to perform the abortion—kinder than any wayward girl could hope for, and Hannah knew how lucky she was. Any other sporting house in the city would have thrown her out until the pregnancy was over. The only thing Carrie had asked was that Hannah take care of customers until she started to show. Hannah knew she'd better not let her down.

"You just calm yourself, Miss Hannah," said Vina. "I'll see if I can't borry you a dress that's a little bigger."

Vina headed to the door; then she looked back. "Second thought, I'll have better luck if I offer *this* in exchange." She swooped Hannah's beautiful green dress off the bed and, before Hannah could argue, had taken it with her.

Vina walked down the third-floor hallway, figuring. Best thing was to find a big girl who had lost weight. That way she might be able to trade this nice new frock of Hannah's for something larger. Vina knew that *trading* one dress for another was a more viable proposition than asking to borrow one. The girls here placed a lot of importance on their gowns. They knew that expensive dresses helped them fetch higher prices for their services.

They were right about that, too, Vina thought. In this house everything was all show. The men who came here every night—they weren't poor men. They were rich! There was no reason why they couldn't get sex from their wives because those leisurely ladies still had strength left at the end of a day. So it must be that the rich men just wanted something more interesting.

Poor women, now that was a whole different story. A poor woman had to work! She had to carry water and scrub and cook all day. At the end of all that, a poor overworked woman was just too tired to let her man interfere with her. Vina knew because it had happened to her. She figured it was why Joe had bolted a few months after they moved up from Savannah.

When Vina and Joe had arrived in Chicago ten years before, he'd had a bad time getting work. It was a scary time, and Vina had no choice but to get a job cleaning and cooking for a big family. At night she was just too tired to let him bother her. Many's the time she'd wished Joe could drop in on someone else, do what he had to do, and then come on home. If Joe had just had an inexpensive whore, Vina figured he might still be with her.

After he had left her, Vina was so destroyed that she could not find a reason in her to leave her room. She stayed there for two whole days until her food ran out, and it was during that time that she developed her philosophy about whores. She came to believe that prostitutes did many a good deed for the hard-working woman. She thought that a good whore could keep a family together.

With these beliefs firmly in place, Vina took herself to the red-light district and knocked on the front door at Carrie Watson's and asked for a job. Carrie was so taken by Vina's kindly thoughts about prostitution that she hired her. It was an easy job. Vina was happy making the beds and being helpful to those who were preserving family life in Chicago.

Of course, Carrie Watson's place didn't cater to work-ingmen like Joe. This was a showplace for white men, a palace built just for sex. So it made sense that it didn't do for a girl to wear a dress that was ordinary. And Vina knew that getting someone to relinquish a cherished dress would be as tough as parting Lake Michigan. Her chances would be better if she could strike up a trade.

While Hannah was waiting for Vina to return with suitable clothing, she studied herself in the mirror. She was so pale she pinched her cheeks to give them color. She was happy to notice that they had filled out since she arrived here that cold, dreadful day months ago. The food here had helped, that was for sure. Then again, maybe carrying a child inside her had filled out her cheeks as well as her waist.

Hannah felt a familiar sense of grief flow through her. Lately, whenever she thought about the baby inside her, she thought of her mother. She could still remember how big her mother's body had looked when she was pregnant with Han-nah's sisters. But unlike her own, her mother's face had *not* filled out. Without enough food to eat, Mama's face had become gaunt and her neck stringy.

What a shame, Hannah thought. How sad that her mother—a good woman—had been cheated of the food and security that Hannah had found in a bad life. She missed her mother terribly. If Hannah had known that her dreams of riches would lead to this, she would never have gone downtown for the department store job. But how could she have known?

It wasn't that she minded prostituting all that much any-more. Now that Miss Watson was teaching her the business of running a house, Hannah could view prostitution as a means to an end. When a strange man touched her, instead of feeling cold and dead inside, she could simply redirect her thoughts to the wonderful life she'd have managing Miss Watson's property. She'd not let a man touch her *then*, she promised herself. Not unless she really loved him.

In the meantime, Hannah was learning how to run a business. It wasn't too complicated because everything was on a cash basis. But there was a lot of ordering to do: food, whiskey, champagne. Most often Carrie got her provisions at a cut rate because she made a point of knowing people and making sure they owed her plenty of favors.

Vina hurried back into the room, carrying a dress made of pale ivory taffeta. "This ought to do," she said. "Let's get it on quick."

"But it's soiled." Hannah was disappointed with the dress.

"Don't have time for that now," said Vina. "Miss Carrie sent word that your boyfriend's here. She wants you downstairs in a hurry."

"My boyfriend?"

"Mr. Cudahy. That old banker who likes you so much. Miss Carrie said he was askin' for you."

Hannah forgot her displeasure and quickly dressed. If Mr. Cudahy had asked for her, he must be partial to her. That would make it easy to tell him about her new arrangement with Carrie. Maybe he could help her buy property.

Hannah hurriedly combed her hair as Vina fastened the buttons. When she looked down at herself, the dress was practically hanging on her. "Vina!" she said. "I can't wear this. It's too loose."

"Just you hold your arms in tight against your body," Vina said, "and think pretty thoughts. That's more important than keeping that old man waiting. You make him wait too long he'll likely be dead by the time you get there."

When Hannah reached the bottom of the stairs, she ran into Carrie Watson in the hallway. "Where is he?" she asked.

"He's sitting in the Mikado Room, of course, looking at himself. Git on in there. That old man's never happier than when he can look at a pretty girl sitting beside him in the mirror."

Hannah walked down the hall into the Mikado Room. Sure enough, there he sat, staring across the room at himself.

"Mr. Cudahy," she said, "I'm delighted to see you again."

Old Mr. Cudahy turned to look at Hannah and smiled. He stood courteously and took her hand. As he drank in her pretty face with his eyes, he couldn't help noticing that something was different about her. She had filled out and become more confident of herself. It was attractive, of course, but he couldn't help missing the shy, insecure girl he had last seen. It was a pity, but in a place like this, it couldn't be helped.

"I bet you say you're delighted to everyone," he commented.

"Of course, I do," Hannah said, her green eyes sparkling. "But I really mean it with you."

Mr. Cudahy laughed. The girl *had* changed, but the change was charming.

"I ordered some champagne, my dear," he said, filling her glass. "I hope you'll enjoy some with me."

"Of course." She lifted the glass in a small salute to him and glanced across the room at her reflection. "Here's to you, my favorite friend."

He chuckled. "Oh, 'friend' is what I am, eh? Well, why not? I can certainly use one today." He lifted his glass and looked across the room at their reflection. "Here's to us. My favorite looking-glass couple."

Hannah took a tiny sip and studied him over her glass. He did look as if he needed a friend tonight. Perhaps there were more problems with his bank.

"My *dear* friend," she repeated. She impulsively leaned forward and laced her fingers between his. He smiled, enjoying being touched. He reflected that a month ago she would never have been so forward as to touch him.

"You seem downcast," she said. "What's wrong?"

"You won't believe it, but a damned pirate is trying to take one of my biggest depositors."

"A pirate? You mean another banker?"

"Yes, if you can call that ugly old dog Phillip Woodruff a banker. Can you imagine, going after a friend's customers?" He shook his head disapprovingly. "I've known that rogue for years. He's a damned dreadful man."

It seemed perfectly logical to her that even bankers would compete for business, but she clucked her tongue. "My, my. Why would he do such a thing?"

"Because he's got the unhealthiest bank in the city. You talk about bad loans! Phillip Woodruff has bit into many a bad apple in the last few years."

"Well, I'm sure he won't succeed in taking your customers from you," she said smoothly. "Who could compete with you?"

"Why, thank you, my dear." He smiled gratefully. Under the influence of this lovely girl, he could feel himself relax. "Tell me, what have you been up to lately?"

"Well," she said as if this were going to be a pleasant surprise for him, "I've been thinking a lot about what you taught me about the banking business."

"My, my, my." He frowned slightly. It bothered him that this girl would have given much thought to his complaining. He should have known better than share a confidence with a whore. "I would think a pretty girl like you would forget idle talk from an old man. You didn't discuss our conversation with anyone else, I trust."

"Why, no," Hannah said, smiling at him as she lied. "Of course, I didn't. But I do have an idea about all that bad property you've made loans on—the property you said you wanted to sell for less than its face value?"

"Oh? Did I say that?"

Hannah looked at him closely. Was it possible that she could have misunderstood? "Why, yes, I thought you did."

"Well, what about it?" he asked.

Hannah noticed that his voice had developed an edge of impatience. She was bothered by it but couldn't think of anything to do but push ahead.

"Mr. Cudahy, I have found a buyer for you."

The banker put his champagne glass down on the table. He narrowed his eyes and looked at Hannah closely. This was not the lighthearted evening he had hoped for. The girl wanted to discuss business! How absurd. Thomas Cudahy didn't like to mix business with pleasure—certainly not with a woman in a whorehouse. If she persisted in talking about the banking business, he would have to ask Carrie for someone else.

He sighed deeply. "All right now. What's all this about?"

"Mr. Cudahy," she said with excitement, "I know someone who has a great deal of cash. Someone who could buy some of those troublesome buildings—if the price were right."

"Ah, if the price were right."

Mr. Cudahy nodded and smiled to himself. The girl was so obvious. If she weren't so clearly a business novice, he would have been offended. "And who, may I ask, is this person?"

Hannah smiled broadly. "Carrie Watson."

Cudahy looked at the girl through flinty eyes. So she *had* discussed his predicament with someone else. How many others, he wondered, had heard about his banking problems? "I see," he said. "So Carrie Watson wants to get into the real estate business, does she?"

"Well, yes, she does," Hannah said. "But like I say, the price has to be right."

Cudahy laughed out loud in spite of himself. He was deciding rather quickly that he didn't like little Miss Hannah.

"That's too bad," he said with a cruel edge to his voice.

"Too bad?" said Hannah. She had assumed that the hardness in Mr. Cudahy's attitude was his demeanor when he did business. But it had rapidly grown worse. Now he almost seemed hostile.

"I can't sell property to a whore! Why, if word got out that a property was owned by a woman like that, she'd never be able to rent it out anyway. It would be tainted."

Hannah could almost see her dreams evaporating into the air. She felt numb.

"Tainted money, my dear," he repeated. "Upstanding people in the community wouldn't allow it. You can appreciate my position, I'm sure. If word got out that I had sold property to a whore, my reputation would suffer greatly. Then that dog, Phillip Woodruff, really would take my customers."

Hannah was stunned with disappointment. So it wouldn't work, after all. Mr. Cudahy wouldn't let her buy property because Carrie Watson's money was tainted.

Suddenly she realized that there was no reason for him to know who's money he was taking. If she hadn't told him, the property could have been purchased in a different name. Well, it was too late, now. If she wanted to pursue her scheme, she'd have to go to another banker and keep Carrie Watson's identity a secret.

Hannah looked at Mr. Cudahy's face. His mouth was set in a grim line. She could see that instead of wanting to help her, he resented her for bringing this up. Apparently he liked seeing her as a pretty girl who catered to *his* needs, not as a person with needs of her own.

Mr. Cudahy noticed the dismay in Hannah's face, and it softened him. There was no telling what silly plan she had had in mind. "You understand, my dear," he said, as if the matter were closed, "it would be different if your buyer were respectable. Respectability is very important in this city."

"Respectability," Hannah repeated, with a faraway look in her eyes. "Royalty would be considered respectable, would it not?"

"Royalty!" Mr. Cudahy chuckled. "Royalty can get by with anything in America these days."

Hannah had an idea, but it was clear that she should leave the subject and give Mr. Cudahy the glowing attention he expected. It wouldn't do for him to complain to Carrie.

"I can see that all this talk about business isn't fair to you," she said. "You came here to relax and drink champagne."

"Indeed," said Mr. Cudahy, softening toward her again. He raised his glass and smiled. This was more like it. This was the girl he had come to see.

Hannah reached forward and squeezed his hand again. "Let's toast each other and forget about that Mr. Woodruff and his awful bank." Hannah looked in his eyes for a moment before she smiled. "By the way, what *is* the name of his bank?"

The handwritten note to Phillip Woodruff was a private announcement that the Countess Alexandria Nichelovich was quietly visiting the United States.

"I am sure that a man of your quality can understand the necessity of discretion," the note said. "I do hope my presence will not attract the torrent of reporters who all too often have marred my visits abroad. I am, however, interested in investing in property in Chicago and I will send my secretary along to discuss such purchases."

The secretary, the note advised, would arrive at Woodruff's bank at 2:00 P.M.

Woodruff received the letter at ten o'clock in the morning. The troubling memory of his encounter with his wife vanished quickly. This was the opportunity he had been needing. With only four hours to prepare for this visit, he threw himself into frantic preparations. Every cleaning woman in the building was summoned to polish the wooden counters and brass fixtures until they were gleaming. With the maintenance staff occupied, he dismissed clerks to purchase flowers and a silver samovar from which he could serve tea.

When Hannah arrived at the First Commerce Bank, Woodruff was not sorry he had made such elaborate preparations. She was dressed as a secretary to royalty in a new daytime costume. Her black ankle-length skirt was topped with an expensive lace-trimmed blouse with leg-of-mutton sleeves. An expensive straw hat was perched on her head.

Phillip Woodruff gave the secretary every courtesy, even when she indicated that the countess, though fabulously wealthy, was extremely thrifty. The countess viewed property in America as outrageously overpriced, the secretary said, and would pay nothing more than one third the appraised value. Absolute confidentiality, of course, was also necessary.

To Phillip Woodruff, beleaguered with bad debts, less than a third was good enough—especially if his deals with this woman remained quiet. He supplied the secretary with a list of "available" property and wrote down the purchase price as well as the rents the property had commanded before the depression.

Hannah shook his hand and left. She knew that the idea of picking up valuable property at such a discount would appeal to Carrie's avaricious nature. She also knew that if she presented it correctly, Carrie would be amused to own property under the absurd name of Countess Alexandria Nichelovich.

22

THE DAY AFTER THE meeting in Chicago with George Pullman, Josef reported to work in the machine shop at 6:30 A.M. A few minutes later Karl Lubek stumbled in bleary-eyed and disheveled.

"Something's wrong," Lubek said under his breath. "Something's very wrong."

Josef picked up his wrench and began to work. He didn't even want to look at Lubek. Lubek reeked of whiskey and was in a foul mood. His dark, stringy hair was plastered against his head. Under his arms his shirt was already dark with sweat. "You hear what I said?" Lubek hissed. "Something's wrong."

Josef kept his eyes fixed on the underside of the car.

"There's guards outside," Lubek muttered. "And more just arrived on the train. Something's up."

Josef felt his mouth get dry. He worked hard on the wheel base under the Pullman car and tried not to think. Soldiers? What if the company had decided to punish the committee because of the meeting.

An hour later his foreman walked toward them with a belligerent look on his face.

"There's not enough work around here," Rufus McFarr said to Lubek. "Go home. You can check back next week."

"This mean I'm fired?" Lubek said.

"You got kraut in your ears, Lubek? I *said*, 'Check back next week.'"

Josef looked at his foreman and fear spread through his body. "You mean, me, too?" he asked.

The foreman checked his list. "Nope. I still got work for you. At least as long as you behave yourself."

Josef's fear dissolved to numbness. The foreman's message was clear: Don't make trouble. Make trouble, and you're out of a job.

Lubek swaggered over to the toolbox, a large wrench in his hand. "What're you gonna tell me when I come back next week, Mr. Foreman? You gonna tell me there's still no work?"

Lubek's face was glistening with sweat. His arm muscles were in tense knots.

"I might tell you I'm sick of your mouth," the foreman said. "Depends on how I feel."

"You big shit," said Lubek.

The foreman opened the toolbox and took out a hammer. "You got something else you want to say, Lubek? 'Cause I got something I'd like to *do*. I'll do it, too, unless you get outta here like I told you."

Lubek looked at the foreman and then at Josef. "See, kid?" he said arrogantly, as if proving he was right. "Didn't I tell you?"

Josef looked away. He was sorry for Lubek, but he was sick of the man's temper. At first, when he had thought he was fired, he was sure it was because he'd gone to the city with the committee. But now he felt relieved. Maybe Lubek was fired because he had a big mouth. Maybe it had nothing to do with the delegation. If so, it was Lubek's problem, not his. He was still safe.

Josef didn't want the foreman to think he was a friend of Lubek's, so he turned away without acknowledging him. Lubek slammed down his wrench and hissed at Josef, "You shit bag!" before he walked up the aisle. Other workers watched silently as Lubek walked by. They knew what had happened.

When Lubek reached the door, he turned back to the room. "Hey!" he shouted.

The workers looked up from their work. "They *fired* me. I went to the city to talk to Pullman—I went for *you*—and they fired me. How much are you gonna take before they fire you, too?"

The foreman ran up toward Lubek with the hammer raised to strike him. Lubek pushed open the door and went outside before the foreman reached him.

Josef could hear the workers at their machines whispering to one another. The word spread that Lubek had been fired for his part on the committee. But Josef was so fearful about being fired himself that he didn't want to believe it. After all, the men who ran this company were respectable men, and they had promised no reprisals. Lubek was a troublemaker. It had nothing to do with the committee—or with him.

Josef stayed at his machine until lunch. As the workers walked by on their way outside, one of them whispered, "Three others on the committee got fired. Pass it on."

Josef felt a stab of anxiety. "But if it's for being on the committee, why weren't we all fired?" he demanded.

"Who knows?" the informant shrugged. "Maybe they're trying to set an example, show us what they'll do to the rest of us if we have more meetings."

This explanation made enough sense that it destroyed the delicate peace of mind Josef had been maintaining. "Who else is fired?" he asked, hoping to hear that they were troublemakers, too.

"Petersen. Filipek. Gustafson."

Josef heard this information with a sinking heart. They were good men, but they had been on the committee.

"Meeting tonight at nine," whispered the informant. "Pass it on."

Josef spent the afternoon in a dark mood. He was convinced that his family was going to suffer again because of him. The guarded optimism he had felt about the committee meeting soured into despair. Being at the meeting had been a mistake, a pointless waste of time. He saw that it had been only a foolish attempt to help Corliss—perhaps even make her feel grateful to him. Why, in heaven's name, had he valued her welfare more than his own family's?

Anyway, what good had it done him? There was only scant evidence that the woman even liked him. The night they walked home from the union meeting, he had tried to kiss her, but she pushed him away.

Josef frowned as he thought about his foolishness. Hours later, as soon as it was dark, he walked reluctantly to Kensington to the union hall. He told himself that he didn't want to be there. The only reason he was going was to keep Lubek from inflaming them into a strike.

The meeting started late and went on until almost dawn. In addition to the men on the committee, other workers had come. The room was so full that men and women flowed out onto the porch and down the steps. Many of the workers felt the way Josef did: They were disillusioned and angry but grateful that they still had jobs. Others thought that the company had broken faith with the workers and they wanted to take a stand. They were worried that if they accepted the firings, the company would be encouraged to oppress them even more.

Josef had taken a seat early in the second row. He felt muddled as if the events going on around him had nothing to do with him. He didn't even bother to look around at the men who spoke. He let the angry words wash over him.

"The company violated its word."

"They're intent on destroying the union."

"If we submit to this, it's the beginning of the end of the union."

Josef didn't care about the union. He cared about putting bread on his family's table. To him, the union was good only if it guaranteed that. And now it appeared to him that the union would bring more misery to his family.

After hours of debate Lubek demanded a resolution to strike. Josef, still staring ahead, could not agree. During the vote he could not hold his hand in the air to signify yes.

After the vote the hall erupted into shouts.

"I cannot recommend a strike with four votes against it," Heathcoate said. When a loud groan rose in the room, he pleaded with them. "It's too dangerous. This vote represents only the opinion of the committee and the people here tonight. Go to work tomorrow. Talk to the people in the shops. We can't risk walking out without wide support."

The sun was rising when Josef went home to wash and eat before returning to work. He had not slept all night.

A short while after he took his place in the factory, a tall mechanic named Harris walked by and whispered, "A spy was at the meeting last night and reported the strike vote. The Chicago office sent a telegram to Middleton, ordering him to close the plant at noon. Pass it on."

Josef was dismayed. "How do you know this?"

"A Western Union messenger told one of the workers."

"God!"

"Listen, we can't let them lock us out. A lockout means the company's *punishing* us. We've got to strike. They've got to understand we won't be treated this way."

Word moved through the factory like locusts across a field. "Pass it on. . . . Pass it on. . . ."

The workers whispered instructions to each other. To protect individuals from reprisal, they all had to leave at the same time—every one of them. If only half of them walked out, the company could ignore the strike.

They would leave their posts when they heard the signal. Someone was to hammer a drumbeat on metal. That was the sign.

Josef swallowed hard, but he was no longer afraid. His confusion lifted like a troubling cloud. He felt cheated by the company, and his anger gave him clarity. The company had broken its word. It would fire him or lock him out no matter what he did. He would join the strike.

At ten-thirty, Josef heard a loud, rhythmic pounding from somewhere in the factory. Someone was hitting a hammer against metal.

Rap rap rap-rap-rap rap rap rap-rap-rap.

This was it! This was the signal.

Josef stopped working and looked around. He was so nervous he thought his heart would stop. Near him a man picked up a wrench and began to hit a pipe: Rap rap rap-rap-rap.

In another moment the sound was repeated somewhere else: Rap rap rap-rap-rap.

In moments the signal was being hammered out throughout the factory: RAP RAP RAP-RAP-RAP RAP RAP RAP-RAP-RAP.

The sound of rebellion was everywhere. Josef timidly banged his own wrench against a pipe under the car. Then he hit it harder. Lying there on his back, seeing nothing but the underbelly of the car, he felt released by the action, as if hitting the pipe were a strike against the evil he felt in the company.

It was eerie. No one said anything. No one shouted. There was just the rapping.

Then it stopped.

Gradually, one by one, the machines and power were turned off, and the familiar din of machinery and work became silent. As if one man, the workers near Josef opened their tool chests and laid down their tools.

Josef put his wrench away. Quickly and quietly the men were leaving their work stations and moving into the aisle. Now they were walking down the aisle, almost marching toward the door. It was thrilling! One, two, three, four, their feet shuffling against the floor in cadence.

Josef glanced at a worker walking by. For a moment the worker looked back. In the man's eyes Josef saw his own determination reflected back at him. Suddenly Josef felt so close to this stranger that he wanted to lock arms with him, but he did not because he saw the man's fear, too. In putting down their tools, they had declared themselves strikers.

One, two, three, four. The only sounds in the factory now were the shoes scuffling on the floor and the voice of a foreman shouting somewhere in the plant, "Stop. Stop. Think what you are doing! Stop! You're destroying yourselves!"

From what Josef could see, his entire section was walking out. This was good: The body shop was one of the largest units in Pullman.

The question on everyone's mind was how many from the other departments would join them. Would there be enough departments to make the strike successful—or only enough to result in being fired?

Josef fell into line in the aisle. Except for the shush-shush-shush of their walking, the plant was silent. They walked in step, disciplined and orderly, until they were outside and had reached Florence Boulevard. There they waited expectantly in front of the gates.

As more and more people came through the door, the crowd began to cheer. Workers were streaming from the factory. The street was filling with people!

Tears filled Josef's eyes. He was part of this! When he saw

Corliss and the girls from the embroidery department walk through the gates, he began to shout and cheer. Even the women had joined!

It was wonderful! Suddenly everyone was cheering and screaming and hugging each other. Every department had walked out!

Josef threw his arms around the workers near him. They had won! The strike was company-wide. Not one department had held back. Now the company would *have* to negotiate. With all of them out, the strike would soon be over, and they all could go back to work on terms that made sense.

An elderly man from the foundry, grit worn into his wrinkles, hugged Josef and slapped him on the back. "This is the greatest day for the workingman in American history," he cried. And Josef, who knew little of American history, hugged him and wept.

When Harry Elston, a newspaper reporter from the Chicago *Daily News*, arrived that afternoon, he was astonished. He had expected unruly mobs and fires. Instead, he found the workers outside, having a picnic. As he walked from group to group, interviewing the strikers, one of them offered him a cup of cool water. He was a tall kid with slanted eyes.

"I'm Josef Chernik," the young man said. "We're glad you're here. We don't have much food, but you're welcome to our water."

Harry Elston took off his plaid jacket and sat on the grass in the park. This was the strangest thing he had ever seen. The strikers were joyful. They seemed to think that in showing that the little guy had a right to a voice, they had done something wonderful for America.

Problem was, Elston wasn't sure his paper would print this story the way he saw it. Even papers as liberal as the *Daily News* were owned by wealthy people who equated striking with rebellion. Just a few weeks ago one of the other papers in town had suggested hanging bums and Communists from the nearest lamppost.

Victor Lawson, the esteemed publisher of the *Daily News*, was known for his freethinking, but Elston figured that when push came to shove, Lawson would side with his own upper class. He wished he could bring Lawson here to meet these workers.

"Share some bread with the newspaperman," the young striker said to another who had food.

Elson was touched by the simplicity and kindness of these people. What he wanted to write was that the strikers seemed like peaceful, honorable people who had been pushed into rebellion. He felt sympathetic to them, and for their sake he hoped they were right about one thing: They were convinced the strike would be over in a matter of days.

That was what Harry Elston wrote for his paper on May 11, 1894.

George Pullman carefully removed his wire glasses and put them on his desk. "So they've got pickets at the gates, have they?" he said to Wickes. "Well, I am disgusted."

Pullman got up from his chair and looked out the window at the Chicago street below. "I would have thought my talk would give those men some appreciation of the company's position," he said. "I will never understand why they voted that strike."

"I believe it may have been firing those men in the delegation, sir," said Wickes. "Our spy at the union meeting said that was what got them stirred up."

"So you said," said Pullman, irritated, "and I don't care to hear about it again. As far as I'm concerned, it was generous of the company not to fire the whole lot."

Wickes decided to keep his comments about the firings to himself. Before he went on, he paused for a moment, wondering if there was any point in trying to soften George Pullman toward the strikers. "Sir, I understand that they were also concerned about the lockout."

"The lockout was to teach them a lesson!" said Pullman. "Any fool would know that. After the factory had been closed a few days and they'd felt the sting of unemployment, I'd have opened it up again. Why, if they hadn't pushed the confrontation to this point, they'd be back at work now."

"Sir, they didn't know—"

"Don't be a fool, Wickes!" Pullman exploded. "Of course,

they did. Anyone with a lick of sense knows that a businessman doesn't keep his own factory closed for long. This whole thing is an expression of disloyalty and ingratitude."

"I received a telegram from the union again today," said Wickes. "The men would like to go back to work. They want to arbitrate."

"No, sir," Pullman said abruptly. "No, sir. I will not meet with those hooligans again. Meeting with them the first time was a ridiculous mistake I won't repeat. We have nothing to discuss."

The two men were interrupted by a timid knock at the door. It was typical of Pullman's secretary Bob Eagan to knock so softly that he could barely be heard.

"What is it, Eagan?" demanded Pullman angrily.

"Sir, there are a number . . ." Eagan's voice was muffled at the door.

"Will you open the door so I can hear you!" said Pullman.

Eagan opened the door and, red-faced, stepped into the room. "Sir, there are a number of reporters from the papers here. They want your comments on the strike."

"You tell them the strike is a wanton, ungrateful, and suicidal act directed at a generous and fair employer," said Pullman. "That is all I have to say."

"Yes, sir," said Eagan, quickly closing the door.

"There's one other thing, sir," said Wickes after Eagan had left. "In the last two days we have received new orders for cars. I'm afraid we won't be able to fill the orders if we can't end this thing quickly."

Pullman sat down and smiled grimly at his gray-haired official. "You remember that little strike the ironworkers staged at Christmastime in '86?"

"Yes, sir," responded Wickes.

"Do you remember how we handled it?" Before Wickes could answer, he continued. "We deliberately did nothing until the men's ability to resist had crumbled. What'd it take them . . . ten days before they came back, begging for work."

"Something like that," said Wickes.

"There are times when waiting is the very best thing to do. I tell you, Wickes, we're in a war here. The side that will win this war is the side that can hold out the longest. Let me assure you that this company's financial power surpasses that of the workers. We'll wait them out."

Pullman struck a safety match against the underside of his wooden desk. It popped loudly before it ignited. "I've got a few tricks up my sleeve," he said, lighting his cigar and looking out the window again. "By God, we'll break them if we have to starve them out."

Josef wheeled his bicycle outside onto the dirt yard in front of his family's shack. He looked up at the sky. It was overcast, but the air was warm and sultry and his clothes were sticking to him. He wished it would rain and cool things off.

He turned his bicycle upside down and spun the wheel listlessly. He was tired. Heathcoate had ordered the strikers to guard the factory because he didn't want vandalism to turn public opinion against them. Josef's guard duty was from 2:00 A.M. to 6:00 A.M. During the day, while others picketed the gates, there wasn't much for him to do except work on his bicycle.

He gazed at the wheels. It was ridiculous that someone couldn't figure out a way to put brakes on a bicycle. Even the Pullman sleeping car had brakes.

He looked up and saw his mother trudging back from the grocery store in the Pullman Arcade. For a moment he thought of slipping away before she arrived, but it was too late. She'd already seen him. He knew she'd start worrying him about the strike again. She must have asked three times a day for the last two weeks when it was going to be over.

As if he knew! The word from union headquarters was that the company was still refusing to meet. This thing could go on for a month. He didn't feel like sharing this kind of news with his family because he didn't want to frighten them. But it made him feel even more burdened to try to reassure them when he himself knew how bad things were.

When his mother came into the yard, her eyes were distracted with fear. Josef noticed that there were no groceries in her arms. "Josef," she said, "the shops in the arcade are refusing to give the workers credit."

"What? All the shops?" he asked.

"All." She began to wring her hands. "All of them."

This was bad. If everyone had stopped giving credit, the order must have come from Mr. Pullman himself. Without credit there was no way to buy food. The family was already out of money.

"What if it isn't over soon?" his mother said, fretting. She was imploring him as if the situation were something he could fix. "What are you going to do?"

God, I wish I knew, he thought. *I wish I could end it. I wish I could go back in time and undo everything that led to this point.*

"What are we going to do, Josef?" his mother pleaded. "We have no food."

The waiter at Darrow's favorite restaurant approached his table. "May I recommend the chicken tonight?" he said. "It's delicious."

Isabelle looked up at the waiter and smiled. "Thank you. Chicken will be fine," she said.

Isabelle had become accustomed to speaking first and ordering her own meals when she was with Darrow. Clarence squinted at his menu for a second before he folded it. "I'll just have the pot roast again, Jimmy," he said.

When the waiter had left them, Isabelle smiled at Darrow. He was sitting across the table from her, and he had a peculiarly uncomfortable expression on his face. "Do you always order the pot roast?" she asked.

"No, but I surely can't eat chicken," Darrow answered. "One year, when I was a kid, my folks went through a tough spell and forced me to eat my pet. It was a Rhode Island Red."

"Oh, Clarence," said Isabelle with affection. She started to laugh and then thought better of it. Darrow had a humorous manner and always gave the impression that unless he was very serious, he was joking. This time she realized he wasn't joking. "That must have been dreadful for you."

"Yep," he said, looking glum at the memory of that meal. "But at least we had a chicken to eat. In all likelihood those poor workers out in Pullman don't even have that."

"People all over town are forming a relief committee to gather money and food for the strikers," Isabelle said. "Mayor Hopkins has donated flour and potatoes and meat."

"It's about time. The papers said some poor chap out there had convulsions from hunger. Why doesn't that damn fool Pullman meet with those workers and settle this before someone dies? I hope Debs can make sure the strikers keep their heads and don't destroy property. Pullman would love to have a reason to put them in jail."

"If that happens," she said, "will you defend them in court?"

"I certainly will. I turned in my resignation at the North Western Railway Company today. I'm free, Isabelle. If I can afford to pay the rent on my flat and office, I can follow my conscience at last."

Isabelle studied him. It occurred to her that she had never before known a man who would give up money for his principles. *He's a good man*, she thought, *a good man whom many people think bad.* She stared down at her plate so he wouldn't see the tears in her eyes.

She looked so worried sitting there that Darrow misunderstood. "I'm sorry, dear," he said. "I didn't mean to distress you more than you already are." He discreetly averted his eyes to spare her feelings. "How are things at home?"

Isabelle shook her head to indicate that she did not want to pursue this topic. "We don't speak," she answered simply. "He comes and goes—the way he always has, I suppose. At least I know about it now and have taken some freedom for myself."

Darrow leaned forward and cleared his throat. "Isabelle," he began tentatively, "I don't know what awful things happened that night in your home, but I want you to understand that I accept as, ah, natural . . . any reluctance you may have to get near a man . . ."

Isabelle felt her face get hot at the mention of that night. She hadn't told Darrow what she had seen—the very idea of discussing it was unthinkable—but the day after her discovery she had surprised him by showing up in his law office. She told him that she had discovered something dreadful going on in her home and that she needed his friendship.

That day in his office Clarence had taken her hands in his and studied her face for signs of what had happened. He could see that whatever it was had changed her.

Now at the restaurant Isabelle finally looked back into his eyes. "It would be impossible for me to explain the jumble of emotions that torment me now, Clarence. I hate Phillip, yet my reason tells me to stay with him. I feel close to you, but something powerful in me keeps me away."

She hesitated before she continued. In the silence her eyes again filled with tears. "But, Clarence, of all those feelings . . . the one I feel most strongly is . . . how much I admire you. You're so good. . . ."

"Oh, my, my, Isabelle," he said softly, reaching across the table to take her hand. "I'm not good. It's just that I'm attracted to unpopular causes. The sight of injustice makes me angry."

Isabelle quickly wiped her tears away before she called the waiter over to the table. "May I change my order to pot roast?" she asked. "I don't want the sight of a chicken dinner to make my friend remember a previous injustice."

Buffalo Bill Cody unwillingly stepped into his wife's parlor. He'd just received yet another letter from the Bureau of Indian Affairs and realized he'd have to do something about that missing Indian.

Louisa was sitting in front of the window on the prickly horsehair-stuffed love seat. She was reading a book of some kind. Hell, he wouldn't be surprised if it were the Bible. It was just the kind of book she'd be likely to read, even though by now she surely knew it by heart. He knew she'd never so much as looked at a novel about him.

Louisa turned a page without looking up at him. He was happy to be getting out of the house, but it was clear she wasn't going to make this conversation easy.

"Lulu?" he said.

"What is it?"

"I'm going to Chicago, dear, and I just wanted to say good-bye."

She raised an eyebrow and looked up. "Chicago, eh?" she said. "I didn't know you were doing a show in Chicago this year."

Louisa knew darned well he wasn't doing a show in Chicago. And without a show she figured the only thing that would take him back there was some little floozy of an actress.

"I'm *not* doing a show there, my dear. The Indian bureau won't let me do any show at all—or least not one with Indians—

unless I can find that damned renegade and get him to go back to his reservation."

"Why didn't you handle that last fall when you closed the show?"

"It was an oversight, my dear. It was easy to let that one detail fall through the cracks."

"I suppose it *would* be easy for one whose mind has been pickled in whiskey."

"My dear . . ." he said, feeling anxious to get out of there.

"And just how do you plan to get to Chicago?"

"By train, of course. Without a show to do, there's little reason to take my horse to a city with paved streets."

"Yes, I suppose it would look odd," Louisa said, "seeing that old horse clatter up and down in front of all those houses of ill repute."

"Now, Louisa," he said reproachfully, "you don't think I'll find the Indian in a house of ill repute, do you?"

"No, Bill. But I am thinking that if I have to come in search of *you*, that's where I'll look first."

Hannah settled back in Phillip Woodruff's beautiful lacquered carriage. Mr. Woodruff himself wasn't showing her the property he had repossessed, because that task was beneath the president of the bank. Since Hannah had represented herself as only a secretary to the countess, it had been left to Charlie Miller, a clerk who could be counted on to keep this particular business quiet. Even so, the banker had shown her every courtesy, and Hannah enjoyed hearing the clerk answer her questions with a respectful "yes, ma'am" or "no, ma'am."

It had been more than a month since the Pullman strike had erupted, and the news worried Hannah for her family. She didn't know whether they were living in Pullman because it seemed unlikely that they would move away from the old neighborhood. But she did know that her brother had been working there before she had left home.

She was deeply worried about the family's welfare. Alhough she didn't dare show her face in the old neighborhood, she felt she had to do something. One day, dressed in her secretary's outfit, she had taken money to one of the collection centers for the strikers relief fund. "I want my aid to go to a particular family," she had said. But the response had been no, that would be impossible. All the strikers were needy, she was told. They all would appreciate her help.

Now she realized that the financial impact of the strike must have rippled out and further worsened other businesses, for the banker had seemed more anxious than ever to sell his repossessed property. Before she left the bank today, Woodruff emphasized, "All prices are negotiable." He demonstrated his willingness to haggle by slashing the price of one property in half with a stroke of his pen.

"The countess will be pleased," Hannah had said. "I will try to reach her. She is presently away, seeking other property."

The young clerk rapped on the ceiling, and the driver brought the horses to a stop. "This is one of the properties Mr. Woodruff thought you'd be interested in," the clerk said, opening the door for her.

Hannah looked at the factory in amazement. The name above the door was Illinois Rawhide. This was where her brother had worked before the plant had been closed.

"This building is for sale?" she asked.

"Yes, I'm afraid it closed months ago." The clerk nattered on, unaware of Hannah's concerns. "But really, you know, when this depression is over, it's a good business. Those leather pulleys are indispensable to many factories. If you just hold it till things pick up again, you could easily double your money."

Being so near the place where her brother had worked made her feel oddly close to him. Memories of them as children flooded back. She wanted to see the building where her brother had spent so many days.

As soon as the clerk unlocked the lock and pried open the rusty hasp, she stepped inside the deserted factory. For a few moments she looked around, trying to imagine where Josef had worked. She was drawn to a machine with large gears, and when she walked over to it, she fancied she could feel her brother's presence. It was almost as if the air were still charged with him. She closed her eyes and sighed to breathe him in. She realized that he had been unhappy in this dark, dreary place, sacrificing his youth for the family.

"Are you ill, miss?" the clerk finally asked.

She opened her eyes. "No," she answered. "I'm all right.

But I need more information about this building. I want to know when it closed and what happened to the people who worked here."

"I can easily get you the date on the closing, ma'am," said the clerk. "But as for the people who worked here, I doubt that anyone knows—or, for that matter, that anybody cares."

I *care*, thought Hannah, looking around her one last time. *What has happened to them?* she wondered. *Where are they now?*

Josef hoisted himself onto his bicycle and rode out of the little dirt yard. He wanted to get over to union headquarters fast. He'd just heard that the American Railway Union had voted unanimously to support the Pullman workers. Unless Pullman agreed to arbitrate within four days, *all* ARU members would boycott trains carrying Pullman cars.

This was wonderful news. It meant that switchmen would refuse to couple Pullman cars onto trains. It meant that if a train was pulling a Pullman car, engineers and brakemen would get off rather than operate it. Most important, the boycott was nationwide! This was clearly the breakthrough they needed to bring Pullman to the table for talks.

Josef was anxious to hear more about the rumors, but he watched his speed cautiously. He was still limping from the time he had hurt his leg showing off for Corliss, and he was afraid of having to stop quickly. As he coasted to a corner and slammed his foot onto the spinning front wheel, an idea occurred to him. If he could just get a small sheet of steel and bend it into a little drum, he could make it cover the axle of the rear wheel. Then, if he attached a lever to it, he could force the drum against the axle. It would work like a brake.

No, he thought. Metal on metal. That wouldn't work. Then he remembered: He still had some leather scraps he'd taken home from Illinois Rawhide. What if he could line the drum with leather? That way, instead of sparks, he'd get friction.

He needed steel, but he knew he could slip inside the factory and pick up some scrap—maybe even borrow some of his old tools. After all, he was guarding the factory at night!

23

_____

HORACE HILL SMASHED HIS cigar in an onyx ashtray. "Damnation!" he shouted. Hill owned the Chicago, Minneapolis and St. Paul Railway Company, and he was accustomed to expressing his emotions openly.

The other railway owners who were at this meeting of the General Managers' Association felt pretty much the way he did. The news that workers from their companies had joined the Pullman boycott was unsettling.

"You mean to tell me I can't roll my trains out of the yard if they're pulling Pullman cars?" Hill demanded.

"I'm afraid those are their terms," replied Edwin Walker.

Walker was the attorney for the General Managers' Association. The members of the association—the owners of twenty-four railroads that terminated in Chicago—heard the union's demands sourly.

"The union gave Pullman until June twenty-sixth to meet with the workers before they started their boycott," Walker said. "Regrettably he refused."

"Any damn fool who won't meet his employees halfway in these times is an ass!" grumbled Horace Hill. "Pullman's bullheadedness is leading us all to ruination."

The brotherhood of railway owners solemnly agreed. These were troubled times indeed.

"I say, if the stubborn fool led us into this," announced John Porterfield, another owner, "let's just stop pulling his cars."

"I don't think that's advisable," interrupted lawyer Walker. "We have a more serious problem here than Pullman. This strike has led to the solidification of a national union. It's the first time this kind of thing has ever happened, and the workers must think they have us over a barrel."

Another railroad owner grumbled. "Obviously they wouldn't make this kind of demand unless they thought they could get away with it."

"Well, by God, I don't like it," said Lyman Whitaker, owner of the Illinois Central. "I don't like anything that gives those hooligans more power."

"Yes, and we're talking about *unlimited* power," said lawyer Walker. "If they can create a national union that joins engineers and office workers with common laborers, it'll put them in charge. If they bring Pullman to his knees, what is to prevent them from destroying your company—or yours?"

The railway owners looked at one another fearfully. They had never in their wildest moments envisioned such a thing.

"That's why we have to take the bull by the horns," Walker continued. "If we handle their boycott properly, I think we can destroy Debs's union before it gets off the ground."

"Here, here," said the owners, forgetting their anger against George Pullman. They hit their toddy glasses on the table in approval. Brandy sloshed over the sides of the glasses onto the tooled leather that covered the meeting table. The dark stains spread across the leather like blood.

"There're a couple of things we should do," said Walker, posturing a serious attitude to show off his legal expertise. "First, we'll charge the strikers with conspiracy to stop interstate commerce."

"Well, by God, a conspiracy is exactly what it is!" announced Horace Hill.

"In the second place, all of you should attach Pullman cars to any trains that are carrying the mail."

"Wait a minute," said John Porterfield. "I thought we had decided to uncouple Pullman's cars and let him take his lumps."

"That's right," said Horace Hill. "In heaven's name, why should we take *extra* pains to attach Pullman's cars to our mail trains?"

Walker cleared his throat. His colleagues were going to love his next idea. "Because it will provoke the strikers into *obstructing* the U.S. mails," he said slowly. "And that's a federal crime."

Lyman Whitaker again rapped his toddy glass against the table. "Excellent idea! Excellent!" he shouted.

"I can get an injunction from the federal court prohibiting both the obstruction of the mails and interference with interstate commerce," continued Walker. "That will make their little boycott doubly illegal."

"You think you can get an injunction like that?" asked Horace Hill.

The other members of the General Managers' Association glanced at one another and chuckled. This Hill was certainly a dim-witted fellow.

"Of course, I can get it," replied the lawyer. "One of the founders of our association is at this very moment the attorney general of the United States."

"Oh, so he is," replied Hill. "So he is."

Richard Olney, the attorney general of the United States, knocked briefly before he entered President Cleveland's Oval Office.

"We have quite a serious situation brewing in Chicago, Mr. President," he said. "The strikers have gotten out of hand."

Grover Cleveland rubbed his tongue against the top of his mouth and pushed himself away from his desk. The artificial upper jaw his dentist had made from vulcanized rubber was hurting again. For a moment it worried him that maybe the cancer might be coming back. He remembered the day, just a little more than a year ago, when he had shuffled drowsily into the presidential bathroom to brush his teeth. It was an ordinary act, but it had led him to find a rough spot on his gum that had turned out to be cancer in his upper jaw.

Now, with his mouth hurting again, the last thing he needed was this overeager nincompoop pressing yet another unpleasant issue upon him.

"I've been trying to keep up with it, Richard," responded the President noncommittally. "Can you fill me in?"

"Yes, sir," answered the attorney general. "I have telegraphed an injunction to Eugene Debs, the head of the American Railway Union, forbidding interference with the mails or interstate commerce."

"Oh, the mails are involved in this, are they?"

"Indeed, they are, sir. Edwin Walker, the lawyer for the General Managers' Association, tells me that the strikers are specifically refusing to handle mail cars."

"How odd," said Cleveland. "You'd think they'd know not to do that sort of thing."

"These are a lawless group of men, sir," the attorney general replied.

"Indeed?"

"Oh, yes, sir. Only a couple of days ago they derailed a train. And the boycott is growing. Do you realize, sir, that there are fifty thousand men out across the country?"

"Hmm," said Cleveland. "I was given to understand that things were quite peaceful."

"Sir, I believe the situation is potentially dangerous. It is my recommendation that troops be sent from Fort Sheridan into Chicago to keep the peace."

"I hardly think that's necessary," answered Cleveland. "I'm sure Governor Altgeld will call out the militia if things go that far."

"I'm sure he *won't*," countered Olney. "Altgeld's sympathies tend toward the *unpopular* causes." Olney raised his eyebrows to remind the President that the governor had supported workers in the past. "Furthermore, sir, as bad as business has been for the last year, I don't think you can afford to let a *boycott* stifle such business as we still have."

"That is a troubling thought," agreed the President.

Cleveland recalled that only two months after he had taken office the year before, the country had been shaken by a financial panic. The policies of his predecessor, Benjamin Harrison, had depleted the U.S. Treasury of a hundred million dollars. That drain, combined with a farm depression and a business slump abroad, had left the nation in desperate condition. The country needed business, and it needed confidence in him.

That was why he had kept the operation for the cancer in his jaw such a guarded secret. That was why instead of going to a hospital, he had boarded a friend's yacht in New York Harbor and smuggled the team of surgeons on board to avoid arousing the suspicions of reporters. The country needed to believe that their President was strong—strong enough to head off this disaster.

The attorney general pressed his case. "Sir, Chicago is a powder keg of social disorder. The city is home to an enormous population of foreign anarchists. Put them together with the shiftless adventurers who moved there for the fair, why, it's hard to imagine a more dangerous place for a strike."

President Cleveland leaned his corpulent frame back into his chair thoughtfully. When he had been silent for a few moments, Olney continued. "Allow me to call up the troops, sir," he pleaded. "You cannot afford to let violence spread throughout the country."

"Are there troops enough on the ready?" the President asked.

Attorney General Richard Olney smiled to himself. The President's question indicated that he had just handed over his authority. "Perhaps not," replied Olney. "I'll instruct the deputization of additional U.S. marshals in case we need them."

G. G. Mattingly pushed open the swinging doors to Alderman Hinky Dink Kenna's saloon and looked around. It was just past noon, and the bar was crowded with the usual swarm of drifters and loiterers who came there for Hinky Dink's free lunch.

Mattingly was a tall, robust man, and his square face was set off by a handsome black handlebar mustache. He exuded power and determination. Mattingly stepped to the bar and banged a silver dollar on the counter. Although he was an executive with the Illinois Central Railway Company, he had been directed by lawyer Edwin Walker to deputize U.S. marshals.

"Bartender," he bawled loudly so as to get everyone's attention, "I'm going to buy every brave man in the joint a drink."

His announcement was greeted with chortles of approval. Men who had been sprawled at the tables abruptly pushed back their chairs and stood up to hear what this well-dressed stranger had to say.

"Boys," said G. G. Mattingly to the attentive crowd, "how'd you like to be deputized as U.S. marshals? You can shoot yourself some strikers and do your country a favor at the same time."

"What's in it fer us?" yelled a man at the end of the bar. He was so filthy that his blue jacket appeared black.

"A dollar a day and as much as you can drink at this here bar," said Mattingly, winking at the bartender. "We'll deputize you and issue you a gun."

A murmur of astonishment went through the crowd. To men who had spent much of their lives avoiding the law, the offer of money as well as guns by a representative of the government was an unexpected boon indeed.

"If you really mean for us to shoot them strikers," asked the filthy man, spitting a quantity of tobacco juice through his dark teeth, "then I reckon you'll keep us out of jail when we do."

G. G. Mattingly smiled expansively. "Boys, as long as you make it look lawful, you can bag yourself a boxcar full."

"Hey, Chernik! Come out here. Quick. We need you."

Mama heard the voice outside calling her son. She opened the door a crack and looked out. It was that tall worker Lubek. The ugly, dirty one. He was standing with five or six others.

She slammed the door and tried to block it. "Don't go," she begged her son. "It's that bad man. Whatever he wants of you, don't do it!"

Josef shook his head. "You want the strike to be over, don't you, Mama? You want the workers to win?"

"But what can you do—"

"I have to support the union," he said. "It's our only hope."

When she reluctantly stepped out of his way, Josef went outside. "What is it?" he asked Lubek. "What's going on?"

"The railroad companies are trying to break the boycott. They're attaching Pullman cars to the trains and running them out of the yards. We need every able man to keep those cars from leaving the yard."

"But I thought the boycott was going well."

"It was. Now it looks like the bastards want to fight."

Josef knew how much Lubek loved a fight. But if that was all this was about, he didn't want to get involved. On the other hand, if the railway companies were breaking the boycott, it was his duty to support the workers.

He questioned Lubek cautiously. "Where is this happening?"

"The Rock Island yard in Blue Island."

"But that's ten miles away. The commuter trains aren't running."

"So we'll walk. If we hurry, I figure we can be there in less than two hours." Lubek saw Josef's hesitation. "Come on, Chernik!" he said gruffly. "We need you."

Josef hesitated. "Debs said no violence."

Lubek laughed bitterly. "And look what that's done for us. The railroads want to destroy us, and our glorious union leader wants us to starve while he waits for talks to begin."

Suddenly Lubek flared with anger. He had known this guy Chernik for several years and had never known him to stand up for the union. During normal times that soft-handed approach wasn't all that damaging, but now—now they were at war!

"I shoulda known," he said low and mean. "Ain't it just like you people to stay at home when we need every man?"

The men with Lubek stared at Josef, and their expressions changed very subtly. They saw a man who was afraid to fight. Josef understood the look in their eyes.

"I'm no coward," he said. "I'll go."

"You mean to tell me that federal soldiers have been called out against the citizens of this state because strikers have assembled at Blue Island?"

Clarence Darrow repeated Debs's news with agitation. He pushed himself away from his desk and began pacing. Eugene Debs was sitting quite still in Darrow's big wing chair. He was trying to hold on to his composure in order to think through a strategy. "I cannot imagine Governor Altgeld asking the federal government to send troops," said Darrow.

"The governor didn't," answered Debs. "The orders came direct from the President of the United States."

Darrow was perplexed. "What possible grounds could he have for this, I wonder?"

Debs shook his head remorsefully "It hardly matters. Edwin Walker, the lawyer for the railway owners, has just been named attorney general for Chicago. With a man from the railroad companies in charge, the legality of the matter isn't even an issue."

Darrow shook his head in disgust. "My God! How could they appoint someone so clearly biased at a time like this?"

"Apparently someone has gotten to the President and has made it appear that the strikers are endangering the peace."

Debs had such a sense of insurmountable odds that he was forced to his feet. "First they hit us with that injunction against obstructing the mails and I respond by offering special crews to work the mail trains—with only the stipulation that Pullman cars not be attached. Then they continue to create ways to put us in violation."

"The strikers have every right to gather at the railyards," declared Darrow.

Debs paced angrily. His restraint was cracking.

"Yes, but it's given the government the excuse to bring in troops. Dammit, Clarence, it's obvious what their real intention is. President Cleveland wants to get those trains rolling again no matter what. When that happens, we'll have no way of forcing Pullman to the bargaining table.

"And then we'll lose," he said, looking hopelessly at Darrow. "We'll lose everything."

When Josef arrived at suburban railway yard in Blue Island, he felt parched and exhausted. The months of inadequate food had taken its toll on his stamina, and the ten-mile walk had been hard. He had to sit down on the curb before he could go on.

Just ahead, hundreds of men were milling about the yard. A handful of railroad executives in shirts with starched collars were attempting to couple a Pullman car onto a train. As soon as they got it attached, they ran back and shouted to the engineer to go on, go on.

The workers saw what they were doing and a loud cry went up. "Stop it! Stop the train."

A swarm of workers ran in front of the train to block it from moving. Other strikers ran to the Pullman car itself. After a few minutes of struggle they managed to detach it. A cheer went up.

The railroad executives, their white shirts now soiled and oily, had run up the steps to the railway office when the crowd surged. As they rubbed the soot off their hands, they angrily watched the scene below. When they saw that the car had been disconnected, they went inside to telegraph for help.

Seeing the men retreat, the crowd cheered. Josef felt reassured because the workers had not harmed the men from the company. He finally pulled himself to his feet and, moving like a sleepwalker, walked deeper into the crowd. He saw Lubek and the group of men from Pullman drinking water from a barrel with a tin dipper. He was so thirsty he felt dizzy. He staggered toward them for a drink.

Josef raised the dipper to his lips. Someone jostled him, and the water splashed on his chest. His shirt stuck to his skin, but it felt cool and good. For a while the workers moved about, chatting aimlessly. Then the sound of a voice shouting above the din was heard. The crowd became quiet. Someone was addressing them.

Josef spotted a man in uniform standing on the locomotive. The man identified himself as a federal marshal and ordered the strikers to disperse in the name of the U.S. government. The men grumbled among themselves, but they didn't know what to do. They weren't destroying property. Why should they leave?

While they were still deliberating, a striker climbed to the top of a boxcar. He was drenched in sweat as if he had been running. "Chicago," he yelled. "They're running trains out of Chicago! Right now!"

The indecision about obeying the marshal was immediately forgotten. "Chicago!" Lubek shouted. "Every man go to Chicago."

The workers fled into the streets outside the yard and swarmed north. It was another ten-mile walk, maybe more.

There was no food. No more water.

Josef was exhausted from the effort of the journey. Trudging heavily, he forced himself to put one foot in front of the other. For a while the sky glowed red with the setting sun. Now, as the evening deepened, gaslights began to illuminate the windows of buildings. He stumbled onto the open plaza of

Grand Boulevard and leaned against a train that had been stopped in front of a Chicago post office.

Thousands of people were around him, scurrying back and forth, shrieking news and instructions to one another. After a while there was an uproar at the northern edge of the crowd. A train was approaching. Workers thronged forward to meet it, but Josef was too tired to join them. He stayed where he was, resting on the boarding steps of the abandoned train. From this distance he could see the top of the locomotive over the heads of the crowd as it chuffed toward them.

The smokestack belched a blast of gray smoke. For a few seconds, fog blew across the men in the yard, shielding them from view. Even from this distance Josef could hear the commands being shouted.

"Company A! Company C! On the double! On the double!" Josef could hear men leaping from the train onto the street. Then he heard the staccato sound of drummers rattling their sticks on the rims of their drums.

In a few seconds he heard a metered cadence. Then he saw the soldiers. They were marching, their feet hitting the cobblestones in unison, and they were coming in his direction. They were coming toward him! The crowd parted and pushed back against one another.

On the soldiers came, and Josef could see the red, white, and blue of the American flag floating above them. He stood up in slow alarm. What was happening here? This was the American flag! His flag.

Suddenly he felt uneasy. He had felt so right about what he was doing. But now he wondered. Was he actually taking action against the United States of America? Against his own adopted country?

Then the throng began to stampede away from the soldiers and the flag. They were shouting in fear. Now Josef heard the blast of another train heading toward him from the opposite direction. As the strikers surged by him, he could hear them yelling: "A Blue Island train. It's pulling a Pullman car."

Hundreds of people were running toward the new train. Lubek ran by a short distance away. "Let's go," he yelled to Josef. He swung his big arm in the direction of the train. "Let's go!"

Josef was afraid. He began to run along the tracks, following Lubek toward the oncoming train. The train slowed to a crawl. The crowd was growing, gathering around the locomotive. A man up in the locomotive shouted,"Get off the tracks or I'll run you down!" He gave the engine some steam, and smoke belched from the stack. The train jerked forward. People on the tracks screamed and fell backward over one another to get away.

"Scum!" yelled Lubek at the engineer, shaking his fists. Then he shouted to the men around him. "Come on."

Lubek led the crowd to a nearby boxcar. It was ahead of the engine on an adjacent strip of rail. They began shoving the boxcar.

"Now," Lubek cried. *"Now. Now."* Josef found a place to put his hands on the boxcar and began to push, too. It started to rock. Back and forth. Back. And forth. Josef was afraid it would fall back and crush him. He pushed against the car with all his might. After an agonizing moment, it toppled in the other direction and fell across the tracks in front of the moving train. The locomotive hissed and screeched and stopped. Josef could feel the hot cinders from the smokestack on his cheeks.

The men around Josef sent up a cheer. The train was blocked. Lubek was excited by his victory. "Come on," he yelled. "Come on." Josef watched Lubek lead the men toward another freight car. Now that car rocked back and forth. He saw it topple over.

It was growing dark. Suddenly an orange flare glowed, and a flame leaped into the air. A freight car had been set on fire. The orange flames twisted and danced higher. People around Josef stopped running and watched.

The fire licked its shimmering red heat into the warm night sky. It was both thrilling and frightening. It proclaimed the workers' solidarity in their resistance, but it also announced that a line had been crossed.

Suddenly someone behind Josef shoved him hard. People were lunging against him. There were screams all around. The troops and newly deputized marshals were charging into the crowd, hitting people with their guns. Josef stumbled forward trying to regain his footing. He glanced backward. For an instant he saw the reflection of the fire glint on a bayonet. A man near him screamed and fell. Josef regained his balance. Another man ran by with blood streaming from his shoulder.

Josef wanted to get away from the crowd, but in the darkness he didn't know which way to go. People packed around him, running, pushing, shoving. He ran with the mob.

Ahead of him he heard a loud sound. Gunfire.

Someone is shooting, he thought. *Someone is shooting at us.*

Josef heard a woman in front of him scream. She fell to the pavement.

The crowd behind Josef kept coming. He fell and was crushed onto the woman. Something warm and wet was oozing from her back. He could feel it on his hands. People continued to race over him, stepping on him as they ran. He put one of his hands on the back of his head to protect himself.

It seemed like a long time before the crowd had passed. He was dazed. He could feel something sticky covering his arm and shoulder. Its moist, earthy smell nauseated him. He began to stagger forward blindly. He felt driven to get away from there.

In the darkness, a burning torch floated before him. Suddenly it was thrust in his face. His head snapped back to avoid it. Angry voices surrounded him. Arms grabbed him and hurled him to the ground. A crowd of tough, dirty men were standing above him. "Look at that," one of them said. "He's covered with blood."

"So what?" said another. "You know them strikers ain't human."

Josef could feel the weight of their boots as they kicked him. Pains shot across his back and groin. Lights flashed before his eyes as something struck his head.

"Git him in the boxcar," one of them said. "Git him in there, and hold him. By jingo, we're going to scrape some scum off the streets tonight."

Strong hands yanked him from the pavement. "Get up," the voices said. "Get him over here." Josef stumbled as he was pushed up the steps into the boxcar. His knee slammed into the metal and he cried out.

"Get in there," a voice said, and strong arms sent him sprawling across the floor of the dark car.

Two men followed him inside. One of them carried a torch.

"Be careful you hold that torch down low," said one. "Don't want to set the car on fire."

"Why not?" said the other. "Instead of lockin' him up, I have a notion to roast this striker."

The man thrust the torch in Josef's face. Josef fell back against the wall to get as far away as he could. The man enjoyed this game. He shoved the torch so close Josef could smell his hair burning. The other deputy got bored.

"Come on," he said. "Let's go outside. It's too hot in here."

As the deputies climbed down the stairs to leave, the deputy with the torch looked back at his captive.

"We're gonna git you, striker," he said. "You just wait."

24

_____

A SEARING PAIN BURNED through Josef's unconsciousness, something hurting so much that his brain first recorded it as a jagged yellow flash. Then he became aware of a tearing sensation near his ankle. He heard himself scream and opened his eyes to a murky darkness.

In the dim light he saw a man lean over him and flap his hands toward the floor in a flailing motion. "Get away!" the man shouted. "Get away." Then Josef felt the weight of a furry body move across his foot, heard claws scratch across the iron floor. "Damned rats," the man said to Josef. "One of 'em get you?"

Josef wondered what the man was saying. Gradually, one perception at a time, he became aware that he was lying on a floor somewhere. It was cold and hard. His hands became aware of rough patches of rust and bolts on the iron floor.

"Hey, bud," said the man standing over him in the darkness, "you awake?"

"Where am I?" Josef asked.

"Why, mister, you're in jail. They threw you in here last night. I kinda thought your head might of got hit when you fell. They weren't any too gentle."

Josef tried to sit up, but the lights in his head flashed again. The pain in his leg was throbbing.

"Come on, friend," said the man. "Rats'll bite you if you lay on the floor. You'd best get up on a bench."

The man leaned over and slipped his hands under Josef's shoulders. "Come on, buddy. Let me help you."

Josef let the man pull him to his feet. When his knees were almost straight, his vision blurred, and he felt himself sinking back into unconsciousness.

"Oh, jeez," the man gasped, struggling with his weight. "Come on, Jasper, help me. He's going out again."

Another set of arms surrounded Josef's waist, and he felt himself half dragged, half carried. He was gently turned, and his legs lifted onto a bench. He felt a tentative touch near the ache in his calf.

"Criminy, look at that bite!" the man said. "I'd best ask the guard for some vitriol. Don't move, friend, I'll git you something for it."

The pains in Josef's head and leg pulsed insistently. With effort he opened his eyes to watch the activity of the man who was taking care of him. The room was indirectly illuminated by a pale yellow light somewhere down the hall. Even in that dim light Josef could see the outline of the thick steel bars.

The man banged a tin cup on the bars, and the noise slammed against Josef's head like a blow. He closed his eyes.

"Hey, Charlie," the man called. "We got another rat bite here. Can you bring us the vitriol?"

"You yelling about something again, Lacey?" a voice responded.

"It's these rats," the man named Lacey answered. "They're bigger than my dog."

The jailer appeared at the door. "Who got bit?"

"The new guy."

"That striker?"

Josef could tell from the jailer's tone that he was less friendly to union men than to the prisoner he was talking to.

"Come on," said Lacey. "He's hurt bad."

"Maybe not bad enough," said the jailer. "Christ, can you imagine walking away from a job! I bet you that poor bastard Duane would of been happy to have this guy's job."

The jailer paused, apparently in recollection. "Jeez," he finally breathed, "did you ever see a man want to die so much?"

The memory of the man who had recently shared his cell cast a pall on Lacey's mood. "He couldn't stand being alive in here, while his wife and little girls were out there starving," Lacey said. "Poor Duane. He knew he was going to be in jail for a long time for stealing that money. He just couldn't stand thinking about his kids suffering."

"I know," the guard sighed. "But to beat his head on the goddamn wall like that . . . Jeez."

Both men stared silently at the bloodstains still on the wall. Finally Lacey interrupted their sorrowful thoughts. "Come on, Charlie," he said, wheedling at the guard. "Give us the vitriol. This guy's young, and he's hurtin' bad."

The jailer eyed Lacey appraisingly before he walked off down the hall. Lacey returned to Josef and patted his arm. "He'll get the medicine for you, friend," he said. "He ain't a bad guy. You'll see."

In a few moments Josef heard a key working in the lock. The jailer handed the bottle of vitriol to Lacey. Two policemen stepped into the cell behind him. Josef was still lying on the bench, following the scene with his eyes.

"Josef Chernik in here?" one of the police asked.

Josef cleared his throat and licked his lips to moisten them. "Yes, sir. That's me."

"OK, Chernik. You're wanted upstairs."

Josef tried to sit up, but a stab of pain jolted through his head.

"I said upstairs, Chernik. Now."

"He's sick," said Lacey. "He's real bad. I better put some of this vitriol on his bite."

The guards watched while Lacey opened the bottle and dabbed at Josef's leg. When the chemical seeped into the wound, it seemed to set the hole in his leg on fire. Josef exhaled a sharp cry.

"Burns like hell," agreed Lacey. "But it's the best thing to keep from getting blood poisoning."

While Josef was still writhing on the bench, one of the police pulled him to his feet. "You think that hurts, buddy, you ain't seen nothing yet."

Josef swayed, and the policeman drew Josef's arm high over his shoulder. "Come on, Coot," he said to the other guard. "Give me a hand."

With his arms stretched wide across the shoulders of the two police, Josef was dragged up a long stretch of stairs and taken into a room on the floor above. The unaccustomed light from the window assaulted his eyes, and the pain in his head throbbed again. He slumped into a chair and didn't open his eyes until he heard footsteps at the door.

A short man in a high, crisp collar was standing in the doorway. Behind him, leaning angularly against the door, a tall lanky man in a rumpled brown suit peered over his shoulder. They both stared at him for a few seconds without speaking. Then the short man walked deliberately to the window and pulled down the shade. For a few seconds Josef was in twilight again. The tall man ambled to the table, pulled a safety match from his pocket, and touched the sulfurous-smelling flame to a kerosene lamp.

The short man looked at the policemen who had dragged Josef upstairs. "Git outta here," he said abruptly.

When the policemen had gone, the tall man took a pencil and paper from his pocket and slapped them on the table. He spun a chair around and lifted his long leg to straddle it. "You Josef Chernik?" he asked.

Josef squinted at the man; the kerosene light was beside his face. "Yes."

"I'm Detective Wheeler. You're in a good deal of trouble, son," he said. "You better tell us what happened."

"You mean, last night?"

"Sure do."

"I don't know. People were running everywhere, and I fell. When I got up, some men threw me in a train car."

"Was that before or after you shot the woman?"

A flicker of panic crossed Josef's mind. Until now he had assumed that he had been jailed for being a striker. "Shoot a woman? I didn't shoot anybody!"

The shorter man abruptly put his knuckles on the table and leaned into the light. His face glowed yellow in the kerosene flame. "Chernik, I'm putting you on notice right here and now that we are not going to put up with your lies! You can make this as hard on yourself as you want, but we know you shot an innocent bystander last night and we want to know why."

"But . . . I didn't! I don't even have a gun!"

"That's not what the deputy said that saw you shoot it."

"What!" Josef's chest felt so tight, he had trouble breathing.

The short man bristled and took off his collar. He seemed furious. "Big Wheel," he said to the tall detective, "why don't we just throw this scum down the stairs? I think the ride might improve his memory."

The tall detective spoke to the short man under his breath. "I don't think the chief will be too happy if we kill our prime suspect."

The short man ignored this comment and walked around the table and yanked Josef to his feet. He shoved Josef against the wall and hit him in the abdomen. Josef fell forward, gasping for breath. He remembered the long flight of stairs and opened his eyes in terror.

"Wait," he said. "Wait, please. I want to explain. There is some mistake."

The man shoved Josef back into his chair. "You talk to him, Wheeler," he said to the tall man. "He makes me want to puke."

Wheeler pulled a broom straw from his shirt pocket and stuck it between two of his front teeth. He dangled his elbows over the top of the chair and leaned forward conspiratorily. "Don't make Sylvestra mad," he said, indicating his partner with a jerk of his head. "When he's mad, he gets hot as a cheap pistol."

The tall detective named Wheeler eyed him thoughtfully. "I keep looking at you 'cause I know I seen you somewhere before. You ever been arrested?"

"No."

"Even the name means something to me. Chernik." The detective drew out the sound of the name. "Chernik. Hmm. I don't never forget names, you know. Never."

"Get on with it," grumbled Detective Sylvestra.

"No. It'll drive me crazy." Wheeler kept staring at Josef. Suddenly he looked relieved. "Now I remember! Hell, that woulda bothered me all day unless I'd got it. It was at the Buffalo Bill show! Didn't you win a prize?"

Josef stared dumbly at the detective. He sensed danger and felt paralyzed. He didn't know what to say.

"Yeah, you're the one, all right." Wheeler turned to the short detective. "Hell, I *knew* I'd seen him somewhere. This guy plugged a bull's eye from a hundred paces."

The short detective turned to Josef sharply. "Is that right?" he demanded. "You won a shooting contest?"

Josef looked from one detective to the other. He was frightened that the shooting contest would incriminate him in some way.

"Hey, if you did, you might as well admit it. There's no crime in it, is there? Anyway, we can find out as easy as that." Detective Wheeler snapped his fingers. "It'd be in the records."

Josef's mind raced. The records! Of course, someone must have written his name down somewhere. If he denied winning the contest and they found out about it, they might think he was lying to conceal something. His denial would make him appear guilty. Josef watched intently as the large detective shrugged his shoulders and looked at the other. He felt a compelling urge to make this detective like him and believe him.

"Yes, I won the shooting contest," he said. "But I didn't shoot anybody last night."

The two detectives quickly glanced at each other. The tall detective leaned forward and smiled. "That's good," he said. "It's good to tell the truth. Tell me"—he winked—"where'd you learn to shoot a gun like that?"

Wheeler and Sylvestra stepped outside the interrogation room. They had been working on Josef for four hours, but the suspect had continued to plead his innocence in the shooting.

"I say, let's beat the hell outta him," said Sylvestra.

"You already did," said Wheeler. "It won't do no good."

"The hell it won't."

"Nah. He *wants* to talk—keeps telling us how he walked downtown with the strikers. He wants to tell me what he knows. He just doesn't seem to know anything about the shooting. Anyway, he's hurt pretty bad. If we damage him much more, he might not make it."

"Chief Brennan ain't going to like it."

Detectives Wheeler and Sylvestra called a guard to watch the interrogation room while they strolled down the hall to

Chief Brennan's office. When they arrived, the door was open. The chief was chewing out a man dressed in an expensive suit.

"I don't like it, Mattingly. The men you hired to protect the railroad's property stole tons of stuff. Jesus, you put badges on men that were nothing better than riffraff! There's even talk that one of them fired into the crowd. If that's why the woman was killed, the press is going to rip you to shreds."

"Chief," said G. G. Mattingly placatingly. He spread his hands to explain. "You can't expect men under fire by a mob to keep a loaded gun in their pocket, can you?"

"Maybe not. But an innocent woman was shot, and I don't think her family or the press is going to take kindly to an explanation like that."

Detective Wheeler banged his fist on the door. "Excuse me, Chief."

Chief Brennan turned and presented a sour face to Detective Wheeler. Lately Wheeler's work had been disappointing. After months of sleuthing in the city's brothels, Wheeler's investigation of the whore killer had turned up nothing—not even a description of the suspect. The chief had taken him off that case and assigned him to handle some of the police activity the riots had created. Right now the chief figured that Wheeler's interruption was strictly unnecessary.

"What is it, Wheeler?" he asked severely.

"Thought you'd want to know this. One of the strikers we arrested—a kid named Chernik—is a sharpshooter. I remember seeing him at the Buffalo Bill show. He won first prize. Shot out the center of the target at a hundred paces."

The chief took a moment to digest this new information. "Think he had something to do with the shooting?"

Wheeler hesitated for a second. He didn't really think Chernik had shot the woman, but he was suddenly reluctant to say so. It was obvious that the chief was still annoyed with him, was maybe getting ready to fire him. Plus the chief needed a suspect. The fact that federal troops had been called out made the police department look unprepared and incompetent. In response to the chief's question, Wheeler waffled. "Can't tell yet," he said.

For G. G. Mattingly, this moment offered a rare opportunity. "Why, I heard about him! A real troublemaker. He's your suspect, Chief. I'll ask around and see if any of the boys remember seeing him do it. Get a newspaper artist to draw me a sketch."

Within minutes the detectives led Josef from the interrogation room to the front desk. "Book him," said Detective Sylvestra to the sergeant sitting there.

"What's the charge?" asked the sergeant, unconcerned.

"Murder in the first degree," answered the detective.

Josef gasped as if he had been hit again in the stomach. Panic rose in him, and his heart started to pound so hard he was sure everyone in the room could hear it. Even so, in some odd way this devastating trouble, so long dreaded in Russia, had a feeling of familiarity—like a dream that recurs during illness. Without realizing it, Josef had always felt guilty. Now it seemed that he was finally being charged for a crime he simply didn't remember committing.

Even in the dim light downstairs Josef could see that the man being led into his cell was Eugene Debs. He had no idea how many days had passed since he'd been there.

Night was not discernibly different from day down here, and even though the ghastly images in his dreams were even more terrifying than his waking fears, he was drawn to the opiate of sleep. He nodded off in the middle of conversations, and even when he was scratching welts from the prison lice, he could hardly keep his eyes open. When he was alert enough to wonder about his state of mind, it occurred to him that he might be delirious or in the grip of a fever of some kind.

"Hey, Lacey," the jailer called into the cell. "Got you another striker since you like 'em so much." Lacey waved away the jailer's teasing comment. "Be nice to him now," the jailer persisted. "This one's the big guy."

Lacey couldn't resist being friendly to the new inmate, especially now that his curiosity was piqued. He hobbled forward to greet him. "You'd best sit on a bench," Lacey announced to Debs, "and keep your feet offa the floor."

Debs looked around him and remained standing. Four prisoners were lolling about on benches against the iron walls. Lacey continued to introduce the new inmate to the cell. "This boy here," he said, indicating Josef, "he's a striker, too."

Debs stepped over to the bench and looked down at Josef. "Are you with the ARU, son?" he asked quietly.

"Yes, sir." Josef was so groggy he could barely push the words past his teeth. "From Pullman."

"I'm Eugene Debs."

"Yes, sir. I know," said Josef, trying to stop the shiver that suddenly made his teeth chatter. Finally, when he was able, Josef gingerly pushed himself up on the bench. "Mr. Debs, sir?"

"Yes."

The desperation and fatigue Josef had been silently enduring rushed to the surface. In the presence of this friendly, powerful man, tears welled up in Josef's eyes and ran down his cheeks. His voice broke, and his chest heaved with sobs. When Josef thought he had finally finished, more tears sprang up to replace the ones he'd wiped away. There seemed to be a river inside him, an endless deluge of sorrow. Debs watched quietly. He waited until the boy had recovered before they began to talk.

An hour or more passed. Doors were opened; men were shoved up and down the corridor and locked in cells. Occasional moans and shouts echoed against the iron walls. Finally the jailer appeared at the gate again with a tall, sturdily built man.

"Got your mouthpiece here, Debs," the jailer said, turning the key in the door.

"Hello, Clarence," said Debs.

"Hello, Eugene," said Darrow. "I just arranged to get you out on bail. Let's get out of here."

"Get your money back. I don't want this damned state to be one more cent richer because of me. I'm not leaving."

"Gene, for heaven's sake!" said Darrow impatiently. "We have a lot to talk about."

"We can talk in here," said Debs. "As long as they're locking up innocent strikers, I don't feel right leaving."

Darrow squared his shoulders impatiently and remained at the open door. Everything in his being made him feel revolted at the notion of being trapped in a jail cell.

"Oh, come on in, Clarence," Debs said. "It won't kill you to sit on this bench with me. Just be sure to keep your feet off the floor."

Darrow hesitated at the door before he stepped into the

cell. "Keep an ear open for me," he said to the jailer. "When I'm ready to get out of here, I don't want to have to wait."

Darrow walked carefully in the dim light, feeling his way with his foot until he reached the bench. He sat down and patted Debs's shoulder with his big hand. "How are you, Gene?" he asked quietly.

After a short pause Debs answered. "I'm sad, Clarence. More than anything, I feel sad."

"The troops are riding shotgun on the trains. They're getting the trains back on schedule," Darrow said.

Debs shook his head with dismay. "The troops have destroyed our boycott, Clarence. They've killed the union."

For a few moments, silence hung in the cell. Darrow had bad news for Debs and dreaded breaking it to him. In the gloom, the men in the cell listened intently.

"Eugene, they're holding you accountable for the destruction of property and for conspiracy in disobeying a court injunction against obstructing the mails."

Debs laughed bitterly. "Ah, yes. Of course. Obstructing the mails. You do remember, Clarence, that I offered special crews for the mail trains to make sure they would not be slowed down? Of course, no one from the railways ever *responded* to my offer, but I meant the offer nonetheless."

"The charges against you are ridiculous," Darrow agreed. "Gene, I'll do everything I can to get you free of these charges. I want you to know that."

Despite his quiet voice, Darrow's barely suppressed rage filled the cell. "Come on, Gene," he said. "I can't stand seeing you locked up like this. Let me get you out of here."

"I'll think about it," Debs answered. "But in the meantime, there's another urgent situation in here."

"What is it?"

"This boy here is a striker"—Debs nodded in the direction of Josef—"and from what he's been telling me, I think they're going to pin a murder on him. I would consider it a great personal favor if you represented him, too."

Darrow sighed. Debs obviously didn't understand the extent to which he himself was in trouble. Darrow knew that he had enough to do just to keep Debs out of prison for the rest of his life. He had no desire to take on the problems of other

strikers—strikers who, by finally responding with violence to
the traps set by the deputies and police, were responsible for
Debs's being in jail.

Darrow wanted no part of this. But even in the dim light
Darrow could see in his client's pale face that he had shifted his
concern for all the union workers to this young man. And
Darrow knew that Eugene Debs would do whatever had to be
done to protect this forlorn-looking man who was lying on a
bench shivering.

"If this is really how you want me to spend my time, Gene,
that's what I will do."

25

_____

CARRIE WATSON FINALLY LOOKED up from the sheaf of papers on her desk and slipped her tiny reading glasses off her nose. She studied Hannah thoughtfully. "So, according to this banker's figuring, I can buy myself more than a million dollars' worth of property for just under two hundred thousand dollars cash? Is that what you're telling me?"

Hannah answered carefully. "That's what Mr. Woodruff says."

"Can we believe him?"

"I think so, Carrie," Hannah answered. "I got the home addresses of a couple of the owners he had foreclosed on, and I took the carriage around to visit them. They seem to hate Woodruff for what he did to them, but they did agree that the value he told us was correct. That leads me to believe—"

"Yep," Carrie interrupted. "The rest is probably close to right, too."

Hannah's enthusiasm for launching Carrie Watson as a property owner had, over the weeks, grown into something akin to an obsession. Day and night she thought of little else. She had personally visited more than twenty properties offered by Woodruff and had narrowed them down to thirteen. By reading the information he had provided for the "countess" and asking keen questions of Woodruff's bank clerk, she had picked up some good ways to evaluate how sound a business might be when normal times returned. The clerk had also taught her to look at an existing structure with an eye to whether it could be adapted for other manufacturing.

All this checking and rechecking were not merely the result of a desire to learn and execute a new business. It offered her the more compelling motive of springing free from the unwanted personal attentions of Carrie's customers. But now, after all her single-minded determination, she was afraid the plan would fail.

What if Carrie was unable to sell the property later on and lost her money? Whether it actually ruined her or not, Hannah knew she would no longer be welcome here. Even though it had been months since Hannah had been cold and hungry, she knew that her own situation was basically unchanged. She was still an unmarried pregnant woman, and she needed Carrie's support to survive.

"Carrie," Hannah said, anxious to remove the gloss she had placed on the investments, "I do want you to understand that you're not going to get rich with this for a while. Worse yet, if the depression doesn't end, you might even be stuck with those buildings."

"Oh, it'll be over sooner or later," said Carrie. "I seen panics come, and I seen them go. Somehow they always do manage to come to an end. You know, it always did make me envious to see other people cash in after a bad spell. Why, I've seen the stupidest men in this city make fortunes just 'cause they knew when to buy and could afford to wait until things were in the pink again."

"Can you really wait, Carrie?" asked Hannah. "Can you really afford to hold those buildings?"

"I expect so. I got a good business here, Hannah, and it don't seem to be affected by a depression the way others are. It has long been my observation that a man troubled by decreased revenues is no less inclined to splurge on his recreation than he is when his pockets are jingling. There's just something about a woman's thighs that seems to squeeze away a man's concerns about his bank account."

Hannah smiled. Over the past few months she had come to appreciate Carrie's wit.

Carrie faced Hannah directly. "Frankly, the depression isn't the worst of my concerns. The thing that worries me is that I'll be plunkin' down two hundred thousand dollars on properties deeded to a Countess Alexandria Nichelovich."

"But that's so the bank will sell to you. Surely you remember that Mr. Cudahy said that he wouldn't sell to you because your money is tainted."

"I remember, I remember," said Carrie. "But still, it puts me in a bad position. As I see it, Hannah, you're the only one Woodruff has seen. What's to keep you from skipping off with that property? Claiming that it's yours?"

Hannah knew that if there was ever a time to confront Carrie calmly and directly, this was it. In the beginning, when she first arrived here, she had been so intimidated by her madam's forcefulness that she could hardly talk to her without blushing and stumbling for the right words. But in the last few weeks, working with Carrie in her office had helped her overcome much of that intimidation. She took a deep breath and looked deep into Carrie's eyes.

"Whatever assurances you want, I will give you."

"How about signing a paper stating that I am the real owner and that you have simply been acting for me? Would you do that?"

"Of course, I would." Hannah was surprised. "Carrie, surely you realize that I wouldn't cheat you. You took me in when I was dying, and you have saved my life since then."

Carrie could see Hannah's sincerity, and it made her feel somewhat reassured. But as Hannah continued to talk, Carrie could sense that the girl was about to get sentimental. That kind of thing always embarrassed Carrie, because deep inside, she was afraid that the expression of sincere feelings would make her cry herself.

"Oh, well, now, Hannah," she said to stop the declaration of appreciation she knew was coming, "you worked right along. You pretty much paid for yourself."

But Hannah was not to be stopped. "Carrie, do you realize that my own family would have turned me out?"

"Oh, I expect so," answered Carrie, casting an eye toward Hannah's very full figure. "Most families would—given your circumstances."

"You did what my family would never have done. You took me in." Hannah awkwardly pushed herself up from the chair and walked over to the window. "I don't deny that there were nights—more nights than I can even remember—when I missed my family so much I wanted to die."

As Carrie had feared, she felt herself swept along in Hannah's emotion. For the first time in months she began to miss her own mother. "I've lived through it myself," she agreed mournfully. "My mother wouldn't never understand any of this. The life of a prostitute is a lonely one."

"Carrie, all those nights when I cried for my family, I didn't realize it, but I had found one here. Why, you've been a mother to me!"

Carrie and Hannah gazed at each other. They felt so close that tears glistened in their eyes. Carrie shook her head in embarrassment.

"Carrie," said Hannah softly, "you are my family."

Carrie sat quietly for a few moments. She knew that what the girl had said was partly to prove that she wouldn't cheat her. Even so, it had given her a tender feeling. Carrie herself had arrived as a young girl alone in this bad city. She had built her life so entirely on her own that she was still pretty much cut off from every other living soul. The idea of being a family to this earnest young girl here, why, this was wonderful! It was nice to think of Hannah this way, as part of a family.

While Carrie was digesting these feelings—questioning them, evaluating them, savoring them—she had an idea. It might be an idea she would regret later, but at the moment it seemed right.

"Hannah," she said, "we haven't discussed how you're going to get paid for acquiring and handling the business of those properties, but I want to deal with it now. How about I pay you the same way I pay the other girls here?"

Hannah looked confused. In the house Carrie collected the girls' earnings and paid them half of what they brought in. The girls, in exchange, got their room and board and the prestige of working at the city's finest. But she wondered what that method had to do with the real estate investments.

"Here's the deal," Carrie said, pushing herself ahead so that if she later changed her mind, it would be too late. "I put up the money—just like I did for this house here. And you put in your time and effort—like the girls do here. Now the problem is, with this business, it's hard to know what your time and finagling are worth because we don't know how things are going to turn out. So why don't I just pay you, oh, say twenty-five dollars a week, which ain't much I know, compared to what you was earnin' upstairs on your back?"

Hannah thought for a moment. The girls in the establishment often earned as much as fifty dollars in a single night, but that was by prostituting. This was a legitimate business. Anyway, compared with the four dollars a week she had earned at Marshall Field's, twenty-five dollars was a handsome sum.

Carrie saw Hannah's hesitation and misunderstood. She figured her silence was a rejection of the offer. "Oh, heck, Hannah, I have to keep your pay small because right now your investments ain't bringing in anything! But what I figure is when I get around to sellin' the property, I'll give you half of the profits."

"Half?" said Hannah wonderingly. If those businesses would indeed bring the eight hundred thousand dollars' profit that she had been told, then she, Hannah Chernik, would be a rich woman. Rich beyond her wildest dreams.

Carrie corrected herself quickly. "A third. A third," she said, her eyes suddenly glinting a hard light. "But there is a catch. To make sure you work as hard as everybody else does around here, I want you to share in my risk."

"I don't understand," said Hannah.

"What I mean is, if you buy a property that's no darn good and I lose money on it, why, then, you'll have to cover a third of the loss. That's fair, Hannah. And it'll keep you from pissing away my money."

This notion stopped Hannah. Pay a third of an expensive property? "But, Carrie," said Hannah, "I don't *have* any money."

"Well, if what you been telling me is true, Hannah," said Carrie, "one of these days we're both gonna have lots of it."

Hannah left Carrie's office feeling breathlessly light. The closeness she had shared with Carrie and the promise of riches had put her in the brightest mood she could remember. She felt too good to go back upstairs and sit in her room alone. She craved company. When she passed the back dining room, she decided to go inside.

A number of the girls were sitting around the table, smoking cigarettes and reading the papers. Some were eating their late-afternoon meal before the customers showed up for the night. A few of the girls glanced up at her, but no one really spoke. Except for Marie, Hannah had kept herself apart from Carrie's girls.

As she entered the room, Hannah heard Nellie Trace, a pretty brunette, arguing with two girls over an item in the paper.

"It says here he's cunning and sly," said one, pointing to a newspaper. "A real mean character."

"You can't believe everything you read," said Nellie. "Anyway, the paper says he's got Clarence Darrow as his lawyer. If he was so bad, would Darrow work for him?"

"So I suppose you know more than the police?" said one of the girls.

"I suppose any fool would know more than the police!" said Nellie.

Hannah glanced in their direction, and what she saw stunned her. A sketch of a young man looked out at her from the front page of the paper. Though the eyes were a little too far apart and a little too slanted, the resemblance was unmistakable. It was her brother.

Above his picture a headline read: ANARCHIST SHOOTS BY-STANDER. Under the headline, a smaller caption: "A Tell-tale History of Sharpshooting."

Hannah reached out to steady herself, her good mood swept away by the assault of the news. Nellie looked away from her argument.

"What's the matter?" she said. "You sick or something?"

Hannah clung to the table and closed her eyes. Memories of her brother came flooding back: Josef running past her to get away from the police in Svislovich, the hushed terror when his young friend was taken away by the police, the family's fearful departure in the middle of the night.

After all this, could Josef have finally shot someone? No, she thought. That was something he could never have done.

Not after all this. Hannah was filled with an excruciating sense of wasted effort. All the running and suffering. And now this.

For just a moment Hannah felt that her dress had become terribly tight. It seemed to be pressing in on her chest so hard that she couldn't get her breath. She gasped loudly for air just before the dizziness started and the light behind her eyelids faded into darkness.

"Catch her," she heard someone call out before her fingers let go of the table and her knees gave way. "She's gonna faint."

26

ISABELLE DIDNT SEE CLARENCE Darrow often these days. A polite dinner in a simple restaurant now and then was about all. But tonight at Hull House, while she was helping Jane in the parlor downstairs with a party for the neighborhood youngsters, Darrow was upstairs lecturing on Walt Whitman. Isabelle had stayed later than she had meant to, hoping to have a few moments alone with him, but it seemed he hadn't yet finished his speech. She finally gave up hope of seeing him and was at the door, saying good-bye to Jane Addams, when he clumped noisily down the stairs.

"Guess I'm through tonight, too, Janie," he announced from the middle of the stairs. "My lecture on Whitman led quite naturally to a discussion on free love. I hope I didn't shock your guests too much."

Jane Addams pursed her lips. "If your evening wasn't tinged with shock value, Clarence, I can't imagine that it would have been very interesting for you."

"Well, that certainly is true, Janie," he said. "You seem to understand me quite well."

"At any rate," Jane said, "I'm glad you're here. Isabelle was

307

just getting ready to walk downtown so she could catch a hansom cab. She actually thinks she can protect herself with a pair of knitting needles! Go with her, Clarence, and see that she's safe."

"My pleasure," said Darrow, and he offered Isabelle his arm as they walked down the front steps.

"Why are you walking, Isabelle?" Darrow asked after a few steps. "That pretty carriage you used to bring down here was the envy of the neighborhood."

"Oh, Clarence, I have no desire to make the people around here feel envious. Life is too hard here to flaunt wealth. I think it makes people feel even more miserable when they can see what they're missing."

Darrow looked at Isabelle and smiled. "You've changed, Isabelle. My, how you've changed."

Isabelle recognized Darrow's approval, and it warmed her. She *had* changed. There had been a time when Isabelle thought the main joy of owning something was showing it off to people who didn't have it themselves. What a cruel vanity, she thought, recalling her earlier values.

Since she had started working at Hull House a year ago, so much had changed for her. Even Isabelle's clothes had become less ostentatious. These days she left her fragile silk dresses in the armoire at home. A simple cotton blouse over a black skirt was much more practical for the work here. She had even given up wearing corsets because they were too restrictive for a day of lifting and carrying small children. She had come to discover that she enjoyed the sensation of letting her body and breasts move without restraint beneath her clothing.

"But, Isabelle," Darrow continued as an afterthought, "surely your husband could provide you with a less showy carriage. This is a very dangerous area for a woman to walk in." He emphasized his point by kicking a pile of refuse on the sidewalk. "Those knitting needles Janie mentioned won't give you a lot of protection."

"I'll be all right, Clarence," she said. "Frankly, using my husband's driver and carriage revealed to him more about my whereabouts than I care for him to know."

Darrow clucked his tongue. "Why, Isabelle," he chided with mock seriousness, "what could you possibly be doing that you wouldn't want him to know about?"

Something in his tone annoyed Isabelle. While it was true that she valued respectability, the idea that she was not even *capable* of indiscretion suddenly struck her as a terrible condescension. Surely she didn't appear so tame and bland that he couldn't imagine her being a little bad. Was that why he had stopped pursuing her?

"Well, Clarence, there are a good many things in my life that you don't have the slightest inkling about," she said, trying to pique his interest. "Why, even my involvement with Hull House has made trouble for Phillip. After Jane and I went to George Pullman's office to ask him to arbitrate with the strikers, he sent Phillip a telegram telling him to keep his wife at home."

"That old fool!" Darrow shook his head angrily. The more he learned about Pullman, the more he hated that old tyrant. "Did Phillip actually threaten to keep you at home?"

"He did before I laughed at him for it. Can you imagine such an idea—in this day and age!"

Isabelle hoped that her comment would impress Darrow with the notion that although not a "new woman," she was quite up-to-date. She wanted to surprise Darrow with some as yet unrecognized qualities that he might find fascinating.

"Phillip makes as many demands as he thinks he can these days," she continued, "though since that awful night his power over me has diminished considerably."

Darrow walked on a few moments without speaking. He let Isabelle's reference to that undisclosed night hang in the night air.

"Does Phillip know about us?" he finally asked.

Now it was Isabelle's turn to walk in silence. It had been troubling her lately that the rapt attention she had once felt from Darrow seemed to have cooled. When she had been aloof and refused to answer his messages, she heard from him constantly. But now that she had created a little freedom for herself, she found that she had to wait for *him*. Her mother had always warned her that men valued a woman only when they couldn't have her. "Hunters are what they are," her mother would say. "Once they've captured their prize, most of them don't even take the time to enjoy it."

"Why, Clarence," she finally said, "what is there to know? We hardly even see each other anymore." Isabelle had a teasing quality in her voice, but Darrow knew that under it she was serious. He stopped walking and took her hand and turned to look at her.

"Isabelle," he said seriously, "the evening when you said I was keeping you away from Hull House by pressing my attentions on you, you made a great impression on me. When I reached home that night, I spent a long time trying to put myself in your shoes. The longer I thought about living the way you do, the more I realized that *all* the things that make my life pleasant would simply not be allowed me if I were a woman like you."

"What things are those, Clarence?" asked Isabelle.

"Oh, Lord—everything! Speaking my mind. Aggravating my opponents. Seeing whomever I want, despite the fact that I'm married. Why, heavens, if you carried on the way I do, you'd be put out on the curb like yesterday's ashes."

Isabelle nodded.

"Well, that night I vowed I would not do anything to hurt you, no matter how it troubled me to stay away. Frankly it also occurred to me that if anything happened to your living arrangement because of me, I'd be in no position to take you in."

Isabelle recalled the night when she had pleaded with Darrow to let her be. Now she found herself in the unlikely position of having to encourage him to renew his interest. "Well, Clarence," she said, feeling the heat of her blush in the darkness, "as I said, my situation has changed somewhat."

"Isabelle, you're still a married woman! If there were a scandal about you, even Janie would have to keep you away."

Isabelle, of course, knew all this was true. She had explained it to Darrow herself. But now, having accepted that her husband would never again be important to her, she had been allowing herself to feel just how much she craved Darrow. More than once she had gone to sleep, staring into the darkness while she remembered how small and protected she had felt in his arms that night in the Hull House parlor. The overwhelming giddiness when he kissed her had all but left her in a swoon.

But these thoughts were not the kinds of ideas Isabelle believed a lady should bring up. Since she had no idea what else to say on this topic, she decided to change the subject. "How are things with Debs?" she asked.

"Bad. Bad. They're holding him accountable for all the

damage to property that occurred in the riots. On top of that, there's a man named Josef Chernik in the cell with him—not more than a kid really—who's accused of shooting a bystander."

"Yes. I saw the drawing of him in the paper."

"My guess is that one of those so-called deputies was firing at a striker and accidentally hit the woman Chernik is accused of killing."

"What will they do to him?"

"They want to hang him. And they seem overly anxious to get him to a speedy trial—no doubt to wash their own hands of blame as soon as they can. His sister came into the office today to talk to me and give me money. Seems she's an employee of the notorious Carrie Watson."

"Oh, my. You didn't take her money, did you?" It seemed shocking to Isabelle that Darrow would accept money earned through such a disreputable trade.

"Why, of course, I did. I can hardly afford to take on unpopular causes, Isabelle, unless someone occasionally pays me for my time."

Isabelle reflected for a moment about all the contradictions built into this man. One minute he seemed to be a pure idealist, a man who would defend any unjustly accused victim without charge. The next minute he seemed as interested in money as her own husband.

"Why did you become a lawyer, Clarence?" she asked.

In the darkness Darrow grinned. "Oh, I guess I was impressed by the speeches country lawyers used to make on the Fourth of July back home in Ohio. People would sit up and cheer for any damn thing they said, so it seemed like a pretty good profession to me."

"Be serious, Clarence," Isabelle chided.

"I am serious. Or course, these days the thing that gives me the biggest kick about lawyering is putting an unpopular idea before a jury. I enjoy looking at their hostile, stubborn faces and trying to crack open those rigid, closed minds."

Darrow and Isabelle turned the corner and were suddenly in front of his office. he paused for a moment uncomfortably, as if weighing what he should do. "Well, I guess I'd better go upstairs to work," he finally said. "I'll find a cab for you."

Isabelle felt profoundly disappointed. There was not a

thing in this world that she desired more than for Darrow to hold her and kiss her again. Yet it appeared that he might not have given that notion a thought.

"Explain to me your doctrine of free love," she said abruptly. "I want to understand it."

This request, which came just as a hansom cab pulled up to the curb, struck Darrow as a fairly stunning idea.

"You, of all people, want to hear about free love?" He stared at her from under a raised eyebrow. "My, my, a discussion of that magnitude will certainly involve more than a quick curbside exchange. If we're going to get involved in that subject, I might just have to ride home with you."

Isabelle nodded and stepped up into the carriage. Before Darrow joined her, she heard him tell the driver to meander through Lincoln Park. "Just keep moving until I tell you," he said.

When the carriage started on its way, slowly following the clop-clop of the horse, Isabelle and Darrow stared at each other in the dimly reflected light from the streetlamps. The evening was sultry and the walk from Hull House had left a tiny bead of perspiration on Isabelle's upper lip.

"The main issue, Isabelle, is to realize that free love is no different from any other freedom." Darrow was speaking softly. He pulled a handkerchief from his front pocket and began punctuating his words by rhythmically dabbing the handkerchief against her lips and face. "Whether it's the untrammeled expression of a political point of view"—dab—"or a desire to do something others wouldn't understand"—dab—"or an amorous attraction—" dab—"it's all the same. And it's all so important."

Isabelle's face was tingling. She was being mesmerized by his touch and the soft resonance of his voice. She felt her attraction for him expanding uncontrollably, like steam in a closed kettle that had finally found an opening for release.

"So you think people should do what they want regardless of other vows?" she asked.

"You mean marriage vows, I suppose?"

"Yes."

"Isabelle, no agreement is so important that it should enslave the very people it was meant to benefit. I may want you, Isabelle, but I would never want to enslave you."

Isabelle was momentarily taken aback by Darrow's shift from a theoretical discussion to such a personal declaration. Though she knew her pulse was racing, she fought to maintain her composure by moving the conversation back to the safety of theory.

"So you see no virtue in faithfulness?" she whispered.

Darrow smiled at her tactic and answered softly, his voice resonant and low in the darkness. "No. And certainly no virtue in long, unhappy marriages."

"Yet, Clarence, you yourself are married."

"Yes," he said simply.

Darrow lightly stroked the handkerchief across her forehead. He was reassuring her the way he would a little child.

"Isabelle, my wife and I were married years ago when we were little more than kids. The years between then and now have changed both of us a great deal. Both of us know that we are completely unsuited to each other."

"And you have agreed that you can maintain your freedom?"

"Of course," he said. "She could, too, if she wanted it. What could be more important than personal freedom?"

"Does she . . . see . . . others?"

"Well, no. But it'd be fine with me if she did," he answered.

"You wouldn't feel . . . embarrassed?"

"Isabelle," he said, looking at her intently, "I would be relieved if she did."

Isabelle felt mollified about Darrow's marriage, and the way he had been touching her made her feel cared for and protected. She suddenly put aside her desire to impress him because she felt safe to bare her inner feelings. "I don't think I've ever been free," she said earnestly, "not for one minute in my life."

A troubling idea occurred to her. Awhile ago she had bragged about taking some little freedom into her life. Yet she knew she had never exercised this freedom to do anything she wasn't *supposed* to do. It seemed to her that she was like a very well-trained poodle, a little pet that's been confined and trained so long that when given its freedom, it still waits meekly to be taken somewhere.

"I thought I had grown away from caring so much about what people think of me," she said, "yet I fear now that I have not."

"Of course you have, Isabelle," Darrow said.

"No. I think I have merely changed the people whose opinions are important to me. Instead of worrying about Phillip's opinions, I concern myself with Jane Addams and Bertha Palmer. I honestly think it is my desire to please every single child and mother who walk into Hull House."

Darrow took her hand. "Can any of those people possibly feel what I am feeling right now, touching you? Can they possibly know or care what you are feeling right now?"

For a few moments Isabelle did not answer. She was amazed by Darrow's open reference to what was happening between them. Did he mean that he, too, was feeling the excitement and desire that were pulsing between them? His ability to read her was a little frightening, but even so, Isabelle did not want to pull away from this delirious intensity.

Instead, she gave herself to the sensations that her heightened awareness was presenting to her. She was aware of everything: the warmth in the still night air, the gently rocking carriage beginning its first turn through Lincoln Park, the shimmering tension that seemed to charge the very air inside that carriage.

"I daresay," she finally answered, "they could not possibly feel what I am feeling."

Darrow took her hands between his. Rather than urgently importune her, he seemed content to touch her in light ways, letting her thoughts catch up with her passion. "Then is it not unthinkable to give strangers the keys to your life? To keep your whole life locked in their beliefs and attitudes?"

Perhaps it was the wonder of experiencing this intoxicating excitement for the very first time. Perhaps it was the knowledge that she had done so very little in her life. But in that moment it seemed achingly critical to Isabelle that she finally do something for herself, something for her own life. Finally, finally to forget the approval she so often sought and abandon herself to this moment. It seemed profoundly important not to live her entire life without at least once embracing sensation and closeness and love.

Rather than coyly wait for him to act, as she had always been trained to do, Isabelle leaned forward to close the space between them, took his face into her hands, and kissed him. It was a long, tender kiss, yet it was breathtaking in its intensity. Finally, with a subtle resignation that told him she had at last yielded to herself, she leaned back against the seat. And when he had released the fastenings on her blouse and skirt, she offered him her soft uncorseted nakedness.

The carriage continued to bob and sway as it wound through the lovely treelined paths in the quiet dark park. The horse, established in its slow pace, never varied from its plodding rhythm. The driver rested his elbows on his knees and nodded off into a peaceful nap. And no one noticed that the carriage was swaying to and fro just a little more more than usual.

27

IT WAS ONLY A little past noon when Buffalo Bill Cody staggered into his fourth saloon of the day. He'd been looking for his renegade Indian for three days now, and he feared that finding him might be more of a task than he'd anticipated. Of course, the job of looking through Chicago bars wasn't exactly what he'd call *hard*. As far as Cody was concerned, it was a relaxing, hazy way to combine business with pleasure.

At any rate it was a darn sight more pleasant than trying to please his wife at home. He grinned when he thought how irritated Louisa would be if she could see him now. If she knew he had found a justifiable reason to be tossing back shots in the middle of the day, the thought would give her a conniption fit.

But that was what had happened. Since Cody had no idea where Running Wolf might be, a saloon *was* the best place to look. The young Indian had always had a weakness for firewater. During a tour, whenever he didn't show up on time for a performance, the fastest way to find him was to comb the bars.

Cody's upper torso swayed unevenly as he approached the bar. The bartender glanced up and, while he didn't know who his new customer was, guessed that he must be involved in a dramatic production of some sort. The man had an unusual manner about him—a kind of elegant formality—and his flowing silvery hair reached past his shoulders. He certainly wasn't one of the poor drifters who frequented the saloon for the free lunch that went along with a five-cent beer. Chances were good that this one was here to drink.

"Afternoon," said the bartender pleasantly. "What'll it be?"

Cody realized that his equilibrium was shaky when he tried to put his boot on the footrail and swayed backward. "Whoa!" he said to let the bartender know he was not trying to conceal his tipsy condition. Cody smiled at the bartender confidentially and leaned forward to put his elbows on the bar for support. "I think some earlier shots may have done me in for a spell," he said. "Maybe you'd better make it a beer."

"Sure thing," said the bartender as he filled a glass with brew. "Say, are you somebody?" he asked, referring to Bill's theatrical appearance.

"Well, I reckon everybody's *somebody*." Cody picked up his glass and silently saluted the bartender before he drank. "But I am in show business if that's what you mean. Name's Buffalo Bill. I run a little show about the Wild West."

"Buffalo Bill!" The bartender whistled through his teeth. "Well, you are somebody all right. I always did want to see that show. Don't know why I missed it last year. I've heard it's the best show on earth."

"Very kind of you," said Cody, pleased. The compliment made him feel called upon to control his slurring. "And just what is your name, sir?"

"Eddie Holmes," answered the bartender. "It's a pleasure."

"Well, Eddie, next time I've got a show in town, you just tell the ticket taker that Bill Cody hisself invited you and said there'd be a free seat for you anywhere you want to sit!"

"That's a fine offer, sir," responded the bartender. "Very fine indeed. And I believe it, too, since it comes from you. You know, there's a durned, crazy-acting Indian that comes in here whenever he has a nickel in his pocket, and he keeps telling me the same thing. I don't believe *him*, of course, but I do believe you."

Cody nodded and smiled at the compliment for a second or two before the thought penetrated his alcoholic muddle that the Indian the bartender was talking about might just be Running Wolf.

"Well, here's a coincidence," he said. "I come in here specially to find one of my redskins. This fella's name ain't Running Wolf, is it?"

"Don't know what his name is, but he's a tall, mean-looking fellow. Thin face. Strange kind of eyes—a little too close together maybe. When he gets a few under his belt, I throw him out before he gets riled up. If I can get him out before he starts with the customers, he just hangs around outside in the street and dances."

"How often does he come in?" Bill asked. "I need to find him and get him back to his reservation in the Nebrasky badlands."

"He shows up around here every week or so," the bartender said thoughtfully. "I 'spect he's about due for a visit. Want me to tell him you come looking for him?"

"Hell, yes!" said Cody, without thinking how Running Wolf would respond to his message. "Tell him the U.S. gov'ment wants him and I got to take him back. I'm staying at the Clarion Hotel over on Dearborn. Tell him I'll buy him a full-out binge when he shows up."

Two days had passed before Running Wolf stalked through the doors at Dugan's Pub and stood silently at the bar. Eddie Holmes had never taken to having the Indian at his bar, so he was delighted to have a reason to send him on his way. The redskin always had an odd, smoky smell about him, and his silence was troubling to the other customers. The way he stood stock-still at the bar, not saying anything unless it was to wheedle a free drink, was enough to make a drinking man go next door.

"Your name Running Wolf?" Holmes asked of the Indian.

By way of response, Running Wolf narrowed his eyes and stared at the bartender. There was a threat in his expression that goaded the bartender to continue.

" 'Cause if it is, there's a man named Buffalo Bill in here a day or two ago, looking for you. He says the government wants you and he's here to take you back. So you just git now. Go on over to the Clarion Hotel. He's waiting for you."

Running Wolf looked silently at Holmes. Funny how some

white men reminded him of the underbelly of a possum—all
pink and white and covered with a light dusting of thin, pale
hair. He could see that he wasn't going to get any whiskey there
today and, for a moment, concentrated on the more pressing
problem of Buffalo Bill's presence in town.

He had no intention of returning to the reservation—certainly not now that the weather was warmer. He had slept in
makeshift shelters and freezing alleys all winter, wrapped only
in his blanket. He had killed cats and dogs and rats all over the
city and roasted them on a stick over open fires for his meals.
Whatever he had to do to stay away from the barren land the
government had reserved for the Indians, he had done.

The notion of being pursued sent a tremor of excitement
and anger through him. It was the kind of emotional tickle that
made him want to drink. Whiskey always kindled his anger and
fear. It generally had the effect of building an irritation into a
fury that would cause him to destroy something to experience
the good release that came after. Sometimes, if he couldn't find
anything else, he'd destroy something a white man valued—a
prize pet if he could find one. Tonight, if he were lucky, he
might be able to find another white woman.

One of the policemen at the station led Hannah downstairs
to the iron cell where her brother was being held. She was
nervous and in the murky, foreboding darkness acutely felt her
anxiety. She had stayed away for almost a month now, each day
obsessively thinking about her brother. She yearned to contact
him, yet she was deeply concerned about how he would react
to seeing her.

She had stayed in her room at Carrie Watson's all day,
agonizing over whether she should visit him at the jail. In addition to the shock of seeing her alive, she knew it would be
immediately and painfully clear to him that she was late in a
pregnancy—no oversized dress could hide that now. She had
no idea how her brother would respond to her presence or her
condition. Even though she and Josef had been very close, so
much had happened to change their lives that she didn't know
if he would even want to see her.

During her months at Carrie Watson's, Hannah had often

been distressed by thoughts about what her family had done when she had not returned home. She knew they had been terrified, for they certainly would have assumed that she had been killed or kidnapped—at least at first. Yet though it would have been so easy to assure them that she was alive and well, the knowledge of her whereabouts would be even harder for them to accept. A disgraced daughter was worse than a dead one. Had they known of her pregnancy, they would have pronounced her dead anyway.

Hannah had seen the forceful rage of parental disapproval back in Russia. When she was still a little girl, her mother had taken her along on a condolence call to neighbors whose son had married a Gentile girl. When Hannah and her mother arrived, the little dirt-floor house had been draped in black, and the family was sitting *shivah*. It was as if the son had not merely disobeyed their wishes but died. Her mother had whispered to her that as far as the family was concerned, the boy had ceased to exist. His name was never to be spoken in their presence again. It was an awe-provoking experience Hannah never forgot.

But the quandary she felt about her brother's attitude was different. She had been his friend when he was in trouble. Would he—he, of all people—turn his face from her? Would he be grateful to know she was alive and could offer assistance, or would he be too ashamed of his own situation to find her presence anything but an embarrassment? It was a big decision for Hannah to make. Finally she realized that no matter what might happen, she had to go.

When she arrived at the cell, she stood still, nervously staring into the shadows. It was a few moments before she could identify her brother in the gloom, lying on a bench.

"That the man you come to see?" asked the jailer.

"Yes," she said. "I think it is."

"Chernik," said the jailer, "you got company."

The jailer walked away and left Hannah standing outside the cell in the hallway. Once he had gone, she felt uneasy. She was in a jail with the brother she had deceived. In the shadows she could see other prisoners sitting on benches.

Josef peered toward the light in the hallway. He couldn't make out the face on the figure in front of him because the light was behind her. For a few moments he thought the large-bodied woman in front of him might be his mother. But when he heard her voice, he knew it was Hannah.

"Josef?"

What a powerful rush of feelings swept over him! At first it seemed like a dream, like some impossible answer to all his prayers for her safety.

"Hannah!" he exclaimed. He pulled himself to his feet but was still too weak to move quickly. As he stumbled to the door of the cell, tears filled his eyes. The joy of seeing her was so great that he was sure it would break his heart if this did turn out to be a dream. His eyes studied her closely to make sure they were not deceiving him, but there was no question but that this was his sister standing in front of him. This was real. He sobbed loudly. "Thank God," he said. "Oh, thank God."

Hannah stretched her arms through the bars and grasped his shoulders. She knew his tears were a sign of relief, but within his joy she could hear the deep grief she had caused him. She felt sick with shame and sadness.

"I'm sorry," she cried. "I'm so sorry."

They leaned against the bars and huddled against each other, weeping, Josef sobbing about how he had searched for her and never given up, how he had prayed for her and had never believed she was dead. Suddenly he became aware of his situation. "I'm not guilty, you know," he said, wiping tears away from his cheeks. "I didn't do it."

"Hush, *tateleh*," Hannah said. "Of course, you didn't."

When the rush of their emotions had subsided, they rested together, leaning against the bars, touching their arms and hands.

It was awhile before Josef could realize that the size of her body had changed. When he did, it shocked him.

"Hannah, you are with child?"

Hannah looked away. Now that the moment had arrived to tell him about her life, she realized she could not. She knew the disgust her brother would feel about her life as a prostitute because she knew how *she* herself had felt about the women at Carrie's. Despite his love, there was no way in the world that he could ever understand her choosing life in such a shameful circumstance—even if her only alternative had been death.

Hannah took a deep, jagged breath. "Yes," she said quietly. "The baby will soon be here."

"No!" he moaned. "That's what Etta told Papa! She said you had been seen downtown with a blond man. Please don't tell me you let this man disgrace you, Hannah! Don't tell me that! Here I am, ruined, and now you—you also ruined!"

Hannah had come to offer her brother moral support and love. She could not bear to see that she was increasing his distress. Without hesitating, she decided to tell him whatever would make him feel better.

"I am not ruined, Josef. Not at all. In fact, I am a somewhat wealthy woman."

"How is this?" Josef asked.

"I am married to that blond man," she answered. "I am married, and my husband is rich. But he is a Gentile, and that was why I had to leave home. Mama and Papa would have disowned me anyway."

"Papa would have!" Josef's voice choked with anger. "But Mama wouldn't, and I wouldn't! *We* would not have disowned you."

In the darkness one of the men in the jail called out. "Quiet down. Jeez!"

The intrusion reminded Hannah and Josef that they were not alone. Josef tried to pull himself together. The notion that Hannah was married was certainly better news than her condition had first led him to assume. But if this was true, there were other issues almost as unforgivable.

"Then why didn't you let me know, Hannah?" he asked. He had lowered his voice so the others in the cell couldn't hear him, but he was amazed that his sister had treated him so badly. "How could you let me suffer and worry without letting me know?"

Hannah realized that her lie had condemned her for callousness. "I'm sorry, Josef. Forgive me. I simply did not know what to do."

Josef pulled away from her to ponder this situation. He was deeply hurt that she had let him agonize over her disappearance while she blithely went off with someone. On top of it she had left him completely responsible for supporting the entire family!

"I—I just don't know what to say to you," he said hoarsely.

For a few moments Hannah herself could think of nothing to say. She had known Josef would be upset with her regardless of what story she told him about her situation. But she had chosen to risk it because his imprisonment as a murder suspect seemed to overshadow everything else.

"Well . . ." Josef said haltingly, "who is he? Where do you live?"

Hannah wanted to distance herself from her lie as quickly as possible. "Josef, let's not discuss that now. Let's talk about how I can help you and the family."

"The family! Papa would never take your money. He won't even come to visit *me*! I don't need your money either."

"I already gave money to your lawyer, Josef."

Josef was stunned by this announcement. His sister had actually gone to his lawyer before she had come to him! She must have told Darrow to keep her payment a secret. He felt betrayed, like a child who discovers he's been lied to. "Well, you didn't have to do that! Mr. Darrow was handling my case for free!"

"Of course, Josef," she answered, "but that was because he didn't think you had any money. Believe me, he will pay more attention to you if he *is* receiving money. That's the way people are."

Josef shook his head in amazement. Hannah had changed. She had become coolly knowledgeable about manipulating people.

"Maybe Mr. Darrow took your money," he said petulantly, "but Mama and Papa won't. Not ever."

The bitterness Josef felt filled his chest like something hard and solid.

"Please, Josef," she asked softly. "Help me find a way to get money to them."

Josef told himself to put aside his anger. He knew she was right about the family. Mama and Papa had no way to earn a living out there in Pullman. He had heard that the town was in shambles, the streets filled with workers moving away to wherever they could find work. Josef knew his father *should* move back to the old neighborhood, but he knew that Yankel's fight with Etta—and now the charges against Josef—would make returning a hard pill for a proud man to swallow.

"Give the money to Mr. Darrow," he said finally, "and let

him give it to them. Tell him to say it's from someone who knows their son is innocent."

Hannah watched her brother closely. He had not met her eyes since she had told him she was married, and he was still looking down at the floor. "I will do that, Josef," she said softly. "But please, tell me what can I do to help *you*? There must be something."

Finally Josef looked at his sister. When they were children, he had confided in her. Somehow even now that they were separated by bars and the circumstances of their lives, it felt right, so very familiar to be telling her his secrets. Despite all the emotions he was feeling about her betrayal, he still wanted to make her proud of him. He wanted to give her a reason to see him as something more than a hopeless failure.

"I have invented something, Hannah," he said. Then, because he knew there were others listening in the darkness, he whispered, "It's a drum brake for a bicycle. With my drum brake, a rider will be able to stop a bicycle without hurting himself."

Hannah reacted with amazement. A bicycle brake! Even here in this cell, her brother was still dreaming. They could accuse him of murder, they could lock him up in jail, but no one could stop his dreams.

"If you could just bring me some writing paper and a pen," he continued confidentially. "I could draw my invention on paper. Then you could take it to the Patent Office—"

"Of course, Josef," said Hannah, finally understanding that this was how he wanted her to help him. "I will do whatever you want."

A somber thought entered Josef's mind. "Be sure to bring the paper right away. Mr. Darrow says I go to trial soon because the courts want to impress the public with how they deal with troublemakers. If I am convicted and they hang me, I want to have my invention registered so I can leave something behind for the family."

Hannah's throat tightened. Darrow had told her that Josef's chances for acquittal were not good. Until this moment she had not realized that her brother understood the extent of his trouble. She wanted to comfort him and assure him that he would be vindicated, but she did not want to give him false hope.

"You do know I didn't do it, don't you, Hannah?" he said. "I hope you understand that I'm innocent."

"Of course, I do," she said. She wanted to reach forward and hold him again, but she was afraid he was still upset with her. "How could I ever believe that you would do such a thing?"

Hannah leaned against the bars. Finally brother and sister were able to talk quietly again. He told her how frightened he was, and it was just like old times.

In a few minutes the jailer appeared. "Your time's up, missus," he said.

Hannah said good-bye to Josef and left with the jailer. The meeting had left her exhausted, and she climbed heavily up the long flight of stairs. When she arrived in the bright light of the station upstairs, she pulled a veil over her face. It would not be good for anyone to recognize her here.

At her instruction the driver was waiting with the carriage a short distance away. Because of its white body and yellow wheels, the vehicle was too distinctive and recognizable to be parked in front of the jail.

It was earlier, when she left the carriage to walk to the jail, that Running Wolf had first caught sight of her. A pregnant woman in the street after dark. What a trophy this would be, he thought. A woman with a baby inside her.

After the bartender at Dugan's had kicked him out without a drink, Running Wolf had finally been able to buy his whiskey at another saloon. As always, it had inflamed him into a murderous mood. Waiting in the shadow between two buildings in hopes that the woman would return had done nothing to lessen his tension. With the liquor wearing off, the ache in his head made him eager to avenge the bloody assault on his mother so many years ago.

Running Wolf heard a woman's footsteps on the sidewalk, and he flattened his body against one of the buildings. This was the first woman who had passed since he had seen the pregnant woman. Quietly he waited, barely breathing, until he could see who it was. Yes. It was the same woman, the one who was so big with child.

Running Wolf leaped from his hiding place, but the alcohol buzzing in his head threw him off balance. Hannah turned in the direction of the sound in time to see a man lunge at her. She tried to run away but couldn't move quickly enough. The man grabbed her arm and jerked her toward him, and Hannah could feel the jolt run through her shoulder and down her back. She searched the street for the carriage. The driver was still sitting up on the driver's seat, waiting for her. Without hesitating, she screamed loudly. "Joe! Joe, help!"

Her cry stopped Running Wolf for a second. The fact that this woman had shouted a specific name—rather than an anonymous cry for help—caused him to pause. He knew she must have someone waiting nearby. Running Wolf saw a man leap from the top of a carriage and run toward him. He saw the man pull a pistol from his belt.

"Let her go!" the man shouted as he ran. "Let her go or I'll shoot."

Running Wolf knew that by the time he killed the woman, the man would be upon him with a gun. He also knew that if the woman were dead, the man would shoot him as he ran away. He gripped the woman's arm and viciously hurled her to the ground. As he ran back through the shadows between the buildings, he heard her cry out as she hit the sidewalk. He smiled to himself. He knew the man would be too occupied with the pregnant woman to take the time to catch him.

Spasms in Hannah's abdomen—sharp, gripping sensations that appeared and intensified for a few seconds before they vanished—started a few minutes after she had arrived at Carrie Watson's back door. Hannah's back hurt, too, with a heavy pressure low against her spine.

She managed to get upstairs to her room by herself, but within two hours the pains were coming regularly—terrible, cascading waves that would start just as soon as she thought she had gotten over her attack. Now, at eleven o'clock at night during the peak earning hours at Carrie Watson's establishment, she was alone in her room and frightened.

Her mind began to dwell on her encounter with the doctor months before. She remembered that he had not seemed to care whether she lived or died. That recollection had a chilling effect on her now. It was terrible to think that she could die at the hands of an uncaring physician. During the lull between her pains she would decide to do without him and take her chances with one of the women acting as midwife. Yet when she was in the throes of a bad pain, it terrified her that she didn't have a doctor.

Of all the people in the house, Vina would best know what to do. But Hannah didn't know where to find her. Vina was surely moving from room to room, making sure the sheets were changed and that the rooms always ready for new customers. But Hannah was alone on the third floor of that big house. To yell for help and disturb the guests was not a sensible action to take. There was serious work going on here, and Carrie would be very displeased if Hannah interrupted it. Her problem now was to find Vina without creating a disturbance.

She pulled herself to her feet and limped to the door. By the time she was halfway across the room, something had happened inside her, and she felt water rush down her legs. She had heard women talking about when their "water broke," but she didn't know what that meant. In her panic she forgot her concerns about disturbing the customers and dragged herself to the hall. She stood there, leaning against the door, until she saw one of the girls strolling to her room with a client. Against her better judgment she interrupted her.

"Maude!" she called to the prostitute. "Maude, get Vina," she said.

Maude shot Hannah a look of pure resentment. *Now that Little Miss Uppity wants something*, Maude thought, *she feels it's her right to interrupt me with a big spender.* "I'm with a gentleman," she said, bristling slightly. "Get her yourself."

"I'm sick, Maude," Hannah begged, whispering so as to keep the gentleman from being too distracted. "I'm real sick."

"You know the rules," said Maude irritably. Then she opened the door to her room, led her gentleman inside, and closed it a little louder than necessary.

Hannah did know the rules. Interrupting a girl with a customer was strictly against the principles on which Carrie's house was run. Equally bad was Hannah's letting a customer see her looking big and pregnant—especially since Carrie had insisted some time ago that she hide in her room at night. As far as Carrie was concerned, the basic tenet of prostitution was simple: "If a customer has money jingling in his trousers, keep his rod hot until his pockets are empty."

Hannah knew she couldn't be seen downstairs in her condition, but she was too frightened to stay upstairs alone. She headed for the back stairway and carefully made her way down the steep stairs. When she was halfway down to the second floor, she felt a sharp, tearing sensation that made her think her pelvis was being ripped apart. She eased herself down onto a step and, when she thought she would surely have to scream, crammed part of her skirt in her mouth to block the sound.

When the pain subsided, Hannah was wet with perspiration. She found that she was unable to stand and resigned herself to sitting there, crouching on the stairs. It was a terribly insecure way to wait out the birth of a baby, and it made her feel despairing and helpless. The house was filled with people— she could hear people talking and walking around downstairs— yet there was no one around to help her.

While she was curled up with her head on her knees, hoping for someone to come along, she became forcefully aware of how alone she was. It made her unbearably sad to realize it, and a cloud of self-pity descended upon her. Other women, she thought, would see this as a joyful occasion. They would have their husbands or mothers beside them to help them through it. She wondered why it had fallen to her always to be so solitary.

She let her mind play back over her younger years, all the times when she had had her brother to talk to. After her meeting with him earlier this evening, she knew their friendship would certainly never be the same as it had once been. Her brother was angry and hurt. When she left the jail, the last thing he said showed her how much he distrusted her.

"Well, Hannah," he had said, "if you don't decide to come back, I hope you'll at least get me that paper and pen so I can draw my invention. It's all I ask." Hannah knew his comment was intended as a stinging criticism. She feared that his resentment toward her would stay with him forever.

As she sat there reflecting on her loss of an ally, her mind opened up just enough for her to realize how alone her *brother* must be feeling at that very moment. Other men were with him in the cell, but the fearful thoughts that surely filled his mind every waking moment—those were his. There was no one inside his mind but him. The burden of his life was his, his alone.

She realized that was the way it had always been. Not just for him, back in Russia worrying about arrest, but for her, too.

For even though he would have listened willingly, she usually had chosen *not* to confide her problems lest she distress him. The thoughts that most troubled her and the dreams that most thrilled her—those were the images she had always held inside.

It suddenly seemed to her that the part of a person that was never touched by another was the largest part of all, that the human condition was, after all, one long yearning to find someone with whom secret thoughts could be shared and accepted. The most significant things in life, she thought—being born, giving birth, dying—those were the things you did alone, no matter how many people were gathered around the bed to watch.

A door from one of the rooms downstairs opened, and for a moment she heard more clearly the music and the laughter that attracted the men who paid so dearly to be there. Those men, too, she realized, and the prostitutes who pretended to listen and accept them needed this same closeness. And she knew they would certainly never find it here.

Even this baby, which was forcefully trying to separate itself from her, was simply a pathetic remnant of her attempt to find that closeness with Roland Girard. This baby, too, if it lived, would search all its life for human closeness. And it would probably fail to find it.

Suddenly a vision came to Hannah, a vision of the generations of humanity, each of them moving down a staircase. One generation after the other, walking alone, single file, until they reached the end of their journey at the bottom of the stairs. Each would be followed by their sons and daughters, who walked those stairs in their own time. But all of them would go the distance alone.

The thought made tears come to Hannah's eyes. As she sat there, huddled up, curled over the baby she carried, it seemed to her that she was weeping for everyone. She was weeping for the women in the house who secretly despised their customers, weeping for the foolish men who paid for the opportunity to be superficial and unconnected. She wept as much for the rich people who lived in big expensive houses as for those in shacks who wondered where their next meal would come from. For in this essential way, she thought, they were all alike.

In the quiet there on the stairs with the distant tinkle of

music and glasses, it seemed to Hannah that it didn't really matter what happened to her. If she lived, she would spend her days either searching for human connection or denying her need by staying busy with other activities. In the end, she realized, it didn't matter. She would die someday—sooner or later—and take her place in the ground beneath the crust of this growing city or under grass somewhere on a hill. Whether it happened now or later didn't seem to matter too much.

She stayed that way for a while, peacefully surrendering to whatever fate had in store for her. *It wouldn't be too bad to die,* she thought. *If it happens now, I will be happy.*

But in a few moments the baby began to force itself against her again, and the pain grew until she thought she would scream in spite of herself. The overwhelming immediacy of the pain harshly thrust her back into her present situation, and her philosophical acceptance turned to fear. With the dress fabric clenched between her teeth, she began to moan and pray. "Oh, God," she begged, "please just don't let me die here alone."

She was still muttering to herself when Vina appeared on the steps below her.

"Child, what you doin' sittin' here on the steps like this? This ain't no way to do."

"Vina, help me!" Hannah cried. "The baby is coming. I think it's almost here."

"The great I am!" said Vina. "You stay here a minute, honey, whilst I send someone to fetch the doctor."

Now that the threat of dying alone seemed less likely, Hannah allowed herself to whimper like a child. "Do you think Carrie will be mad that I'm having the baby during work hours?" she asked.

"Lord, honey, don't you worry about that," said Vina. "Babies is always born in the middle of the night. Miss Carrie knows that."

When Carrie Watson stepped into Hannah's room the next evening at six o'clock, she was shocked to see how pale and lifeless Hannah looked.

"Jesus, Doc, don't just let her agonize herself to death!" Carrie said.

Hannah's labor had gone on all night and through the day.

Doc McGinnis had come by at midnight, but he had been away all day. He had returned and had just finished a hearty supper downstairs in preparation for a long night's vigil. Hannah was resting now between contractions, but it was clear she was exhausted.

"Can't you give her just a little morphine, Doc?" Carrie urged.

Hannah opened her eyes in time to see him shake his head and glance at his pocket watch again to time her contractions.

"No sense in that now," he said. "She should be ready anytime."

Hannah felt the beginning of another pain. Against her will a groan started in the back of her throat. The doctor heard it and picked up the pillow to have it ready. Hannah tried to control herself. She didn't want to scream because it terrified her when the doctor held the pillow over her face to mute the sound. It frightened her that he might smother her to death.

Between pains she'd promise herself that the next time she would control herself; she'd stay on top of the pain and not cry out. But when the agony became too intense to bear, she would scream despite herself.

"Come on, Doc," said Carrie, trying to wheedle the drugs out of him. "She's getting weak."

The doctor looked balefully at Carrie over his glasses. "Miss Watson," he said, "the timing is in God's hands. Not mine."

"Well, just make sure you don't kill her with that pillow," Carrie said. "Seems like you keep it on her face a lot longer than you need to."

The doctor shrugged to indicate that it was out of his hands. "It was your request that we keep the girl's cries from disturbing the entire house. I don't see how I could do other than I have done."

Dr. McGinnis was not happy that he had been bothered in the middle of last night by a sporting house and had been forced to return there again this evening. He had a bottle of ether in his bag, but he didn't like to use it until he was sure the woman was ready. Sometimes anesthetic slowed things down. It helped for the woman to be awake so she could push.

Anyway, it was his personal opinion that the pain was good,

as long as it didn't exhaust the woman so much that she died. It seemed to him that the pain made a girl understand what she was doing when she got pregnant. He didn't have any surefire ways to avoid pregnancy; many women had asked, and he had never been able to give them a satisfactory answer. But it was his opinion that if a woman didn't want a baby, she should just stay away from sex altogether. If she was going to have sex, this was just the risk she took.

But perhaps, he now thought, this demanding madam was right. Maybe the girl would die. Doc McGinnis took the ether from his bag and poured some onto a cloth. This time, when Hannah started to scream, she felt a small cloth against her nose and mouth instead of the large pillow. For a second before the room started to spin and she closed her eyes, she wondered what the doctor was doing.

From the darkness of her sleep Hannah could hear a baby crying. She tried to open her eyes, but the room was still spinning. She heard a voice say, "It's a girl, Hannah."

A girl! Hannah reacted to this knowledge with dismay. Even though she wasn't completely conscious yet, knowing that she had a girl distressed her greatly. Someone was putting the baby in her arms. She turned her head away so she wouldn't have to look at it.

Hannah didn't want to see the baby, for she knew that if she did, she'd probably want to keep it. If it had just been a boy! A boy would have been so much easier. She knew she'd have to send the child away to be raised, of course, but if it were a boy, she wouldn't have to worry about it as much.

But a girl! A little girl born in a sporting house! How could this child grow up in polite society after being born in a place like this? How could she make her way through life without being mistreated? She might even wind up in the same spot Hannah was in. How could a little girl even have a chance?

The baby was crying, and its small voice seemed no louder than the noise a cat would make. That tiny, vulnerable sound hurt Hannah just to hear it.

"Take it away from me," she said harshly.

The doctor made a clucking sound with his tongue and shook his head. These whores really were just too inhuman in their feelings, he thought. Disgustedly he began to pack his bag. While he was still in the room, Carrie glared at him, daring him to say anything.

After he had left, Carrie sat down on the bed beside Hannah. "Where did you learn to make your heart so hard, missy?" she asked. "Don't you even want to see this child you brought into the world?"

Hannah opened her eyes and looked at Carrie. She still did not want to see the baby, but there it was, in her arms, and Carrie was staring at her as if there were something wrong with her.

Hannah finally looked down at the baby at her breast. She felt the coldness in her heart melt and a burst of love shine forth. It was her baby. She could feel that now. It was bawling, red-faced, and wrinkled, and it was the most beautiful thing she had ever seen.

Carrie had been shocked at Hannah's coldness, but now that she could see the loving tears in her eyes, she hoped she hadn't made a mistake by encouraging Hannah to look at the baby.

"You better not want to keep it," Carrie said dourly. "You remember our agreement."

"No, Carrie," Hannah said. "I won't keep it here. It wouldn't be right for any of us."

Carrie nodded. "Well, if there's anything I can do for you . . ." She was ready to leave now that the crisis was over.

Hannah suddenly remembered her brother's request. It seemed years since she had sat with him in the jail. She knew he had probably been watching for her all day. "Please have the driver take some paper and a pen over to my brother, Josef Chernik, in the jail," she said. "Then send the driver to Mr. Darrow's office. Have him tell Mr. Darrow to do whatever has to be done to help my brother acquire a patent."

Carrie looked at her favorite boarder and shook her head. The girl certainly was strange.

When Hannah was alone in the room with her daughter, she watched the baby as it sucked at her breast. Reluctantly she felt her love for it grow. God, how it hurt to care for something this much! Hannah almost wished she had never had the ill fortune to love anyone—let alone this baby.

When the child had finally finished feeding, it smacked its lips together, and Hannah felt a reminder of something unpleasant, a glimmer of a thought that gave her pain. For in the child's tiny action of smacking its lips, Hannah could see a trace of her old lover, Roland Girard.

28

―――――――

THE FIRST DAY OF Josef's trial the courtroom was jammed. By early morning all the available chairs had been filled with newspaper reporters, union members, and curiosity seekers. Those who arrived too late to get seats stood around the sides and back of the room.

Josef was taken to the courtroom with his hands cuffed behind him. When he appeared at the front of the room, excitement rippled through the crowd. Spectators lunged to their feet to get a look at the violent anarchist in their midst. Someone called out, "There he is!" and waiting deputies swarmed around him to form a barrier while they unlocked his handcuffs.

Josef lowered his face. He felt ashamed and vulnerable to be seen this way, shackled like a dangerous animal. Then he heard his mother cry out his name. She was weeping loudly, repeating his name in a high, hysterical voice. He felt his knees weaken. He knew that if she was in the courtroom, his father must be there, too. The dull fear he had been trying to control deepened into a sense of impending doom.

He lifted his gaze to find his parents in the crowd and saw his father leading Mama to the door. Before they vanished into the hallway, Papa cast Josef a dark look and shook his head miserably.

The crowd murmured again. Josef was confused and frightened. For a few moments all he could see was a blur of the spectators' clothes. Then, through the daze, he saw the faces—all of them unfamiliar. It seemed so important to find someone in that large crowd with a friendly face, but in those odd paralyzing moments he did not see a single soul that he knew.

When he turned away, Clarence Darrow was walking toward him. Darrow grasped his hand, and Josef was filled with enormous gratitude that his lawyer had even shown up. Darrow put his hand on Josef's shoulder and smiled before he led him to the defense table.

After they were seated, Darrow whispered, "How are you holding up, son?" But Josef was too stunned to answer.

Just as Darrow started to whisper to Josef again, a loud voice interrupted them. "All rise," the voice announced. "The Superior Court of Cook County is now in session. The honorable Peter Rhinehart presiding."

Josef heard the crowd stand as the judge entered the room. As he rose, his heart thumped heavily, and he felt unsteady. Then the voice made another imperious proclamation: "The People versus Josef Chernik."

None of his meetings with Darrow had prepared Josef for the shock of hearing his name used this way. The people *versus* Josef Chernik! What an impossible idea. The people against *him*!

Ever since his arrival in America Josef's greatest desire had been to become one of the citizens here, to be part of this free, high-spirited land. He hadn't tried to *distinguish* himself; he had merely wanted to fit in. He had even been willing to change himself—to strip himself of every mannerism and trait that marked him as an outsider. Others might indulge themselves in stories about the old country, but Josef had always remained silent, keeping his past to himself. From that first day when he arrived here, Josef Chernik had wanted nothing so much as to be an American.

Now he realized how badly he had failed. By detaching himself from his own kind, he had made the people who *were* like him—Lubek and many of the union workers—hold him in contempt. And now the very Americans he had wanted to emulate were against him, too.

He took his seat again and watched as Darrow and three lawyers from the other side moved to the judge's bench.

"Gentlemen, are we ready to call for a jury?" the judge asked.

"We are, Your Honor," said a lawyer wearing an immaculate blue suit.

The lawyer made a brief, crisp bow, and Josef realized that he must be the chief prosecutor, Samuel Rais. Josef had heard the men in the cell talk about Rais. He had sent two dozen men and six teenagers to the gallows. He was said to be relentless.

"Don't give Rais a chance to question you," Lacey had warned him one night after overhearing a meeting in the cell with Darrow. Josef had been insisting that he wanted to explain to the jury himself that he had had nothing to do with the killing. He felt the jurors would believe him if only they could hear him.

"Rais will twist your words and turn your meanings to his," Lacey had said. "You'll feel like a rag flapping in the wind."

Now, standing before the judge, Rais looked clean-shaven, his hair so slick that it glistened. The sharp creases in his trousers stuck forward above the toes of his shoes. Beside Rais, Darrow looked so unkempt in his rumpled gray suit that Josef fleetingly wondered if he had slept in his clothes.

"We are ready as well, Your Honor," answered Darrow, "even though, the defense has hardly been given adequate time to prepare the case."

"Oh?" said Judge Rhinehart as he coolly raised his eyebrows. The judge certainly did not want a criticism of the pretrial politics of the case voiced in the courtroom. "Mr. Darrow, you have been given ample opportunity to speak with the state's witnesses, have you not?"

"Yes, Your Honor, I have. But considering that thousands of people—most of them as yet unknown to me—were present at the time of the shooting, I would have liked a little more time to find more witnesses of my own."

"Do you think that with more time, Mr. Darrow, you actually could have winnowed these unknown witnesses from that crowd?"

Darrow understood the futility of arguing with Judge Rhinehart about the court date—there had been great political pressure to go to trial as early as possible—but he had made his statement in the hope that it would be written up in the newspapers. For if it were, material witnesses might read of his need and come forward to testify.

"I certainly would have tried, sir," Darrow answered. "However, we are prepared with such evidence as we have been able to accumulate."

Judge Rhinehart took his wire-rimmed glasses from his eyes and stared at Darrow. Rhinehart had been presiding over this courtroom for twenty years now. He had seen and handled every grandstand maneuver a person could imagine.

I know you'll be a handful, Mr. Darrow, he thought. *But I do know how to handle you.*

Rhinehart narrowed his eyes and gazed past Darrow at the courtroom audience. "We do hope that your comment is not meant to excuse a poorly prepared case, Mr. Darrow. If it is, I doubt any of us will be impressed."

Somewhere in the back of the courtroom a spectator laughed.

Darrow grinned. "I've never made the mistake of assuming that anyone will believe anything but the worst about me. That way I'm never disappointed."

"In your case I'd say that's a wise decision," chimed in Prosecutor Rais. Rais's assistants chortled at his wit.

"That's enough, gentlemen," Judge Rhinehart said gruffly. "Let us proceed."

Josef watched as the prospective jurors were brought into the courtroom. The judge explained to them that they would be asked to sit in the jury box, four at a time, for questioning. On the basis of their answers, twelve of them would be chosen for the jury. Before the questioning began, he said, he wanted to explain the case to them.

"As I'm sure you know," Judge Rhinehart began, "the United States has been in turmoil for more than a decade. The bombings and violence caused by strikers have turned America's great cities into citadels of terror. As we all are aware, much of this tumult has been caused by anarchists from foreign lands."

Darrow sat erect. He knew that to interrupt the judge when he was addressing the jury was a serious breach of courtroom etiquette, but he could not allow the judge to begin the trial by prejudicing the prospective jurors against Josef.

Darrow paused for a moment before he slowly brought himself to his feet. Rather than speak, he stood silently in hope that the judge would correct himself. Instead, when the judge saw Darrow on his feet, he immediately took offense.

"You have something to say, Mr. Darrow?"

Darrow ran his hand through his hair to push a lock of straight hair back from his forehead. "With all due respect, Your Honor, the state of Illinois is not trying the thousands of union members who have been struggling for fairness over the past decade. As far as I know, there is only one person on trial here today."

Judge Rhinehart looked irritably over his wire-rimmed glasses at Darrow. "I was making a point with the jurors, Mr. Darrow—if you will be so kind as to allow me to continue."

Darrow remained standing. "Judge, the fact that a few union men have occasionally engaged in violence should not be held against the defendant. The question of whether *he* was engaged in such violence is what has brought us here."

"I believe I can instruct the jury without your insights, Mr. Darrow. Now if you will be kind enough to allow me to continue, I'd like to make my point."

Darrow scratched his head and angled his jaw to one side. He sat down reluctantly.

"As I was saying," Judge Rhinehart continued, "the fact that these troublesome anarchists have shown contempt for the laws of this country should not be held against the defendant *until such time* as the prosecutor proves that the defendant shares this contempt of law and order."

The judge turned to Darrow with a sarcastic air. "Now that I have finished my statement, Mr. Darrow, I do hope it has met with your approval."

Darrow again rose to his feet respectfully. "Your Honor, I'm not sure that the time will *ever* arrive when the prosecutor can prove my client's contempt for the law. I hope the jurors won't be too disappointed when he fails to do so."

When the first group of men went into the jury box, Darrow

whispered to Josef, "I want you to keep your eyes on these people. Be sure you meet their eyes when they look at you—they expect that of an innocent man. If any of them looks particularly friendly while I'm questioning someone else, let me know."

The selection of the jury was perplexing to Josef. The questions Prosecutor Rais asked seemed to be not so much questions as statements intended to convey his belief that Josef was a craven criminal.

Rais asked one older man, a bald chap with a pinched, sagging face, "Do you accept God's holy commandment not to kill?"

When the man answered, "I do, indeed," Rais nodded in such a way as to show the jurors that he thought this attitude was to be commended.

Interviewing another prospective juror, Rais asked, "What do you think of people who wantonly destroy property?" To another he asked, "Do you believe in the Christian values?"

But when Darrow interviewed those same people, he asked unassuming questions in a such a quiet tone he might have been sitting in a juror's living room with no one else around. Darrow's lack of theatrics troubled Josef somewhat, but it bothered him even more that the questions seemed to have nothing to do with the case at all.

"Mr. Miller," Darrow asked one wrinkled man after he had learned that he had been a farmer, "did you ever have an egg thief in your hen house?"

"I did indeed," answered Miller.

"What did you do about it?"

"I sat up all night in the hen house to catch it."

"Did it occur to you that your dog might be an egg eater?"

"It did."

"Did it occur to you to shoot the dog on the suspicion that he was?"

"Shoot my dog on suspicion?" Miller said. "What damned fool would do that?"

"So you're not a man who would punish someone merely on a suspicion, are you?"

"I think not, Mr. Darrow," said Miller. "I am not a fool."

Darrow smiled and agreed that Miller was not a fool.

As the questioning wore on, Josef listened and watched.

When it appeared that the procedure was over, Darrow whispered, "Got any notions about who likes you?"

When Josef pointed out a couple of men who had glanced at him with friendly expressions, Darrow nodded his head. "That's good," he said. "They're farmers. I like having farmers on a jury. When I talk to those fellows, at least I know who I'm talking to."

Once the jury was selected, the judge declared a recess for lunch. The trial was to begin that afternoon.

Josef sat in his cell for two hours before he was handcuffed and led back to the courtroom. He had not been out of jail since his arrest and, as time passed, had grown used to it. But being outside today, seeing people behave brightly and energetically, had reminded him of what normal life was like. After the morning, returning to the tomblike cell and the defeated lethargy of the prisoners was intolerably bleak. By the time he left his cell, Josef was trembling. He knew the preliminaries were over. The trial that would determine the rest of his life was beginning in earnest.

That afternoon he watched the judge and the lawyers get the proceedings under way. He could feel his heart thumping in a dull, hard way, and for a short while he had the odd feeling that all this was happening to someone else.

When the prosecuting attorney finally stood to begin his opening statement, Josef tried to pay attention, but the things the prosecutor was saying about him were so unpleasant that he could hardly bear to listen. Fearful thoughts suddenly sprang to his mind and crowded out what he was hearing. No matter how closely he listened, he repeatedly had the sense that he had just awakened and had missed something that had just been said.

"In all my years at the bar," Rais was now saying, "I have never seen a more contemptible criminal come into a court of justice than this man."

Josef was suddenly snapped back to awareness. Rais was pointing a finger at him.

"Engaging in a needless violent strike that will surely cause thousands of women and children to cry out in hunger this winter—that was not enough for this scoundrel. No! He had to take up a gun and fire it into Kathleen Kelly, an innocent bystander, before he was satisfied."

Josef felt the blood drain from his face. The jurors were straining forward, listening to Rais's statements as if they were true. He wanted to cry out, "No, no, it's not true!"

"The state will show by facts and circumstances, by witnesses who are no less than U.S. deputies, that this man"—Rais pointed to Josef again—"is guilty of the most cowardly murder ever committed in the annals of American jurisprudence."

Rais paused to pull a well-pressed handkerchief from his pocket and dab at his forehead. Then he concluded his opening remarks. "In the name of all the innocent women and children in the state of Illinois, we will demand the death penalty for this savage, senseless murder."

Josef sagged in his seat. Darrow caught his motion from the corner of his eye and reached over to pat his hand. When Josef had calmed himself somewhat, he noticed that several of the jurors had seen Darrow touch him. It was such a friendly gesture that Josef hoped it would show the jury that he was innocent. Surely they would understand that no one could touch a person as foul as the man Rais had described.

Darrow waited until the prosecutor had taken his seat before he rose to his feet and removed his glasses.

"For the past hour," he said, gesturing to Josef with his glasses, "I have heard this young man characterized as an assassin, a brute, and a criminal fit only for condemnation. But this is not the Josef Chernik it is my good fortune to know. The Josef Chernik I have come to admire is a young man who—like many of you—spent his youth doing backbreaking work to help his family survive. He is a man who has toiled while those he worked for grew rich."

Darrow walked away from the defense table toward the jury.

"Mr. Rais has told you that in all his years at the bar he has never seen anyone more guilty than this young man. He knows his statement will impress you because most of you have never been in a courtroom before. Well, I *have* been in court before, and I can *always* count on a prosecutor to declare that the defendant is guilty of the most atrocious offense he has ever seen."

Rais stood to his feet. "Objection," he shouted. "Argumentative and improper. This is no time for speech making."

"Your Honor," Darrow said, "counsel's objection comes with a striking lack of courtesy—considering that he has been making a defamatory speech for the last hour. In that time he has also insulted a man who cannot reply. And that is cowardly and unethical in the extreme."

Beneath his slick, shiny hair, Rais's face flushed. "I don't have to take lessons from you in ethics or bravery," he shouted.

Darrow turned his back on Rais. "Then you ought to take lessons from someone."

The judge banged his gavel angrily. "Mr. Darrow, you may think these remarks are cunning, but they are out of place here. We do not need your legal advice in this courtroom, sir. Not at all."

"I beg your pardon, Your Honor. I certainly meant no offense to *you*." Darrow glanced over his shoulder to indicate that he *had* meant offense to Rais. "May I continue my opening remarks?"

"You may," the judge replied stiffly, "if you keep them to the subject."

Darrow walked toward the jurors and stood in front of them. His shoulders were slumped, and his face looked sad, as though he were weighed down by the sorrow of all the workers who had ever suffered.

"Mr. Rais has talked to you a good deal about the Pullman strike," he said. "He wanted you to remember how frightened you felt that week because he knows that the violence made you wonder if everything you love about America was coming to an end.

"Well, I want to tell you right now that that was exactly what was happening. On the Fourth of July, the very day on which we celebrate our independence from tyranny, the laws of this state were twisted to be used *against* the people of this state!

"Not by strikers, as Mr. Rais would have you believe, but by the men who run and influence this government. As it happens, those laws were twisted against this boy. But they could just as easily have been used against *you*."

Darrow leaned forward so that his elbow was resting on the

railing in front of the jury. His voice was so soft that even Josef had to lean forward to hear him.

"You see, in contrast with what the prosecutor has told you, this is not a *criminal* case. This is but one more episode in the age-old battle for human liberty. This is merely one more instance of evil men using the law to bring righteous men to prison or death."

"Objection, Your Honor," Rais said. "Mr. Darrow is intentionally attempting to prejudice the jurors."

Judge Rhinehart looked down from his bench at Darrow and shook his head. "Mr. Darrow, if you don't confine yourself to the facts, you can consider your opening statement finished."

Darrow did not answer the judge except to nod. Then he began speaking to the jurors again.

"You will hear that Josef Chernik is a good shot and that his skill with a gun marks him as a murderer. But I know from our conversations earlier that several of you gentlemen are good shots. Mr. Miller, Mr. Haywood, Mr. Ford, from what you told me, you all are excellent marksmen.

Darrow nodded slowly as he looked each juror in the eyes.

"As this trial progresses, I want you to evaluate carefully the *quality* of the prosecutor's so-called evidence. Because," he concluded, "I think you will find that if you had been anywhere near Grand Boulevard on the night of July Fourth, you might very well be sitting where Mr. Chernik is today. Then you, too, would have the honor of hearing Mr. Rais call you the most despicable murderer he had ever set eyes on!"

29

THE PROSECUTION'S FIRST WITNESS was sworn in early the next morning. He was a deputy named Kendrick Hanson. When Hanson first walked to the front of the courtroom, Josef didn't recognize him. His dark hair was combed smoothly behind his ears, and his red mustache was neatly trimmed. He hardly resembled the rough, uncouth man who had shoved him into the boxcar. After staring at him for a few minutes, Josef remembered how the man had threatened to burn down the car with him in it.

Prosecutor Rais's handling of this witness was so expert that it took Darrow by surprise. Before Rais even asked Hanson about the shooting incident, he began with personal questions about Hanson's scurrilous background. Hanson admitted that he had been arrested and jailed numerous times, but he also claimed that he was now a repentant Christian, anxious to atone for his sins.

It was only after an impressive display of penitence that Rais asked Hanson to identify Josef as the man he had seen shoot into the crowd. Even Josef could see that the jury was impressed with his testimony, coming, as it did, on the heels of his confession of religious rebirth.

GRACE MARK

"That son of a bitch knew what I'd do to his star witness," Darrow grumbled to Josef. "He took all the sparks out of my fire."

When Rais finished questioning the deputy, Darrow stood. He did not hesitate to let the jury see his contempt for the man.

"Mr. Hanson," he asked, "how did you come to be a deputy?"

"I was appointed."

"And what were your qualifications for this job, sir?"

"Oh, just that I'm patriotic, I guess." Hanson shrugged his shoulders modestly. "I just wanted to make sure the city could survive that strike."

"That's an unusually noble sentiment for a man who has been arrested six times in the last four years."

Rais sat back in his chair and smiled. He had already shown that the man had repented and was now the most honest of men.

"I was asking about your *qualifications*," Darrow continued. "There are many men in the city who profess religious feeling, but most of them are never called upon to play the role of deputy. I notice that you deputies were given guns. Can I assume you know how to shoot?"

"I do, sir," said Hanson, reluctantly as if he wished to put his past behind him.

"You once shot a man yourself, did you not?"

Rais was on his feet. "The shooting of others," he shouted, "has nothing to do with this case."

"You introduced this line of questioning yourself," said Darrow.

Judge Rhinehart looked at Rais and hesitated. "Indeed, you did, Mr. Rais," the judge said reluctantly. "Continue, Mr. Darrow."

"Under what circumstances did you shoot a man?"

"Aw, I was just scared," Hanson answered. "It was self-defense. A man pulled a gun on me."

Darrow asked his next question quickly, not giving the witness a moment to think. "Can you describe the scene the night of the murder, sir?"

"Which murder?" Hanson asked. When Darrow smiled at the mistake, Hanson covered himself quickly. "Oh, *this* murder. Well, sir, it was terrible. Strikers were running everywhere, settin' fires."

THE DREAM SEEKERS 347

"Sounds frightening," Darrow said.

"Yes, sir. I reckon it was."

"Frightening enough for you to shoot someone again—the way you did before?"

Rais was on his feet, shouting, "Objection!"

"Sustained," said the judge.

Darrow had been leaning forward as if fascinated by Mr. Hanson's testimony. Now he acted as if he were hardly interested in his next answer.

"Mr. Hanson, since you claim you saw Mr. Chernik fire a gun that night, would you show us how he did it?"

Hanson thought for a moment before he lifted his left hand and pretended to fire the pistol.

"You're sure that's exactly how he did it?"

"Yes, sir," Hanson said eagerly. He jerked his left hand up from an imaginary holster and aimed it. "He shot just like this."

"Now, sir, you already told us that the person you saw shoot that gun is in this courtroom."

Hanson agreed that he was. "Yes, sir. Josef Chernik."

"Just to make sure that this is Josef Chernik, I want to ask the defendant to sign his name."

Josef seemed embarrassed. "I can only write in Hebrew."

"Then write your name in Hebrew, Mr. Chernik," Darrow said. "We will trust that your name is the same regardless of the language."

As Josef was writing his name, Darrow said, "Mr. Hanson, would you please demonstrate again the exact way you say this defendant fired that gun?"

Josef was still writing when Hanson resumed his imitation of the shooting.

"I would like to point out to the jury that the defendant is writing his name with his right hand," Darrow said, "while the witness is testifying that he shot with his left."

Rais was on his feet. "This is ridiculous," Rais sputtered. "Obviously Mr. Hanson is left-handed himself. Since he was in front of Chernik, it would appear to him that Chernik was shooting with his left hand."

"Mr. Rais," Darrow said, "this witness has just made an error in his testimony. I think it's a pretty big mistake, considering that a young man's life is at stake."

Darrow walked quickly toward the deputy. Whatever restraint he had shown toward this witness was gone. Now he seemed enraged that Hanson had told such a brazen lie against his client.

"Now, Mr. Hanson, I want to know what happened to the gun?"

"The gun?" Hanson asked innocently.

"You claim you saw the defendant shoot a gun, did you not?"

The deputy paused for a moment before he answered. The look on his face told the courtroom that he knew he was about to step into a trap. He answered a bit too loudly. "Yes, I did."

"Then where is the gun? Surely you took it from him."

"I don't know."

"You and a group of men grabbed this man after you say you saw him shoot someone. Wouldn't you try to get his gun? Wouldn't you make sure you had it for a trial like this one?"

"I guess it's hard to believe, but we was too busy to remember everything," Hanson said.

"Yes, Mr. Hanson," Darrow said dryly. "Even though you kept yourself busy kicking and beating the defendant, that is very hard to believe."

The day dragged on as painfully as any Josef could remember. The prosecution called three deputies, all of whom testified that they had seen Josef shoot his pistol into the crowd. Each of them, in turn, pointed confidently at Josef when asked to identify the murderer. It was only their unimpressive backgrounds and the issue of the missing gun that kept Darrow from looking completely foolish before the jurors.

Later that afternoon Detective Wheeler was called to the stand. Josef recognized Wheeler as the man who had interrogated him in jail.

Under Rais's questioning, Wheeler described how he had questioned the accused. He explained to the jury that Josef admitted he had been at the scene of the crime and how, even hours after his arrest, he was still covered with blood. Wheeler smiled proudly as he described how he had recognized Josef as the sharpshooter who had won five dollars in the Buffalo Bill show.

Wheeler's testimony moved forward in an easy, unpretentious fashion, and it wasn't long before Rais realized that this witness offered his case a credibility that the deputies had not.

To enhance Wheeler's status with the jury, Rais decided to draw him out about his trained memory.

"You mean," Rais asked, "you were able to identify this young man from an event that had occurred more than a year before?"

"Yes, sir," answered Wheeler, crossing his long arms across his chest and smiling complacently. "I do that kind of thing quite often."

"And you have been on the force with an unblemished record for more than twenty years, is that right?"

"Yes, sir." He nodded. "Sure is."

Rais looked at Darrow smugly. Darrow had been able to cast doubt on the testimony of the deputies, but Rais felt confident he would be unable to damage this witness. "Cross-examine," he snapped.

Darrow stood slowly and leaned forward so that his knuckles were resting on the table. "Mr. Wheeler, is your memory the reason you failed to extract a signed confession from this defendant?"

Wheeler was suddenly off guard. "No, sir," he said slowly. He glanced at Rais for help.

"But after questioning the defendant for a number of hours, you did not get a signed confession from him, did you?"

"No, sir."

"Why is that?"

Wheeler slouched in his chair. His pleasure in being praised for his memory was quickly fading. "It was pointless."

"Pointless?" Darrow leaned forward as if he couldn't quite hear. "Did you say *'pointless'*?"

"Yes. Well, we knew he was guilty."

"But he did not confess, did he?"

"No."

Still staring at Wheeler, Darrow walked slowly to the jurors' box. "In fact, during the entire interrogation he continued to insist that he was innocent, did he not?"

Wheeler leaned back in his seat and crossed his legs. He managed to sneak in a small grin at the jury. "Well, most all of 'em that we get in there swear they're innocent."

"Even after they've been thrown down the stairs?"

Darrow's question surprised Wheeler so much that he almost coughed.

Darrow bored in on the witness. "You did throw the defendant down the stairs, didn't you?"

For a moment Wheeler's eyes showed that he couldn't remember whether he and Detective Silvestra had pushed Josef down the stairs or not. "No," he said finally, and then he shook his head definitively to cover his confusion.

"You don't seem too sure about it," said Darrow. "For a man with your memory, you seem to be in some doubt."

Darrow put one of his feet on the rail in front of the jury box. He made his next comment without even looking at the detective. "I'm sure his cellmates will testify as to his physical condition if you can't remember."

Wheeler could feel his face beginning to sweat. All the detectives on the force beat up suspects to extract confessions from them, but it was a practice frowned on by people who didn't understand the legal system. The discussion of this practice in a courtroom filled with reporters made him feel pressured.

Suddenly he lost control of himself and shouted, "We did not throw the bastard down the stairs!"

Darrow knew that the detectives had only threatened to throw Josef down the flight of stairs, but this line of questioning had unsettled the witness and eroded his credibility. To keep the issue alive, Darrow made one last jab. "I guess he was just strolling on the landing and happened to fall?"

A spectator laughed, and Darrow glanced at the jurors. Several of them were staring at him dumbfounded. It was clear from their expressions that they had never realized that beatings were commonplace in the police department.

"But surely, as a murder suspect, he was not pampered?" Darrow continued. "Surely you gave him a tough, thorough police interrogation, did you not?"

Wheeler's face showed dread. "Yes, of course," he said irritably.

"And throughout an interrogation that you yourself describe as tough, he continued to insist on his innocence, didn't he?"

Wheeler slumped further in his seat. "Yep," he finally said.

Darrow stood erect and moved in front of the witness. He had lost every sign of anger. His expression was that of a man trying very hard to understand something.

"Detective, I don't mean to cast doubt on your ability as a member of the police department. We have all come to recognize what a fine memory you have. But what I'm curious about is what happened when the decision was made to charge the defendant with murder. I don't understand. At the end of a tough interrogation during which the defendant continuously upheld his innocence, someone decided to charge him. Was that you?"

"Of course not," Wheeler said. "It was Police Chief Brennan himself."

"Ah," Darrow said, as if that clarified matters for him. "And was the police chief *with* you while you interrogated Josef Chernik?"

"He was in his office."

"Alone?"

"No, sir. With Mr. G. G. Mattingly."

Darrow had no idea who this Mattingly was, but he knew it was to his advantage to act as if he did. "And who is G. G. Mattingly?" he asked as if for the benefit of the jury.

"He's the guy that deputized the marshals during the strike."

"Does he work for the police department?" Darrow asked.

"Of course not," said Wheeler. "He works for one of the railroads."

This news took Darrow by surprise. "You mean, the man who pinned a badge on men with police records and armed them with loaded guns—this man worked for the railroad? And, you're saying he was with the police chief when the state decided to charge Josef Chernik with murder?"

"Objection," shouted Rais. "What difference does it make *who* was with the chief when Chernik was charged with murder?"

"Sustained," said Judge Rhinehart.

"Don't you think it curious, Your Honor," said Darrow, "that these railroaders seem to be everywhere these days?"

A stir passed through the courtroom. It sounded a little like the fall leaves outside when a wind blew through them. Darrow knew he had better not venture deeper into unknown waters.

"No more questions," he said.

30

HARRY ELSTON WAS BARELY twenty-four, but he had already been a newspaperman for eight years. As he raced to the newspaper office to write his story on the trial, he had a lot on his mind.

Elston had a nose for corruption, and for weeks, whenever he got near the upcoming Chernik trial, he'd been getting the scent of City Hall. Elston remembered meeting Chernik the day he was out in Pullman covering the strike. The young man had given him water, and Elston had liked him. Elston's impulse was to write a piece that was sympathetic to the young striker, but he was almost afraid to file it. Lately the newspaper had taken a hard line against the unions.

As Elston pumped his short, chubby legs up the stairs to the newsroom, he decided he'd take his chances and write the story he wanted. If his editor threw it back at him, he'd take it over his head to Victor Lawson. Lawson was unpredictable, but he might run the story.

As the publisher of the *Daily News* Victor Lawson had often used his paper to engage in controversy. Though Lawson's editorials had irritated a variety of citizens, ranging from the city's most upright to the downright scurrilous, it was the breach of old-boy decorum that had caused him the most trouble. These days he seemed more inclined to back away from trouble. The problem for his reporters was never knowing just how close they had to stay to the line.

Elston wrote his story, and his editor ran it by Lawson, who thought Elston's personal recollections of Josef during the strike gave the story a unique slant. He was fascinated that Elston would describe Josef as kind and gentle. Until then the press had characterized Chernik as mean and shifty. Lawson was so interested in Elston's report that he called him into his office.

"Young man, explain this story to me if you please."

Elston had anticipated trouble, and he was spoiling for a fight. "This story tells the truth," he snapped, squeezing his roly-poly face into a grimace of indignation. "The circumstances surrounding Chernik's arrest just don't make sense!"

"Sit down," Lawson said. "I want to hear all about it."

So it happened that Elston's front-page story was supported by an editorial written by Victor Lawson himself. Readers who were enthralled by Elston's unusual portrayal of the gentle striker on trial for murder could turn to the editorial section and read the paper's concerns about the legal system. Could any striker, the editorial asked, get a fair trial in the city of Chicago?

By early evening the special edition was on the streets. Readers, who had deplored the biased trial that sent the Haymarket anarchists to the gallows several years before, felt once more the chill of injustice. Could it be happening again?

One of the readers who read the paper closely was Judge Peter Rhinehart. Rhinehart had hated the *Daily News* for quite some time. It was the *News* that had first publicly accused Judge Joseph E. Gary of misconduct in the famous Haymarket trials a few years ago. An accusation like that was something he wanted to avoid.

When Rhinehart was appointed to the Chernik case, he had felt sure that public opinion would be strongly against the young striker. But this article made him aware that he should rethink his position. At the very least he'd be careful to conceal his personal bias against the defendant. The last thing he needed was for the public to start seeing this kid as a victim.

*   *   *

Hannah was beside herself. She lay in bed, surrounded by four of the evening newspapers. Under the headline

FOUR WITNESSES SAW CHERNIK KILL!
DEFENSE FALTERS, STATE DEMANDS HANGING

the Chicago *Tribune* told its story: "The overwhelming number of eyewitnesses to the brutal shooting death of Kathleen Kelly on July 4, have built an impregnable case against radical striker Josef Chernik."

The same story was found in the *Examiner* and the *Journal*. Only Harry Elston's article in the Chicago *Daily News* offered a different perspective.

Despite his favorable report, what made Hannah feel completely hopeless was that no matter what their perspective, there was no disagreement about one thing in the newspaper accounts: The state's evidence was strong. It seemed certain that Josef Chernik would be sentenced to hang.

From her bed Hannah heard giggling outside in the hallway. She knew it was some of the girls in the house playing with the baby. It was nearly suppertime, and the girls were enjoying their last chance to frolic with the child before the customers arrived. Hannah was so despondent she didn't even lift up her head when they came in.

"Here's little Sonja" called May-Belle Simmons as she burst through the door without knocking.

She was followed by Nellie Trace, who waltzed across the floor toward Hannah with the baby in her arms. Marie, Hannah's special friend, followed them closely.

"Be careful, Nellie," Marie said. "You'd kill it if you dropped it." Marie had developed a strong proprietary feeling for the child, almost as if little Sonja were her own.

As Hannah had expected, Roland Girard's fascination with Marie had cooled shortly after he had given her the necklace, and he had dropped her abruptly. Being abandoned this way had left Marie listless and depressed because she had fancied that Girard loved her. The baby had helped Marie recover, for it had given her a much-needed distraction.

Marie wasn't the only girl who had been changed by the child. Hannah had been surprised to notice that the baby seemed to touch something different in each of them.

One girl, holding Sonja's soft little body in her arms, might be reminded of a young sister she still missed. Another, looking into those pale green eyes, might be painfully moved to remember her own lost innocence. Another might simply enjoy the experience of making Sonja smile.

The baby had quite a different effect on Carrie Watson, who couldn't wait for Hannah to send it away. Carrie had made inquiries about a suitable wet nurse the first week of the baby's life, but her network of suppliers had come up with no ready answers. As a result, the baby was still in the house, Hannah was still nursing it, and Carrie was spoiling to get rid of it.

The fact that the girls were making fools of themselves over that kid had put Carrie in a bad mood that evening. She knew that somehow or other the baby was costing her money. How could it not when it was distracting her girls from their work?

Carrie and Vina walked through Hannah's door just as Nellie Trace was nestling little Sonja in Hannah's arms.

"Come on, Mother," Nellie said to coax Hannah when she didn't respond. "Give her your tit. This baby's hungry!"

When Hannah felt the warmth of her daughter against her breast, all her sadness about Josef intensified, and she burst into tears. As she lay there, sobbing mournfully, Vina shook her head.

"I think she's got the baby sadness," Vina said. "Lawd, I seen that happen once to a girl, and she wound up killing her baby and herself, too."

"She'd better not kill *this* baby," said Marie, alarmed that little Sonja was in danger.

"Don't be ridiculous," said Carrie. "She's sad about her brother. The poor kid's accused of killing that woman during the riot."

Since this news was not generally known in the house, it was met with the sounds of shock and sympathy.

"You mean, the man they said did it is her *brother*?" said Nellie Trace. "Why, heck, her brother didn't do it."

"How would *you* know? asked Carrie.

" 'Cause some muckety-muck railroadman come in here and spent an evening with yours truly!"

Hannah became alert. "Who is he?"

"None other than G. G. Mattingly."

"What's he got to do with it?" Carrie asked.

As Nellie Trace described what Mattingly had talked about the night she entertained him, the sense that there was an answer to this impossible situation opened Hannah's eyes. She sat up in bed so fast the baby lost hold of her breast and started to howl. "You've got to tell that to the police!" she urged. "I'll take you there in the carriage now."

Nellie was suddenly taken aback. She had been fearful of encounters with the police ever since an unpleasant episode several years ago when she was still working alone as a street-walker. During one of City Hall's rare morality sweeps, Nellie had been thrown in jail. Without money for bail, she was worrying about how she'd get out when a randy police officer offered her the opportunity of covering her bail in trade. When Chicago's finest discovered the arrangement, they all wanted a share, and after a week Nellie began to think they'd never let her go.

After that experience the idea of going *back* into a police station—especially with unpleasant news for the officials—was not appealing.

"Go to the police!" she squealed. "Not me!"

"But you know he's innocent!" Hannah wailed. "It's your duty."

Nellie looked slyly at Carrie Watson. Like many of the girls, Nellie had felt replaced in Miss Watson's affections by Hannah. She was happy now to have a chance to accuse Hannah of a lack of concern for Carrie's house.

"Duty!" she said. "My duty is to keep myself from starving. And, I might add, *not* to do anything that would get the police riled against this fine establishment."

Hannah caught the tone in Nellie's voice. *You're Carrie Watson's pet*, the tone said. *You don't live like us. You've had a baby, and you don't entertain men.*

Carrie caught it, too. And it annoyed her that this little flibbertigibbet would refuse Hannah in a bald-faced attempt to discredit her. She looked at Nellie severely and shook her head.

"Hell, if you don't stand up to the police every once in a while, they take advantage of you. If I hadn't stood up to 'em, I'd be paying half my earnings to keep the cops off my back to this day."

"But, Carrie," Nellie said, in a last-ditch appeal, "I got a full night tonight."

This argument was more persuasive, for Carrie had never been known to discomfit a customer unless she had to. "Who said anything about tonight?" she said impatiently. "We'll go tomorrow at noon—after we get up."

While Nellie stood by, looking chastised, Carrie had another thought. "Actually, you know," she said, "going to the police would be dumb. The person you should talk to is Clarence Darrow."

31

THE NEXT MORNING RAIS declared the prosecution's case closed. As he stood before the judge, cheerful and well groomed, he exuded confidence that his witnesses had given him a conviction. Before he returned to the prosecution's table, he took a moment to pause before the jurors. With a slight smile on his lips, he clearly conveyed his belief that since the jury already knew the facts, anything the defense had to say would be irrelevant.

When Rais was seated, Judge Rhinehart turned to Darrow. After reading the editorial in the *Daily News*, Rhinehart had decided that the best way to avoid charges of unfair bias was to show Darrow courtesy.

"Is the defense ready to present its case, Mr. Darrow?" the judge asked in a conciliatory tone.

Josef heard something new in the judge's voice. It sounded so much like sympathy that it scared him. When Darrow sighed and rose slowly to his feet, Josef's heart sank. His lawyer's face looked ravaged with worry and sleeplessness.

Darrow had spent much of the night thinking and pacing in his office. He knew he had put together a slim case for the boy, and he blamed himself. It was true that he hadn't had much to go on. The boy had not been able to come up with anyone who might have seen someone else shoot Kathleen Kelly. Josef hadn't even been able to suggest witnesses who would speak highly of his character. It seemed to Darrow that Josef had called so little attention to himself that few people outside his family had any opinion about him at all.

Even Lubek, whom Darrow had interviewed when he was preparing his case, had not had the highest praise for Josef. "He is uncommitted," Lubek had said. "Too cowardly to be with the union."

That wasn't much, Darrow knew, but it was something. Because Lubek was the kind of striker the jurors would dislike, Darrow thought his criticism of Josef would appeal to them. With luck, they would see that Lubek was right: Josef was too mild to commit a murder. But Lubek's opinions certainly weren't enough to build a case on.

Darrow knew that if he put Josef on the stand, Rais would attack him, but he saw it as his only chance. He wanted the jury to get to know the boy. The issue of Josef's marksmanship also needed to be addressed, and he thought it could best be handled by Josef himself. If he could just make the farmers empathize with the ordeal of being a foreigner, he thought he might be able to get them to like Josef instead of hate him.

The night before, Darrow had ordered G. G. Mattingly to be served with a subpoena. He didn't want to lead off his case with Mattingly because he had no idea where the questioning would lead, but at least he wanted to have this railroad executive standing by. If nothing else in Darrow's case was working, he knew he could hammer away at the police's motive for charging Josef in the first place.

To open his case for the defense, Darrow first called Karl Lubek. The big man had the desired effect on the jury, alienating them with his rough appearance and language.

"Was Josef Chernik a strong union supporter?" Darrow asked him.

Lubek made a face to show his contempt. "No," he growled. "He didn't really care about the workers."

"Do you think Josef Chernik would kill someone who opposed the union?"

Lubek laughed with disdain. "Him? No. He's too weak," Lubek answered. "Too chicken-shit scared all the time."

Under Darrow's questioning, Lubek described Josef's commitment to his family and his reluctance to go downtown the day of the riot. When Darrow finally turned Lubek over to Rais, the prosecutor decided to minimize the importance of Lubek's testimony by declining to cross-examine him.

Rais merely glanced at Lubek and shrugged. "No questions."

Darrow returned to the defense table and leaned near Josef for one last consultation. "It's your turn now," he whispered. You're going to do fine. Just tell your story the way we discussed."

Josef felt his stomach flutter with nerves as Darrow addressed the judge. "The defense calls Josef Chernik."

The spectators stirred excitedly. Darrow nodded, and Josef walked unsteadily to the witness stand. After Josef had been sworn in, Darrow began his questioning.

"Son," he said to emphasize Josef's youth to the jury, "first of all, I think most of us are curious about why you and your family came all the way from Russia to America. Tell us, what did you hope to find here?"

Josef nervously cleared his throat. "Justice."

Josef was hunched forward in his chair and spoke in such a low tone that the jury could barely hear him. Darrow knew that Josef's physical attitude would not give the jury a good impression.

"Son, we all know you're nervous," said Darrow kindly, "but we aren't going to be able to hear you if you don't speak up." He smiled and glanced at the jurors to include them in his recognition of the young man's discomfort. "Why don't you sit up straight so we can hear you?"

When Josef assumed a more alert posture, Darrow said, "Now give us that answer a little louder."

"We came here to find freedom and justice," Josef answered loudly, as Darrow had coached him.

"Justice?" Darrow asked. "That's interesting. Now, as I understand it, you were raised in a small town in Russia and moved to a big city in Lithuania in order to prepare for your move here. Is that right?"

"Yes, sir."

"You know, over here we hear a lot about Russia but not

much about Lithuania. Do those countries have anything to do with each other?"

"Yes, sir. The czar of Russia rules Lithuania."

"Ah," Darrow said. "So Lithuania is really under Russia's heel, is that right?"

"Yes, sir."

Darrow knew that his jurors had read a great deal about the dreadful tyranny of the czars. He intended to use their abhorrence of Russia to make his next point.

"Son, did your family have enough food over there?"

"No, sir."

"Did you have good job opportunities?"

Josef shook his head. "No, sir. The city we lived in was poor and crowded."

"But why didn't you move to another city over there and find work? That would have been easier than coming all the way to America. Moscow is a big city. Why didn't you just move there?"

"The czar won't let certain people live in Moscow."

"Certain people?" Darrow threw back his head as if this were a new idea to him. "You mean, Jews?"

Josef dropped his head and nodded. He was very afraid that once the jurors knew he was Jewish, they would find it easier to decide him guilty. Darrow knew that Rais would bring out Josef's faith anyway, so he smiled and walked toward the jury.

"Son, this is America," he said, spreading his hands to show the jurors how foolish it was for Josef to be afraid of their prejudice. "These people believe that it's just fine for you to be Jewish because they believe in the Bill of Rights. Isn't that right?"

A couple of the jurors were so caught up in Darrow's patriotism that they bobbed their heads up and down to agree. Darrow nodded his approval before he turned back to Josef. "But I'm still curious about your comment on finding justice. Isn't there justice in Russia?"

"No, sir."

"If a person wanted to have a fair trial there, could he?"

"No, sir," Josef answered. "The police decide. If they think you're guilty of something, you go to jail."

Rais stood to his feet slowly. His face wore an expression

of utter astonishment. "Your Honor," he said, "this is the most ridiculous line of questioning I have ever heard. What on earth does Mr. Darrow think he is doing here?"

This was the opportunity Darrow had been hoping for. He turned to Rais and shot back, "I am about to show that this poor boy's family came all the way to this country to find a system of justice they could trust. But instead, they found a nightmare equal to the worst in czarist Russia—"

Rais's face turned a bright red. "That's a lie!" he shouted.

Darrow raised his voice to shout over Rais. "—where the police, once again, can decide who is guilty and who is innocent—whether they have any evidence or not."

Bedlam broke out in the courtroom. Rais shouted over the uproar, "That's a damnable lie, and I won't stand for it!"

Judge Rhinehart banged his gavel loudly to restore order. "Mr. Darrow, this is intolerable! The reason we are here at all, sir, is so Josef Chernik *can* have a fair trial. One more comment about unfairness in this courtroom, and I'll hold you in contempt, sir."

Darrow became silent. His brooding eyes were fastened on the floor in front of him. When Rais resumed his seat, Darrow continued.

Under his questioning, Josef described why he had taught himself to shoot a rifle. He described the pogroms in Russia, how soldiers and peasants would ride into the Jewish communities to terrify the Jews. He spoke of how houses and shops were burned to the ground, how the women and girls were dragged away, screaming, to be raped or beaten.

During Josef's testimony the courtroom spectators sat spellbound. For all their prejudice against foreigners, his description gave them a glimpse of a world they had never known. In the stillness of the late morning they sat silently, imagining the horror of life in an oppressive country. As they thrilled to the danger of the czar's authority, they felt grateful and protected to be American.

When Darrow felt they had heard enough to appreciate Josef's gentleness and honesty, he paused for a moment. Then he walked over to stand directly in front of Josef.

"Josef Chernik," he finally said, "do you believe in God?"

"Yes, sir," Josef answered.

"As God is your witness, did you shoot Kathleen Kelly on the night of July fourth?"

Josef sat up straight and answered clearly. "No, sir. I did not."

"Did you have a gun in your hand at all?"

"Not that night, sir."

Darrow stepped back and spread his hands as if Josef had satisfied all his questions. "No further questions," he said softly.

As Darrow returned to his seat, Judge Rhinehart leaned forward to address the prosecution over the bench. "Mr. Rais, it is now eleven-thirty. Would you like to break for lunch or begin your questioning?"

During Josef's testimony Rais had observed the favorable impression the young man was making with the jury. The confidence Rais had felt earlier had somewhat faded. Darrow had already impugned some of his witnesses' credibility. Now, with the good showing Chernik had made, he did not want the jury to be left with a good impression of the defendant over the lunch hour.

"I want to question Chernik *now*," he answered harshly.

Rais sat quietly for a few moments before he rose to his feet. He slipped his hands into his neat, unwrinkled trousers and threw his head back contemptuously. "Well, now, Mr. Chernik, that was an interesting little tale you told about Russia."

Josef said nothing. He had calmed somewhat during Darrow's questioning, but the way Rais was looking at him frightened him.

"You have told us that you learned to shoot a gun in Russia, is that correct?"

"Yes, sir."

"Interesting," Rais said thoughtfully. "I'm surprised that in a country with the persecution you described, Jews would be allowed to own guns."

Again Josef sat still. He had a growing alarm that Rais was going to discover truths about him that would be very bad.

"Mr. Chernik," said Rais, "were Jews allowed to own guns in Russia?"

"No, sir."

"Then, where did you get the gun you learned to shoot with?"

Josef hesitated just long enough for Rais to know he had hit a nerve.

"I got it from a soldier."

"You got it from a soldier?" Rais smiled and shook his head incredulously. "Mr. Chernik, don't you mean that you *stole* it from a soldier?"

Josef slouched in his chair and spoke very quietly. "Yes. A friend of mine did."

"Speak up," said Rais impatiently. "The jury can't hear you."

Josef had a desperate sense of helplessness. He felt that he was being drawn inexorably down a passage where his secret life would be drawn from him against his will. He answered obediently. "We stole it."

Rais smiled and turned so that he was facing the jury. "Ah," he said. "So you stole a gun in Russia. Just, I daresay, as you stole a gun in Chicago on the night of July Fourth."

Darrow was on his feet. "Objection, Your Honor! What the defendant did years ago in another country has nothing to do with his behavior in Chicago."

Rais laughed, "Is that why you bent our ear for the last hour about the defendant's childhood in another country? Because it isn't relevant?"

Darrow shouted, "No, sir. That was different. You are drawing *conclusions* from past events that have no connection to the present."

Judge Rhinehart banged his gavel loudly. "Objection overruled. As Mr. Rais has pointed out, Mr. Darrow, you cannot have it both ways. You introduced the defendant's past to make a point about the present. Now it is the prosecution's turn."

Darrow sat down heavily at the defense table. In the face of the judge's hostility, he felt lost.

"And, again, Mr. Chernik," Rais asked, "what did you do with this gun—this gun that you stole in Russia?"

"I took it out in the woods with my friend, and we practiced shooting."

"Why were you practicing?" When Josef hesitated, he smiled. "I see you don't understand me. What I mean, Mr. Chernik, is why did you *want* to become a good shot?"

Josef was suddenly terrified that Rais would extract the

story about the soldier who had been shot in the small village. He began to stammer. "I don't know," he said.

"Oh, tut-tut-tut," Rais replied contemptuously, taking in the jury with his look. "Of course, you know. You wanted to be a good shot so you could protect yourself from those soldiers, so that, if the occasion demanded it, you could kill them. Murder them. Is that not true?"

Darrow was on his feet, yelling, "Objection! Objection!"

This time the judge didn't even look at Darrow before he ruled against him. "Overruled. Answer the question, Mr. Chernik."

Josef felt confused. He didn't quite remember the question. It had something to do with protecting himself from the oppressive soldiers. He saw nothing wrong with that, but he wondered why Mr. Darrow was so concerned. His mouth felt dry. People were looking at him.

"Yes," he said.

"So even as a young boy you were practicing with a gun in order to shoot soldiers." The prosecutor looked at the jury and smiled ruefully. "Well, Mr. Chernik," he said, "it would seem that the Pullman strike finally gave you the opportunity you have been wanting for so long. The problem, of course, was that you didn't fire upon one of the brave lads in the American Army. You shot an innocent civilian."

"Objection!" Darrow shouted.

Rais paused and looked around to make sure the jurors had understood everything that he had said. When he was satisfied that they did, he curtly nodded in a gesture of dismissal.

"No further questions."

Carrie Watson and Nellie Trace were waiting in the hallway when Darrow left the courtroom. He was walking slowly, and they could see that he was discouraged. Darrow was, in fact, deeply concerned. He knew Rais had undermined the gentle image of Josef he had created earlier. Darrow feared that putting the boy on the stand had thrown him to the lions.

"Mr. Darrow!" called Carrie, hurrying after him. "Mr. Darrow!" When he didn't stop immediately, Carrie called out, "Well, that's just fine, Mr. Darrow. If you don't want the evidence that'll save your client from the hangman's noose, just keep on walking."

Darrow turned around. He was in such a dark mood that he didn't even smile, though he had always been amused by Carrie Watson. But after he had heard Nellie's news in a deserted alcove under a staircase, he grinned from ear to ear.

As he stopped at the curb to offer Nellie Trace his hand gallantly, he had another thought. "Tell me, Miss Trace," he said, "do most men reveal their deepest secrets to you over a simple glass of champagne. Or did Mattingly happen to have his pants around his ankles at the time?"

Though she was an experienced prostitute and could have been expected to take the question in stride, Nellie blushed.

"Ah, well," said Darrow, "it's a good thing I decided to subpoena Mr. Mattingly yesterday. If I can get as much information out of him on the stand as you did when he was out of his drawers, it'll be a good day."

When Judge Rhinehart called his courtroom to order that afternoon, Darrow sprang to his feet with a light step. Rhinehart noticed that the weary creases on Darrow's face in the morning seemed to be completely gone. This afternoon the lawyer for the defense seemed almost sprightly.

Darrow approached the bench and smiled cunningly. "Your Honor, we have uncovered new evidence that has great bearing on this case."

Rhinehart looked at Darrow over his glasses. Something about the defense lawyer's eagerness irritated him. "Proceed, Mr. Darrow," he said dryly.

Darrow turned to the courtroom and announced loudly, "The defense calls Miss Nellie Trace."

As an employee of Carrie Watson Nellie had not failed to learn the importance of displaying her wares. Instead of the black skirt and modest mutton-sleeve blouse that another woman might have selected for day wear, Nellie was done up in a vivid, blue silk dress cut so low in the bodice that the cleavage between her breasts was discernible even at thirty feet. On her head, a matching ostrich plume bounced and swayed as she moved.

As she walked toward the witness stand, Nellie's appearance created an immediate sensation. It was clear to everyone in the room that this newest testifier for the defense was a high-priced whore. Spectators gawked and whispered. Some stood in order to get a better view. They were still whispering when Nellie settled herself and tucked her matching parasol against her voluminous skirt in order to fit her costume inside the witness box.

During this excitement Rais rose to his feet, grinning broadly. Lacking his courtroom skill, Rais's assistants were tittering like small schoolboys.

"Is this the latest character witness for your client, Mr. Darrow?" Rais asked. He winked at the jurors so that they could readily understand that only a lowlife would call a whore as a character witness.

Darrow turned to him and smiled back. "No, Mr. Rais," he drawled, enjoying himself immensely. "To my knowledge, Miss Nellie Trace has never met my client. She's here to testify about that railroadman you were so protective of. Maybe, if we're lucky, she can share some secrets about you."

As Rais turned red and sat down, a few of the jurors smiled.

After Nellie had taken her oath, Darrow asked her, "Miss Trace, will you tell us your occupation?"

"Indeed, sir," she said prettily. "I work for the finest sporting house in the entire Midwest, Miss Carrie Watson's."

Darrow waited until the courtroom had quieted before he continued. Looking at her seriously, he asked, "Now, Miss Trace, there are many who might say that a prostitute is a bad woman whose testimony should be discounted. For the sake of gaining their confidence, I want to remind you that you just took an oath to tell the truth."

"I always tell the truth, Mr. Darrow," Nellie said, miffed at the insult. "And I'll oblige you not to call me bad. At Carrie's house we don't water no drinks, and we never accept pay without giving satisfaction. As businesses go, it is more honorable than most."

Darrow ignored the titters her comment provoked. "I understand, Miss Trace," he said, "and I meant no offense. But there are some respectable folks, who, though they cheat and lie routinely, might nevertheless be inclined to doubt *your* testimony."

With her dark eyes snapping fire, Nellie nodded to indicate that she accepted his apology.

"Then, with the warning I have repeated about your oath, I am now going to ask you if you know the defendant, Josef Chernik?"

Darrow gestured broadly toward Josef, who was sitting in his chair with a look of utter confusion on his face.

"Never seen him before in my life," she answered crisply.

"Do you know a Mr. G. G. Mattingly?"

"Indeed, I do," she answered. "He's a customer. Not a *good* customer," she clarified. "But he was my customer once."

In the next few moments Nellie Trace recounted the night Mattingly had celebrated with her.

"And why was Mr. Mattingly celebrating?" asked Darrow.

"Well, he said he'd been worried that the deputies he'd appointed had got him in trouble—looting and shooting into the crowd and all. He was in a happy mood because he said he'd found someone else to pin it on."

Rais was so upset by the disclosure that for a few moments he was speechless. "Your Honor," he finally sputtered indignantly, "I will not stand by and hear the reputation of a respected businessman slandered by this—this whore."

"You watch your mouth," Nellie snapped.

Judge Rhinehart was suddenly very concerned about the way the state had handled its case. He rapped his gavel to quiet the chatter that Nellie's testimony had stimulated. "This is a very serious charge, Miss Trace," he said severely. "Very serious indeed."

"I would say so, sir," Nellie answered, unabashed. "I certainly wouldn't be sitting up here if it wasn't important."

Rhinehart quickly pondered the best action to take. Rais interrupted his thoughts. "Your Honor, it would be unthinkable—if this—this prostitute's testimony were admitted into evidence. In the first place, it's slanderous. In the second, it's hearsay—"

Darrow interrupted Rais. "The girl's testimony is as good as gold," he said. "Certainly as good as those deputies you called. But if there's any question and you wish to waive your right to cross-examine, let's just call Mattingly to the stand right now."

This suggestion provided the judge with a solution to this problem. "Is Mr. Mattingly here?" he asked.

After a long pause a small man in the courtroom stood self-consciously to his feet. "Your Honor," he called nervously, holding his hand in the air for recognition. His appearance was so softly effeminate that he himself caused a small stir. Spectators could not resist discussing the likelihood that this little man had visited Nellie Trace.

"Yes?" the judge said. "Are you Mr. Mattingly?"

"No, sir," the man said. "I'm Edward Long, a secretary of Mr. Mattingly's. Mr. Mattingly said to say that he was sorry, sir, but that he's been unavoidably called away on business to New York."

Darrow spun back to the judge and pounded his fist on the defense table. "This is an outrage, Your Honor! Mattingly deliberately slipped out on a subpoena!"

"Mr. Darrow," said the judge wearily, "*I'll* handle this if you please." The judge turned his attention back to Edward Long. "You mean that after Mr. Mattingly received his subpoena to appear in court, he left town?"

"Yes, sir," said the small man softly. "He said it was unavoidable."

"Your Honor," said Darrow, "I request that the case against Josef Chernik be dismissed."

"What?" shouted Rais. "On the basis of this little floozy here? Your Honor, that would be—"

"Do you mind, Mr. Rais?" Rhinehart said sternly.

The judge was troubled and needed time to think. He feared that the state had bungled its case so badly that it would cast doubt on all the union trials that were scheduled over the next few months. He didn't want to take the word of this chippy on the stand, but with Mattingly's flight to New York, the conclusions were disturbing. He wanted to delay his decision until he had seen the papers. He knew they would give him a sense of the public's attitude.

He studied Darrow over his glasses. "Court dismissed until tomorrow at ten o'clock."

32

DURING THE NIGHT WARM air brought Indian summer to Chicago. The next morning spectators at the trial found that the change in the weather had made the crowded courtroom uncomfortable. They withdrew pocket handkerchiefs and folded their newspapers to fan their necks and faces. When Judge Peter Rhinehart seated himself at the bench and looked out at the room, he stared into a sea of flapping handkerchiefs and fans.

Rhinehart had read accounts of the trial in the newspapers the night before. They were so mixed that he was left without a clear sense of popular opinion to guide him. It was late evening before he felt he had come up with a solution that would protect him from criticism.

When Darrow and Rais were standing in front of him, Rhinehart made his announcement to the courtroom. "I have deliberated on the testimony of Nellie Trace for the last eighteen hours," he said as if wearied by his effort. "I have concluded that being the sort of woman she is, she is of questionable credibility. I therefore believe that it would be unwise to allow her testimony to take precedence over that of other witnesses that we heard for the prosecution. It is my decision, therefore, that stopping this trial and releasing the prisoner, as Mr. Darrow has requested, would be grossly improper. Indeed, if there were ever a case when the outcome should be decided by a jury, it is this one."

Darrow glared at the judge. Rhinehart caught his look and ignored it. He had expected Darrow to be disappointed but thought it far more important to his future as a judge that he wash his hands of the decision and leave it up to the jury.

Having satisfied himself that the press had had time enough to jot down his words, Rhinehart turned to address the jury. "I am not going to strike Miss Trace's testimony from the record," he said, "but I do want to instruct you jurors to bear in mind the nature of this woman when you weigh her testimony against the facts in this case."

Without giving Darrow a chance to object to his characterization of Miss Trace's testimony, Rhinehart turned to the defense attorney. "Mr. Darrow," he said with an edge to his voice, "do you have additional witnesses to call?"

"Since G. G. Mattingly has chosen to ignore this court's subpoena," Darrow said tersely, "and since Nellie Trace's sworn statement has been denigrated, the defense will rest."

When Darrow answered, he conveyed the idea that he didn't think there was any *point* in calling other witnesses. Nevertheless, despite the judge's criticism of Nellie Trace, Darrow knew she had made quite an impact on the jury. Even if he had other witnesses standing by, Darrow would have been inclined to let her revelations ring last in the jurors' ears without reducing their impact with weaker testimony.

The spectators continued to fan themselves as Samuel Rais began his summation. He reviewed the testimony of Darrow's witnesses and denounced Nellie Trace as a perjurer and the vilest of liars. Only such a woman, he said, would have had the gall to step forth and tell such brazen lies.

As Rais spoke, he projected an air of simple honesty. His manner was so sincere that the jurors appeared transfixed by his performance. Several of them seemed to forget the discomfort of the hot weather and the perspiration that trickled down their faces.

"Kendrick Hanson, that fine deputy who has been reformed through a powerful spiritual rebirth," Rais warned, "will be attacked by Mr. Darrow in his argument for the other side. Darrow will call him a liar. And he will call the other eyewitnesses you have heard liars. But gentlemen of the jury, let me assure you that there is a Providence in Kendrick Hanson's testimony. Yes, I say a Providence, for surely this man's testimony has come not from the man himself but from the power of divine grace working in his soul to bring one of the nation's worst criminals to justice."

Rais spoke for six hours, stopping only for lunch and two five-minute breaks. At the end of the day, when he concluded his talk, the jurors looked more exhausted than he did.

"Gentlemen of the jury," he said, wrapping up his argument, "I have searched my own soul, and I can come to only one conclusion: This man, whom we graciously admitted into our land—a land where peace and prosperity were his for the taking—has brought his own form of injustice to our shores.

"Perhaps it was because of his demented hatred of Russian soldiers that Josef Chernik came to this country a self-trained assassin. But one thing is clear: With malice aforethought, he took aim against one of our sworn deputies, and not caring whom he would destroy if he missed, he thoughtlessly and willfully took the life of an innocent woman."

Rais stepped close to the jury for his final comment. Before he spoke, he looked long and hard in each juror's eyes.

"This jury must put aside soft-minded sympathy and perform its duty. When you review the evidence with a clear mind, I know that you will find no alternative but to hang Josef Chernik."

As Rais finished his talk, Josef covered his face with his hands. In the persuasive words of the prosecuting attorney, he heard his doom being sealed.

By the next morning the temperature had risen another seven degrees. The Indian summer warming had become hotter than anyone could remember. The courtroom was steaming. Not even the open windows and hand fans could bring relief to the crowded room.

After hearing Rais's closing argument the day before, Josef had hardly slept. He was so despairing that he was barely able to walk from the jail to the courtroom without being assisted.

As Darrow began his closing argument, Josef couldn't bring himself to watch. He sat, slouched over the defense table, staring forlornly into his hands.

Darrow rose to his feet. He seemed to have given more attention to his appearance for this important day, and he stood before the jury in his black three-piece suit. A stiff white-winged collar framed his sorrowful face. When he began speaking, it was slowly and softly.

"I'm sure it seems like a long time ago when I told you that this was more than a criminal case," he said. "After listening to the trumped-up evidence the state has put before you, I hope you can understand that now. The villainy and infamy of the prosecution reek from beginning to end with corruption and heartlessness.

"Yes, this is a great deal *more* than a criminal case. What this case is really about is the right of workingmen in this country to earn a decent wage."

Darrow moved closer to the jury and leaned against the railing in front of the jury box. His tone became so low and confidential that spectators in the back of the courtroom assumed he was telling secrets to the jury that they were not allowed to hear. Except for the soft flopping sound of the audience fanning itself, the courtroom was completely silent. Many spectators strained forward. They were not aware that Darrow's voice was so well pitched that they could have heard every word even if they hadn't been paying particular attention.

"You see, gentlemen," he was saying, "this case is about the destruction of a movement which represents the dreams of *all* men who labor to sustain their daily lives.

"Why do I say that?" he asked the jurors, and paused as if he wanted them to think about it. "Because Josef Chernik is innocent. There is not one shred of evidence against him. Not one. His only crime is that he was present at the site of the crime—along with thousands of others. Yet because he is a worker, because he was known to be able to shoot a gun, and because he committed the crime of being born in a foreign land, he was chosen to be a sacrifice. Yes. Josef Chernik was selected to be the sacrificial lamb that would cover up the behavior of criminals whom the state had supplied with guns and uniforms."

Darrow now changed his attitude, as if he were interested

in the logic of the government. "Just ask yourself why our government would behave so foolishly as to hire and arm criminals—especially during a time when reason and understanding were essential.

"Why? The only reason that holds any water is that throughout the Pullman strike the government had become unduly influenced by those with money and power.

"I am speaking now, of course, of the power of George Pullman. Over the years George Pullman has become a czar in this country as surely as Nicholas is czar in Russia. Through his influence and money, he reached out his long arm to change the laws and traditions that make us free. And, my friends, for that reason Czar Pullman is a greater threat to the welfare of this great nation than Czar Nicholas could ever be."

Though Darrow's back was to the spectators, he could sense their attention. While he was talking about Czar Pullman, not one person had coughed. That, he knew, meant that they were listening so hard that they didn't have time to fidget.

"Czar George," he continued. He shook his head with strong judgment. "Was it enough that he should take the toil, sweat, and lives of his poor men for starvation wages? No. Was it enough that he should import spies to dog and incite them? No, indeed. Like a czar posting Cossacks in the homes of the serfs, George Pullman deliberately *set in motion* the violence that racked this city and even destroyed his own property.

"Now, you may well ask yourself, 'Why would a man want to destroy his own property?' And I will tell you right. Because breaking the will of his workers was worth more to this despotic man than the cost of his sleeping cars."

The courtroom was stirred. Even Josef could feel it. People were listening and being angered by what Darrow was saying. Josef began to feel alive again as sparks of hope returned to him.

When court was adjourned for lunch, Josef turned to Darrow eagerly. "Mr. Darrow," he said with admiration and hope glowing in his eyes, "you were wonderful."

Darrow grunted noncommittally. He was so concerned for the young man's future that it hurt him to see the pitiful eagerness in his face. He could not bear to give him false hopes. When Josef was being led back to his cell, Darrow looked away.

At noon word got out on the street that Darrow had attacked George Pullman. "Why, he acts as if it were George Pullman on trial—not the striker," one spectator announced loudly outside the courtroom. By the time court resumed, a thousand people had pushed their way into the hallway. They shoved against one another to get near the courtroom door in order to catch whatever they could hear of Darrow's speech.

Darrow started off the afternoon by castigating the state's star witnesses. He criticized them and spoke of their past troubles for more than two hours. He scoffed at the testimony of the deputies, but he saved his strongest words for Kendrick Hanson.

"I want to say to you, gentlemen," he declared righteously, "that if Kendrick Hanson has religion now, I hope I never get it myself."

Toward the end of the afternoon, his stiff collar now limp and wilted, Darrow walked back to the defense table so that he could reach over and touch Josef on the shoulder as he talked. He spoke quietly as though weary with sadness.

"You have heard it said that when Josef Chernik's family arrived on these shores, it was to find a dream. Now I know that when you hear Josef's accent, it makes you feel that he is *different* from you. I know that his accent makes it hard to sympathize with his dreams and disappointments. I don't criticize you for it, for it is only natural. But I do want you to understand that at some point or another *most* of us have been foreigners here ourselves.

"When I first moved here from Ohio, I was a foreigner in this city. When you moved to Chicago from your small town, Mr. Miller," Darrow said to one of the jurors, "and when you came here from your farm, Mr. Atkins, in a sense, you were foreigners here, too. Can you remember how hard that was?"

Darrow saw two of the jurors nodding in recollection of their own bewilderment when they had first moved to the big city. Even Judge Rhinehart was listening attentively, his chin resting on his clasped hands.

"Yes, I see that you do remember," he said gently. "But hard though it was for you, think how much *easier* it was than for this young man. At least, you spoke English. Just imagine—if your every word had marked you with the stigma of having been born elsewhere!

"You have heard Mr. Rais charge this young man with coming to this country to take advantage of our laws," he said. "But ask yourself this: Who is the criminal here? Is it the innocent man who is standing up for his rights to earn a living wage? Or is it a responsible man like George Pullman who keeps food out of the mouths of that man's children and calls out an army of criminals to provoke a riot?"

Darrow paused and looked into the eyes of each juror. He saw that they had understood his point. He knew that they finally realized that George Pullman had intentionally inflicted hardship on his workers.

"No, gentlemen, this is not a criminal case," he finally said, returning to his main point. "Those people who would destroy your right to a decent living are using this court of justice to their own evil ends. That is why this trial is important to every man, woman, and child in America. For it threatens justice itself. And in threatening justice, it is an attack on the way you will live, and the way your children and grandchildren will live, in this great land.

"Gentlemen, don't ever think that your own life or liberty is safe when under evidence like this and circumstances like these, this boy has been brought here and placed in the shadow of the gallows."

Darrow walked toward the jurors. He stretched out his arms to them imploringly. He was speaking emphatically, yet softly, and his eyes were filled with tears.

"Are you ready, gentlemen, in this day and generation, to take away the life and liberty of a human being upon the testimony of rogues and liars? If so, I don't want to live. I don't want to live in a world where such men as these can cause the undoing of another human being."

Darrow finished his plea so quietly that it was hard to know where his voice had finished and where silence had begun.

In the crowded courtroom the silence lasted thirty seconds. Then a full minute.

Finally the judge broke the quiet to instruct the jury. When he finished, a bailiff gave a signal. The jury rose and left the box. Judge Rhinehart abruptly left the bench.

No one else stirred. Darrow sat quietly; Rais and his prosecutors sat silent, their eyes down. In that room so filled with spectators, there was hardly a breath or a movement. It was not merely that people did not want to speak. It was that they sensed something extraordinary had happened and didn't want to break the spell.

The jury was taken out at four-thirty in the afternoon. At five-thirteen there was a buzz from the jury room, which announced that the jurors wanted to return. Still, no one in the courtroom had moved. Now people looked at one another in amazement.

Josef felt his heart lurch in his chest. He looked at Darrow with fear. "What does it mean?" he asked. "Have they decided so soon?"

Darrow, fearful that the jury had so easily found Josef guilty, told a white lie. "Maybe they want more instructions."

But the jurymen were grinning as they filed into their box. Judge Rhinehart took his place on the bench and broke the tense silence.

"Your pleasure?" he asked.

"A verdict," replied the foreman.

"Read it," ordered Rhinehart.

"Not guilty!" cried the foreman.

The courtroom erupted with excitement. For a moment Josef did not dare to think that this could be over. Then Darrow jumped up and dragged Josef to his feet to hug him. Only then did Josef have the slightest understanding that he was free.

Spectators at the trial hurried down the aisles to pat Josef on the back; some of them hugged him as they congratulated him.

Darrow himself was so excited that he rushed over to the jury box where two of the jurors reached out and embraced him. "We knew." They smiled with tears glistening in their eyes. "We knew it wasn't right!"

Josef, in a daze, continued to accept the buffeting and hugging from spectators until he got a glimpse of his mother and father pushing toward him through the crowd. His mother was sobbing, but as he held her to him for the first time in such a long, long time, Josef knew she was weeping because the agony was finally over.

33

IT SEEMED LIKE HOURS before Darrow and Josef could get through the crowd and onto the courthouse steps. Josef blinked in the sunlight. Even this late in the day his eyes were unaccustomed to so much light. People were still pushing against him, congratulating him or trying to get statements for their newspapers.

He realized he could walk away anytime now, and his freedom was disorienting. He had somehow expected to be sent back to his cell—perhaps to await a more formal dismissal—but here he was. Free. The knowledge made him feel incomplete, like a timid little animal off its leash. The fear that had slaked him, been part of his life for as long as he could remember was gone, and he felt its loss almost like the death of a familiar friend. He was afraid that he would lose control of himself and weep.

Darrow could see Josef's confusion. He held Josef's elbow and was helping him through the crowd when he heard Josef's father answering the reporters' questions.

"We knew he was innocent," his father was saying. "Like Mr. Darrow said, the czar here same as there. Only there Josef could not have a fair trial for shooting the soldier."

Darrow was jolted by the old man's statement. He had no idea what shooting Yankel Chernik was talking about, but he didn't want it repeated to the press. Darrow abruptly reached past a couple of reporters and pulled Josef's father toward him.

"This family has been through a lot of strain lately," he said loudly to cover the man's confusing comment. "Justice was done, and we're happy about it. But I would like to ask you fellas to kindly leave these folks alone now so they can try to resume a normal life."

A few reporters groaned, but Darrow continued. "This family has been through enough," he said nicely, not wanting to offend the press. "Please. Let them be."

He could see that Josef was too disoriented to control his father, and he was concerned. Although Darrow had started thinking about Isabelle minutes after he had heard the jury's verdict and wanted to get over to Hull House to tell her about his victory, he knew he couldn't trust Yankel Chernik to resist the reporters' probing.

He spread his arms protectively over the shoulders of Josef and his father. "Come on, folks," he said, including Josef's mother in his look. "Let's go home."

Darrow led Josef and his parents to the seclusion of his office a couple of blocks away. When he got them inside the door on the first floor, he turned back to the few reporters who had followed them there. "So long, boys," he said. "You'd better get that story written. Tell the people it is still possible to get a fair trial in America."

Once upstairs, Josef sank heavily into Darrow's wing chair. His parents stood respectfully, impressed with the lawbooks that covered the wall, while Darrow brought in a couple of chairs for them.

"You will come to our home to celebrate," announced Yankel. "You will tell the neighbors of the law and Josef's innocence."

Before Darrow answered, he glanced out the window. There were still reporters hanging around on the street below. He didn't dare send these innocent, excited people away on their own.

He sighed. Seeing Isabelle would have to wait. This troubled him, for he knew he had neglected her lately. During the trial he had expended all his emotion thinking and worrying about the case. For weeks now he'd had no time for her.

One day early in the trial he had found a note from her slipped under his office door. "I would like to watch you in court tomorrow," her note said. "May I come?"

He had been so agitated and fearful about the outcome of the case that he had scribbled a note in response and sent his law clerk to Hull House with the answer. "Please stay away," his note said. "This case is so dismal that it will only upset you. The probability of a disastrous outcome does not allow for pleasurable viewing."

But now with the trial behind him, he yearned to see her. More important, he didn't want to hurt her feelings. Darrow decided to pen her a note. As he raked through the papers on his desk to find an empty sheet of paper, he noticed a document that in all his consternation about the trial, he had forgotten.

"More good news, Josef," he said, handing the paper to the young man. Josef took the paper and stared at it. It was official-looking and written in English.

"Just give me one minute," Darrow said graciously to the Cherniks as he sat down at the desk. "There is a little matter I must take care of before we leave."

"My dear Isabelle," he wrote. "Josef is free. At this moment I want nothing more than to celebrate by holding you in my arms, but I must accompany the boy and his family to their home. Please forgive my recent absence from you and meet me later tonight at my office. I will have Mrs. Hastings leave the door unlocked. Yours, Clarence."

Darrow folded the note and sealed it in an envelope. He stepped out into the hallway to speak to his elderly receptionist.

"Is Jim around, Mrs. Hastings?" he asked, inquiring about his young law clerk.

"Oh, Mr. Darrow," the lady said, as if the fault were with herself, "I am afraid I have not seen him all afternoon."

Darrow shook his head indulgently. Jim had been at the trial, and Darrow knew he'd probably stopped into a bar to brag about the acquittal. "I expect he'll be back soon," he said to Mrs. Hastings. "Have him take this note to Isabelle Woodruff over at Hull House. Tell him I want it delivered to her personally."

Darrow returned to his office, feeling pleased with the notion that his message might reach Isabelle before she read the outcome of the trial in the newspapers.

Josef was on his feet now, dumbly staring at the document in his hands. "Mr. Darrow," he asked, "what is this?"

"It's your patent. For the bicycle drum brake. Remember?"

For a second Josef didn't remember, and Darrow saw the confusion in his eyes. He almost slipped and said, "Your sister sent it to me," but he realized that Josef's parents didn't know Hannah's situation, and he stopped himself in time. "Remember?" he repeated.

Josef did remember, and he nodded. He was happy that his sister had come through. "But what does this mean?" he asked of the paper.

"It means you own the idea," Darrow said.

Darrow had never been on a bicycle and had not been too impressed with Josef's idea of putting brakes on those ungainly things. But at Hannah's insistence, he had followed through and submitted the drawing with a written description of the invention.

"I don't know if there's a use for brakes on a bicycle," he said, "but you could try to sell the idea to a manufacturer. Of course, if you had the money, I suppose you could manufacture it yourself."

Since all that seemed highly unlikely and had nothing to do with the problem of getting the Cherniks home and safely away from the press, Darrow changed the subject.

"Well," he said, rubbing his hands together in an outward display of eagerness, "it's a big day. Where can I take you? Are you still living in Pullman? Can we ride by and thumb our noses at Czar George?"

"No, no," said Yankel Chernik. "After the strike and the trouble we moved back to the old neighborhood. Today, in my part of town, you are a big hero. Josef, too," he said, glancing at his son, who was still staring at his patent. "Today we can walk down the street with our heads up."

When Isabelle saw Jim standing at the door of her nursery with a note in his hand, she felt a shiver of anxiety. She knew the note was from Clarence, and she hoped desperately that the news was good. Clarence always agonized over his cases, but

this one had been particularly difficult for him. He had believed
in Chernik's innocence so strongly that she knew if the young
man were convicted and hanged, Clarence would feel a devastating torment.

"Well, Jim," she said in a businesslike way to cover her
apprehension, "how is the trial going?" She wiped her hands
on her apron before she took the note from him.

"We won!" said Jim, flushing as if the triumph were his own.

"Thank God!" breathed Isabelle. She closed her eyes for a
brief moment as if in prayer. "Is Mr. Darrow all right?" she
asked.

"Yes, ma'am," he said, trying to keep the smile off his face.
"It's him that sent you this note."

Isabelle tried to ignore the possibility that Jim might have
opened the note and read it. "Thank you, Jim," she said, a little
formally.

As she turned away and left him at the door she saw the
smirk on his face. This bothered her. The worst thing about
her affair with Darrow was the fear that others knew her secret
and were talking about her behind their backs.

She knew she shouldn't care what others thought. Darrow
had taught her that it was her fear of others' opinions that had
made her feel enslaved for so long. After all, he said, once she
truly accepted that love was meant to be freely bestowed on
whomever the heart had chosen, then whose opinions could
possibly be important enough to worry about?

All that sounded reasonable, and she wanted to believe it,
but she was still fearful of being discovered. For if she were,
she surely would be told not to return to Hull House. She had
gotten over her worry that her husband might divorce her.
Obviously he no longer cared what she did. Jane Addams, however, would be *forced* to care.

Now, eager to read her note, Isabelle asked the children to
clean up their modeling clay. While they were occupied, she
stepped into the corner to read Darrow's message. When she
got to the part about how he wanted to celebrate with her in his
arms, her heart filled with joy.

For some time now she had not felt loved. Darrow's involvement in the Chernik trial had made her feel displaced and
ignored. No matter how hard she tried to be understanding,

she felt abandoned. She knew that Darrow's preoccupation with the trial was different from her husband's abandonment of her, but somehow it *felt* the same. No matter what the reason, being ignored caused her intense emotional pain.

But reading Clarence's note changed all that. All her doubt about his feelings evaporated like dew on a sunny morning. She gaily set about washing the children's faces and hands. She wanted them to be ready to leave the minute their mothers came so that she could hurry over to Darrow's office. She had not felt so light and happy in many a week.

The mothers straggled in, one or two at a time. When all but one child had been taken home, Isabelle was so anxious to get out of there that it was hard to control her impatience. When the mother finally arrived, it was after nine o'clock.

Isabelle followed the mother and child out onto the large front porch and waved good-bye. "Be careful," she called. "See you tomorrow."

She stepped back into the foyer to grab her shawl and handbag. Because it was already dark outside, she checked her handbag to make sure she had her knitting needles ready as protection. She wanted to get away as soon as she could, so she left the house without finding Jane Addams to say good-bye.

She stepped out onto the porch and closed the front door. A breeze had come up, and the warmth of the day had cooled into a fine evening. As she pulled her shawl around her shoulders, Isabelle felt exhilarated. She hurried down the street and enjoyed the way the large trees were swaying above her in the wind.

I'm a blessed woman, she thought. *I have a wonderful son and a houseful of children I love as my own. And now I'm going to see Clarence Darrow.*

For the first time since she had received Clarence's note, she had time to think about the trial. Darrow had won an acquittal. That meant that he would be in a happy frame of mind. She hoped he would tell her what he had said that swayed the jury. She so wanted to see him in a trial. How thrilling that would be.

She passed a corner where a small boy was selling papers and bought one. It was too dark to read it here, but she thought it would please Clarence to see it. She rehearsed in her mind what she would say to him and whether she should tell him that she had missed him. She didn't want him to feel pressured, but she wanted him to know how much she cared. She was so involved in her thoughts that she didn't notice the tall, muscular man standing in the shadows.

Running Wolf was leaning against a door. He had been drinking, and the rustling of the large branches blowing back and forth had almost lulled him to sleep. The sound reminded him of the tall grass in the plains when he was a boy, long, long ago near a creek called Mini Pusa before Buffalo Bill and the soldiers had ridden into the village to destroy it. All that killing to rescue a couple of white women!

When the slender woman walked by, Running Wolf was aroused from his reverie. He smelled her lavender scent before he saw her, and he noticed the rustling sound of her dress—so tiny a sound compared with the wind in the trees.

He felt a jolt of awareness, a pang of anger. He stepped quickly into the shadows and followed her.

Isabelle reached an alley and had almost crossed it to continue on up the street when a noise stopped her. A few feet up the alley a back door opened. Light and the sound of an argument spilled out behind the buildings.

"Lissen, you son of a bitch," a voice yelled, "you've been treatin' yourself to me food and whiskey for months now."

Something crashed. "Aw, Criminy," answered another voice. "Shut the door and set down."

The light from the open door had shown her that the alley was empty. Now that it was dark again, she considered it. Cutting through the alley would shorten her trip. Against her better judgment, she turned into it. In the shadows the man stepped quietly behind her.

She had traveled nearly a block and was approaching the street up ahead when she heard a noise. Something had fallen to the ground behind her, and she looked around in alarm. For a moment she didn't see the figure crouching behind the pile of boxes.

Then he stood erect. The streetlight up ahead reflected on something in his hand.

She turned to run away, ran a few steps, and felt him grab at her arm. When she jerked to get free, the movement threw her off-balance, and she careened toward the wall of a building.

When she recovered her balance, she spun around to face him. Even in the dark she could see the hatred in his eyes.

"Who are you?" she asked, trembling.

He growled a response, and instinctively she put her thin hands up in front of her chest. "What do you want?" she cried, knowing the answer, knowing that she was as good as dead.

The tall man watched her run sideways along the wall to get away from him, racing back up the alley. When she reached the pile of rubbish, she stopped, trapped between the wall and the trash heap. He came near and waited.

He grinned to himself. He could practically stand still and watch her wear herself out.

Isabelle knew she was trapped, and terror pounded in her chest. "Oh, God, please . . ." she repeated frantically. "Please. Oh, God."

Suddenly her perspective changed. Instead of looking across at the man's face, she found that she was looking down at the frightened woman in the dark alley. Outside herself, high above the street, she could see the scene clearly even in the darkness. She saw the man moving toward the woman. She saw how frightened the woman looked but no longer felt the fear. She was sorry for the woman pleading with the man. The woman was so terrified that she had started to weep.

Up there, watching the woman weeping and pleading, she saw her life so clearly. How silly her girlish loneliness had been and how much she loved the poor little babies that came to her at Hull House. Defiance flashed through her mind. *I have much yet to do*, she thought.

Suddenly she was back on the street again, in herself, her heart racing as she faced the man. The knitting needles! She pulled them from her bag. When he came at her, she stabbed them toward his face and raked them down his eye and cheek. He howled in pain and furiously shoved her against the wall.

Now with his eyes a scant twelve inches from hers, she gazed at him, barely able to breathe with fear. For a moment the eyes looked into hers, and her words came racing forth uncontrollably. "Oh, please, no. Please, no." She noticed as his eyes saw something else, recalled a memory, watched the memory for a moment, then saw her again.

Then she felt the knife. It felt like a stinging burn. Her heart fluttered with fear. She was above herself again. Watching sadly. All her dreams gone now, her only thoughts now on the cruel blade flashing between each searing cut. She saw her hand reach out to stop it, saw the thin hot line of scarlet open into a river of blood. Saw the knife slash open the white blouse and expose her breasts. Saw the knife held steady for a second, felt the hope that perhaps the rage behind those eyes would stop.

For a moment she was back in herself again, feeling her heart pounding as though it would burst. Now she heard the soft pop as the knife pushed through the soft white skin, felt the powerful thrust glance achingly off the bottom of her breastbone.

Now she was above the scene again, no longer feeling anything, watching the woman. No longer pleading, no longer resisting, no longer weeping. Her dreams gone. Now a loud buzzing in her ears. Now, gratefully, the silence. The peaceful silence.

34

DARROW WAITED IN HIS office for Isabelle until he fell asleep in his big leather chair. He was awakened the next morning when Mrs. Hastings came in, carrying a jar of sugary coffee and the Chicago *Tribune*. The old lady had come in early in hopes of tidying up Darrow's office before he arrived. She figured he'd be too upset by that story in the newspaper to be able to deal with a lot of disorder.

When she came upon him in his chair, she was startled. "Why, heavens, Mr. Darrow. Did you spend the night here?"

"Yes," he said, coming awake and stretching his long frame. "I had work to do." Darrow shook his head to wake himself. He wondered why Isabelle had not shown up.

"Mrs. Hastings, did Jim take that note over to Mrs. Woodruff yesterday afternoon like I asked?" he asked.

Mrs. Hastings hesitated. She knew Jim had delivered the note. She also knew that Mr. Darrow had been having a relationship with the Woodruff woman because of the notes the two sent back and forth.

It was nothing to her, of course. She was used to his ways and had long ago learned to keep her nose out of it. She personally had liked Mrs. Woodruff on the few occasions she had seen her in the law office. If she hadn't disapproved of the whole situation, she would have found much more to like in her than in those radical women who bothered him at the office. But that was none of her affair.

Now it seemed that he might not have heard of the death, and she didn't know quite how to tell him about it.

"Oh, dear, Mr. Darrow," she said, "I suppose you haven't seen the papers yet, have you?"

"No, Mrs. Hastings," he said. "Lots of coverage on the trial, I suppose."

Mrs. Hastings put the paper down and backed her way to the door. She did not want to be around when Darrow discovered the news. "Well, sir, something quite dreadful has happened, and I think you should drink some of this coffee before you look at that newspaper."

Darrow opened the paper immediately, but even when he saw the story, it took a few moments before it could sink in that the ghastly report was about his Isabelle. Above the story about Josef Chernik's trial was a large, bold headline:

BANKER'S WIFE FOUND SLASHED TO DEATH

Darrow read the report with shock and growing horror. The paper told the gruesome story of the stabbing of Isabelle Woodruff. It described how the body had been found by a bartender when he was emptying his trash in the alley, how the police had quickly suspected an Indian of some foul misdeed when they saw him staggering down the street splattered with blood, still carrying a large buffalo knife in his hand. It described the slash marks that ran down one side of his face and the bloody knitting needles that had been found beside the murdered woman.

Darrow realized that Isabelle had been killed while she was coming to see him. He was overcome with despair. Then images of how frightened she must have been and the grotesque circumstances that had destroyed her flashed through his mind. He could see her eyes bright with tears, could feel her terror. A sense of her beauty and tenderness came to him so vividly that it almost seemed she was present in the room.

A dreadful groan escaped from his throat. What kind of city was this—what kind of world—where such cruelty could happen to one as gentle as Isabelle? He blamed himself that he had not rushed to her after the trial. He blamed himself that he had stayed distant from her during the last few weeks. He had gotten so caught up in his work that he had abandoned her to the lonely task of reconciling his love with his long absences.

He was seized with a powerful yearning to go back in time and change what he had done. The words "if only, if only" filled his mind. How foolish to have taken her love and her life for granted.

So many mistakes. So many missed opportunities.

He paced in his office for a long while before he could bring himself to face anyone. Finally he emerged from his office. When he spoke, his voice was hoarse. "I'm going for a walk today, Mrs. Hastings."

"It's raining, Mr. Darrow," she cautioned. "It's just a terrible day."

"Yes, it is," he replied, walking heavily down the stairs. "A terrible, terrible day."

The news spread throughout the city quickly. In the Nineteenth Ward, people who had known Isabelle at Hull House met there to discuss the shocking event. Little children in the nursery asked for her and stopped only when they sensed that something was very wrong. Jane Addams, usually so good at comforting others, stayed in her room all day with the door closed.

Later editions of the papers quoted Bertha Palmer as saying what an upstanding member of society Isabelle Woodruff had been. Phillip Woodruff, using this opportunity to enhance his position in the community, praised his wife's work at the settlement and called her a saint. He spoke of the impossibility of telling his son what had happened and asked well-wishers to stay away. He announced that he was taking his son on a trip to protect him from the shock.

Privately Phillip was relieved to be rid of his wife and saw little point in distressing his son with this gaudy story. It seemed easier to tell the boy that his mother had abandoned him. If he kept him home from school and took him abroad until the story died down, the boy might never have to know the truth.

That night Buffalo Bill Cody grimly followed a guard down into the jail. The sound of his boots echoed noisily on the iron stairs.

"You be careful now. That big Indian's dangerous," the guard warned Bill. "If you wasn't with the Bureau of Indian Affairs, I doubt the police chief would let you see him."

"Is he actin' crazy?" Cody asked.

"Oh, yes. Singing mournful and dancing. Had to put him in a cell all to hisself. Can't have him killing nobody else."

When they arrived at the cell, Cody peered into the dark to see Running Wolf. His cell was solid iron on three sides. Only the side facing the corridor had bars. The Indian was still chanting and shuffling his feet energetically.

"Can you imagine?" said the guard. "Killing a woman and then carrying on like that? They say he's been at it for hours."

"I'd like to go in there and talk to him," Cody said.

"Into that cell! No, siree," said the guard. "I'd get fired if I let you in there."

"I'll be all right," said Cody. "I know how to handle Indians."

"Can't do it," said the guard.

"Then at least leave me alone with him."

When the guard hesitated, Buffalo Bill added, "Mister, I'm here on official United States Indian affairs business. I never like to push my weight around, but when I tell you to leave me alone with him, I'd appreciate it if you could understand that it's an order."

After the guard had disappeared down the dark corridor, Buffalo Bill Cody stood watching Running Wolf.

"So, you're still doing that dance, are you?" he said more to himself than to the Indian. "Don't you know nothing will ever bring back life the way it used to be?"

Cody recognized the vigorous forward and back steps of the ghost dance. He'd seen it in early December four years ago out near Sitting Bull's reservation in the Bad Lands. It was the ghost dance that had led to the massacre at Wounded Knee.

Cody recalled hurrying to the Bad Lands to find out what

was going on. He had just returned from a tour in Europe and was stepping off the ship in New York when he got General Miles's telegram.

SITTING BULL PLANNING TO LEAD A MAJOR WAR was what the telegram said. Cody knew his old friend Sitting Bull had neither the inclination nor the manpower to do such a thing, and he told General Miles so. But Miles insisted that Cody go to the Bad Lands to handle the situation.

By the time Cody got out there, Sitting Bull was dead. Shot down by soldiers who claimed he was trying to make trouble. The truth was that all Sitting Bull had wanted was to visit a nearby reservation so he could see the ghost dance for himself.

The old Indian never got to see the dance, but Cody got a glimpse of it before he returned east. It was quite a sight, watching hundreds of Indians dance until they passed out. It must have been the frenzy of that dance that scared the soldiers enough to start firing at them at Wounded Knee. Surely they hadn't really believed that the dance would bring the Indians a messiah who would roll back the earth, bring the dead Indians to life, and bury the white man.

Seeing Running Wolf in the cell now, Cody wondered how the Indian had learned that dance. He couldn't remember if Running Wolf had been on that European trip with him that year or not. Running Wolf's home had been near the Cheyenne River. If he'd been in the Bad Lands that year, he might have been part of that puny attempt to defeat the white man with a spiritual uprising.

Running Wolf saw the shadowy outline of a tall man standing behind the bars, but he paid little attention. He had danced long enough in the dark cell that he was hardly aware of his surroundings. He knew he was nearing the moment when he would have the small death that would bring him visions of the Great Spirit.

Running Wolf could still feel the tribe's excitement when Kicking Bear had returned to the reservation with news of a dance that would bring them a messiah. As he danced now, Running Wolf could still hear the words of Kicking Bear when he spoke to the tribe.

"My brothers," Kicking Bear had called out. "I bring you the promise of a day when there will be no white man to lay his hand on the bridle of any Indian's horse."

Running Wolf remembered how he and the braves had shouted: *"Hau! Hau!"*

"I bring you the promise of a day when the red men of the prairie will not be turned from the hunting grounds by any man."

"Hau! Hau! Hau!" they had shouted, joy filling their hearts.

"I have seen the wonders of the spirit land and have talked with the ghosts. I traveled far. Now I am sent back with this message: Get ready for the coming of the Great Warrior Messiah."

Running Wolf slumped to the floor of the cell in exhaustion. He awaited the moment when a beautiful vision would fill his mind. He yearned to see the land as it had been, to see his tribe and feel his horse under him.

Instead, he again saw the bad vision, an old memory that returned to him often. It was a remembrance of that time four years ago when the Indians were starving on the reservations. He had been standing near when one of the tribe's leaders had tried to make a white leader understand why the tribes were doing the spirit dance.

"We hold our dying children and feel their little bodies tremble as their souls go out and leave a dead weight in our hands. Where is there any hope for us on this earth?"

Running Wolf gnashed his teeth in anguish. This was not the beautiful vision he had danced to find. This vision was so bitter it brought the taste of gall to his mouth. When he could, he opened his eyes to dispel it.

"Hello, Running Wolf," said Cody when he saw the Indian open his eyes.

Running Wolf stared at Cody mutely. Now that he had heard the voice, he realized who was at the door. There was a time when this man had been good to him, but Running Wolf knew it was only because of what he had done to his tribe.

He didn't respond. His face was pressed to the cold iron floor. He was exhausted and hot, and the iron felt good against his skin.

"It's over, Running Wolf," Cody said. "The animals are gone. Your land is gone. The way you lived is no more. Doing that dance isn't going to bring it back."

Running Wolf heard Cody's words and sorrowfully knew they were true.

Cody watched the Indian shiver for a few moments.

"That's a real bad thing you did, Running Wolf," Cody said. "Killing that woman. Poor lady who never did anything to hurt you."

Running Wolf stared at Cody with hatred. In his mind he raged, *All of you hurt me.*

"Look, Running Wolf," Cody said, as if he knew the Indian's thoughts, "I know it's hard for you to understand this, but once your pa had dragged off those women and killed 'em, there was nothing else we could do. We had to destroy the tribe."

Running Wolf squeezed his eyes to shut out the memory. Even with them closed he could see his father and Cody racing toward each other, Cody firing just as his father was taking aim.

"You were just a skinny little kid at the time, half crazy with what was happening." Cody said. Then he paused and thought. "I always hoped I could help you, make things all right for you again. That was why I put you in the show and took you with me."

Cody looked remorsefully at the exhausted man lying in front of him. "You should have gone back to the reservation. There's no way an Indian can exist in a city. Cities aren't what you understand. What you understand is gone."

The two men stared at each other, realizing that the past they loved was over for both of them. Finally Cody shook his head resolutely. "Well, Running Wolf, that's all behind us, and there's nothing we can do about it now. But I will tell you this. They're going to keep you in this cell until you're half crazy, and then they'll put you on trial for that murder. When they convict you, they'll hang you."

Running Wolf sat up and listened intently. "I don't want that for you," Cody continued. "I was with you in the beginning when things started to go wrong for you. I'm going to be with you now at the end."

Cody pulled a lariat from his coat jacket. "This is for you," he said. "It won't help you get out of here, and I know you won't be able to get close enough to the guard to hurt him. I brought it so you could give yourself an honorable death without a lot of people rejoicing at your demise. It's awful, and it's painful, but it's the only way."

Running Wolf stood to his feet, and Cody passed the rope

through the bars. Running Wolf took it in his hand and gazed at it.

"You understand what I just said to you, don't you?" asked Cody.

Running Wolf nodded silently.

"I guess the only thing I ever brought you was death and destruction," Cody said. "And I'm sorry. But I guess sometimes that's just the way it is."

When the guard returned, Cody glanced at Running Wolf one last time. "Good-bye, Running Wolf," he said. "Better do it soon."

Then he turned and walked down the long corridor.

35

HANNAH COULDN'T STOP CRYING, and Carrie Watson simply could not understand why.

"For a girl who has everything," Carrie said, "you surely do carry on. You got a legitimate business. That brother of yours got off free as a bird. And we finally found a wet nurse to take the baby off your hands."

Hannah didn't answer. She stepped away from the little basket where the baby was sleeping and wiped her tears.

"Well, all I have to say is there ain't much time," Carrie said impatiently. "So you better get busy and pull yourself together."

When Carrie left the room, Hannah was relieved, for she needed to be alone. It was hard to give the baby away. Just knowing that the woman was coming today troubled her more deeply than she had anticipated.

Sometimes it seemed to her that the child had given her pain from the moment she had known she was pregnant. Now that she was about to confront the most agonizing part of the experience yet, she felt strengthened by another emotion that had been coming up a good deal recently: her hatred for Roland Girard.

During Hannah's long agonizing labor, her mind had plucked Roland Girard from the shadows of her memory and given him a new role. As the hours of pain had worn on, Hannah had focused on him, using hatred to strengthen herself. *I will not die*, she had told herself. *I will not die and leave him without regret for what he did to me.*

When the delivery was finally over, her first sight of the child had transformed Hannah's hate into love. But once her hatred for Roland had been evoked, it was always lurking in the back of her mind. It even affected her feelings for the child. As the days passed and the baby's face lost its red, distorted quality, Hannah became increasingly aware that when the child opened her mouth in a certain way, she looked like Roland Girard.

It confused her, seeing Roland in little Sonja's face. Hannah loved the child mightily, but when the baby took on his look, Hannah could feel hatred boil up inside her. Now, knowing the woman was due to arrive, she was sad. When she heard the knock on the door, she knew her time with the baby was short.

"Hannah," Carrie said, opening the door, "Mrs. Spatafore is here."

Hannah turned to see Carrie standing in the hallway with a tall, stocky woman who had dark hair pinned back from her face. Hannah stared at her in a penetrating way. She wanted to be able to look into this woman and make sure she had a kindly disposition.

"Well, really, Hannah," chastised Carrie. "You might at least invite us in. Mrs. Spatafore just rode a train all the way from Galena."

"Oh, yes," Hannah said. "Come in."

The woman was uncomfortable in Hannah's room with its ornate furniture. When she spotted the baby lying in the basket, she went over to look at it.

"So that's it, eh?" she said, peering at little Sonja curiously. Mrs. Spatafore needed the money, but she hoped the child would not be colicky and cry all the time.

"Yes," answered Hannah, moving a step closer to the baby as if to protect her from this stranger. "And you want to take care of her?"

"I think I do."

"And you have milk?" Hannah asked.

"Lots of it," said Mrs. Spatafore. The woman opened her coat to show Hannah the large wet spot on her blouse where milk had spurted forth on its own. "My child was born last month. There's milk enough for two."

"Did you bring your baby with you?" Hannah asked, curious to see the Spatafore child.

"I didn't want to take it on the train. I made up a sugar tit and left it with my neighbor."

"Then you're in a hurry?"

"Somewhat, I suppose."

Hannah gestured to a chair beside the baby's basket. She had a number of questions to ask this woman. "Please sit down, Mrs. Spatafore," she said. "Would you like coffee?"

The billowy woman settled herself erectly in the brocade-upholstered chair. She held a huge knitting bag in her lap.

"I would, as a matter of fact."

While Hannah poured coffee, Carrie leaned against the door and relaxed. Hannah seemed to be warming up to the wet nurse.

"So," Hannah began, "you will provide milk and care for my child?"

"Yes, ma'am," the woman answered. "Of course, it's a great deal of work, raising an extra one, so there is a charge—I already mentioned this to the man who contacted me. Plus my husband was fired this year and times are hard."

"Yes, of course," Hannah said, trying to get a sense of the woman's suitability. "There is no question but that you will be paid. But what I want you to understand is that merely providing care is not enough. What I want is—I want you to promise me that you'll love my child."

The woman was taken off guard by this stipulation. "Well, I do like children," she said rather unconvincingly.

Hannah looked at the woman testily. At the door Carrie Watson cleared her throat. The sound was intended to warn Hannah not to offend the woman. It had been hard to find a decent woman with milk who was willing to raise an illegitimate child. Carrie's sources had been forced to go all the way to Galena to find her.

Carrie's signal made Hannah feel pressured. She was grateful that Carrie had found a woman, but before she could give her only daughter to her to raise, she had to be sure about her.

"I want you to listen to me and never to forget what I'm saying," Hannah said. "I will pay you the terms you agreed to. I will even pay you more when you need it—if your claims are just. But know this. As long as you have my child, I will never take my eyes off you. I will send spies to check on you, and you will never know when they are watching. If I ever, ever hear that you have been mean or unkind to my child, I will kill you myself."

Carrie raised her eyes to the ceiling and sighed loudly. If Mrs. Spatafore hadn't been saddled with a bunch of kids, she surely would have walked out. Carrie wondered how on earth she could have developed such a close relationship with Hannah. The girl had always been such trouble.

"Will you take the child under those conditions?" Hannah asked a little more calmly.

The woman blinked and put her coffee on the table. She would never have gotten on that train this morning if she had anticipated this kind of attitude. She had counted on the mother's being *grateful* to her. After all, it was obvious that the child was illegitimate. Why else would a mother give it away? Especially a woman living in a nice house like this.

Mrs. Spatafore bit her lip and thought. She didn't like the idea of spies snooping around, but to be fair, it did seem reasonable that a mother would want her baby to be loved. She knew if she were giving away a child, she'd want the same thing.

Mrs. Spatafore looked over at the baby. It seemed like a sweet little thing sleeping there quietly. Plus she had three kids of her own, and God knows, she needed the money. She decided that she would accept the terms.

"What's its name?" she asked, picking up the baby.

"Sonja," Hannah answered, watching the woman closely.

"I agree to your terms," Mrs. Spatafore said. "I think I could love it." The baby smacked its lips in its sleep. Without ceremony Mrs. Spatafore unbuttoned her blouse and held her big breast against the baby's mouth. The baby began to suck, still in its sleep.

Hannah watched. The woman was grinning at Sonja as if she already liked her. "There is one last term," Hannah said, and her voice began to break. "I want my daughter to believe that you are her mother. I want her never to know about me. Is that clear?"

"Why, yes, ma'am," Mrs. Spatafore said, somewhat surprised. "I'll be her mother if that's what you want." When she looked up, she saw tears in Hannah's eyes. "Don't you worry, miss," she said. "I don't have it in me to be mean to a child. I'll treat her as good as I treat my own."

Downstairs the white carriage with the yellow wheels had been loaded with dresses and toys from the girls in the house. Hannah carried the baby downstairs, and a few of the girls followed. When Hannah was beside the carriage, she brought the child's little face close to hers.

"You will never know," she whispered. "You will never know what a disgrace your mother was. I will never make you feel ashamed."

Hannah held her child that one last time. When she felt the baby's breath and warmth against her face, she thought her heart would break. The baby made a little sound with its mouth—not a cry, just a little sound—almost like talking.

Hannah handed her child to the dark woman from Galena. When the woman was seated securely, the driver climbed up to his seat. As the carriage clattered away, the woman held the baby up to the window so Hannah could see her daughter's face for the last time. It was such a dreadful moment that the only way Hannah could bear the aching sadness was to fill herself with hatred.

It is time, she thought. *It is time I got even with Roland Girard.*

She knew, of course, about the jewelry he had given Marie, and it had occurred to Hannah long ago that he had probably taken it from Marshall Field's. She knew from her own experience that he dipped freely into the store's luxurious stock for his own purposes.

An idea had come to Hannah the week after the baby was born, and she felt ready now to put it into action. She went down the hall to have a talk with Zorrine.

"Zo," she said, "you're such a pretty girl. I believe you could get a rich man to marry you if your dresses were of a higher quality."

Hannah's declaration took Zorrine by surprise. In the first place, she had no idea Hannah appreciated her beauty. In the second, she didn't see anything wrong with the dresses she was wearing now.

Hannah explained to her that there was an executive at Marshall Field's who, in exchange for her favors, was willing to provide dresses. Not just any dresses—the most gorgeous dresses in the store! When Zorrine agreed that she would discuss the matter with the gentleman, Hannah went downstairs to Carrie's office and wrote Roland Girard a letter. In it, she identified herself as the most beautiful girl at Carrie Watson's and said she wanted to discuss a business arrangement with him. She hinted that it would be entirely to his satisfaction. Then she signed Zorrine's name.

That evening Roland Girard appeared downstairs and sent up his card. When Zorrine greeted him at the foot of the stairs with a smoldering look, he was not disappointed. The woman was stirring! As she turned to lead Girard up to her room, he could feel himself becoming titillated. He followed her up the stairs, watching her hips sway under her dress.

"Well, Mr. Girard," Zorrine said seductively when he was seated on her chaise, "you wanted to discuss a business proposition with me?"

Girard wanted to say that he thought he was responding to *her* proposition, but he decided she was indulging in a woman's coquetry by putting the idea back on him.

"Certainly." He smiled. His eyes met hers for a moment, and he sensuously twisted the end of his mustache. "Go ahead."

"I understand you have beautiful dresses you would like to trade for evenings of rapture."

Ah, Girard thought. *So that's it.* He quickly evaluated the proposition. It certainly wasn't hard for him to slip clothes out of the store. He merely had to move them into his office for some excuse and then never return them to the proper department.

When he nodded, Zorrine responded. "Just to make sure we both are satisfied"—she lowered her voice to a soft, warm richness—"we'll keep an accounting. When you give me a dress, I'll credit you with a night here."

Girard smiled at the audacity of the woman. Keep an accounting! "What will that night include?" Girard asked, raising one eyebrow voluptuously. "Food? Wine?"

"No," she said simply. Zorrine knew Carrie would charge her for food and wine the same as she'd charge any man.

He reached forward to tickle her arm. "Will it include you?"

She smiled. "Why, yes, of course. Isn't that what we're talking about?"

"What if I wanted to sample the merchandise before I agree to the deal?"

This ploy irritated Zorrine no end. As far as she was concerned, he was the one who had proposed this arrangement—not she. She lifted her chin and gave him her most regal look. "It is my pleasure, Mr. Girard, to satisfy my customers. But I have no desire to let a man drop anchor with me unless he *is* a customer. Do you get my meaning?"

Roland Girard closed his eyes and smiled. It was so tasteless for this girl to negotiate her body this way. If she hadn't been so beautiful, he would have been too disgusted even to touch her. It was a good deal for him, though. Quite a good deal. A prize like Zorrine would run at least seventy-five dollars a night, not including wine.

"Let's agree to our transaction," he said. "But as long as I'm here . . ."

"Fine," she said, getting his meaning. With a smirk she began to unfasten her bodice. When she had stripped herself down to her whalebone waist corset and her breasts were fully exposed, she stopped. She could see that she had his entire attention.

"Well, Mr. Girard," she said, "until I get my hands on *your* merchandise, this look is all you'll get of mine."

The next few months went quickly for Hannah. She threw herself into the task of finding healthy companies that might purchase Carrie's new property, and she met with some success. Though the depression was not over, business was showing signs of recovery. By posing as an agent of the owner, Hannah had sold one of the buildings at a nice profit.

Though Hannah stayed away from Zorrine's transactions with Roland Girard, she spent a fair amount of time thinking about them. After his first meeting with Zorrine, he always

arrived with a beautiful dress that he would present at the
beginning of the evening. The following day Zorrine would
show Hannah her new trophy.

"Look," she would say, spreading the dress across her bed
in front of Hannah, "think this is good enough to attract a rich
husband?"

"Indeed," Hannah would reply, exploring the inside seams
with her fingers. When she would find the label hand-embroi-
dered with Marshall Field's own name, she would take a pair of
manicure scissors from her pocket and snip it out.

"For my collection," she would say sweetly.

But though she occupied herself with her work, the arrangement troubled her. Knowing the day after that Girard
had been with Zorrine was bad enough. Sometimes Hannah
could still smell his fragrance in Zorrine's room, and it would
stir her with an obscure longing that she found maddening. But
it was even worse if Zorrine happened to mention in advance
that he was coming. Knowing that he was in the house, being
enthralled by Zorrine's stories and manipulations, bothered her
mightily.

She often thought what a treat it would be to see Roland
Girard humiliated and manipulated by Zorrine. Nobody knew
how to toy with a man the way Zorrine did. Perhaps, Hannah
thought, that could be part of her revenge: watching.

Once she had conceived that fantasy, she could hardly wait
for his next appointment. She stayed close to Zorrine so she
would be sure to hear about it. When the evening finally came,
Hannah was ready.

She was actually sitting in Zorrine's room when Roland
Girard's card was brought upstairs to announce him. When
Zorrine went downstairs to greet him, Hannah opened the fake
panel in Zorrine's room and hid in the small room.

It wasn't long before she heard the two of them enter
the room. She had expected them to enjoy the entertainment
downstairs first, but then she recalled that wine and food were
not part of the arrangement. Evidently Roland was spending as
little of his own money as he could.

"What is your desire tonight?" Hannah heard Zorrine
ask him.

Though Hannah did not dare open the panel and look at

him, she heard every word he said. He wanted Zorrine to take off the dress she was wearing so she could try on the one he had brought. Then the talking stopped, and Hannah wondered what was happening. She thought he must be embracing Zorrine.

In the silence Hannah pushed the panel open a small bit and peeked out. She saw Roland staring silently at Zorrine as he raised his glass—just the way he had always done with her.

So much hatred welled up inside her that the force of it surprised her. When Hannah saw him strip down to his garters and socks and fold his trousers over a chair, she asked herself in disbelief how she could have loved this man so much that she would ruin her life for him. He seemed so silly now, with his white, hairless chest and narrow shoulders. Like nothing more than an arrogant popinjay.

When Girard stepped forward to embrace Zorrine, Hannah closed the panel and put her hands over her ears. Her emotions were so strong that she knew she would be unable to watch. It was hard enough to be this close to him. The only thing that enabled her to remain quiet a few feet from where her former lover was moaning and tossing on the bed was knowing that she was finally going to destroy him.

The next day Hannah folded one of Zorrine's most expensive dresses into a hatbox and, leaving the ostentatious carriage at Carrie Watson's, took a train to the Loop. She got off the streetcar and walked up State Street to Marshall Field's department store.

She was dressed so elegantly that as soon as she presented the card that proclaimed her a secretary to a countess, she was shown to Field's office. The thin, graying man rose to his feet as she entered. Hannah had glimpsed Field once when she was employed there but had never spoken to him. She had not anticipated how stiff and uncomfortable he would seem.

Field had never seen this lovely woman before but assumed that she was paying him a visit to establish an account for the countess—perhaps even discuss a method by which gowns could be specially created for her by his sewing department. He offered coffee, and when the woman declined, he raised his eyebrows in an attitude of helpfulness.

"What may I do for you?" he inquired.

Hannah had thought about this moment for so long that she now found her mouth dry with nerves. After all her planning, what if her words failed to rouse him? She made her voice as formal as she could. "I regret that I am here on a most difficult matter."

"Oh?" The muscles in Field's face sagged, and his face relaxed into its habitually cold expression.

"Though she is a newcomer to Chicago," Hannah continued, "the countess has become very involved in the reform movement here. She spends a good deal of her time quietly visiting the poor and working with distressed young women at Hull House."

Marshall Field pursed his lips. He hoped this was not going to be another request for him to donate clothing. He was already giving away far more than he wanted just to stay on the good side of the wealthy women who concerned themselves with such things. A businessman had to do many things in this town to maintain an air of Christian propriety.

"On a recent visit to the less fortunate, my lady discovered that something quite shocking has been going on here in your fine establishment."

"And what might that be?"

Hannah took a deep breath and cleared her throat. "A young woman revealed to the countess that one of your executives was taking dresses from your store in order to lure girls to their downfall. She was so penitent that she gave this dress to my lady when she renounced her wicked life."

Hannah opened the hatbox and presented the expensive dress with a flourish. Field leaned forward, staring at it. Hannah noticed that his entire scalp seemed to move back with the shock of her revelation.

"This is a serious charge," he said.

"Indeed, it is."

"How can we be sure that this fallen girl is telling the truth? Could she not have purchased—or stolen—the dress herself?"

"My dear Mr. Field," Hannah said, "a girl earning four dollars a week is not likely to be able to purchase a dress like this." She stood and stepped closer to his desk. "Nor would she be able to steal all the dresses from which she clipped these."

Hannah hurled the Marshall Field labels onto the desk in front of him. His head shot back as if he had been slapped.

When he finally spoke, his voice was a deep growl. "Who is this executive? Have you his name?"

"Yes," she said, her heart skipping a beat. "His name is Roland Girard."

When their conversation was concluded, Field courteously escorted Hannah out of his office and down the hall to the elevator. As they waited in silence, Hannah was still unsure of what—if anything—Field would do. She was trying to formulate some last thing to say when the elevator door opened and out stepped Roland Girard.

It was only after Girard had nodded politely to Field that he glanced at Hannah. They had not looked at each other since the night before he had had her fired so long ago. For a moment he didn't recognize her. Then, when he realized who she was, his jaw nearly went slack. She was so well dressed and self-possessed that she didn't seem the same girl at all. When their eyes locked, Hannah covered her nervousness with a haughty bravado. But he, taken by surprise, seemed alarmed.

Hannah, now in control, gave him a long look of contempt before she turned to wish Mr. Field a good day. As she stepped onto the elevator, she saw uncertainty in Roland Girard's eyes and knew he was wondering what on earth she was doing there.

For several days Hannah searched the papers for news of Girard's dismissal. The only news she could find was mention of an upcoming dinner at Marshall Field's own house on Prairie Avenue. She had heard about the dinners Field gave his executives. It was common knowledge that he would invite his chief officers to a formal party on Christmas Day and announce that by the end of the evening one of them would be fired. It seemed likely to Hannah that Girard would be handled this way. Publicly and meanly.

The day after the party Hannah turned quickly to the business section. It was only later that she read the first page, but that was where the story was. It was too important to be buried in the middle of the paper. It seemed that one of Field's executives had gone home from a party at his famous Prairie Avenue house and unexpectedly shot himself.

When Hannah realized that Roland Girard was dead, she could hardly get her breath. She was shocked that her plan to get him fired had resulted in his death. She hadn't meant for that to happen. She had merely wanted to see him struggle with poverty and alienation the way she had. But not to kill himself!

The knowledge of his death gave her a sense of loss so profound that it was almost as if she had never stopped loving him. She was suffocating with it. She knew she had killed him as surely as if she had pulled that trigger herself.

She felt desperate to get out from behind these heavy draperies and into the sun. She needed to breathe fresh air and rid herself of the feeling that she was trapped in a nightmare.

"Let me take the carriage, Carrie," she said. "I must get out of here today."

Carrie looked at Hannah for a few seconds before she agreed. The girl was in another of her moods. *She's such an intense little thing*, Carrie thought, *so different from the other girls*. Carrie shook her head, wondering what it was that had driven her into such frenzy.

Hannah told the driver to take her anywhere, anywhere away from here.

"It's a nice day, Miss Hannah," he replied. "The leaves are out, and the park is full of blooms. Maybe you'd like to ride along the lakefront."

The lake was beautiful. It seemed that every flowering tree and shrub in the whole city had chosen that day to burst into full bloom. The green plants and the fecundity made the news about Roland even stranger than it was. It seemed that everything in the world was alive except Roland Girard.

The driver slowed the horse to a leisurely walk. As it ambled along the paths in the parkways beside the lake, something outside the window caught Hannah's attention, and she suddenly sat erect. The carriage was nearing a large tree. She had passed that tree many times in the last year, but her attention was drawn to it today because she saw a girl leaning against it.

Could that really be the same tree, she wondered, the tree she herself had leaned against when she had been so ill with morning sickness? She remembered the moment vividly. How lost and desperate she had felt, knowing that Girard had fired her and that she could not return home. She signaled the driver to stop, curious if the girl standing there now was also sick.

The girl was leaning against the tree, but in a second it was clear that it was not illness that had made her bend over shaking. It was laughter. In another moment a young man appeared from behind the tree and surprised her. The girl giggled and pulled her hands up in front of her face. When she brought her hands down, the young man kissed her on the cheek.

The driver opened the door in the ceiling. "You want me to keep going, Miss Hannah, or stop here?" he asked.

She was caught up in the sight of the two lovers. "Just wait a moment," she said.

That could have been the two of us, Roland, she thought bitterly. *That could have been me, being kissed and teased, and loving you so much I couldn't stand it.*

Hannah remembered again the despair she had felt at that tree and tears burned in her eyes.

"God damn you, Roland," she whispered out loud. "God damn you!"

Hannah sat in the carriage lost in her thoughts until the young man at the tree noticed her. He recognized the carriage as the trademark of Carrie Watson. "Git away from here," he called out. "What do you think you're doing, watching us?"

Hannah turned her head away.

"Go on," he yelled. "Git!" He turned to the girl beside him. "That's a damned whore over there in that carriage watching us!"

The girl tried to see into the carriage and got a glimpse of Hannah's profile. "She sure is pretty," she said.

"That's what they want you to think—that it's all honey and cream. But you just stay away. I hear they lure girls with that carriage." He turned the girl's face to him. "Anyway, you're my girl now. Ain't no reason for you to ever find out about such things."

Hannah tapped the ceiling of the carriage. "Take me away from here," she said.

The driver snapped the horses' reins, and the carriage lurched forward. They had been traveling only a few minutes when she told the driver to take her back to Carrie Watson's. She didn't feel right out here in the daylight where people with normal lives were enjoying nature. She didn't feel right because she knew she didn't belong. Somehow seeing the girl and her sweetheart had taught her that.

It was time to let go of the past, let go of her regrets. She inhaled resolutely. Regardless of what had happened to Roland Girard, regardless of what had happened to her, she knew that someday she would be rich. And when she was, she hoped that no one would ever hurt her again.

Chicago

July 1896
The National Democratic Convention

THE NEBRASKA BOYS WERE decked out with red bandannas around their necks. They pushed through the crowd, dragging their banjos and drums, to be near the platform when their candidate began his speech. By the time William Jennings Bryan bounded to the platform, they were ready to strike up a lively tune.

Hannah leaned forward in her seat. It was hard to hear the little band in this angry, sweating crowd. More than twenty thousand had filled the Coliseum that day, and from what she had observed, there were at least that many outside, shouting and pleading to come in.

Gaining admittance had not been a problem for Hannah or her brother, for contributors to the Democratic party could always expect special privileges. As a favor, Darrow had asked Hannah's financial support for the silver platform—a Populist cause that he and Governor Altgeld were backing at the convention—and she had not hesitated to contribute. After all, Hannah felt immense gratitude to Darrow for saving her brother's life. In addition, through her work with Carrie Watson, she had come to understand the benefits of making political gifts.

The convention audience today was angry and noisy. De-
bates on the silver issue had stirred up dissension among the
delegates. They were still arguing and cursing the previous
speaker when the young William Jennings Bryan strode to the
lectern. He waited until the Nebraska Boys had completed their
tune, and during the delay Hannah had time to appreciate his
tall, slim body and straight raven hair.

This fellow had a presence about him that was serene and
self-possessed, and he seemed to have a splendid consciousness
of his power. Before he uttered a word, he stood comfortably,
smiling at the crowd with his right hand raised. When the pandemonium had dropped to a murmur, Bryan's voice filled the
hall.

*"It would be presumptuous, indeed, to present myself against the
distinguished gentleman to whom you have just listened if this were a
mere measuring of abilities; but this is not a contest between persons."*

Hannah glanced over at Darrow and Governor Altgeld.
They were across the aisle and just a few benches ahead of
where she and Josef sat. While Hannah was looking at Darrow,
a tall, dour man walked down the aisle between them. He was
leading a young boy who appeared to be about nine years old.
When the man turned to find his seat, Hannah realized it was
Phillip Woodruff, the banker from whom she had purchased
most of Carrie Watson's properties.

When Woodruff took the only empty seats in the row in
front of Darrow, Darrow leaned close to the governor.

"What's that damned capitalist doing here?" Darrow whispered.

The governor shrugged. "Probably bought his way in."

Seeing Phillip Woodruff here today was the last thing Darrow wanted. In spite of himself, he studied the boy. So that was
Isabelle's son. The child bore little resemblance to her, but
seeing him brought Darrow a flood of regret.

With a sharp pang he wondered what the banker had told
the boy about his mother's death. He wondered if the boy had
any idea how cherished Isabelle had been by people the boy
would certainly never know. Darrow could not guess that Isabelle's son believed his mother had abandoned him.

"The humblest citizen in all the land, when clad in the armor of righteous cause, is stronger than all the hosts of error."

Being present at this convention pleased Hannah no end. It had taken money and a considerable bit of political pull to be invited, and she squeezed her brother's hand conspiratorially. For a moment they smiled at each other. They had come a long way together.

Josef's life had taken on enormous changes. The trial had revealed to the public the railroads' machinations to trample the rights of workingmen. As the intended victim of their plot Josef had become famous as a symbol of a poor workingman suffering at their hands.

With a loan from Hannah, he had started a small bicycle manufacturing company in one of Carrie Watson's old buildings. It had become successful immediately, for his invention gave his bicycles the unique advantage of having a drum brake. Recently he had been working on a modification of his brake, enlarging it for a new type of vehicle that was called a horseless carriage. Josef believed this new motorcar could have a future if it had a reliable braking system.

"The man who is employed for wages is as much a businessman as his employers; the farmer who goes forth in the morning and toils all day is as much a businessman as the man who goes upon the board of trade and bets upon the price of grain. . . ."

Hannah sighed with satisfaction. She could feel people staring at her beautiful dress, wondering who she was. Even if this orator was correct that working for wages had the dignity of owning a company, she was glad she no longer had to rely on being paid a salary.

The depression was slow to end, and many farmers and workers were still in desperate straits. However, pockets of prosperity had begun to appear. She had already sold three of Carrie's buildings, and her percentage on those had made her rich. After the sale of the first building, she had moved to a lovely mansion on Ashland Avenue. Because she had ended her life of prostitution so quickly, few people knew she had been one of Carrie's girls. Most assumed she was the daughter of a rich man or, at the very least, married to one.

"Principles are eternal, and this has been a contest over principle."

She had only the best of things now. Her daughter was safe in the country, a pretty little girl with green eyes and curly hair. Hannah visited her occasionally, posing as a distant rich aunt. "She looks just like you," Mrs. Spatafore had said last week when Hannah had arrived laden with gifts. But Hannah knew better. *She looks like Mama,* she thought. *Though I can never see my family, I can have some part of them through little Sonja.*

But this thought was not troubling Hannah now as she sat in a special seat for contributors to the Democratic party. As William Jennings Bryan's words filled the air with promises that he would uplift the common man, Hannah was deep in reflection, considering—after all was said and done—how well she had done. She recalled the strange sadness she had felt after the baby's birth. She had been certain then that all the good things in life were gone from her forever.

Vina was right, she thought. *That dark mood was only the baby sadness. Life is a balance. I gave up a great deal along the way, but you can't have everything. I don't have a family, and I'll probably never have a husband. But I do have money. Having lost so much, I would be silly not to enjoy what I have gained. Fortunately, money makes up for so much.*

Hannah smiled to herself again as she caught another admiring glance. She smoothed the silk skirt and let her eyes meet the gaze of the anonymous admirer. While she was caught up in her thoughts, Bryan continued his speech.

"The great political questions are in their final analysis great moral questions. Who will save the people from themselves? Who?"

That's the beauty of this country, she thought. *If you're determined enough, you can get what you want. Perhaps it doesn't matter what you lose along the way.*